The Curse

The Curse

Xenanique Clarke

To order additional copies of this book, contact:
Xlibris
1-888-795-4274
www.Xlibris.com
Orders@Xlibris.com
776367

For Caroline
I never would have done it without you

Chapter 1

Not This Time

Zylan

August 14, 1468

Father had just gotten home from a rough month at sea. He decided to skip dinner and go straight to bed, so it was just Mother and I at the table. She had just asked me about my day out with Cristoforo, Aurora, and Marco when there was a knock at the door. I stood up to answer it, but Mother grabbed my arm.

"Get Father up," she said. Her eyes were filled with something I couldn't read. She looked scared, but why? It was just a knock at the door.

I hesitated but did as she asked. I quickly moved down the hallway to the end. I passed my room then Wendy's old room then what would have been Nathan's room. I missed them so much. I wished that they could be here for my birthday. I was turning seventeen today, and I couldn't be with most of the people I loved.

I knocked on Father's door and pushed it open slightly. "Father, someone knocked at the door. Mother looked . . ." I tried to find the right word, but I didn't know it. "She just told me to come get you."

He jumped out of bed. "When?"

"Not but thirty seconds ago."

He ran down the hall. Why was everyone acting so strange? It was just a knock. . . . We got back to the table. The door was wide open, and Mother was gone. I didn't understand what was going on.

Father turned back to me. He put his hands on my shoulders and bent down, so he was looking right into my eyes. "Go to my room, lock the door, and hide under the bed. Do not open the door for anyone. Your Mother and I are the only ones with a key. Do you understand?" he ordered. I nodded and turned back down the hall.

What was going on? Where did Mother go? And why did Father look so worried? I know that we were right on the sea so sometimes pirates docked, but why would they come to our house, especially while it was still light out.

I locked the door like Father asked, but I didn't go under the bed. I wandered around the room for a minute looking around. I was never allowed in here. I had no clue why, but I was curious as to what it looked like. There was a large bed in the centre of the right wall with one nightstand on each side of it. They had a small closet in the back, right corner. There was a dresser in the centre of the left wall with a large mirror, and Mother had her cosmetics scattered all over it.

I made my way around the bed and to the closet when I heard footsteps coming down the hall. I slid under the bed as fast as possible. Just as I was hidden, the lock clicked, and the door swung open.

"It okay to—" My mother was cut off by a loud bang, a bang I knew all too well, a bang that would ring through my nightmares for years after that day. I didn't scream. I didn't make a sound. I just lay there and watched my mother bleed out in front of me, her eyes blank.

A few seconds later, I saw black boots walk in and around the bed to the closet. The person wearing the boots paused. I heard the squeak of hangers being pushed. When that person saw nothing, they turned to the bed. I thought I was going to die. I thought he was going to lean down and look under the bed and then he was going to kill me. I took a silent, deep breath as I saw that person's right hand coming into view. It was definitely a man's; his hand was big, with two large rings. One was on his forefinger; the other was on his ring finger. Just before I would have been in his sight, he stood up straight and walked out the door. Something must have called his attention away, but I didn't know what. All I could think about was Mother lying dead on the ground.

I felt tears roll down my cheeks. I tried to slide out from under the bed so I could hug Mother one last time, but my body wouldn't move. For a few minutes, all I could do was lie there and watch as her blood pooled out farther. Finally, I managed to slide myself out from under the bed and over to her. I rolled her onto my lap and brushed the hair out of her face, her blood staining my white nightgown.

"I'm so sorry, Momma," I whispered as more tears started pouring out of my eyes. "I love you, Momma. Please don't be gone."

There was nothing but silence. I sat there for a long time, hunched over and crying into my mother's shoulder.

The sound of someone running into the room made me look up slightly. I saw black boots in front of me.

"Kill me and get it over with," I said, keeping my eyes down.

The person said nothing. He just reached down and grabbed my arm, pulling me up and away from my mother. Her body rolled off me into a position I didn't know a human body could make. I let tears pour out of my eyes as the man holding me drags me out of my house.

I saw a puddle of blood on the floor by my table. I wondered if it was my father's. I wondered where he was and what happened. I shouldn't have been hiding. I should have been trying to help. My mother was dead, and I had no clue what happened to my father.

I looked over at the person holding onto me for the first time. It was a young man, probably about my age. He wouldn't look at me, so I could only see the right side of his face. How could this boy murder my parents without blinking an eye, but not have the stomach to look at me?

I looked down at the hand gripping my arm. The rings were gone, and the hand looked different. Something wasn't right, but what?

"Where are you taking me?" I asked, my voice barely a whisper.

"Neverland."

September 20, 2011

Carefully positioned on the highest branch of the smallest oak tree, I peered down over Pan's camp. The girls and I have something special planned for him and the boys. They've been messing with us for far too long, and you see, it's time to get even. My job is to get the layout of the camp. Although we all live on this island together, Pan keeps us on opposite sides. Apparently, we "distract the boys," so we aren't allowed to know where the camp is. This means none of us have seen the camp, well, recently anyways.

Willow and Iris saw Klaus and Hunter walking around just outside our camp and figured it would be the perfect opportunity to strike. I followed them from one side of the island to the other, but I stayed in the trees to keep them from seeing me. It wasn't easy either. They walk super slow and stop every five minutes. Oh, and don't even get me started on the things I overheard, which reminds me I have to have a serious talk with Elena.

But here I am, crouching on a branch, scanning every inch of their camp. I look for exit and entrance points for the knot tiers and hiding spots for the shooters, as well as counting people to make sure they're all there. Unfortunately, there's no sign of Pan, which is not good.

"Spying? Didn't your mother ever teach you that was wrong?"

Of course, he knows I'm here. I stand up slowly but only turn my head enough to see him out of the corner of my eye. His face has dirt smudged on it but his chocolate brown hair is as perfect as always. It waves to the right with a shine I'm so jealous of. He's a few inches taller than me but carries himself like he could be seven feet. His arms are crossed, showing a slight bulge of muscle under his white long-sleeved shirt. He has rolled the sleeves up to his elbow. He has skinny skinny jeans and black boots. His laces are tied low enough that the top of his boots can be folded and loosely enough that he could kick them off at any moment.

"She didn't get the chance. You killed her." With that I flip over him, landing gracefully on top of the tree, before diving over to the next one. I grab hold of it and swing myself around so I land crouched on the branch. I turn around to see Pan standing there frozen, which is weird because he's never at a loss for words. I smile before disappearing into the trees.

He and I have been on this island for about the same amount of time. That means I've been seventeen for a very, very long time. I was the first person Pan ever took, and even though it's been hundreds of years, I remember like it was yesterday. No matter how much time passes, no matter how many other things have happened, no matter how much I want to forget it, that night is crystal clear.

The worst part about that whole night is that he pretended like it never happened. As soon as we got here, he made dinner over the fire—I guess it's because he saw the untouched food on my table—smiled and got blankets that he said he made himself, even though we both know he just "poofed" it up.

I couldn't eat anything. When he wasn't looking, I tossed my food into the fire and ran. I ran until my lungs couldn't handle it and I collapsed onto the forest floor. Then I cried until my eyes wouldn't stay open anymore.

The next morning, I woke up in front of a fire with Pan sitting on a log across from me. He was whittling a branch. He smiled when he saw I was awake. He offered me breakfast. I jumped to my feet and told him to stay away from me. Then I ran again. I avoided him as much as possible after that.

I guess that's probably why he started getting other kids. All of them love him. They tell stories of him rescuing them, or stories about how lonely they were until he came around, or how this is the best thing that ever happened to them.

Some of the new people even talk about something called a movie. Apparently, it's a collection of something called pictures. But it's not just the new kids who heard of him. When Elena first came, she had heard of him. It's the same with Ace. . . . Peter Pan is supposed to rescue children and take them to Neverland, but he didn't rescue me. He kidnapped me and brought me to a place where I can't die. A place where I will never forget what happened to me. If he really rescued children, he would have rescued my sister from the ally she was killed in.

The boy who brought me here isn't Peter Pan. He's a monster.

I've only ever told one person what happened that night, but that was over 450 years ago. I haven't thought about it since then. It feels so weird, thinking about it now. I just wish I could forget.

I make my way back to camp, jumping and swinging from tree to tree. For twenty years, I was alone for most of the time. I would climb trees and jump from tree to tree, just to keep myself busy. I'm basically a professional at this, but one of the branches I grab is too skinny to hold my weight and snaps. I close my eyes and believe I won't hit the ground. Sure enough, just before I would have hit the ground, I land on a bed of leaves.

I learned how to do magic basically right away. I never hurt myself or let anyone else hurt themselves while they were fooling around. Pan says that not everyone can do it, but I know that's a lie. Magic flows through The Island, and anyone can tap into it with a little practice. Honestly, I don't understand why everyone loves him so much. Okay, well he does favour the boys, so that explains that, and all the girls think he's massively attractive, so I guess that would explain that one. But really, the girls only see him once every couple of weeks so, they shouldn't love him that much.

Today is the day we were supposed to prank them. (Well, not actually today. It was like an if-y plan depending on whenever we found out where they were.) But now that Pan saw me, it's going to be a lot harder. They'll be on red alert and probably move their camp somewhere else. "Oh well, time to give the girls the bad news," I say to myself as I continue the rest of my long walk back.

***

I knew something was wrong before I even got close to camp. I look around quickly for a tree I can climb. I take three running strides to my left and jump, pulling myself up. Just in time too. As soon as I'm hidden in the leaves, a herd of boys come running out, laughing, led by Ace. "Crap! Not again. I'm going to kill that boy someday," I mutter to myself. Once I'm sure they're clear I jump down and run in.

"Get down!" Delilah yells.

I stop dead in my tracks and drop to the floor, just in time to see a huge bucket full of crushed berries get released. I roll closer to it, as fast as I can, so I'm out of the splash zone. But then I realize that it's going to swing back and release whatever is left. So as soon as it passes me, I jump to my feet and step out of the way.

"Girls, we're moving." I cross my arms. "Then it's time for some payback." Cheers all around. "Today's the day we say no." That's when a huge gust of wind comes by, pulling my long dark brown hair to the right.

"Girl, you look like you just stepped into a movie," Ryan observes, tilting her head to the side.

"How many times do I have to tell you? I'm 559 years old, and I've been on this island for 543 of those years. I DON'T KNOW WHAT A DAMN MOVIE IS! You darn kids and your—What do you call it?"

"Technology," Elena assists.

"Ah yes, technology. I know nothing about that." Some of the older girls nod their heads in agreement, but the newer ones just laugh and shake their heads at us "old folk" as they say.

"Anyways . . ." I clap my hands. "Who's ready to move?"

***

"No! Over to the right! Little more, little more, little more, perfect!" I say, looking up to where a Clover and Elena are helping me set up my bed.

After a few minutes of arguing, I convinced them that not only do we have to move over, but we have to move up as well. That way, the boys won't be able to find us. They never bother looking up and all of us can climb. Plus, if they ever come looking for us again, we have the upper hand.

"Great! That's the last of it," Elena says, climbing down the tree.

"Okay, everyone, bring it in!" I yell. Pan took one kid every ten years since he grabbed me. That's fifty-five kids in total, twenty-eight girls, including me, and twenty-seven boys, not including him. This means I lead twenty-seven girls, and Pan leads twenty-seven boys.

"So, the boys have been messing with us for far too long! And it's time to get even." The cheers are so loud that it echoes around us, like there are 280 people as opposed to twenty-eight.

I nod over to Clover, who smiles her devious smile. Her blue eyes sparkle in mischief. "Okay, so everyone with a good shot, you know where to go. Everyone who ties a good knot, with me. If you can do both, Elena's your girl. Let's go!"

I get Lydia, Willow, Autumn, Iris, Ryan, and Unique. "All right, girls, our job is the hardest. Come with me."

I lead them over to the other side of the camp, away from the others. All our bows are leaning up against a tree and the arrows are carefully positioned in front of six trees that have the outlines of six boys. Clover, Elena, and I put them up while everyone else was setting up themselves. "So our job is to keep boys from escaping while everyone else is tying them up, which, I can promise you, will be harder than you think. Pan may or may not be there when we strike, so not only does that mean we're keeping them in, we're keeping him out. Everyone follow?"

"Not really . . . I mean I get the plan, but why aren't Elena, Noel, Kathryn, Trixie, Faye, Raven, and Brandi with us?" Willow asks.

"Because the more girls tying at first, the better. Each girl picks a boy and gets them tied up before they ever know what happened. The less people we have to shoot at, the better. Make sense?"

Everyone nods and turns to their assigned outline. I explain that the purpose of these outlines is to *scrap* them, not hit them.

"All right, guys, you're doing great! I'll be back in a few minutes. Keep doing what you're doing." I step away from my group and signal Clover and Elena over.

"What's up, girl?"

"Pan saw me scouting earlier . . . I think that's why he sent the boys over . . . Plus, he may have moved his camp."

"Why wouldn't you say something sooner!" Elena hisses, her brown eyes filling with rage.

"Don't hiss at me! In case you haven't noticed, I've been having a bad day! Now I'm going to fix it."

"How?" Elena asks sarcastically, rolling her eyes.

"Clover, how do you get in touch with Justin?"

"Remember how we heard Ace and Justin talking about us that one time?"

"Oh god! That was so funny. They thought we were mad." I laugh. "Can you tell him I need to meet with Ace?"

"Where do I tell him?"

"He'll know where. You know that. Just make sure that Justin calls him out front of everyone. Make it as loud as possible okay?"

"So you're ready for everyone to know?"

"No, but we need to find out where their new camp is. And I can only do that if I go through his memories. I need a reason to backtrack. Me wanting to see everyone's reaction when Justin calls him out is the best way."

Elena looks shocked. "No way! Why do I never find out these things? Why did you never tell me?"

"I honestly thought you knew. Otherwise, I would have told you, I swear."

"Well, I didn't. At least I know now."

"So now that El's in the know, is he, you know, good?" Clover raises her left eyebrow and smirks slightly.

"Oh my god! You've asked me a million times, and I will never tell you!"

"That means he sucks," Elena chuckles. I hope that means she won't hold a grudge, at least for very long.

"He doesn't, and this conversation is over."

"Wait, so am I the only—"

"Nate, Luke, Griffin, Pan, Sh—" I don't mention Hunter because . . ., well, there's a reason her list is so long.

"Shut up and leave!" Elena hisses some more.

I smile and walk back to the girls, who have done a number on their targets. Each one has every arrow on the outside of the border. "Wow! You guys are killing it! I have some last-minute shit to deal with, all the technical stuff, but I'll be back as soon as I can. In the meantime, Elena is your go-to girl."

"Bye! Good luck!" They all say before turning back to their target. They all draw back at the same time then release. The scariest part is that all the arrows hit the same spot on the different targets. Those boys don't stand a chance.

I smile and walk over to Clover, just to make sure Ace got my message. "He's on his way," she whispers,

"Thank you! I'll be back soon!" I start to walk away but, at the last second, turn back and smirk. "Ish."

"I'm sure." She smirks back at me.

***

"I thought we were only supposed to meet at night." Ace raises an eyebrow as I walk over. I always love when he does that.

His hair is styled up, so this is a rare opportunity to see his eyes. Soft blue eyes that you could get lost in, dirty blond hair perfect for running my fingers through, and a smile that can brighten anyone's day. Today, he wears a black T-shirt, gray skinny jeans, and black combat boots. I love it when he wears black. He looks so good in it because it highlights his pale complexion.

"Yeah, but I really wanted to see you," I smile and stop in front of him.

He smiles back, wrapping his arms around my waist and pulling me down so I'm sitting on his lap. I wrap my arms around his neck and lean closer like I'm about to kiss him, but at the last second, I grab his hair, pulling his head back, and hammer fist him in the nose. I jump off him as he goes to lean forward, hand covering his face.

"Ow! What the fuck!" he exclaims.

"I saw you leading the pack, running out of there! Giggling like a bunch of little girls, I might add." I cross my arms and admire my work as the blood drips down between his fingers, leaving little tiny droplets on the forest floor. "I was the one that almost got splashed, and you know how much I hate getting dirty!"

"Didn't seem to mind so much last night." His voice is muffled, but the smirk is very prominent.

"Do you want me to hit you again? 'Cause I will. Oh, better yet, do you want to have sex again? 'Cause that could stop."

"I'm sorry. I had to!" He chuckles. "You left yourself open for that one. But seriously, I'm sorry. Pan ordered it."

"Of course, he did . . ." I roll my eyes. "So I have a question for you."

"And what would that be?" He raises an eyebrow.

"Clover told me that Justin called you out in front of everyone . . . How did the guys react?"

"You know how to do that thing. The one where you can see what I see."

"Your point?"

"See for yourself."

I shrug. The bleeding finally stopped, and he wiped a little dry blood from under his nose. "Alright, give me your hands." He stands up and holds them out. "Okay, close your eyes and try to rewind what you did."

***

Something in the distance is making a weird buzzing sound. It distracts me as I walk, following Ace like a ghost. Well, we aren't walking really. It's more like getting pulled backward from the rock. This was my goal. Through him taking me back, I can find out where the camp is. My eyes scan every direction and every tree as fast as it passes until we end up at Pan's new camp.

Ace is standing on the left side of the camp next to Pan. He was the second one to get grabbed, so he's second in command, Pan's right-hand man. They're as close as Elena, Clover, and I. It's weird because they're so different. Ace is six foot, blond hair, perfect smile. Pan's five ten, brown hair, evil grin. Ace is sweet, kind, and loveable. Pan is evil, manipulative, and cold-hearted.

"Yo! Ace! Come 'ere, bud," Justin yells across camp.

He's sitting with Tyler, Damon, and Klaus. I don't know why Pan decided that all of the boys have to dress the exact the same every single day, but he did, so they do. Navy blue T-shirts, black pants, gray combat boots, and brown capes. The only two people that dress differently are Pan and Ace.

"What's up, man."

"Someone wants to meet with you." He smirks.

"Who?" Ace sounds slightly irritated with him.

"Ze," he drags out finally, smirk deepening. "She said you'll know where."

He's not exactly being quiet, so he starts getting a lot of looks, including from Pan. I can't read his face, but it looks blank, like when I said he killed my mom.

"Dude! How did you pull that?" Dylan exclaims. "She doesn't even look at us."

"Yeah. I was just figured she wasn't into that . . .," Damon mutters under his breath.

Ace smirks. "Continue thinking that. . . . I'll be back later."

"Wait, Ace. Come here for a minute," Pan calls.

"What's up?" he asks, walking back.

"You and Zylan . . . How long has—"

***

The memory cuts out.

"What happened?" I question, opening eyes. I pull back to see Ace fall off the rock and onto his knees, then his left shoulder hits the dirt, then the side of his head. He's going to have a wicked headache when he wakes up.

"I know what you're doing. Neat trick too, getting Ace to show you where our new camp is." I turn around to see Pan leaning on a tree.

"So what? You're going to move again eventually. We *will* find you."

"That's why I'm not moving. Do whatever you want. Once it out of your system, you guys can move into our camp or stay where you are. Your choice." With that, he disappears in the shadows of the trees.

"I choose for you to fuck off," I whisper kneeling in front of Ace. "Now, how do I wake you up?"

I lay him flat on his back, so when he wakes up, he'll be in a more comfortable position than the one he fell into. "Hey." I slap his cheek lightly. "Hey, come on, sleepy head. Time to wake up." I slap him a little harder.

His eyes flutter open. "What happened? How long was I out?" He pushes himself into a sitting position.

"Must be a side effect of looking through your memories." Yes, I hate Pan, but he was Ace's best friend, and I respected that, mostly because he wouldn't believe me if I told him the truth. But I also had the perfect opportunity to fuck with him. "And about a day."

"What!" He flies to his feet.

I burst out laughing. "I'm kidding."

"Fuck you."

"You wish." I smirk.

"Do I now?" He raises an eyebrow.

"I know you do."

"Well, I won't be in a second." He smirks.

I break into a run, and he chases me.

Chapter 2

Time to Strike

Zylan

"He said that?" Clover sounds like she just shit a brick, and kind of looks like it too. I don't blame her though. It took me by surprise as well. In fact, that's probably what I looked like when Pan told me.

"Yeah. What if it's a trap? We've been living separately for over 543 years. I can't imagine him having a change of heart today of all days."

I nibble on my bottom lip and look over at the other girls. They're all practicing and laughing in their different groups.

"Do we postpone? Or maybe we could just warn them?" Elena suggests.

"I thought about it . . . Honestly, I think we need all the arrows we can get." They look at me really confused. "I know that has nothing to do with either plan, but I came up with my own."

"Of course, you did." Clover chuckles. "Girls! Bring it in."

"So while I was out I ran into Pan." Camilla, Tara, and Jasmine look at each other and giggle. I roll my eyes and continue. "Anyways, long story short, he knows we're planning something for today."

"So what are we going to do?" Dawn asks.

"Well, this is where things get tricky. He knows something's up, and he knows it has to do with the camp, *but* he doesn't know exactly when or how. So we can go ahead as planned, *or* we can postpone it. It's all up to you, guys, because we'll have no idea what we're walking into. And if you don't want to do it, we won't force you to."

They murmur to each other before Iris nods. "We're doing it."

Clover, Elena, and I smile. "Alright! But before we get going, there's one more thing you should know. Pan said we can move into their camp after this is out of our systems."

I knew the answer before I even asked the question. Man, these girls have a good set of lungs. Moving here was completely pointless.

***

After calming the girls down, I get the chance to talk strategy. The plan involves me going in first. Well, not *in* per se but getting a look at what we're up against. Elena is going to lead the group of shooters while Clover gets the tiers ready. We planned out signals so that, if the boys are expecting us, Elena goes first, and I shake a tree branch. If they're not, the original plan is back on, and I whistle.

I lead them to the spot I met up with Ace for one more quick run over the plan before we head out. I get the feeling that the girls are kind of nervous. None of us know what's going to happen once we get there. And if Pan is messing with us, they'll be very disappointed.

Just outside the entrance, half the girls stand waiting for my signal to find out whether they will be in the trees or on the ground. The other half takes off the rope wrapped around their upper body, getting ready to grab someone. Elena and Clover are following close behind me, carrying a basket of extra rope, bows, and arrows.

I leave my bow and arrows where they are, so I can climb the tree. I look around for a good one that's easy to climb. Over to my left, there is a large, thick oak tree similar to the one I climbed earlier, when I first found their camp. I jump to the lowest branch and pull myself up, so my hips are resting on it. Then I swing my legs, so I am crouched, ready for the rest of the climb. After I hit the third jump, the branches get closer together, so I can just step from one to the other. Once I'm in the shelter of the leaves, I scan the clearing. One, two . . . twenty-seven boys all in the camp. They're scattered around in their different groups, talking and laughing. From the looks of it, they're definitely not expecting us.

After sitting here for almost a minute, I realize how flawed our—my—signals are. If I whistle, they'll hear it. And if I had, had to shake the branch they would have seen it. It looks like I've gotten myself into a pickle. I debated whether or not I should climb back down the tree and get them or just sit here and wait.

Just as I am about to leave, my group joins me. Not in the exact same spot, more like they're heads pop out of tree leaves all around the camp. They smile at me, like they figured out the flaw in the signals and decided that my silence was a sign that the boys weren't ready. Once we're all set up with our bows and arrows in hand, I give the signal we made up after the first couple times the boys started messing with us.

The boys jump up as soon as I start, but the girls are faster. They run in from every direction, each throwing a rope around the first guy they see. I see Ace in the corner of the camp watching my girls take out his boys. I point my bow at him, ready to shoot if he tries to run, but he just stands there, smiling and shaking his head.

After a couple minutes, there are only three boys left and Willow and I are the only ones with arrows. That's when I see Tyler trying to sneak out by Ace so I take a shot at him and pull out another. It lands right in front of him and my next one isn't as friendly. This one cuts through his cape and shirt, between his arm and the side of his chest. The back of the arrow catches his cape, pulling him to the ground. Ty hits the ground hard, getting a face full of dirt as Ace stands there laughing. He looks up at me, so I send him a wink before grabbing another arrow.

That's when I see Damon out of the corner of my eye. He's trying to run out by the tree Lydia is in. I pull the bow back and aim for just in front of him. The arrow flies by him slicing part of his cheek before landing at his feet. Noel runs over throwing the rope around his hips and the tree behind him. She uses her entire body thrown backward to hoist him up so his feet are dangling just above the ground.

Back on the other side of camp, Dawn is grabbing a hold of Tyler and dragging him to his feet. Then she tosses the rope around him, pulling him back toward the tree. A couple seconds after that, he's hanging the same way Damon is, except she was nicer and tied his feet. But he is *not* a happy camper. By the time she's done, all the boys are in the trees, and they are *really* not happy about it.

The shooters and I climb down our trees and meet the rest of the girls in the middle of all the boys. We laugh at their misery and high-five while the boys bitch and moan about the discomfort.

"Oh, you guys think *this* is it?" Elena asks as we laugh some more. "We're not quiet done yet."

"Pan's going to be mad when he gets back. And you don't want to make him angry, do you?" Griffin asks in a baby voice, pouting.

At this point, our laughter has evolved with Ryan, Lydia, Iris, Dawn, and Noel rolling around on the forest floor, trying to breathe. A look of confusion crosses the boys' faces. I stop laughing.

"Oh, didn't you know? That's awkward. Pan knows all about this." I pause for a second and look around at the girls. I try not to laugh as I break the rest of the news to them. "So I'm guessing that means he didn't tell you the good news! Guess what!" I exclaim, overexaggerating my excitement. You can hear the leaves being rustled by the soft breeze blowing through the camp as I pause. "Would you look at that! Twenty-seven boys with nothing to say! Who would have guessed? Has anyone seen them at a loss for words?" There are shaking heads from all the girls. "Well, it's okay! We can do all the talking when we move in! Shoot away, girls."

Elena and Clover had brought in the basket while the rest of us were doing our parts so the girls with ropes could join the fun. Though half of them don't have the best shots, they can still shoot.

After everyone has their case of arrows slung over their shoulder, they pick a boy to shoot at. Camila goes to stand in front of Hunter, but Elena stops her. "If you want to continue breathing, you'll pick someone else."

Camila's eyes go wide, and she runs away.

I wish I could say that to Jasmine as she parks herself in front of Ace. I roll my eyes. She's been after him since the day she stepped foot on this island. Oh, how I would love to threaten her, but I'm not as petty as Elena. I'll just hate her from afar.

After everyone's set up in front of one of the guys, I stand back and let them have their fun. There are only twenty-seven of them, so unless Pan lets us tie him up, I'm out of luck.

I find a good tree, out of the way, to climb, so I can sit and watch the game. Once I'm up, I sit in a break of the tree and let my feet hang over the edge. There are three thick branches, actually more like three thin tree trunks, making it feel kind of like a throne. I like it—Zylan, queen of The Island. I smile at myself before focusing back on the girls.

Clover is standing in front of Justin with her back facing me, teasing him. She pulls back the bow, about to shoot, so he closes his eyes, turning his head to the side like he doesn't want to see her shoot him. Then while he's not looking, she lowers the bow and I see her shoulders moving up and down like she laughing silently to herself. He stays like that for a few seconds before peeking one eye open and looking at her. As soon as that happens, she repeats the cycle.

I look over to where Elena is standing in front of Hunter, firing shot after shot after shot all the way around him. She laughs as his feet flail around and he screams for mercy. I chuckle to myself as well. That'll teach him to keep it in his pants. Besides, she's not doing any serious damage. Never mind. That's definitely a low blow.

"I would appreciate it if *your* girls didn't kill *my* boys. I quite like having minions." Pan appears, leaning on the branch to my right. Well, I'm assuming he is. He likes to do that a lot, and his voice travels to my right ear, but my eyes are watching Elena send another shot scraping Hunter's cheek.

"Elena's not going to kill him, just neuter him. Besides, we need blow off steam before we can move in. Fair is fair."

I sense a smile creep up on his lips, as Noel sends a shot at Klaus, skimming the sleeve of his shirt. Blood trickles down his arm to the end of his fingertip and lands on the dirt beside his left foot.

"So you've decided to take me up on my offer?"

I hear the leaves rustle, meaning he *was* leaning on the branch. I move to my left a little as he joins me.

"They have." I look over at him. His jaw is set, but he has a smirk creeping onto his face. "I haven't. I still don't trust you."

He swallows hard, the lump in his throat moving slowly as he thinks about what to say next.

"Smart."

Poof! He's gone.

***

"I hope there are no hard feelings. We just thought it was about time we got even," I say, shaking hands with Ace, who's smiling enough for the both of us. "And we also hope it's not a bother if we move here . . ."

Ace looks around at the other boys. Some of them look a little bit—angry isn't even strong enough to describe them, maybe furious? Nope, something even stronger than that would be a better term. Beyond pissed is probably the closest I'll get. But most of them are nodding and laughing at themselves for getting bested by a bunch of girls. "*Most* of us would love to have you join us. The rest"—he looks at Tyler, Damon, Hunter, Nate, and Luke—"will have to get over it."

All the girls look at each other relieved, like they thought this was all Pan's idea of a sick joke. Clover steps forward and whispers that I can let go of Ace's hand. I look down at our hands still locked together.

"Oops!" I laugh, mostly to myself, releasing my grip. "We'll be back with our stuff in a couple hoursish." Just before I push the branches out of my way at the entrance of the camp, I turn back around. "Anyone with a problem with that better get over it before we do. I'm a better shot than all of them, and I have no problem stringing you up by your ankles and taking a few shots if you make us feel unwelcome." I wink before throwing my hair over my shoulder. "Tata for now, boys."

"Wait! Do you guys maybe want some help?" Cole asks, running through the branches, followed by Ace, Justin, Klaus, Conner, Griffin, Isaac, Shawn, Dylan, and Matt.

We stop and turn to look at each other. We've been doing that a lot today. After a few seconds, Hope turns around and shrugs. "If you want to, we don't mind."

The ten of them start to follow us back to camp. I fall back, so I can talk to Ace. "So it looks like we'll be seeing a lot of each other now."

He smiles, lacing his fingers through mine. They're rough with calluses from all his years of using a bow staff. I remember when he first got here, and I would sneak around to watch him practice.

"Looks like it," I say.

My thoughts bounce around in my head as we walk farther. Are those five boys angry enough to do something stupid? Will it be awkward for me and Ace now that all the boys know? More importantly, will he get sick of me if he sees me every day?

"Hey, what's up with you?" Ace asks, noticing my lack of conversation.

We stop, and I watch the group disappear through the trees.

"Nothing. I'm just a little bit out of it." I shake my head. "But it doesn't matter. The Island will finally be unified, and there'll be no more feuds. Well, there will be, but the more time we spend together, the faster we'll get over it. And now . . ."—I grab his other hand, pulling them both behind my back so his arms wrap around my waist and we're pressed against each other. Then I go up on my tippy-toes and wrap my arms around his neck—"we can see each other all the time."

He picks me up and carries me over to a tree stump I can stand on, so we're the same height. "What if I don't want to see you all the time?" He chuckles a little, unable to keep a straight face.

"Well then, I'd have to kick some sense into you. Or I could just pull an Elena and shoot you multiple times." I smile.

He smiles back, his beautiful blue eyes sparkling as he does, like they always do when we're together.

"Then I guess it's a good thing I want to see you all the time." He pulls me closer.

"Yeah, it is." I quickly kiss him on the cheek before pulling away. "We should go catch up before they notice we're gone."

"But—" he cuts off what he is about to say as soon as I make my "scary face," as he says, by crossing my arms and dropping all my weight to my right leg. I like to think of it more as my sassy stance, but everyone says it's scarier, so I go with it. "Okay! Okay! No need for your scary face! Let's go."

Ace holds out his hands, helping me off the stump before lacing his fingers through mine, again.

***

"Alright! That's the last of it," Ace says, dropping a bag full of our supplies in the centre of camp.

"Thanks so much for your help," I say, smiling at Ace.

"No problem!" Justin yells very sarcastically from across the camp while standing over the heap of supplies he brought in. "Anytime!"

Clover bumps him with her hip and laughs. "No sarcasm out of you," she says sternly, pointing her figure at him.

"Yes, ma'am." He salutes.

"You're a dork." Clover smiles wider and nudges him again.

"Okay, lovebirds, break it up. We have a lot to do before dark." I roll my eyes.

Clover rolls her eyes back. "You don't own me."

"I wish she did," Elena says, entering the conversation. "At least you'd be under control. Now come on. Let's go."

"Are you saying I don't do a good enough job controlling my woman?" Justin asks with a look of fake hurt on his face.

The look he gets from Clover in return, however, is very real and very angry. "Excuse me? You don't control me at all."

"That's the problem."

"Alright, alright. Enough. We're going to have to deal with the angry when they get back. No use fighting among ourselves. No one controls anyone. We're all our own owners. Now, can we please get to work?"

"I think that's a marvelous idea!" Pan exclaims. He appears at the entrance of camp with a huge smile plastered on his face. "I'm going to run around and do a couple things but here." He waves his hand and a fire appears in the middle of camp. "When you're done setting up, sit down and enjoy yourselves. We haven't done a group dinner in a while. Time to catch up."

With that he disappears again.

"Thanks for your help, Pan," I say sarcastically. "Alright, you heard the man. Let's get moving."

Before any of us can even move, Tyler, Hunter, Damon, Nate, and Luke come charging into camp, and they look pissed. Their faces are bright red, and I think if I focus my eyes well enough, I'll be able to see steam coming out of Hunter's ears.

"You actually think it's alright for you to stay here?" Hunter screams, tossing a few of our pillows into the fire.

"You're all stupid if you think this is over!" Luke adds, throwing at least ten of our beds in after the pillows.

"You tied us up like animals!" Nate throws a few bows.

"And shoot at us like them too!" And there go our arrows at the hand of Damon.

I'm too shocked to move. All the girls are. We worked so hard finding leaves strong enough to string together to make beds for all twenty-eight of us. Not to mention how much work actually went into stringing them together. It took days, and it burned to ash in seconds.

Luckily, the boys move for us. They pull the five of them out of camp, still screaming nonsense about this not being over. Once they're gone, I call the girls together.

"I know Pan invited us here, but if they're going to be this angry for a while, I think it might be best if we set up somewhere else."

"But Pan invited us here. If we leave, they win. Wasn't that the point of this? To tell them they're not winning anymore?" Willow says.

"Good point. But I think Zylan meant leave until they calm down a bit."

Clover glances at me and I nod.

"They don't get to win anymore. But this wasn't just about winning. It was about getting even so we could unite The Island. If we unite from a couple clearings over, for now, I'm okay with that. We still have time to move."

"I agree with Zylan. How about we do a vote?" Elena suggests. "If you don't mind moving, raise your hand."

Before we get the chance, Pan comes strolling into camp with his arms full of cloth, followed by Ace and Justin. "Why are you all standing around? I thought I told you to get to work."

"First of all, you don't own us. Therefore, you can't tell us what to do."

"You go, girl," Clover says with a smirk plastered on her face.

I shoot her a look. "Second of all, you're five angry minions destroyed most of our stuff, so we can't get to work even if I felt the desire to listen to you, which I don't."

"Yeah, got that much from your 'first of all.'" Pan rolls his eyes. "To think I even went out of my way to get you these, so you'd be able to sleep." He waves his hands, and the cloth appears in the trees. "They're called hammocks. Sailors use them a lot. They're more comfortable than leaves."

"Thanks, Pan," Jasmine says shyly.

"You're welcome, J. I'm glad someone appreciates me."

He flashes his signature grin, and she giggles. And I thought I couldn't hate her any more than I alright do. Guess I was wrong.

I roll my eyes. "If you two are done flirting, could you magic us up some food? I'm starving and would very much love to go to bed soon. It's been a long day."

"What's the magic word?"

"I'll shoot you if you don't."

"You know that won't work on me, but I get the point."

Seconds later, the fire is replaced by two long tables covered with just about every food and drink I've ever seen in my whole life. There's turkey, chicken, beef, salad, cheese, pasta, pizza, bread, sausage, fish, soups, and so much more. My mouth waters just looking at it.

"Thank you," I say as I pass by.

I surprise myself with the sincerity in my tone. There was no hint sarcasm. There was no venom. There was no bitter taste in my mouth.

"What poor people did you steal all this food from?" Clover asks.

I should have asked that. That's literally my go-to line whenever we have dinners together. What's wrong with me? I'm off my game.

"No idea. I think I actually stole it from a restaurant. Oops, you better eat it all."

"Come on, man," Justin says, stacking up a second plate. "When has that ever been a problem?"

"Normally, Hunt's here. You don't eat as much as him."

"Oh? So this is a challenge? An eat off? Get Hunter. Chain him to a tree if you have to. I'll destroy him. I will destroy him so hard."

"Honey, think about your words before you say them," Clover says as she slides a piece of roast beef onto her plate.

Justin pauses, unsure of what he said that could be taken the wrong way. "I don't get it."

We all burst out laughing.

"I say we get him. The thought of Hunter being chained to a tree again makes me smile. Him actually being chained to a tree again would make me happy." Elena says, scooping mash potato onto her plate. When she looks up and sees no one has moved to find him, she rolls her eyes. "I'm serious. Someone find him and bring him to me. I want to shoot him some more."

"You heard the lady. Ace, Justin with me," Pan says.

Justin says some gibberish with a mouthful of food. It sounds like, "Come on, man. I'm eating here."

"Let's go, or I'll turn your food into a frog."

Justin drops both his plates on the ground and jumps up. "Dude, that is so not funny. You know I'm scared of frogs."

Pan smiles. "Yes, that's why I said it. Ace, do you have any objections? Should I turn your food into a snake?"

"Hell no! Let's go," Ace exclaims, jumping to his feet. As he walks past me, he kisses the top of my head. "We won't be long."

"Take your time. Seeing Elena shoot Hunter again would make me very happy too." I smile and kiss his cheek.

He smiles back. "Well then, we'll find him."

"Come on! We're losing daylight!" Pan yells from the other side of camp.

"It's nighttime, dumbass. There's no daylight left," I say, adding some chicken to my plate. I look down at my plate. I think I have enough for now. There are two pieces of roast beef, three rolls of bread, two chicken legs, and some gravy poured over the beef.

I feel Pan roll his eyes at me from behind me. "You know what I meant. Now, let's go."

Justin and Ace follow Pan out of camp.

I make my way over to where Clover and Elena are sitting. "You seriously want to shoot him more?" I laugh, taking a seat across from Elena. "I think you did enough damage this afternoon."

"No no. I don't want to shoot him. I want you to shoot him. He's terrified of you, and I want to witness his heart attack." She takes a bite of her mash potato, not even cracking a smile.

"You're serious?"

"Do I look like I'm joking? Consider this your retribution for not telling me about Ace for 496 goddamn years." She takes another bite of her mash potato, this time smiling.

"Fine. I'll shoot him." I sigh.

"You sound so enthusiastic. I can do it instead. I like shooting people, especially Hunter," Clover says.

"You're an awful shot! That's why you didn't shoot at Justin. You would have killed him," Elena exclaims with a laugh.

I choke on my chicken. "You almost took off Hunter's dick! At least I can admit I'm a bad shot. You just want Zylan to shoot him so you don't kill him. Just admit you still love him."

Oh no. Here it comes. Elena and Clover have trouble getting along. The three of us are crazy close, but for some reason, the two of them go at it more often than what makes sense. The three of us have been best friends since Elena's first night on The Island, but every once in a while, the two of them get into a huge fight and don't talk for weeks. Then in the blink of an eye, they're hanging out and laughing like nothing ever happened.

"I DO NOT!" Elena yells standing up. Her plate flips off her lap and lands upside down on the forest floor. My heart sinks a little when I see the mash potato hit the dirt. I love mashed potatoes. "THIS IS SO TYPICAL OF YOU. WHENEVER I ASK ZYLAN TO DO SOMETHING, YOU

TRY TO INSERT YOURSELF. GUESS WHAT! SHE NOT
JUST YOU'RE FRIEND."

Now everyone's staring.

"I was just saying she didn't look like she wanted to. I
offered to help. My mistake. Won't happen again." Clover
stands up as well, leaving more mash potato lying in the dirt.
"Why are you so obsessed with her anyways?"

It's time for me to step in. I set my plate on the log beside
me and stand up. "Guys! This isn't about me. You know that,
Clover. Come on. We're dealing with the five angry guys.
The last thing we need right now is you two at each other's
throats. Get some more food, sit down, and shut up. No one
needs to hear you two argue, especially over something as
stupid as this."

"Fine!" Elena storms off to who knows where.

Clover rolls her eyes and heads to the food. I hope they fix
their issue quickly. It's bad enough the five guys are angry at
us. We can't be angry with each other, not when we have to
watch each other's backs.

Chapter 3

Jacob

Pan

Five hundred and forty-three. Five hundred and forty-three years. For 543 years, she's hated me, and I had no idea. I always figured she was freaked out because her mom was murdered in front of her, and she could have died herself. Never did it occur to me that she would think I'm the one who did it. I didn't. All I wanted to do was protect her.

Despite popular belief, I'm not Peter Pan, and this isn't Neverland. Five hundred and fifty-one years ago, my twin brother (yes, he would be Peter Pan) and I lived on Neverland together, saving kids—from evil parents, illnesses, just about anything really—and teaching them that it wasn't their fault and that they didn't deserve what happened to them.

That was until one day, while I was doing my rounds, I saw Zylan. So instead of getting Wendy right away, I watched her despite Peter's instructions. I don't know why he fussed so much about Wendy, to be honest, but his instruction was very clear: "Get the girl. Get out. Don't stop." He was never like that with the other kids. Anyways, I wasn't used to being around kids my age. Peter only saves kids between four and twelve. They all follow the rules until they've settled into Neverland because they're too scared not to. But this girl, she wasn't.

From what I knew about the rules for girls at that time, they had to be proper. This meant hair up, posture straight, long dress to cover their ankles with a corset underneath, hands folded neatly in front of them while speaking to a male, and they had to be home before dark unless they were with their father or husband. She was breaking all these rules when I saw her.

Her hair was let down, coming to an end just under her second rib. She was standing with her shoulders hunched over slightly. She wore a white underdress that ended at her midthigh, and it didn't look like she could be wearing a corset under that fabric without it showing. Her hands were flying in different directions as she spoke to her two male friends, and it was definitely way after dark.

I stood there watching her until her girlfriend looked over in my direction. I figured, because I was standing in a pitch-black alleyway, she wouldn't be able to see me, but she really tried. She got the attention of the other three talking and pointed directly at me. The girl that caught my attention in the first place nodded quickly like she was nervous. The other three shrugged, and they all ran in my direction. I disappeared farther down the alley to grab Wendy before they could find me, but she never left my mind.

Three months after that, I would visit her town every day before I would rescue the child Peter sent me after. I watched her grow up in front of me for three years. I saw her happy with her friends, angry with her mother, cry to her father, frustrated with society. I saw her and her friends get into fights one night then they were fine the next. I heard her ideas about the world and her ideas about legends and magic. While her friends would laugh at her and say, "The world isn't round. It's flat," and "There's no way dragons exist, and we haven't seen one," or "No one can just light a fire with their hands," I would nod in agreement from a distance. I wished that I could prove to her that she wasn't crazy, that it wasn't just her imagination. It was real.

One day while I was trying to find her, I saw her friends sitting together without her, laughing about some of her ideas.

I took this opportunity to show them that she was right. I walked over and sat down beside the girl.

"Who are you?" she asked.

Even though I knew she spoke Italian, it came out in perfect English. It was a little trick I picked up as I travelled the world, rescuing children. It was no good if we couldn't understand each other, so I enchant all of their voices so they speak English and my own voice so it comes out in what even language is needed at the time.

"Jacob, who are you?"

"Aurora. This is Cristoforo." She pointed at the darker-haired boy. "And he's Marco." She pointed at the lighter-haired one. "What are you doing here?"

"I overheard you talking about one of your friends believing in magic. You think she's crazy, but she's not." I smiled and started to stand up. "You see, there are thing about this world you know nothing about. Things you'll never see but are still there. Things you have yet to see but will."

"You're just as crazy as she is," Cristoforo said with a laugh.

"Am I, Christopher?" I smiled, raising my eyebrow. I circled my right hand over my left, making the image of the world appear in spherical form.

They gasped.

"How did you do that?" Marco asked.

"Magic." With that, I vanished to find the girl.

Since her friends weren't with her, I figured she was at home. I reappeared on the roof of her neighbour's house, crouched behind a higher part of it, out of sight. I got there just in time to see her get into a screaming match with her mom again. That time, it got to the point of a chair being thrown across the room. I'm pretty sure it was her mom who did it, but they looked so much alike from the back, I couldn't tell and I still, to this day, don't know.

I wished that I could go in. I wanted to help her so bad, but I wouldn't know what to do. That's when a man, probably a pirate by the looks of his outfit, knocked on the door and I saw the gun. Inside the house, she and her mother looked at each other like they knew what was outside that door. They stood there for a few seconds before the girl ran down the hallway.

Her mother took a slow, deep breath before walking to the door. The guy pointed the gun at her and motioned her to walk down the street. She did. Just as she disappeared out of my sight, her husband came running down the hall, his daughter right behind him. He told her something that made her hesitate but disappear back down the hall, then he chased the stranger and his wife down the street.

I stood up and jumped off the roof. I looked around to make sure there's no one around before I ran into her house. Before I could make my way to the end of the hall, I heard footsteps running in my direction. I hid in the first room I could duck into and looked around. It was definitely the girl's room. On my right, there was a dresser, slightly open, filled with dresses I've never seen her wear. On the left was a desk with a chair and huge mirror was set up on top. In front of me, there was a bed pushed against the wall and a bench under a window. I had watched her fall asleep on that bench so many times. It was the place I talked to her for the first time, and where I had seen her spend many nights starring out that window then writing stuff down in a notebook.

I went to open the door a crack when a shot rang through the house, so I decided to back farther into the room. What if that shot hit the girl? What if it hit her mom and the pirate finds the girl? What will he do with her? Not focusing on my surroundings, I missed the notebook lying on the floor in the middle of the room. I hit the ground, making a small thump covered up by a slightly louder thump just outside the door. Was it her or her father?

I pushed myself up and walked back to the door, my curiosity taking over my sense of survival. I slowly pushed it open a crack to see what was going on. A pirate, with his back to me, was standing over the girl's father. The pirate was bleeding onto the floor from the place his left hand should be. The girl's father was hunched over on his hands and knees, trying to catch his breath.

"Why us?" he asked while trying to stand.

The pirate kicked him, and he flipped onto his back.

"Don't pre'end like yee don't know, Cap'ain." He spat the last word like it was venom to him. "I wants me treasure. All'f it."

"I don't have it."

The pirate pointed the gun at him, and the girl's father put his hands up in defense. "I know where to get it!" He rolled over and stood up, leaving his hands up. "Don't shoot. I'll take you to it."

At that moment, he saw me. He locked eyes with me, and I knew what he was thinking. He didn't want to get shot because he knew the pirate would find his daughter, and if he did that, well, we all know what happens to pirate prisoners. That was all a distraction so someone would find the girl. By the look in his eye, he was hoping I would save her. I nodded my head twice, letting him know I would.

A quick look of relief crossed his face before the pirate waved his gun and pushed him to lead. "Let's go." With the gun pressed to his back, the man led the pirate out the door and down the street.

As soon as the coast was clear, I pushed the door all the way open and ran down the hall, hoping to find the girl quickly in case they came back. Finally, at the very end of the hall, I heard the soft sound of weeping. The door was wide open, and she was sitting on the floor, crying into her mother's shoulder. I really didn't want to ruin her moment, but I also didn't want her to die. As far as I knew, they wouldn't be gone for long. She looked up just a little bit when I moved in front of her.

"Is my father okay?" she asked, her green eyes bloodshot and glossed from the tears welling up.

I knelt down, so I could look her directly in the eyes. "I'm so sorry, but I don't know. I promised him that I would keep you safe, so we need to leave now." I extended my hand to help her up. She kissed her mother's forehead and slid her off her lap before taking it. She blinked, letting all the tears she was holding in spill over her cheeks. "I'm Jacob by the way. Jacob Pan."

"Zylan" is all she said as I helped her up.

On the trip back to Neverland, she fell asleep. I was carrying her bridal style with her arms draped around my neck. The longer we took, the tighter she held on. By the time my feet touched the ground, she was snuggled into my neck, not wanting to let go when I tried to put her down.

"Who is this? Where's Jaden?" Peter asked, appearing in front of me.

"This is Zylan. On my way to get Jaden, I saw her family being attacked by pirates, and if I hadn't grabbed her, she would have been dead," I said, finally getting her to let go of me, as I set her gently on a pile of leaves.

"She's not a child, Jacob. She can take care of herself. What about Jaden? Who's going to protect him? What if he dies tonight because you got her instead?" He crosses his arms. "You should have just done what you were told."

"So what? Just because Zylan's seventeen instead seven, she didn't need my help? You weren't there. You didn't see it. I did and I'm not going to apologize for saving her."

"Fine. You want to help her? Do it from The Island, not from here." He waved his hand, and a splurge of colours poured from his fingers. Then he was gone.

That was the last time I ever saw my brother. I have no idea where Neverland is in relation to The Island, and I had no intention of finding out, but now I think it's about time for a family reunion.

***

"Are we actually going to chain Hunt to a tree? 'Cause I was completely joking. I love the dude. The last thing I want is him to be angry at everyone . . ."

Justin picks at his nails as we walk through the woods.

"We should do what Zylan said she would do," Ace suggests.

"And what was that?"

"She said she would string them up and shoot at them herself if they made her feel unwelcome."

"I love it. Scrap the original plan. We'll collect them all tonight, just before everyone wakes up." I smile to myself.

"What happened to Elena? She's not going to be happy anymore."

Justin kicks a stone in front of him.

"About that . . . Justin, you should go back to camp. Clover's pissed and Elena's gone. You can guess what's happened."

Justin rolls his eyes. "How are those two friends? Alright. Thanks for letting me know." He turns around and heads back toward camp.

"How do you always know?" Ace asks.

We're continuing our walk into the forest. Tyler's probably my best student when it comes to magic. He's the only guy that can cloak himself properly, meaning he's probably keeping the five of them hidden, most likely because they're scared of Zylan, which means Ace and I have to find them the old-fashioned way—tracking.

"I just do." I'm not about to tell my best friend that I know because I can always sense what his girlfriend is feeling, and right now, she was feeling annoyed and unhappy.

"You gotta teach me that."

"You mean like I had to teach you transporting? Or cloaking? Or changing? Or any of the other million things I had to teach you, which you suck at?"

"I don't suck at them as bad anymore! Zylan's a better teacher than you." He laughs.

"Tyler would disagree. I taught him everything, and he got it just fine. *You* are just a shitty student. It has absolutely nothing to do with my ability to teach and everything to do with your ability to retain information."

"Plot twist: Zylan actually taught Tyler everything he knows, and he lied to you about learning from you because he felt bad that you suck. Take that, Mr. I'm A Great Teacher. How's your ego feeling now?"

I stop walking a turn to him. "Are you serious? Everybody went to Zylan? Damnit! I really do suck." I sigh and bowed my head.

"Aha! So you finally admit it? You suck." He smirks.

"You bastard. You lied so I would say that." I shake my head. "Who'd you bet? Justin? He's known for his bets. I should have known better." I laugh. "Yup, I am admitting I suck, but only because I didn't see that coming."

He tilts his head slightly, studying me. "For the record, I did not lie. She really did teach him. Are you okay? Normally, you would have seen that coming from a mile away."

He's been my best friend from the second he set foot on The Island. Of course, he could tell I was off. I don't know why either. I mean Zylan's hated me from the second she stepped foot on The Island. It's not like she was about to sit around for 543 years and not date anyone. I think what's throwing me off is the fact that, of all people, it had to be Ace.

I've seen her talk to other guys but never Ace. He's the last person I would expect her to be with. If anything, I would have thought it was Tyler. They've always been pretty close.

I know that Ace has been here the longest of all the guys, but I can't wrap my head around the fact that he's been with her all this time and he never told me. Mind you, I never told him that I've been obsessing over her for 546 years, six months, two weeks, and three days.

"I'm fine. Just thinking about how weird it's going to be with the girls running around our camp." I force myself to smile and laugh.

He lets out a laugh as well. "Very true." He pauses. "I've been wondering. What made you change your mind?"

"I just thought it was time to bury the hatchet. Five hundred years is a long time to live separately. It's time for a change." *But, in reality, I was keeping the boys on the other side of The Island so that Zylan would be alone forever. No point in doing that now.*

"Today of all days?" He laughs and shakes his head. "You're a terrible liar. You know that right? This has something to do with Zylan, doesn't it?"

"What do you mean?"

"I mean Zylan finally let go of whatever bullshit she was holding on to for five hundred years and settled a truce."

I laugh. "You always could see right through me. Now come on. We have five angry boys to find and hang upside down." I slap his shoulder and turn my back to him.

Ace is the smartest person I know, or second smartest next to Zylan. If he can't put together him telling me about his relationship and my uniting the camps, no one will. I hope.

"So now that we're all together, am I going to find out what girl you've been seeing?"

I snort. "I haven't been seeing anyone."

"Oh, come on. You're telling me that after 542 years, you haven't seen anyone?"

"Actually, fifty-one. Eight years before Zylan."

"Shit. You're telling me that, after all this time, you've never been with anyone? I don't believe that for a second. You're a guy. How have you not exploded?"

I burst out laughing. "Oh, that kind of seeing. No one here, recently anyways. When I leave to bring someone back, I find someone. Starting something with someone here would be too messy."

When she first got here, Elena came on to me pretty strongly. While I hate myself for sleeping with one of Zylan's best friends, I can only control myself so much.

"What do you mean? Zylan and I have been together for like ever. Clover and Justin the same. It takes effort, but it doesn't have to be messy."

"It does when you've been in love with someone for so long, but you can't have them." I sigh. "I'm not seeing anyone because I can't move on."

"Dude, what are you talking about?"

I could tell him half a truth. Come on. Think, Jacob. What could explain me being in love with someone for most of my life, without telling him about Zylan? Something supernatural. My older sister. I could twist their stories and combine them.

"You promise you'll believe me? It sounds a little unbelievable."

"Dude, I've been alive for over five hundred years. I've seen magic. There's a freaking waterfall that heals any injury. Nothing is unbelievable to me."

"I've been in love with a girl for almost my whole life. I've known her for as long as I can remember, and she's perfect. She's smart, funny, sarcastic, beautiful, strong. She's everything good about life. Whenever I see her, my mind goes blank, and I can't think of a word to say. I saw her for the first time in 1465, and before you go telling me that's impossible, you promised to believe me.

"She was fourteen, and it was the middle of the night. You know what it was like back then women weren't allowed out by themselves. To see a girl out in the middle of the night, in the middle of the town's square, was unheard of. I watched her with her friends and I knew that I had to know her. So, watched her and looked out for her.

"When I finally worked up the nerve to talk to her, she already knew I was watching her. She didn't freak out or scream for help or yell at me to get away from her. She wasn't scared. So I sat outside of her window and talked to her. She was going through a rough time, so I wanted her to know I would always be there for her.

"I kept going back every night. Then one night she was attacked and I couldn't save her. The guy who attacked her wasn't human. He was a vampire. He drained the life from her right in front of me. Little did I know she would become a vampire too.

"Every time I go back to earth, I try to find her. Every time I do. It's hard to move on when there's still a chance but you know it will never happen."

Ace drops his hand on my shoulder to stop me from walking. "I, as your best friend, am going to help you move on. Then I'm going to get you a girl. Any of them would drop their guy for you in a second. They all love you."

Not the one that matters. "Not any of them. Besides, there's no one here worth stealing."

"Zylan is. But if you steal her, I'll kill you." He holds a serious face for about three seconds then bursts out laughing. "I know you wouldn't. Now come on. We have five people to find."

I would if I could, but I can't.

Chapter 4

Trip to the Past

Zylan

I think all of us are a little bit on edge, the girls because we don't know if the boys will try something to retaliate, and the boys because they don't know if we have anything else planned.

Everyone's sleeping. I can't. I haven't been able to sleep since I came here. I mean I get a few hours here and there, but I always have these weird dreams I can't remember when I wake up. Everyone says it's normal not to remember, that the longer you're awake, the more you forget. But for me, it's like the second I open my eyes, it's gone, and if I try to remember it, my head hurts. I find the more I don't sleep, the less pain I have in my head, so I try and find things to do.

When I was alone, when Pan first brought me here, I taught myself how to shoot a bow and arrow. I hoped that if I did, the next time Pan came around, I could shoot him and try to leave. That's actually how I ended up meeting Ace. I tried to kill him. Looking back on it now, it's actually a rather funny story.

I was wandering around with my bow slung over my shoulder and my arrows in a case on my back. I found a really nice place deep in the forest that I like to go to whenever I get overwhelmed. It's humbling. It made me realize the beauty that surrounds me.

It's a cliff on the far northwest side of The Island. At the top of that cliff, hidden behind a great deal of thorny vines, is a waterfall. The entrance was hidden at the time I found it, and if I hadn't seen it open, I would have jumped off that cliff. I don't remember how that hidden entrance came to reveal itself, but I'm glad it did.

The day I met Ace, I was wandering toward the waterfall when I heard branches snapping from behind me. I was terrified it was Pan. After all, we were the only two people there, so I removed the bow from my shoulder and grabbed an arrow. I slid behind a tree, getting ready to shoot.

Boy, was I ever surprised to see a tall blur with blond hair walk into view. My confusion led to the accidental release of my bow arm. The arrow just missed his face, lodging itself in the tree beside him. He grabbed the sword he had holstered at his hip, and in the blink of an eye, he was standing in front of me, the tip of his sword poking into my ribs.

"Who the hell are you?" he asked.

His face was still blurry, but I could definitely tell it wasn't Pan.

"I could ask you the same thing."

Faster than he could reply, I used my bow to knock his sword out of his hand. Then I grabbed another arrow and pointed it at his chest. "But the better question is who taught you how to use a sword? A cripple?"

"I'll have you know my best friend is a cripple, and he could do just as well as anyone else. Don't pretend you know anything about one."

"That's where you're wrong. My sister was a cripple. Not born, but made. Don't pretend you know anything about me."

"Was?"

"She's dead. Just like everyone else in my family."

I aimed my bow off and released the tension, sending the arrow just past his ear and into the tree behind him. "Don't follow me unless you want to join them, that is."

I ran past him, back in the direction of my camp.

When my sister was almost eleven, she fell in love with this boy down the street. His name was Robert. I know it sounds young, but back then, we were married off around the age of fourteen. If it was going to happen anyways, it might as well happen with someone you would enjoy. So we came up with plans involving meeting, talking, and getting him to love her back. At first, she would make up entire conversations with him, and we would lay out plans on the floor showing how it would work.

I wish, looking back, I had talked her out of it, though it probably wouldn't have mattered. She was very stubborn. He was a horrible person, not at first and not around my parents, but I saw him with her one day.

They were with a few of his friends, standing on the far side of the square. Back then that was the only place to hang out with your friends, if you had any, that is. Most of our time was supposed to be taken up by family duties, so most of the kids in the village never made any friends. Anyway, she stood there in silence the entire time. Her mouth didn't move once. All she did was smile and nod. When I walked by, I heard a little bit of the conversation.

"What do you do in your spare time?" the fair-haired boy asked.

"She is learning how to horseback ride. She is rather good actually," Robert interjected. Which is a big fat lie. Wendy never rode a horse a day in her life.

"We would love to join you on one of your rides!" one girl exclaimed. The girl next to her nodded, smiling widely.

"I do not think that is a good idea. She gets rather nervous riding in front of people." I know why he lied about that, but I still couldn't figure out why he lied about her horseback riding in the first place.

It went on like that until I walked over. I got really fed up with him not letting her talk, and lying, so I decided to do something about it. "Wendy! What are you doing here? I've been looking for you everywhere!"

"She has been here with us the whole time," Robert said. I could sense a snarl present in his tone. "You walked by twice."

I looked away from my sister to glare at him. "Well, first of all, I don't know if you knew this, but my vision is rather blurry, and normally, I would recognize her voice. But you didn't really give her a chance to speak. Second of all, I don't think I was talking to you. I was talking to her."

Everyone looked at me wide-eyed, like I had killed someone. Women weren't allowed to talk to men like that. Women had to be proper. Women had to do this. Women had to do that. You have no idea how sick I was of people telling me how to act, how to speak, how to behave, but most importantly, I was sick of men thinking we couldn't do things for ourselves. Do you know how much work it is to get yourself into a corset? If we had to wear them every day, the least they could do is let us speak for ourselves.

The worst thing about the situation was that they all stood there and watched as the little prick slapped me across the face. The whole square watched him hit me, and no one did *anything* about it. That's the problem about that time. Woman weren't people, so why shouldn't they be hit in public as everyone watched but did nothing?

Wendy looked at me, horrified. As soon as she did, I knew that wasn't the first time he acted out like that. The mysterious bruises no one could see under her dress came from him. At that moment, I thought of every possible way I could kill him and get away with it, but my plan would have to wait.

"Don't you dare speak to me like that, wench. I am a nobleman. You will address me properly."

Your dad may be a nobleman, but any man who strikes a woman is anything but. The only thing you are is a coward, I thought as I grabbed the ends of my dress, pulling it up a tad so I could curtsy. "Yes, my lord. I am truly sorry, my lord." *For your parents because they raised a monster like you.*

I walked back home, massaging my cheek. I needed to find a way to help Wendy out of that relationship. I suppose I could have told Mother and Father, but it would have been his word against mine. Even though Wendy probably wanted to leave him, she wouldn't speak against Robert. She would be too scared.

Later, when she got home, she ran into my room crying. After I had left, his friends decided they had had enough of him, so they left as well. He brought her back to his family's home shortly after that. She figured if she stayed in the family room, nothing bad would happen to her, but he asked to be excused. He beat her because of what I said, because I embarrassed him, and because of me, my little sister was covered in bruises from her chest to her feet.

I held her in my arms. I promised I would help her no matter what. I helped her get ready for bed because it takes a steady hand to undo a corset and tie the back of a nightgown. She was shaking too much to stand for very long, let alone untie a tightly pulled string.

That night when Mother called us for supper, I told her we weren't feeling well, so we were going to skip it and go to bed. She looked slightly annoyed but let us go. Of course, we didn't sleep. I made her tell me everything, including when it started. They had been together for about six months at that point, and apparently, it only started a month before. At first it was only a light punch to the stomach, the occasional slap across the face. She didn't think it was a problem until last week. That was the first time he left a mark. She couldn't remember what started his fit, but she remembered it was a bad one. She said she'd been having trouble walking properly and standing properly. That led him to hit harder.

Every night after that day, I prayed that someone would save her. That someone would take her away from this abuse. I would stare out my window for hours, hoping someone walking by would suddenly take her away from here. I would rather have her safe than have her with me. I needed her safe, even if it meant she had to leave me. I prayed for someone to help her. But no one ever did, and I never prayed again.

One night, almost a year later, I was walking home from Cris's house when I heard crying from an alleyway. Despite the logical voice in my head, I turned and walked down it. There she was, Wendy. She was lying there, bruises all over her face, blood pouring out of a cut above her eyebrow, and her lip swollen. Her dress was ripped open, revealing more blood coming from her stomach. She was stabbed. The bastard stabbed her.

"Did he do this?"

She tried to speak, but nothing came out, and she cried even harder. I couldn't calm her down. I couldn't stop her tears. I couldn't do anything. I was useless. I tried helping her walk, but she fell back to the ground. I was her big sister. I was supposed to be able to help her. The best I could do was to rip my dress apart to clean her face.

I pulled it over my head and tore it, using most of the fabric to cover up her stab wound, then I used my corset to put under her head like a pillow, and the rest of my dress to cover her before I ran to get help. I told her not to move. I told her I would be right back.

That was the last time I saw her. I ran out of the alley to find my friends laughing. I thought they were all leaving, I guess they were. I just wasn't invited along. By the time I returned to Wendy with them, she was gone. Her blood still fresh, my dress and corset still there. I have no idea where she went. I always thought Robert had just come back to finish her off before dumping her somewhere like garbage. I always blamed myself for what happened. I always wished I had stayed with her. I lost my best friend and sister that night. I thought I was going to lose everyone actually.

When we came back and she was gone, I thought my friends wouldn't believe me. But they did. They dragged me away from that place and back to my house. They explained what happened while I cried into Cris's shoulder. Mother cried with me as the story progressed. I left out the part about Robert doing it when I told my friends, so my parents rushed right over there to tell him.

They sent out sailors, knights, hounds, townspeople, anyone willing to help really. When they came out empty-handed three weeks later, we had to call it quits. That was the hardest night of my life.

She's the reason I became so rebellious. I didn't want to be home to face my parents, and I sure as hell didn't want my friends looking at me with pity filling their eyes every time they saw me. I did anything and everything I could to keep it off my mind until, eventually, I pushed it out of my memories almost completely.

***

"Hey, Ze. Are you still up?" Clover whispers, snapping me out of my train of thought.

Her bed is hanging just beside mine, so I roll to my right so I can talk to her properly.

"Yeah, C. What's up?" I whisper back.

"Nothing . . . I was just thinking about stuff. Would you mind going for a walk with me? I want to talk, but I don't want to wake anyone."

Careful not to flip the hammock, I sit up. "Yeah sure. No problem. I can't sleep either."

I see the outline of her smile in the dim moonlight. "Thanks."

I'm not entirely sure how to get out of one of these things, so I grab one side of the hammock, bring it to the other, so it's all crumpled together. Once it is, I flip myself over, so my feet are dangling, and I use my hands to walk myself over to the nearest tree. Once I'm safely over there, I easily climb down it and plant my feet on the ground.

Clover beat me down, so she's laughing at how complicated I had made that. "Hey! I've never seen one of those before! Stop judging!" That just makes her laugh harder. "Fine. Know what? I'll just climb back up."

I turn around but she grabs my arm. "I'm sorry! I'm sorry! Come on. I was just laughing at the fact that you could pop down, but you had to make it all complicated. It's typical Zylan."

I roll my eyes as she ducks under the branches covering the entrance then I follow. We walk in silence for a while before I can't take it anymore.

"Okay, so what is it you want to talk about?" I ask.

She sighs, letting a puff of air frost slightly as it exits. Though the days are always hot, or at least warm, sometimes the nights can be freezing. Tonight, it isn't freezing but cold enough that we could see our breath.

"This is kind of embarrassing, but . . . I'm worried. Now that our camps are together, Justin might . . . you know . . . get sick of me. I know it seems weird, but I'm wondering if the only reason we work is because we don't spend 24-7 together. What if he gets sick of me? I don't think I could watch him fall for another girl." Clover sighs again, stopping in the middle of a clearing.

I let out a sharp breath of air. It's kind of like a laugh, the kind you do when nothing's funny but you feel like you have too.

"Don't worry. You're not alone." She looks at me a little confused. I wave her off. "This looks like a job for my thinking spot."

More confusion floods her face. I ignore it and grab her hand.

A couple seconds later, we're standing on top of my cliff. Sometimes, walking is good for me to get my thoughts together, which is why I walked back to camp after I found Pan. Right now, however, magic is better.

She blinks, stumbling backward. "You know how much I hate it when you do that with no warning! You could have told me where to go, and I could have joined you myself!" She pauses and looks around. "Where are we?"

"Sorry." I laugh. "I forgot you never saw the outside of the cave. I could have sworn I showed you this spot when I gave you the tour!" She shakes her head. "Well, this is where I come when I'm struggling with something. When I first got here, I was kind of a mess. This is where I came. Every time I thought about doing something drastic, every time I needed a reason to live, and now every time I need an answer to something, this is where I come to think."

I close my eyes and breathe in slowly then out slowly. I feel the cold breeze pulling my hair out of my face, the metal on my glasses chills, and the peace of The Island as it sleeps. I hear the distant sound of wolves howling, of leaves rustling, of the soft thumping of the waterfall behind me.

"What do you mean reason to live? What happened to you?"

"The long version?"

"Yes."

"Well, we better get started."

And so I tell her. I leave out the part about Pan killing my parents though. I'm not ready to talk about that yet.

***

"Wait! You almost killed him?" Clover asks. I nod my head as we laugh together. "So how did you guys end up together?"

"Well, we hated each other for a long time. At least, he acted like he hated me." I laugh. "I remember the day Pan officially introduced us like a year later. I was hunting a deer because I hadn't eaten in a couple days and I was starving. I had the perfect position to kill it mercifully. St least I think I did. My vision was getting worse at that time, but that has nothing to do with this . . . um, where was I? Oh yeah! Just as I released the bow, Pan appeared right in front of it. Of course, he caught the arrow before it hit him. He likes to show off as you know." I roll my eyes and she laughs.

"So I started screaming at him: 'You're so stupid,' 'I'm starving,' 'You messed up my hunt,' blah blah blah. And he stood there, still holding the arrow, laughing at me. He thought my suffering was hysterical. I had half a mind to shoot him again, but I just asked him what he wanted. That's when he dropped the arrow and motioned Ace to come out."

"'I'd like you to meet Ace,' he said.

"'What kind of name is Ace? Who named you? A retard?'

"Ace got really mad. 'I named myself. Pan said I could change my name and leave the past behind me.'

"Then I got mad. 'You didn't give me that option!'

"The three of us spent a great deal of time yelling at each other before Pan got fed up and disappeared. That left me and Ace to yell at each other some more. That went on for a little longer before I got fed up and disappeared myself.

"I had to find something else to eat, seeing as Pan fucked that up for me. I wandered around a bit more until I found Ace practicing with his bow staff. I referred to it as the giant stick because I had no idea what it was at first. I hid behind a tree and watched him. Even as a giant blur, he was so graceful. It was beautiful to watch. Like a piece of art that you can stare at for hours. I think that's when I started to fall for him. Every day I would go back to that spot and watch him.

"For years, he didn't notice, but one day, my vision was getting so bad that I ended up stumbling. I was met with a nice crack to the side of the head. That was not a fun headache when I woke up, I can tell you that. When I came to, Ace was hovering over me, holding a cloth to my forehead. 'How long was I out?' I asked.

"'Almost an hour. I wasn't sure you were waking up.' He chuckled and helped me sit up. That was the first time we talked. I asked him how he ended up here. His story was very different than mine.

"He was a sailor, top of his class. Only seventeen-year-old on the ocean for the good guys at least. That night, when he ended up here, his ship was under attack by pirates. He said that the pirate made the rest of the crew walk the plank. He was the youngest, so he went last. Pan rescued his from drowning.

"After that I told him about my story. He pitied me, asked me if I wanted to learn how to use a bow staff. I said yes. He offered to help if I taught him how to shoot. He's actually the one who gave me these." I pull my glasses off my face and study them. Everything around me is just a blob of different colours. "One day while we were practicing, I almost took off his head, so he asked me about it. The next day, he came back with these." I put them back on and look at Clover. "But enough about me. You never told me your story."

"You never asked." She laughs.

"Well, when we met, we were both trying to forget. If you still are, I get it. You don't have to tell me."

"It's probably about time I talked about it. Where do I begin?"

"Wherever you want."

Her story is one as old as time. She fell in love with the wrong guy. So deeply in love, she was willing to lose everything for him. She came from a noble family in England. She was supposed to marry the prince of Scotland, so she moved there when she was thirteen. When her father found out she fell for a peasant, he gave her an option, demand really: marry Prince James the Fourth or leave and never come back. She chose the second option.

When the peasant found out she lost the family fortune, he was furious. He screamed at her, told her she was stupid, beat her up, and left her for dead. He was clearly only in it for the money, and after that was gone, why would he stay?

While she was lying there, coming to terms with her death, Pan appeared in front of her. At the time, she was more terrified than relieved. She had no idea what this random guy was going to do to her. But he sat down with her, asked if she was okay, asked what he could do to help. He ended up bringing her here.

The rest I knew.

We both helped each other out of a dark place. I was still driving myself crazy, spending most of my time alone, only seeing Ace once or twice a week. Meanwhile, her wound was still fresh. Honestly, I don't know what I would have done if Pan hadn't brought her here when he did. I was a mess, and it probably would *not* have been good.

"Okay, so now I know how you and Justin happened, but what's the actual story there? When did he really win you over?" I smile.

The sun is starting to peek over the horizon, causing the sky to turn pink, with bits of orange and red. It's beautiful. I miss being able to see the lights dance across the ocean as the birds start to sing their songs and the owls stop singing theirs. If I could draw, I would come up here to try and capture the beauty it possesses.

"I hated boys because I thought they were all the same."

"Of course you did." We laugh together.

"I figured Justin would hurt me just like Kaleb did. Every time he tried to talk to me, I would run away, as you know. I didn't want to get my heart torn apart again considering I just fixed it. This went on for a while, longer than I care to admit. Anyways, eventually, I think it was some time in 1520. I found myself having a nightmare about what happened that night.

"I had fallen asleep before practicing my swords lesson with Pan. I asked him to teach me. After all that happened with Kaleb, I never wanted to feel powerless again."

I could relate to that.

"Apparently, it wouldn't have mattered anyways because he sent Justin to cancel it.

"He said he found me screaming, tossing, and turning. He ran over and tried to shake me awake. I remember flying up, gasping for air. He tried to calm me down. He wrapped his arms around me and pulled me toward him. I honestly never wanted him to let go. We sat there like that for a while. I cried into his shoulder while he rubbed my back and played with my hair, trying to soothe me.

"That was the day he won me over. I didn't tell him that at first." She chuckles. "I wanted him to work for it."

"The poor guy! Didn't even give him a break."

"Um! Excuse me! What about Ace? Poor guy told Justin about how he really got impaled!"

"Oh yeah? And how did he really get impaled then?"

"You were teaching him teleportation and teasing him, so when he tried to catch you in the trees, he impaled himself and you laughed!"

I laugh. "Oh, come on, like you wouldn't have. You should have seen his face when he looked down and saw the branch sticking through his right kidney. You would have been dying."

"I would not have! I would have taken him to the waterfall, and once I knew he was safe, then I would have started dying." She smiles. "I missed this, the two of us talking like this without Elena."

"I know you're pissed at her right now, but you guys are best friends. You'll be fine in a couple days."

"Not this time."

"You say that every time and guess what. You never mean it. Besides, this time you started it, you can't stay mad at her forever."

"Yes, I ca—"

"So sorry to interrupt. We need you back at camp."

Clover and I jump up and turn around. Pan is leaning on the rock wall behind us with a smirk plastered on his face.

"How long have you been there? What's going on?" I ask, crossing my arms. "You nearly gave me a heart attack."

"Long enough." His smirk drops only for half a second then returns. "Now come on. You'll see." He peels himself off the wall before disappearing.

"Long enough? How much do you think he heard?" Clover asks.

"Knowing him, probably everything." I roll my eyes.

"Why do you hate him? I mean after everything he's done, how could you hate someone like that?"

"It's a story for another time that I *really* don't want to get into ever."

I turn to leave, but she grabs my arm. She opens her mouth but shuts it as soon as she sees my face.

"Come on. Let's go see what kind of trouble will start today."

Chapter 5

I'm Really Not That Sorry

Pan

Clover and Zylan appear in camp shortly after I do. They look really confused when they do. They probably thought something bad was going on, but it's just the five "angries" hanging upside down by their ankles. Ace and I finally found them. I knocked them out, brought them here, and strung them up.

"Alright! Everyone get up!" I yell.

Slowly but surely groggy faces start to appear out from under blankets and behind the leaves in the trees.

"What's going on?" Klaus asks, rubbing his eyes. "Are we dying?"

"No?" I laugh.

"Then it's too early for this shit." He pulls the blanket back over his head and rolls over.

"Fine. Then you'll miss the games." I smirk. "Ace, lower them."

The girls are starting to climb down from the trees as Ace slowly releases a little rope at a time, revealing Tyler, Luke, Damon, Nate, and Hunter.

"Come on, Pan! Let us down! This isn't fair!" Tyler whines.

The others try to nod but end up holding their heads. They've been up there for almost an hour, enough time for the blood to rush to their brains. It probably hurts a lot to move it.

"So it's come to my attention that you five have been making the girls feel unwelcome. It has also come to my attention that Zylan said she would string you up by your ankles and shoot at you some more. While I like the idea, I think it could be improved slightly. Zylan," I say, motioning her over with a smirk, "if you don't mind coming here."

She looks around like she thinks it's going to be a trap. "What is it that you want?" Her glasses are sliding down her nose, but she quickly pushes them back into place as she walks up. There are bags under her eyes like she hasn't slept in ages. Her long dark brown hair is pulled back, out of her face into a ponytail.

"I know you wanted to shoot them, but that's not very personal, don't you think?"

"I guess. So what?"

She crosses her arms, covering the little bit of skin you can see on her stomach. She always judged me for making the boys dress the same, but all the girls do as well. All of them wear tight cropped tank tops, the colours vary, and black baggy pants. Right now, their shirts are dark green, and they're in pants because of their plans yesterday.

"Well, if you really want to teach them, you have to hit them." I bring my right hand down from my shoulder until it is parallel to the ground. Between here and there, a wooden bat appears. I hold it out to her. "Go ahead. Teach them."

"Let me get this straight. *You* want *me* to hit them with *this*? What's the catch?" she asks, raising an eyebrow.

"No catch. You are just as much a part of this group as they are. They don't know that. You need to teach them." I try offering her the bat again.

"You go first." She steps back, arms still crossed. I look at her confused. "Yeah, you heard me. You first."

I shrug and walk over to Nate. "Come on, man. Please don't do this. I like my face." He lowers his voice. "Brandi likes my face."

I snort. "Brandi?" I call.

She looks up. "Yeah?"

"You like his face?" I ask, pointing the bat at Nate's face. He scrunches up his nose and tries to manoeuvre away from me as soon as I do.

"I guess it's okay. I mean I've seen better." She pauses and glances at Tyler. I think I'm the only one that notices though. "But it doesn't make me want to throw up." She turns her attention back to me and shrugs.

"So I should leave it like that?"

"I don't care. Either way, we're all going to have to hear him complain about it. Actually, if you hit his face it might break his jaw. Ou! Do that!" She smiles at Nate sarcastically.

I shrug. "Sorry man, the lady has spoken." I pull the bat back and swing.

"Stop!" Zylan yells right before the bat would have collided with Nate's face.

"You said. 'You first.'" I'm still looking at Nate. He's shaking slightly with his head turned to the side and his eyes closed.

"Yeah, I've said a lot of things I don't mean. If you hit him, he's going to be angrier with us. If we all take a swing at each of them, they'll hate us even more. The whole point of yesterday was to put the past behind us. I'm totally fine with picking up and moving a couple clearings over, if it would mean all of us putting this little feud behind us. Girls, are we on the same page?" They all nod. "Good. Now, Ace, put them down."

She winks at him. Ace smiles and lets go of the rope all at once. Everyone laughs as the five of them hit the ground. They groan, rolling over. Tyler cradles his left arm to his stomach as he does. Luke holds the back of his neck as he rolls it from his left side to his right. Hunter cries out in pain when he tries to roll his right shoulder back into place. Nate gets a mouthful of dirt that he tries to spit out. And Damon just bounces back up like a cat, not a scratch to be seen.

Elena walks over to Hunter, who's still screaming. "Relax, you baby." He stops wailing long enough to give her a dirty look. That's enough time for her to grab his forearm and bicep and pull. He screams for a second before stopping and making an impressed face. "There. That should help."

"Thanks," he says, smiling slightly.

I can't believe there's still tension between them. They we're apart for so long, I can't believe she's still mad that he changed so much.

When I look over at Zylan, she's crouched in front of Tyler, whispering to him. She lightly brushes her fingers along his forearm. He looks down, smiling. "Wow! Thanks!"

She smiles back saying something too quiet to hear.

***

I haven't been able to find anything related to Neverland. I suppose I could sail blindly, but even if I did, I could be gone for days. It's kind of weird to think about how much I loved that place, and now, I don't even remember what it's like. It seems like such a long time ago.

I do, however, remember the first day there. Or rather, how Peter and I ended up there. It's a memory I have tried so hard to push to the back of my mind. It's the reason I'm happy I haven't thought about Peter since I've gotten here.

I was goofing off with my friends in the backyard when Father came out screaming about how inconsiderate I was being to Mother. All we were doing was kicking around a football, how could it be inconsiderate? I didn't ask, of course. I didn't want to disrespect my father for fear that he would hit me. So I apologised and told my friends it was probably a good time to leave, and I would see them later.

I figured that would make Father happy, but it didn't. As soon as I walked inside the house, he grabbed his whip off the wall where it hung. He struck me once at the back of my knee, so I would fall and several times in the back. I didn't make a sound, so he wouldn't be angrier with me.

Father had gotten very angry once Mother got sick. He wanted Peter and me to stay home all day to take care of her so he could work. We came up with the idea of alternating days, which worked out for a couple months. But the sicker Mother got, the angrier Father became.

The abuse didn't start until three months before the day we left. Because she wasn't getting better, and we were the ones taking care of her, he thought it was our fault. That day, it was Peter's turn so I thought I could hang out with my friends. That was a big no from Father. A very big no.

Afterward, I stood up and apologised again before joining Peter in Mother's room. He was standing on the right side of her bed as she slept. Next to him was a water bucket with a cloth folded neatly over the edge of it. He was looking down at her with a look of sadness on his face. I leaned on the doorway as he sighed and picked up the cloth, dipping it into the water.

"Peter, I've never seen him this angry," I said when he looked up.

"We need to leave." He looked back down and picked the cloth out of the water bucket, twisting it. He watched the extra water pour back into the bucket before placing it gently on Mother's forehead.

"What do you mean? We can't leave Mother like this. He can't take care of her." I closed the door to her room and walked over the other side of the bed.

"She won't need to be taken care of."

He kept his head down as he talked. A single tear rolled down his cheek and landed on Mother's hand.

I hadn't noticed how pale her face looked until that moment. Her normally tanned skin was white as a ghost.

"No. Please no." I knew he meant that she was dead already. "She can't," I whispered. "It can't be true."

But I knew it was. I felt the tears welling up in my eyes. She was my mother; she couldn't die. She didn't deserve to die. I grabbed her hand, hoping that she would open her big green eyes and laugh, that this was all a joke. But her hands were cold to the touch, like she had been gone for hours, days even. "How long?"

"This morning." Peter was still, looking at her, face blank. "We need to leave. Now."

I leaned over Mother and kissed her forehead. When my eyes closed, I felt a few tears roll down my cheeks. They landed on her left cheek and rolled onto her pillow. *Why did she get sick? What did she do to deserve this?* I thought.

"Where will we go?" I asked, pulling the blanket over Mother. I couldn't stand to see her like that.

"Anywhere but here. It's you and me until the end, brother."

We were just about out the front door when something wrapped around my ankle and pulled me to the ground. A sharp pain ran down my spine when I tried to roll over, causing me to cry out in pain. Peter stopped running long enough for Father to do the same thing to him. We both stayed on the ground, knowing he would do so much worse if we tried to run.

He stood over us, brown eyes glowing with rage. It's weird. I could have sworn they were originally green like Mother's.

"And where do you think you boys are going?" he snarled.

His brown hair was all over the place, making him look ten times more terrifying. He didn't even look like himself. It looked like someone hijacked his body just to hurt us.

Peter and I stayed silent, making him angrier. I could have sworn, for a split second, his eyes went fully black. Then he picked me up by the neck and squeezed. I closed my eyes, accepting the fact that I was going to die while Peter screamed for him to stop.

Everything started to fade away, and I thought it would stay gone forever, but I woke up in the middle of a forest with Peter next to me. We both looked at each other, confused beyond belief.

"Where are we?" he asked, like I would have had a clue.

"Neverland," a voice from behind us said.

I knew that voice. It was the voice that sung to me when I couldn't sleep. It was the voice that woke me up every morning. It was the voice I would never forget.

"Mother?" Peter and I exclaimed at the same time, turning around.

There she was, standing on top of a rock, shimmering in the golden light peeking through the trees. Her brown hair was being pulled to the right, out of her face by a gust of wind. She wore a plain white dress that reached her ankles, which was also being pulled by the wind.

She smiled. "My little angels." But her smile slowly faded away. "I'm so sorry that this happened to you. This is all my fault."

"What do you mean?" I asked.

"Oh, my sweet, sweet children. It wasn't your time. I never meant for this to happen." She started to fade away. Each passing second led to her becoming more and more transparent.

"Mom! What do you mean?"

"I don't have much time. Listen to me very closely. There is a way you can change this." Her voice becomes more distant. "Help the people in need. Save them every chance you get. You'll get a second chance." The last bit that she said was cut off as she disappeared completely.

I looked over at Peter, who was nodding. He must have heard what she said. He was crying. We both were again. What did she mean? What was going to happen? What was Neverland? Who are we supposed to help?

"Peter . . ." my voice trailed off, but he knew what I was thinking.

"Don't worry, Jacob. Everything is going to be okay."

And it was for a while. He set up a camp in the middle of this Neverland place, and he began to plan. For what? I had no idea until he came up to me almost a week after being there and told me that we were sent her for a reason. All he said was that there were children just like us all around the world, and this island was powered by magic. What we had to do was save these children from their awful lives and bring them here.

"What will that do for them? What will happen when we die? It's not like we can do this forever, Peter. And even if we could, do you really want to spend forever on this island? Because I really don't."

"Brother, you have to trust me! It will all be worth it! Wouldn't you have been happy if someone had saved us?"

I shrugged but nodded. "I would have, but at the same time, what if they choose not to leave with me? Because if I were them and some stranger came up to me and told me to come with them to a magical island . . . I wouldn't go."

"We're talking about children, Jacob! Children love magic! And on this island, you will never grow old. Who would turn that down!" he exclaimed, smile plastered on his face like it would never go away.

I would, I thought. "Okay, when do we start?"

"Tonight!"

He was way too excited about the whole thing. But instead of saying something, I kept my mouth shut and smiled back. I told myself that everything would be okay because I was here with my brother and best friend. We would rescue children and help them move on from the trauma. I should have known better than to trust a situation without all the facts! Looking back now, I should have known that he was keeping something from me! Why else would he have said 'trust me' instead of telling me what Mother said to him? Why else would he have sent Zylan and I to this island instead of taking her in as well? None of it makes any sense.

***

"Pan?"

I jump up out of my chair, giving myself a mini heart attack. I lean over trying to catch my breath and hold my chest. I was too out of it to recognise the voice, so I am pleasantly surprised to see Zylan leaning in the doorway of my tree house.

I don't like to camp with the other boys. After spending a long period of time, with a large group of them, I realised that I couldn't deal with them 24-7 for the rest of my immortal life.

"What can I do for you?" I ask, standing up.

"What were you thinking? Hanging them upside down like that? If you really wanted us to be on good terms, why would you do that?" She pulls herself off the door frame and makes her way into the room.

She changed out of her last outfit into a blue shirt and black off side, high-low skirt. From what I've noticed about the outfits they chose, blue meant they had their guard down because they were just going to be hanging out all day. I always thought it was adorable how their outfits showed what they were thinking or their intentions on the day.

I smile at her. I knew she wasn't going to let me hit them. My intention was for her to stop me. That way they would see the girls just wanted a little payback, and they weren't going to do it again.

She shakes her head and laughs. "You knew."

"Of course, I knew. Though I was hoping you'd at least let me hit him once. I had been looking forward to it."

She walks into the room more, examining it. She looks over to her right where she sees a large square window in the middle of the wall. The left side has one in the exact same spot as well. Beside the door are my bed and a nightstand with an oil lantern on it. Behind me is a desk with a chair. Right now, there are papers scattered around on top with four large books stacked on top of one another. It was my attempt at trying to find a reference to where Neverland may be.

"Nice place." She runs her fingers along the bed as she walks closer to me. "Lot nicer than the clearing."

"Yeah, I kind of got sick of living in the jungle after 350 years."

She walks over to me, eyeing the desk. I don't want her to know what I'm up to, so I try to clear the papers before she sees what I'm doing, but one gets left behind. "Neverland? I thought this was Neverland . . . That's what everyone says. That's what you told me . . ." she says, snatching up the stragglier.

"Um . . . it is, it's just the new ones always talk about the different stories and stuff, so I decided I wanted to read them." That's the best cover I could come up with under pressure. She definitely doesn't buy it.

"Don't lie to me." She looks at the paper closer. "Are you trying to find Neverland?" Her eyes scan the paper quickly before looking back at me. "If this is Neverland, why would you need to find it?"

"I'm not even going to try and come up with anything because you wouldn't believe me even if I told you the truth." I set the papers back down on the desk and walk over to my bed. I sigh, running my fingers through my hair as I sit down. "I'm not even sure if I would believe myself," I say under my breath.

"So don't tell me the truth. Show me the truth."

"What do you mean?" I ask, lifting my head to meet her gaze.

Zylan walks over to me and holds out her hands. "That thing I did with Ace, where I saw what he did. Give me your hands and show me the truth. Don't tell me."

"Are you sure you want to know?"

"I can leave if you don't want me to know. I have things I would much rather be doing. I don't like you very much. Actually, scratch that, I don't like you at all." She turns to leave.

"Stop! Stop." I stand up. "Fine, but don't tell me that I didn't warn you. The truth is pretty messed up."

"Stop talking and hold my hands." She rolls her eyes and reaches out again.

"I'm just trying to tell you that I'm not making this up."

She rolls her eyes again, reaching her hands closer to me. As soon as I grab them and start to think of everything, a shock sends both of us flying in different directions. I hit the wall behind me, just beside the window, and everything goes black.

Chapter 6

What?

Zylan

I'm standing in the corner of my parents' room, looking at myself under the bed. The door is swinging open, and my mom runs in covered in blood. When a bang sounds, I find myself, back in my body, looking at Mother lying on the floor, her blood covering the stains I saw her run in with. Then the black boots I remember walk in and out. This time when I crawl out to hold Mother, I hear two thumps, one quiet and closer, the other louder but farther. I sit with Mother, and I cry. I feel the presence of someone. I recognize it, but how? I open my eyes to find brown boots in front of me.

"Is my father okay?" I ask. I feel the tears building up in my eyes, but I try to hold them in.

The boy in boots kneels down and looks me in the eyes. I know this boy. I've seen him in my dreams. I've felt him watch over me.

"I'm so sorry, but I don't know. I promised him that I would keep you safe, so we need to leave now." He holds out his hand to help me up, but I kiss my mother's forehead and

slide her off my lap before I take it. "I'm Jacob by the way. Jacob Pan."

"Zylan" is all I can make myself say.

***

My eyes fly open. Was that real? I've never remembered a dream before. Jacob . . . why does that seem so familiar? Everyone called him Peter, yet he introduced himself as Pan every time. "Jacob," I whisper to myself. I push myself into a sitting position. "Jacob?"

"You remember?" Pan is pushing himself off the ground next to the window. His eyes are wide like he just saw a ghost.

"Yes . . . No. I'm not sure. It doesn't seem real."

I look around, trying to figure out what just happened. Could it be real? If so, why do I remember something different? For all I know, he put that idea in my head. He's trying to trick me. I don't know why, but he is.

"What do you remember?" he asks walking over to me.

I jump to my feet. "Stay away from me." I start to back up, slowly toward the door, my left hand in front of me trying to keep him back, my right hand behind my back gripping the dagger I hid from him. "For all I know this is your idea of a sick game. We all know how much you love your games." I make it to the doorway when he tries to grab my left arm. Before he can do anything else my right hand is pressing the dagger into his throat. "You think this is funny? I'm trying to give you a chance and now you think you can mess with my head?" I back him up against the wall, just beside the window. The tip of the blade cuts into his neck when he tries to say something. "Don't," I warn before I step back and think of the cliff.

When I open my eyes, I'm leaning on the wall of the cliff.

It can't be real. I know what I remember. *Do you? Isn't it possible that you only remember what you want to remember? The brain does try to protect itself after a traumatizing experience. Maybe he's—*

"No, it's not possible. He's trying to mess with your head and you're letting him," I say to myself, cutting off my inner voice. "He's just trying to trick you."

I take a deep breath, sliding down the wall as I do. I run my fingers through my hair, pulling it slightly like I always do when I'm stressed. I try and think of anything but what just happened. That's when I realise I was supposed to meet Tyler.

"Crap." I stand up and think of the clearing I told him to meet me at. A second later, I see him sitting on a rock with his back facing me. "Sorry, I'm late," I say, walking over.

He jumps up, holding his heart.

Wow, I'm just scaring everyone today.

"Don't do that! You're like a cat!"

"I don't know how I feel about being compared to an animal. I think I'll just leave you with that broken arm." I turn to walk away, but he grabs my shoulder with his good arm.

"Come on! Don't play me like that!" He pouts. "This is your fault, you know?"

"Fine, but call me a cat again, and I'll break your other arm."

He raises his arms in defence causing him to wince a little.

"Follow me." I start walking in the direction of the cliff again.

"Where are you taking me anyways?" he asks, jogging up beside me.

"When I first got here, I wandered around a lot. It was only me and Pan. You know I couldn't face him after what he did to me, so I tried to keep myself busy."

He nods and gives my hand a tight squeeze.

Tyler and I have been best friends since he got to The Island. He's the only one I told about what really happened that night. We were talking, and I don't know why, but it just kind of slipped out, and we haven't talked about it since.

"One day, I came across this cliff. The view is absolutely stunning, so it became the place I went when I was struggling with something, and well, a year to the day of my parents' death, I went to the cliff with . . . It's not important, but before I did anything, these vines on the cliff moved and I found this cave. Inside this cave, there's a waterfall, and this waterfall healed my aching heart in a matter of seconds. So the answer to your question is I'm taking you to a waterfall."

"Why couldn't you just heal my arm completely when you did that thing at camp?"

We're almost there at this point. The trees start getting closer and closer together, so we have to duck under low hanging branches and step over tree roots sticking out of the ground.

"I'm sure I've explained this to you before, but magic can't heal. It just takes away the pain, which can be super dangerous sometimes. I don't know if you've noticed Luna's limp, but the reason she has it is because of me. She broke her leg just after she got here, running away from Olive. They were playing tag, in case you were wondering. Anyways, I hid the pain, but the bone never healed completely because she wasn't taking proper care if it. If you don't feel the pain, then you do things you shouldn't do with a broken arm. But this waterfall returns things to the way they should be. So long story short, the waterfall will return your arm to the way it should be, and it will be all good again." I smile.

"So if it returns things to the way they should be, why don't you use it on your eyes? I mean that is why you have those, right? And you complain about them all the time. It's quite annoying actually." He points at my glasses.

I roll my eyes and punch his good arm lightly. "Because my eyes have never been good, and they weren't bad because of an injury. Trust me. I tried just about everything to get rid of these things. Nothing's worked. But it'll fix your arm."

"Why did you never tell me about this place?"

"It never came up, and you never needed it before."

"How much farther?" Tyler asks, fixing his hair.

His hair is brown, styled up like Ace's, but it's much shorter, so it's not as much of a bother. I noticed when he first got here that he really liked to play with it when he's nervous or stressed. He'll constantly runs his fingers through it, puffing it up or pulling it back. It's kind of cute actually.

I push a branch out of the way. "No need to stress it's right there." The cliff wall is a light gray, almost white, colour with little chips perfect for climbing. It's tall like a small mountain, maybe a hundred meters high.

Tyler steps around the branch and looks up, looks at his arm, looks back up then looks over at me. "You want me to climb that? With a broken arm?" he asks, sarcasm present in his voice.

"Fine. You don't have to climb." I over-exaggerate, swinging my right arm around me, over to the side. There's a pathway that leads all the way to the top without having to climb it. "How 'bout you walk?"

He glares at me. "Fuck you," he says with a hint of joking in his tone.

"You wish!" I laugh.

"You know I do." He winks and laughs, starting to run toward the pathway. "Come on, slowpoke!" he yells once he's almost out of view.

"Is that a challenge?"

"Maybe it is!"

"It's on!" I yell as he disappears from my sights. "Stupid idiot."

I laugh to myself before disappearing and reappearing on top of the mountain. I sit on a rock and wait for him to catch up. A few minutes later, he finally makes it to the top. He puts both hands on his knees, trying to catch his breath.

"What?" he manages to puff out when he leans back. "That's not . . . even fair." He makes this weird sound, a mix between a moan, a sigh, and a scream.

"Are you okay?" I laugh.

He squints one eye like he's trying to think of something. "Yeah, I think so."

"Alrighty then. Why didn't you just pop yourself up here? You're literally the best student I ever had." I laugh again.

"Because I thought it was going to be a fair race! You cheated!"

"You cheated first!"

"I never cheat! How did I cheat?"

"You told me to race you as you were running up the cliff path, and you know I don't run."

"Alright, you win this one."

"I know."

I smile, stand up, and walk over to the vines. With the wave of my right hand, they pull off to the sides and reveal the waterfall. I hear the light thumping of the water hitting itself over and over again. When the sun hits the mist, an array of colours fills the cave.

"Wow," Tyler says, coming up behind me.

"I know. Now let's fix your arm," I say, scurrying him into the cave and closing the vines back behind me.

"Wow, Ze, you know I love you, but you're a taken woman. I would never do anything to jeopardize that."

Like I said, Ty and I have been best friends since like a week after he got to The Island. I didn't like him for the first few minutes, but he was just so cute and awkward, it was hard to dislike him. We always talked to each other like this.

That's just the way we were. I kind of feel bad doing it in front of Ace, but I didn't mean it, not really.

"Shut up." I laugh and punch his bad arm this time.

"Ow! Fucking shitty ass fucking broken arm! You suck!"

"If I sucked, I would have left you with your broken arm instead of showing you my secret getaway spot." I stick my tongue out at him. "Just stick your hand in the water, and you'll be good as new."

He walks over to the edge of the water very slowly and leans over it slightly. He sticks his fingers in the water, and I stay as far from him as I can, just because the urge to push him in is too tempting.

"Oh my god." He takes his fingers out and wiggles them. "This is literally the coolest thing ever."

"I'm sure that's not true." I laugh.

"You might be right, but at this moment, it is."

"Can I ask you something?"

"You just did." He smiles.

I roll my eyes. "I'm serious, Tyler."

"Oh shit, you really are." He walks over and sits on the rock next to me. "What's on your mind?"

"Why did you throw our stuff into the fire? Why were you so angry? Why did you make us feel so unwelcome?"

"Honestly, I have no idea. I just felt like I had to. When we left camp, we got each other riled up and when we came back and saw the fire, we just kind of snapped, I guess. I never meant to make you feel unwelcome. I was just really mad that you shot me."

"So instead of walking up to me and saying, 'Hey, Zylan, I really didn't appreciate you shooting at me, please don't do it again' you decided to throw all our stuff into the fire Pan left for us to bond with?"

"Yes. I'm a guy. That's what we do, overreact." He slings his arm around my shoulder and squeezes quickly before letting go. "I'm sorry, Ze. I really am."

"You better be. I'm sorry for shooting you, making you eat dirt, and breaking your arm." I put my head on his shoulder and sigh. "Are you still mad?"

"More at myself for my reaction than you guys. Thinking about it today, I realized that we've done a lot worse to you guys a lot more often. I'm surprised you guys even agreed to move in with us."

"We figured if we got you back, we could put it behind us. It would have worked if not for you five assholes." I chuckle a little to let him know I'm not angry with him. "I think it's all behind us now. Hunter's the only one being an asshole, but that's nothing new."

"You know he's not a total asshole, right? He had a really rough life before The Island. His first and *only* love was basically ripped out of his arms, and then he was forced to live on a pirate ship for 190 years. That kind of thing changes a person."

"All he had to do was tell Elena that, and I wouldn't hate him so much. I know he's a good friend of yours and you meet him when your parent—" I stop myself. He doesn't like to talk about his last day at home, which I completely understand, so I didn't want to remind him of it. "Look, I know he's nice to you guys, but to Clover, Elena, and I, he's a dick, and you're not going to change my mind."

"I know that. I just don't like the fact that almost everyone hates him because of one mistake over three hundred years ago."

"I would like to point out that he made multiple mistakes with multiple girls before he was caught."

"Okay, okay. Fair enough. I won't try to change your mind anymore." Tyler smiles and stands up. "We should head back to camp. I'm sure something's happened by now."

"You're probably right." I stand up as well. "Let's go."

***

"Where were you?" Clover asks.

I have just walked back into camp with Tyler behind me when she jumped up and basically attack me.

"I was helping Ty with his arm. Why? What's up?"

"Pan came in and told us that when we found you, we were to tell you you're in charge until he gets back." She smiles like she's proud of herself for remembering everything he said.

"When did he leave?"

"Maybe five minutes ago."

"You're in charge until I get back."

I disappear before she has a chance to argue. When I reappear, I'm surprised to find Pan standing over a boat, mostly because he always keeps himself cloaked. Most of the time, he's impossible to find, which is why I had to track Hunter and Klaus to the camp.

We're at the edge of The Island, on the shore of the beach. Why is he packing up a boat? What could he possibly be up to?

"Where are you going?" I ask.

He whips around holding his sword. Once he sees it's me, he rolls his eyes and holsters it. "What are you doing here?" He crosses his arms.

"Like I said earlier, I don't trust you. I want to know what you're up to." I cross my arms as well and lean on the tree next to me.

"You also said to stay away from you. I can't do that if you're stalking me. So go away. You can't come." He turns back to the boat, dropping a bag in it.

"Look, I don't care if you want to send me back to camp or lock me up in a cage or do whatever it is you do when people don't listen to you. I'm going to find out what you're up to eventually. You might as well take me with you."

He turns around, face burning red. "I don't care. Throw a fit, think I'm a villain, think I'm the reason your life went to hell, think my life goal is to make you miserable, think whatever you want to think, but I don't owe you anything. You're staying here whether you like it or not, and you can't do anything about it," he whispers. Not like a hushed whisper, more like a threatening whisper and as he's whispering he walks forward. By the time he's done he's centimetres away, looking down at me with anger burning in his eyes.

At some point, my arms dropped to my sides, and the only thing keeping me standing became the tree I was leaning on. I feel a wave of fear wash over me before I realize I'm not the girl who needs saving.

I push him away. "What the hell do you mean you don't owe me anything?" I scream at him. "You ruined my life and took me to a place I could never die no matter how hard I tried! Now I spend every day thinking of ways, anyway, it could have been different! I drove myself crazy for twenty years! I haven't been able to sleep in 543 years, and you don't owe me anything? Bull fucking shit! You owe me everything!"

I didn't notice until I finished screaming that there are tears dripping out of my eyes. I make no effort to wipe them away as they rest on my cheeks.

Pan looks at me and I see something I've never seen on him before, sadness. He doesn't even try to hide it.

"I'm sorry. I'm so sorry," he whispers looking down at the ground. "I'm going to fix this. I promise."

Before I can ask what he's talking about, he waves his hand and everything goes black.

***

When I come to, everything's blurry. I see the outline of five people. I'm pretty sure it's Ace, Clover, Elena, Justin, and Tyler leaning over me, based on the colourful blur of their hair.

"Look who's finally up!" Elena chirps.

"Yeah. You've been out for almost three weeks," Ace says.

"Is this a fucking joke?" I scream, jumping up. Three weeks? No way! Where's Pan then? Why the hell did he knock me out in the first place? The next time I see him, I'm going to kill him!

"He's totally fucking with you." Justin laughs. "You've been out for like four hours."

"At least we think. Pan brought you back, put you down then disappeared, so we're not sure how long you've actually been out."

"Where are my glasses?" I ask, rolling my eyes. Ty hands them to me. As soon as I get them on and I can see, I punch Ace in the face again. "Fuck you! Don't scare me like that again!"

"Ouch! Why would you do that?" he exclaims, stumbling backward. "Do you ever get tired of punching me in the face?" His voice is muffled, his hands block his mouth.

"No, because you're a piece of shit!"

"But you love me." He drops his hands and smiles. Blood is dripping out of his nose and over his mouth as he does. Some of it stains his lips, turning them a dark red instead of light pick like they normally are.

"Um . . . I don't know about that." I fake my disgusted face. He looks really offended, and everyone around us starts laughing. "I'm kidding! Relax!"

"Good." He smiles again. Actually, more like a smirk this time.

"Oh god." I take a step back. That look is nothing but trouble. The smirk deepens as he walks toward me. "Oh no! Stay away from me with that bloody nose!" I turn and start running away.

"I'll get you eventually! Just give up!"

"Do you even know me? When do I ever give up?"

I dodge him for a few minutes, hiding behind people and throwing them into him when he gets too close. But eventually, I turn to see if he's behind me, and he's not. I stop and look around. "Where'd he go?" I ask.

Everyone looks around with me, confused. No one knows. He kind of just disappeared without anyone seeing. That's not a good sign. A couple seconds later, I feel arms wrap around my waist and pick me up, spinning me around.

"I got you. What are you going to do now?" he whispers in my ear.

"Stop! You're getting blood on my shirt!" I yell while laughing.

He puts me down, spins me around so I'm facing him, still in his arms, and laughs. "You do know there's this thing called magic and with a poof the blood will be gone."

"Oh right." I giggle. "Sometimes I forget! Don't laugh at me!" I push his shoulder, but he keeps his grip on me.

"Or what? You'll punch me again?" he mocks, rolling his eyes a little.

"Maybe I will!" I go to raise my arm, but he's faster. He holds both my arms at my sides and smirks. "Okay, you got me. Now what?" I ask, moving closer.

"Whatever I want," he whispers leaning over me.

"Careful, people are watching."

"Not anymore."

I'm about to ask what he means, but I pull away and look around first. We're on the shore of the beach. Not the one I found Pan on, but the one in the centre of The Island. This is where he took me on our first date. It was the happiest I had been since I got here. I remember it like it was yesterday.

***

"Come on! Tell me where we're going!" I whine. "I hate surprises!"

Ace dragged me from camp and blindfolded me. He told me that he wanted to show me something, but it had to be a surprise, so I couldn't see until we got there. No matter how much I complained, he said the same thing every time.

"Well, you're going to have to get used to it. I plan on surprising you every day till the day I die." This time I sigh and keep walking. "Okay, stop now. We're here."

"What could be so important that you had to . . ." I trail off once the blindfold drops from my eyes. "It's beautiful," I whisper, trying to take it all in.

We're standing on the shore with the water creeping up to our feet. There's a rock wall behind the lake, about five meters high, tree roots cracking through parts of it. When the sun hits the water, it—and the area around it—shimmers like gold.

"I'm glad you like it," Ace says when I look back at him. "But this isn't it."

"What else could you possibly have? This is already so perfect."

"Wait here for a second." He smiles and holds up a finger before disappearing behind a tree. When he comes back, he's holding a basket full of different foods, like bread and cheese as well as wine.

"Where did you get wine? I haven't had any in forever!" I exclaim when he puts the basket down. He pulls out a wool blanket and lays it on the ground so we can sit.

"I have my ways." He smiles.

"I love this."

"I love you," he says.

This really takes me by surprise, but I smile. "I love you too."

***

I smile to myself, looking down. "Why here?"

"This is where I told you I loved you for the first time, so I figured it would be the perfect place for . . ." he trails off, motioning behind him. In the tree behind him, there is a hole at the bottom of it, revealing stairs leading to a two-story tree house. "So on our first date, I told you I would surprise you every day until the day I die, and I kind of fell short of that promise, so I want to start doing it again. Since this is the place I found out you love me as much as I love you, I wanted to do something special here." He gets down on one knee and pulls a small wooden box out of his pocket. "Zylan Cain, I love you more than anything, and I would be honoured if you would marry me." He opens the box to reveal a gold ring.

I smile, feeling tears sliding down my cheeks. "Yes," I whisper. "Yes, of course I will."

He lets out the breath he had been holding in. "Thank god."

I throw my arms around him once the ring is on my finger and he's standing again. "I can't believe you were worried." I laugh slightly.

"Well, how was I supposed to know? You hated me for . . . I don't know how long, plus it's not like people get married here. We're all like sixteen or seventeen technically. I didn't want it to be awkward, and you didn't want people finding out, but now . . . everyone knows and our camps came together, so I figured it was now or never." He pulls away but keeps his hands on my waist. "I love you."

"I love you too," I whisper before pulling him down towards me. "I love you so much." I smile and kiss him.

Ace

1478

"Please be careful, Jason," Mother said, giving me a hug. I rolled my eyes. I had been on so many journeys. When would she learn that I was always careful? "Do not roll your eyes at me, young man." I could hear the playful tone in her voice as she pulled away.

"How do you always know?" I exclaimed, laughing.

"Call it a mother's intuition." She smiled. "I am going to miss you." Her normally bright smile, fell only slightly but enough.

She always got like this when I left. My father died at sea just after I was born, and so she convinced herself the same thing would happen to me. No matter how many times I reassured her, she was always left thinking that I was going to die. I hated leaving her like this, I hated seeing her cry, and I hated that I felt as though I was going to cry.

"Please, Momma, do not cry. I am going to be alright. I promise." I smiled and hugged her again. "I will see you again in a month. Right here. Just one month, Momma. I have been gone longer. I will be okay." I always said the same thing, and no matter how many times I came home, the words never got through to her.

"I know, baby. I just hate watching you go." She pulled away, smiling through the tears she was trying to keep in.

"I know, Momma. I have to go now. One month, right here." I smiled, backing up. "Give Layla and Charlotte my love!"

"I always do! Have fun. Be safe! I will see you in a month!" she called after me.

I ran up the gangplank onto the ship. I was always the last one on. Luckily, no one seemed to mind, not even the captain. Most of my shipmates were men. The youngest was four years older than me. They did not have mothers to say goodbye to. If they did, we would never leave on time, or maybe at all. Instead, they had wives, who said their goodbyes to at home, which was smart. All the tears left in the walls of a house. Some of them even talk about what their wives did to say goodbye. That would not be a sight for the docks.

I was the youngest on the crew. My oldest sister, Layla, convinced her husband, George, the captain, to take me on as a deck washer. He would only take me on the short journeys; one week was the longest I was allowed to be on board. The only reason I was allowed to go out for even that long was my studies. Mother wanted me to finish my education before I was allowed to sail. I knew this was what I was meant to do, so I studied and studied and I finished early, earlier than everyone. So after Layla convinced George, she convinced Mother. That was last year. This year I was a full member of the crew.

After an incident that left two crew members dead, the captain made me an official member. It had been amazing ever since, even in storms and bumpy seas. As soon as I stepped foot onto this boat, I knew this was where I was meant to be, that sailing ran through my veins.

"Now that we are all here, to your stations!" Captain yelled.

I began to move to my station, up the rope ladder to the main sail, but he stopped me. "Not you, Jason. You are coming with me."

Oh no. What did I do this time? I swallowed and rolled my shoulders. "Yes, captain."

The last time I got called out by the captain, I got pounded for information. I was the newest member, and apparently, the newbie got blamed when stuff went missing.

"Do not look so nervous, boy! This is good news! Buck up," he exclaimed, slapping me on the back.

With that my, shoulders unclenched, and I let out the deep breath I was holding in. "What is this about then, captain?"

"Some people have noticed your good work and would like to have a chat with you." His smile widened. He was leading me to his quarters. Normally, only the lieutenant was welcome into his quarters and only when planning strategy.

"What people?"

"You shall see!" he exclaimed, basically bouncing up and down.

***

"What got you out of setup duty?" David asked.

I barely heard him. Captain thought this was a good thing. I did not. Move ships? No way! It took me a whole six months after joining this crew before they stopped using me as the punch line to all their jokes. A whole new ship with a whole new crew, what if I was not excepted? I was seventeen. No one would take me seriously. The only reason they did here was because of George. Even if I did the best job they had ever seen, I did not believe they would accept me as their own.

"Hey, cheer up, Ace! It is not like you are dead!" David exclaimed with a chuckle and a slap on the back.

Ace was a nickname here. I was not sure why, but when I first joined the crew, Charlie started calling me that. He never told me why. I had asked him about it a million times, but he refused to tell me. Maybe if I did leave, he would. Even though he would not tell me, it caught on, so the whole ship called me that except the captain.

"The captain of another ship wants me to move over there. This is my last sail here." I sighed and looked over the deck. This was the last sail I was going to be standing on *this* deck, looking out over the sea. The last time I would hear *these* people yelling to get everything ready as we left England.

"Then make it count!" There was another slap on the back before he scurried off. He was probably going to tell the whole crew.

"Perfect. Just what I need, everyone knowing and more jokes. This is going to be a long month," I muttered to myself before slugging over to my post.

August 14, 1478

Today is my 268th day at sea as a full crew member of *Mayfly.* I only have fourteen more before—I do not wish to leave this ship. I only wish to stay here with my friends, with my crew.

Over the last two years, these people have become my second family, and now they are being ripped away. All the jokes they said at my expense will be redone. All the time it took to earn their respect was for nothing. What if this new crew does not stop this time? What if they think I am a joke? Will I be allowed to return here or will they just laugh and ask if I need my mother to come get me? The latter seems more likely.

This is not fair! I only wish to have a good last sail here. Maybe I will refuse and just stay on land with my mother and sisters. But then again, that sounds very cowardly. The sea is where I belong, that is why I studied so hard, and why my sister pushed George so hard.

I must transfer. I must go on. For Father, he would have wanted me to do this. This is what he would have done.

Anyways, this voyage was to Italy. Apparently, ten years ago, there was a ship that was supposed to deliver a chest full of gold from England to Turkey. Why the captain took a detour and went home is unknown, but we were tasked with finding the chest and bringing it back. Why ten years later? I have no idea.

When we arrived in Genoa, the people were eager to get rid of it. They believe the chest is cursed. According to them, a pirate ship was after that chest and claimed that it was their treasure, and they were going to get it no matter what.

My shipmates found this rather funny, being a whole ten years later and all. If they wanted this treasure so bad and would do anything to get it, why wait this long? The townspeople could not explain why. They just strongly believed that the pirates would come back.

One woman standing by the docks was in tears the whole time we were there. Right before we loaded up the ship and captain returned from the chandlery, I went to talk to her, ask her why she was so upset.

She said the captain of the last ship to lay hands on that chest was the father of her best friend. Apparently, the evening of August 14, 1468, a pirate ship raided their village, killing all the members of the crew and their families. Those pirates burned the captain's house to the ground. She said that no bodies were found in the fire, that they all just vanished into thin air.

That must have been so hard for her. I cannot imagine losing James like that. One day laughing about the girl chasing me around the courtyard and then, the next, just gone. She cried even harder when I said I was sorry for her loss. She clams it was her fault. She cancelled the plans they had for that night because she was tired of hearing about the boy in the shadows. She said she should have been fine with it, that if she had not been so mad about the night before, her friend would be safe.

I think the weirdest part of it all was when she said that the boy from the shadows came to her that night while she was in the town's square with two of her other friends. At first, she just thought he was a strange boy, but he showed her magic and made her believe all the crazy stories her friend came up with. And then the boy just disappeared, and she knew that boy was the one her friend talked about. But before she could tell the girl that she was sorry for not believing her, she was gone.

Is that not strange? A whole family gone. The girl quickly shut her mouth after that. Her eyes widened as she clapped her hands over her mouth. I guess she realized how her story sounded and figured I would tell someone she was crazy. I would not ever. But she muttered something about learning to keep her mouth shut and not spilling her heart out to strangers then she ran away.

I have heard some very crazy stories in some very different ports, but this one did not seem crazy. It seemed real. I could put myself into the situation. I even thought I saw a boy standing apart from the crowd, leaning on a post. He listened as the girl spoke, sadness filling his face, like he was the boy she spoke of and he could not help her friend ten years ago, just like he could not help her today.

Today is exactly ten years since the pirates attacked. I guess that is why I am writing now. If the treasure is cursed, it makes sense to assume that the pirates are cursed as well. Maybe the reason it has taken them ten years is because they can only come out every ten years. I cannot tell any of the crew. They will deem me as crazy, and I will never sail again. But I am a little on edge today. We still have fourteen days at sea until we return home, having just left this morning. I hope—

"Below deck!" A voice ripped me from my train of thought. "Change the sails!"

That meant pirates, really mean-looking pirates. One of the first things a new crew member learned was the mentality of a pirate. They believed that showing all the members of a crew was a sign of honesty. In order to pass a pirate ship, we had to be deceitful. We passed a fair few pirate ships on our journeys, so captain decided we should carry black sails and two flags. The governor was not too happy about this at first but came around when his son joined the crew. To a passing pirate ship, we were one of their own.

I was already below deck, so I stayed put. We had seventy crew members, not including captain, and seven cabins, so there were ten to a cabin. Only six of my cabin mates joined me, leaving three above deck. So out of seventy crew members, only twenty-one plus captain were shown like always.

I tied up my journal, closed the ink, wiped the quill, and shoved them all under my pillow. The last thing I needed was the whole crew finding out I write down everything. I could already hear the insults bouncing around in my head. I ignored them and jumped off my bed.

"Anyone get a good look?" I asked, trying not to let my voice waver. I did not believe the timing was a coincidence. We had not run into pirates in months but the day we got this cursed chest, we ran into them.

"No. Richard was in the crow. The rest of us were washing the deck. Why?" David replied.

"Oh, no reason. Just curious is all. It has been awhile."

David nodded then walked toward his bed.

Nothing interesting ever happened while I was in the crow! I would really like to see this ship. Captain always kept me below when one passed, so I had yet to see one personally.

I thought that having someone young above deck would make it easier to pass. During my studies, I found that pirates did recruit young men like myself because the crown was less likely to execute a boy. Some of the other men on board could have passed for seventeen-year-olds. Captain should have let us, but he promised my mother and sister that he would keep me safe.

I would see this ship though. How was the question. The answer? Sneak up.

***

"They are sailing rather close. Captain, if we do not shift, they will send us to the locker," I heard Peter whisper.

I was standing at the top of the stairs leading from our quarters at the bow. I pressed myself against the wall as three crew members pass by.

"They would send themselves as well. Just stay on course. They will move."

I waited for the coast to clear before darting for the shrouds of the foremast. I hoped no one would notice me climbing. They had a lot more to worry about than me. Once I reached the bar, I did not have to worry about anyone seeing me, I was blocked. I sat on the bar so that if we hit a wave, I would have something to grip.

Peter was right. The ship was much bigger and was coming very fast. If we did not move, it would bring us down. The ship was dark blue with massive black sails. Wrapped around the bowsprit was the statue of a dragon, mouth open, like it was getting ready to breathe fire.

I had never seen anything like it. I watched as it sliced through the crystal-clear water, not causing a wave. The sun was beginning to set, leaving the sky orange, pink, and purple. If I was not in fear of my life, I would have thought it was the most beautiful thing I had ever seen. Unfortunately, as the ship drew closer, I saw the cannons.

Before I could process what I was seeing, Richard yelled, "Arm the guns! Brace for attack!"

That meant all hands on deck. Every crew member would be needed. I raced back down the shrouds. Where would I be needed? I was never a part of the dummy run. I had to find captain.

"Jason! What are you doing above deck?"

Apparently, I did not have to find him anymore.

"I heard Richard. All hands on deck, right? Where do you need me?"

"The chest. I need you to guard it for your life. Do whatever it takes to keep it away from the pirates, do you understand?" He gripped my shoulders tightly. If I did not know better, I would have thought he was trying to get me out of the line of fire, but the look in his eyes was telling me this was the most important job.

"Yes, captain. I will guard it with my life."

"Good." He smiles slightly.

***

This was the second time I had been in captain's quarters this trip. He hid the chest in a loose floorboard under his desk. His quarters were the largest on the ship, located at the stern. He had a giant map drawn on the starboard size of the ship. The port side was a wall of windows and the back was a wall of cabinets with rolls of papers pouring out of them. His desk was located just in front of that wall, filled with more papers, ink, and a quill.

I heard the sounds of fighting outside the door. Every part of me was screaming to get out there, but the chest was what they were after, and I could not let them get it. I sat behind the desk, my foot over the floorboard. I had my sword sitting on the desk, hand over it. If anyone came into this room, I would die before revealing the location of the chest.

And so I sat there. I did not know how long for. I waited, listening to the screaming and clinking of swords. My crewmates, my friends, my second family, they were dying, and I was sitting here not doing anything. *Damnit, Jason. Why the hell aren't you doing anything!*

"You're doing something. You're guarding the chest."

I jumped up, sword in hand. On the other side of it was the boy I saw on the docks. "You? How did you get in here?" I questioned.

He arched his eyebrow. "Have you ever heard of a thing called magic, boy?"

"Yes. Do not call me boy. You are just a boy yourself." I did not know why I said that.

He chuckled. "I'm older than I look. Eighteen years older to be exact. Why are you in here? Why are you not fighting with the others?"

"Why should I tell you? You are one of them, a pirate."

"I can assure you that I'm not. I'm Pan. I followed this ship from the island I live on."

"Pan? As in Peter Pan? I thought that they were all just stories, saving dying kids and bringing them to Neverland. You are real?"

"Yes, but please call me Pan. I insist."

"I am Jason."

He opened his mouth to say something else, but a one-handed pirate barged through the door. His left hand was missing, replaced by a hook.

"Well, Jason, it's nice to meet yee. Where be me treasure?" he asked, flashing a smile.

"It is not your treasure. It is a chest that was meant for Turkey."

"Me mistake. Where's te chest?"

"You are not getting it."

"Ah, so it be here." He grinned. "That's all I need know." The grin deepens.

I gave him what he wanted, the general location of what he wanted. All he had to do was kill me and trash the room. *Damnit, Jason!* I screamed, mentally slapping myself.

"Calm down. He's not getting the chest," Pan said, stepping into view of the pirate.

"You again," Hook Hand snarled.

"Hello, Hook. I see Zylan's mother really did a number to that hand of yours. If you wish to keep both, I suggest you may want to leave. I wouldn't want to be the one to take it from you." Pan's smile mimicked his.

"I won't be leavin' without me treasure." He ground his teeth.

"Very well." Pan pulled out his sword. "Try to take it."

With that a fight broke out. I did not focus on it. Instead, I tried to figure out how to get out of this mess. I could take the treasure and jump overboard. It is not that heavy. I could try to swim back to shore, get a letter to Mother, or try and get on a ship headed for home. Even if I could make it, I would not want to curse anyone else with this treasure. I had to get rid of it.

"Ace! Where are you?" It was David who ripped me from my thoughts.

"Here!" The pirate and Pan did not break combat. They did not even blink.

David ran in, not even pausing, to look at the two people fighting in the corner. I tried to wave his attention to them before he spoke, but he did not notice. "Captain told us to abandon ship. We are to bring the chest onto a rowboat and get back to shore."

That got the pirate's attention, so much so that Pan managed a shot to his left shoulder. He did not seem to notice though. He ducked out of Pan's reach and dug his hook into David's shoulder. David let out a cry of pain.

"Show me the chest or I kill 'em." The pirate pointed the sword at my throat before I could move.

"Okay! Okay!" David exclaimed. "It is not here. Captain used this room as a diversion. It is one floor below."

"Let's go." He pulled his hook out of David and put his sword at his back. This time there was no cry, just a wince from David.

As soon as they disappeared Pan runs over. "Where is the actual chest? We need to get it to my island where it will be safe."

I hesitated, but only for a second. "It is under the desk. We have to hurry. David is not that good at lying. He will be back up here any minute."

***

"This is Neverland?" I asked.

We each had a handle of the chest, standing on a beach—a small patch of sand is surrounded by trees as far as I could see. Some trees tall, some short, some with holes, some fallen over, some new, some old, some with leaves, some with pines, and some with only branches.

"You could say that."

"So what now?" I asked. "When can I go home? Can I even go home?"

"We have to bury this deep in the forest. As for home, you can stay here and never grow old, or you can return home. But because you have stepped foot on this island"—his head dropped as he finished—"You will not have much time."

I looked around. I could live here. I always loved nature. "Let us get this buried." I smiled.

He looked up and grins. "Good choice! I know the perfect place."

***

"Damnit! This island is so confusing! How hard is it to find one stupid camp!"

I trudged through the forest, occasionally tripping on a tree root sticking out of the ground, or a fallen tree. Pan transported me to the other side of the island and told me to find my way back to camp. I knew he thought he was helping me train, but it sucked!

I pushed a lowered tree branch out of my way. As soon as I stood up straight, an arrow just missed my face, lodging itself in the tree beside me. I grabbed the sword I had holstered at my hip and, in the blink of an eye. I was standing in front of a girl with the tip of my sword poking into her ribs. "Who the hell are you?" I asked.

"I could ask you the same thing." Faster than I could say anything, she used her bow to knock my sword out of my hand. Then she grabbed another arrow and pointed it at my heart. "But the better question is who taught you how to use a sword? A cripple?"

"I will have you know my best friend is a cripple and he could do just as well as anyone else. Do not pretend you know anything about one."

Rage filled me. This girl knew nothing about me, yet she tried to kill me, and now she was making fun of my best friend, James. Well, he had been my best friend before I got here.

"That's where you're wrong. My sister was a cripple. Not born, but made into one. Don't pretend you know anything about me."

"Was?"

"She's dead. Just like everyone else in my family." She shifted her bow slightly and sent an arrow flying past my ear into the tree behind me. "Don't follow me unless you want to join them, that is." With that, she ran past me in the direction I had come from.

1479

"You're so stupid! I haven't eaten in days! That's the first deer I've seen in a year! Why do you insist on ruining my hunt! And my life."

It was the girl who tried to shoot me. It had been almost a year since that happened, and I hadn't seen her since that day. Would I lose my cool again? I hoped not.

"What do you want, Pan?" she asked with a sigh.

Why was Pan laughing?

"Zylan, I'd like you to meet Ace," he said, waving me forward.

Why did that name sound familiar? The ship! Pan said Zylan's mother had taken off Hook's hand! That meant she was in the *Genoa* when it was attacked. Was she the best friend that girl spoke of? The whole family disappeared—a mother, a father, and a daughter. It made sense. No wonder she was like this. She lost her whole family.

"What kind of name is Ace? Who named you? A retard? Or your cripple friend?"

"I named myself. Pan said I could change my name and leave the past behind me," I said through my teeth.

My mother taught me to never hit a woman, but this girl was really starting to get on my nerves. I wondered if she was like this because of what happened. I tried to feel bad for her, but she made it so damn hard.

"So the former then."

This girl had no respect! It took every ounce of will power I had not to smack her across the face. "You didn't let me do that! Why did he get to do it?" She whirled on Pan.

"You didn't give me the chance!"

"So what? That's not on the welcome sign? Oh, wait. There is no welcome sign because you kidnap people!"

"I tried to save you!"

"By bring me here? That's a shit job!"

"Fine!" with that, Pan disappeared.

"Look what you did now. He's not bad guy. What's wrong with you?"

"So much you can't even begin to understand!" With that, she disappeared too.

"Great. Why couldn't someone have taught me that when I got here? Now I have to find my way back to camp . . . again. A year and I still get lost . . . Great job, Jason. Great job." I sighed and started my long walk in the direction I thought the camp was in.

"Ace."

"Jesus Christ, Pan! Why do you do that?" I exclaimed, holding my chest. He was leaning on a tree a few meters ahead of me.

"I figured you wouldn't want to walk back to camp, but if I was wrong . . . " He paused, standing up straight.

"You weren't wrong!"

He grinned. "I figured." The grin dropped. "You recognized her name, didn't you?"

"I did . . ."

He walked over, and put his hand on my shoulder. "Promise me you'll pretend not to. Promise me you won't tell her anything about what happened on the ship. She can't know that the ship that attacked you was the same one that attacked her town. Promise me you won't say anything please."

"I promise."

1486

It had been almost eight years since Pan brought me to Neverland. There wasn't much to do. It was only Zylan, Pan, and I. Zylan stayed pretty far away from me, and Pan was always off doing his own thing. It got pretty lonely. I tried to stay busy by practicing with weapons, mostly my bow staff. I found a small clearing in the middle of the island where I always went to practice.

So there I was, spinning the staff around me, practicing my footwork. When I spun it as a strike to my right, I cracked Zylan in the side of the head.

"Shit! What the hell are you doing out here?"

No answer. Great! She was unconscious. Just what I needed. Pan set up camp a five-minute walk from here. I got there in two, grabbed a cloth, dipped it in water, and ran back. It wouldn't have mattered if I took my time or not. She didn't wake up for another hour, but I sat with her, occasionally dabbing the cloth on her forehead until she came to.

"How long was I out?" she asked, rubbing her temples.

"About an hour. I wasn't sure you were waking up." I chuckled slightly.

"Thanks for not leaving me out here alone. I probably would have if I was you." She smiled a little.

"Well, it's a good thing you're not." I smiled back.

"So, Ace, how'd you end up here?"

That took me off guard. "Well, um . . ."

"You don't have to tell me if you don't want to. Just making conversation, is all."

But I told her anyways, an edited version without the treasure. I told her that the pirates made the remainder of the living crew jump overboard, and being the youngest, I was the last one. Pan got there just in time to keep me from drowning.

Pan told me not to tell her. I had no idea why, but he did, and I promised I wouldn't, so I didn't.

1515

"Zylan!" I called out. "Come on! This isn't funny!"

"I think it's hysterical," she said from behind me. But when I turned toward her voice, she was gone.

She had been doing this for almost ten minutes. She asked me to teach her how to use a bow staff, or "the big spiny stick" as she liked to refer to it. I critiqued one move, and she had a fit. This was how she was retaliating.

"Okay fine. I've had enough. I'm going back to hang out with Matt and Pan, people who actually like me."

I'd been here almost forty years. Pan and I were pretty close, but it almost felt like he wasn't really here most of the time. And Matt was a good guy. It was just, he seemed like he liked to be on his own a lot. He didn't talk much either. Zylan was really the only person I could stand to be around longer than a couple hours.

"Wait." She appeared in front of me, giggling.

"What? Why are you laughing?"

"You just look so cute when you're angry." She giggled again. "I can't help it."

She took me off guard. "Y-You think I'm c-cute," I stuttered. *Damn it, Ace! She probably thinks you're a fool.*

I've had a fancy on her for a long time now. She had never really showed any interest in me, ever. She was very carefree.

She did her own thing, made her own rules. She was really amazing, and I made myself sound like a blubbering idiot.

"Why do you think I spend so much time with you?" She disappeared again.

"Hey! You can't just say that and disappear!"

"I just did. Catch me if you can." Her voice traveled from above me.

I didn't think, I just felt. I felt the wind on my skin, I felt the ground under my feet, and I felt the magic flowing through the island and into my body. The next thing I knew, I was standing on a tree in front of Zylan, and I felt a branch sticking through my side.

She covered her mouth, trying to conceal her laughter as I tried not to cry out in pain. "Why? Why me?" I asked trying to laugh.

"Come on, let's get you fixed up."

Then I was standing in the river flowing from the waterfall. "You make it look so easy! Come on. How do you do that?"

"Don't think. Just do." She smiled.

Don't think. Just do. So I didn't think. I just grabbed her and pulled her toward me, something I had been dying to do for thirty years. And she let me do it.

Chapter 7

Neverland

Pan

As soon as Zylan disappeared from my tree house, I found it. I found the way to Neverland. I didn't know until I saw the paper attached to the one she had picked up. It all became so clear when I read it for myself. I mean I know every inch of the world and never once had I seen The Island on my journeys. It all makes perfect sense. The reason I couldn't find Neverland was because Peter hid it when he banished me here.

For one night, every ten years, I watched Hook's ship sail off. That's because for one night every ten years, The Island is on earth.

Attached to the paper Zylan picked up was actually a letter from my brother. I had forgotten about it. I just tossed it to the side when it appeared to me one morning. Why would I want to read anything my brother had to say? Now I wish I had read it all those years ago.

***

Dear Jacob,

I know you probably hate me. I don't blame you, but there are things that Mother told me, things that she didn't want you to know. I know you're probably going try and find me, but you won't be able to. Neverland and Blankland are on two very different plains. I'm sorry I had to send you there, but I didn't want to ruin my own chances . . . You may have a lot of questions so I will answer a few for you now.

1. You may have noticed Zylan's hatred towards you. That's my fault. I was very angry with you, and I did something I regret. I cursed her to hate you so that you would be unhappy for the rest of your life. She thinks you killed her parents because I changed her memories. She will always hate you because I also made it so she will never remember when she starts to fall in love with you. In case you were wondering, she knew you were watching over her all those years, and she did love you, I saw it when I changed her memories, if that makes any difference.

2. You may have also noticed that there is a pirate ship sailing around your island. That ship is the one that attacked Zylan's village. Because of them, you had to save her, so I decided it was only fair to curse them as well. Every ten years, Blankland will touch down on earth, and the pirates will be able to sail into the world. They will be searching for the chest, and you can't let them find it. If they do, they will be free of their curse and wreak havoc on the world. And they will find it.

3. Well the third question you have, I cannot answer, little brother. That is for mother to answer, and I don't think you will like it.

I hope this helped you a little bit. Goodbye, brother. Maybe one day we will see each other again, and I will be able to apologize to you in person. Or in ghost.

Peter

The reason I couldn't find Neverland is because while I'm in the sky, Neverland is on earth. I don't think he realised how clever I truly am. I know what plains are. He meant the plains of existence, and there are three that I know of. The earth, the heavens, and the skies.

If Blankland is in the skies, which he let slip it is, then Neverland is on earth. When Blankland is on earth, Neverland is in the sky. That meant the key to finding it was leaving The Island while Peter wasn't expecting me too.

So here I am, back in the place I used to call home. It's been so long. I forgot how creepy the vibe of it is. Walking through the forest sends chills down my spine, even though it's an exact mirror image of The Island. It might be difficult to find Peter. I forgot where our camp was, and even if I hadn't, Neverland has changed, and he's probably moved it a few times since I was here last.

The deeper I get into the woods, the more uneasy I feel. I try taking a few deep breaths to calm myself but the goose bumps won't disappear from my arms. Where are all the kids? I got one every day, and if he continued, there should be over 200,000 of them.

After a few minutes of calming myself, I finally relax. Unfortunately, it's a short-lived relaxation. I hear leaves rustling behind me to the right. I stop and spin around. "Who's there?" I call. No answer. I walk a couple of steps forward before I hear it again, this time accompanied by giggling. I forgot how creepy little girls' giggles could be.

"Fuck this."

I yank my sword out from behind my back and throw it to the right. It hits a tree, ten meters away, just in front of a girl. She is mostly hidden by a bush, so I can't make out a face. "Why are you following me?" I yell.

She giggles some more. "You've been gone for so long, I almost forgot you existed."

"Wendy?" I ask as she comes out of the shadows. "It is you! How have you been?" I exclaim, running over and giving her a hug.

All the other kids on Neverland used to bug me. Not Wendy though. She was the only one I ever talked to. Probably because she was the reason I found Zylan in the first place. I remember every time I would come back with a new child, she would be waiting for me on the shore, ready to hear what else I found out about this mysterious girl.

"It is me!" she chirps happily in my ear. "I have been good! I missed you! Honestly, I never thought I would see you again. Peter said you left us." She pulls away and looks down, sadness flushing over her face.

I frown as well. "I missed you too." I use my first two fingers to lift her head. "But I'm here now." She smiles and I smile back. "I wish you had been there when I met her."

Her eyes go wide and she smiles from ear to ear. "Jacob! You found her? That's amazing! Tell me everything!"

"I will. I promise. But right now I need to talk to Peter. Can you take me to him?"

She nods and starts running in the direction I came from. I pull my sword out of the tree it rests in and then follow her for almost ten minutes before she comes to a stop in the middle of a clearing. I laugh to myself, shaking my head. This is exactly where I set up my new camp on The Island. I had no idea we were that much alike.

Peter's standing alone in the middle of the open space with his back facing me. "It's been a long time, brother," he says, turning around.

"Not long enough," I say through my teeth, all the built-up anger I felt towards him is finally boiling to the surface. I feel it burning through my veins as he smiles at me.

"What brings you back to Neverland? Could it be . . . Zylan? Still hasn't forgiven you for killing her parents, eh?" His smile turns into a smirk.

"I didn't kill her parents. You know that. I know that. Make her know that." My jaw is clenched as I speak. I try to remain as calm as I can. It doesn't really work.

"Why would I do that? It worked. It brought you home," he smiles again. "Back to Neverland." He gestures to the space around us before pausing. "Back to me." He takes a step forward.

"Because I'm not staying here. You're going to tell me how to fix this, and then I'm going to leave. I never want to see you again."

"You still don't get it. I did this to help you. Jacob, I did this to protect you. Zylan was going to ruin everything. I couldn't let her. I knew you would come back here, that's why I left those clues." He looks down. "I did hope that it wouldn't take you 543 years to figure it out, but here you are, right where I want you."

"No. I don't think you get it. I'm not here to stay. I'm here to fix her memories, and then I'm leaving. I don't care what it is you think she was going to ruin because you're the only one who ruined something that night. You are *not* my brother," I spit.

Peter's smirk drops. I struck a nerve with that one. I hurt him, just like he hurt me. "I really did hope you would understand without an explanation. Mother wanted so badly for you to not know the truth."

"I don't know what you're talking about, and I don't really want to. Fix. Her. Memory."

"I'm going to show you something. If you still wish to leave after that, I will not stop you, but Zylan is the only one that can fix her own memory."

Peter disappears into the trees behind him. I start to follow despite my better judgment when Wendy stops me.

"Jacob, did you say Zylan?" she asks quietly.

"Yes, why?"

"Jacob . . . Zylan's my sister."

Clover

They have been gone for hours, just disappeared into thin air. I suppose we could go look for them, but now that the camps are joined, I want to see who ended up together. It's harder to hide a secret relationship if you're constantly around each other. So far, I've spotted about five couples trying very hard not to show and two not so, shall we say, discreet about it. I'm not talking just like holding hands and the occasional peck on the cheek. I'm talking full out make-out sessions. It makes me want to throw up just thinking about it. The ones that are disgustingly obvious are Luna and Griffin and Lydia, big surprise there, and Dylan. The more discreet couples are Noel and Klaus, Iris and Isaac, Luke and Ryan, Olive and Cole, and Troy and Gia.

As much as I love people watching, if I see Griffin shove his tongue down Luna's throat one more time, I'm going to cut it off and shove it up his ass. Thank god, Justin rescued me from that sight.

I didn't notice him creeping up behind me until I felt his arms wrap around me. I always love being in his arms. It's like they are meant just to wrap around me. I always feel safe, warm, and loved when I'm with him. Even though, to some, when they first arrive, he looks a little terrifying. His left eyebrow is pierced. He stands six feet above the ground and walks like he could squash you like a bug if you got in his way. He has a few tattoos running up his left arm and along the side of his neck. Plus, he's jacked. That's about the scariest part about him.

His blond hair is long and pushed back. I always love it when strands fall into his face and he pushes it back. His eyes are the most beautiful shade of blue. When the sunlight catches them I swear I can see the ocean. Honestly, he's just a beautiful human being and I love to look at him.

"Hey, babe, haven't seen much of you since the whole joining camps thing," Justin mumbles in my ear before kissing my cheek. "I was wondering if I could pull you away from your intense watching of who's with who."

I sigh sarcastically. "Well, I suppose if it was worth my time, I could pull myself away from visualizing shoving Griffin's tongue up his ass." He chuckles. I can feel a deep rumble coming from his chest as he does. "You think I'm joking?"

"No, I don't, that's why it's funny." He unwraps his arms from around my waist and walks in front of me. "Shall we?" he asks, holding out his hand.

"Sure. Why not?" I smile and take it.

He laces his fingers through mine and leads me away from the camp.

"This whole joining camps thing is a little weird, don't you think? I mean I'm super happy that I get to see you all the time, but I'm kind of nervous you'll get sick of me," Justin says as we walk.

I let out a snort. "You know what? I was thinking the same thing as you this morning, but I think we can handle it."

He stops walking and steps in front of me. "How long have we been together?"

"That's random. Like . . . um . . . 430 years . . . give or take a couple months."

"Four hundred and thirty years, seven months, three weeks, four days, and I have loved you every second of that." He looks away.

"Justin?"

"Sorry. Ace made this sound like it would be a piece of cake . . . but . . . what I'm trying to say is, Clover, I think it would be super cool if you would marry me." He pulls a silver ring out of the pouch in his cape.

"Are you joking?"

By the look on his face, I caught him by surprise just as much as he caught me. It doesn't look like he's joking.

"I . . . um . . . no . . . I'm messing with you! Don't look like I just told you I killed your entire family! Of course I will . . . but how would it work?"

He scratches his head. "Huh . . . I never thought of that."

I smile. "It's okay. We'll figure it out."

***

Shortly after that, I find myself wandering around by myself, smiling like an idiot. I mean every girl dreams about their wedding day even if they don't think it'll happen. Well, I did. Before I got here, I always dreamed about a huge wedding with all my friends and family present, what dress I would wear, the kinds of food that would be served, who the guy would be. When I met Kaleb, whenever I dreamed about the big day, no matter how hard I tried, I couldn't picture him as the guy. At first I ignored it. He loved me and I loved him. What did it matter if I couldn't picture his face as the groom? Thinking about it now, I should have known he wasn't the right guy But with Justin, I can see it.

Everyone on Neverland is sitting on white chairs that have vines twisted around the legs and back, twenty-five on one side, twenty-five on the other. Justin's standing on the right side of a platform, under an arc of green that has a little flower poking out of it. He was smiling. Ace was behind him, whispering in his ear. Justin's shaking his head, his eyes locked on me. This is what he wants, even with the best man doing his duty of trying to talk the groom out of it. Elena and Zylan are walking in front of me, dropping flower petals onto the ground in front of my feet. Even Pan is standing in the centre of the platform, impatiently tapping his foot like this is the most inconvenient thing on the planet. I can picture it, every second of it. And I'm going to love it.

I'm so wrapped up in my imagination that I totally miss the fact that Zylan is right in front of me, waving, trying to snap me out of it. I shake my head and smile at her.

"You'll never guess what just happened!" we exclaim together.

"You first."

We laugh.

"Okay, together then, one, two, three! I'm getting married!"

We both stop and realize we said the same thing. "Congratulations! . . . We need to stop saying things at the same time."

So she stops and waves me to tell my story and I do.

"I can't believe that we both got asked on the same day. What are the odds?" Zylan laughs, shaking her head.

"Apparently pretty good. So what's your story?"

Her story is a lot more romantic than mine, but I could deal with that. "Why does that not surprise me?" I chuckle. "That sound so . . ." I pause, trying to find the right word, "Acey."

"It does, doesn't it?" She smiles. "It's a little weird though. It's almost like the only reason they're doing it is because they're claiming us. I have a feeling if Pan hadn't invited us over, they wouldn't have done anything."

I sigh. "I know what you mean, but I'm not going to complain. I've dreamed about my big day for as long as I can remember. I want this, I need this, and I deserve this. And so do you."

"You're right. We do." She smiles. "But onto other business. The reason I was so eager to find you is I wanted to ask you for a favour."

"Shoot."

"I always wanted a really traditional wedding except I didn't want my dad to give me away. I wanted my sister to do it. Of course, that wasn't a possibility then. Now it is, but my sister isn't here. You are. You are my best friend and the closest thing I have to family. Scratch that. You are family, and I know this is a little weird but can you give me away?"

"That's . . . a little . . . different, but of course! You're the sister I always wanted."

Pan

I take a step back. I'm not sure why. It's like my body thinks the farther away I am from her, the better I'll hear her. I shake my head. It makes since. The reason Zylan was in front of the ally, panicking, was because she knew her sister was bleeding to death. But how could I have not seen the resemblance? Wendy has short, strawberry blonde hair and bright blue eyes. Zylan has long dark brown hair and icy gray eyes. They look nothing alike and don't have the same surname. No way are they related.

"Are you sure it's not a different Zylan?"

She looks at me like I'm the stupidest person she's ever met. Her mouth opens slightly like she's going to say something but shakes her head and laughs instead, rethinking her words.

"Okay . . . Let's say that there is another Zylan Cain running around Genoa, Italy, at the same time as my sister, *Zylan Cain*, and I are there. What are the odds that this other Zylan is standing just outside the ally and my sister just ran out of? Better yet, what are the odds this other Zylan isn't wearing an overdress and corset right after *my sister* took hers off to try and keep me warm, comfortable, and from bleeding out? I'd say that this other Zylan is actually my sister, and if you choose to deny that, you are a lot stupider than I thought."

I laugh at myself. "You're right." Another half laugh escapes my lips. "Just one question. Your name is Wendy Darling . . . Why is Zylan's surname different?"

"Darling isn't my last name. It's more of a nickname. It started with 'my darling Wendy' then it became 'Wendy darling, can you bring me this.' That seemed to stick because everyone just called me Wendy Darling. But I'm actually Wendy Cain."

The reason Zylan hates me is because she thinks I killed her parents. Maybe if I can bring her back to Wendy, she'll see that I'm not as bad as she thinks I am. I don't expect her to love me or anything, but maybe she'll stop looking at me like I'm a murdering psychopath.

It's time to bring Zylan back to Neverland. It's time for her to learn the truth and for her to see her sister again. "Wendy, you continue to be my favourite person ever!" I exclaim, kissing her forehead.

When I start to run back toward the boat I had taken, Wendy calls after me, "Don't you want to know what Peter has to say?"

"I have more important things on my mind right now!" I yell over my shoulder. "I promise I'll be back!"

Clover

1485

"He's here again, miss," my servant girl and best friend said, looking over my shoulder.

We were sitting at a table just in front of the castle. There was a market fair going on. There had been for a week. The first day, a boy had caught my eye. I wasn't sure what it was about him, but I felt drawn to him. I pointed him out to Margret, and ever since she pointed him out to me.

Sure enough, when I turned around, there he was, standing by a trolley three down from where I was sitting. The man behind the stand was handing him a bag. Full out what? I had no idea.

"So what would you have me do about it?" I asked as calmly as I could. I wanted to do something about it. I wanted to go over there and talk to him about something, anything, just so I could be close to him. I just wanted to get to know him, but there was no way that. That would work, not in my current position as soon-to-be princess.

I turned away from him. I should *not* have gone out today. I had a feeling that I shouldn't have come out today! But I did it anyways because I wanted to see him. Why did I never listen to myself? So now I was sitting there, watching a boy I had no chance with.

"I wish to leave now. Let us go," I said, standing up.

"Miss! Wait. he's coming over!" she exclaimed, face lighting up, her smile from ear to ear, like a child receiving their first gift.

"No, he's—"

"Hello. I'm sorry to bother you, but I'm new around here. Is there any way you could point me in the direction of the chandlery?"

It made me smile, hearing that he spoke English just like me. God, I missed speaking English to people other than Margret.

Speaking of Margret, her smile was wider than before, her green eyes sparkling. It was like the boy she'd been in love with since she was ten was standing in front of her, confessing his love for her. My eyes went wide, trying to signal her to calm down before she crept him out so much that he would run away. She didn't catch it at all. She just sat there with a stupid grin on her face like she was frozen. I made a mental note to kill her when we got back to the castle.

I turned around, slowly, very slowly, preparing myself to speak. When I finally made it all the way around, I saw the boy standing was so close to me, I could smell the spices he bought from the man at the trolley. He smiled. He was wearing worker's clothes, a loose white long-sleeved shirt with brown pants and black boots. He had short brown hair—most boys and men would let their hair grow out to at least to their shoulders—but his barely covered his ears. His eyes were bright blue, lit by the sunlight that was making them sparkle.

"I apologize for my friend. She has trouble speaking to boys." I smiled back, letting out a nervous giggle. "The shop you are looking for is at the end of this road to the right. It is the third last. You cannot miss it." I pointed down the road to my right.

"Thank you," he said with a smile before following my outstretched arm down the road. I wondered what he was doing looking for the chandlery.

"Wow, miss! He really is cute!" she squeaked, jumping up.

"Yes, he is. Too bad this is the last day, and I'll never see him again." I sighed, peeling my eyes away from the back of the boy's head. "Let us go. Father shall be waiting." I dropped my voice. "Probably has something to yell at me for by now."

"But miss—"

"Please, just leave it alone." I picked up the ends of my beige dress and made my way toward the castle.

***

I found myself wandering around the left wing of the castle. I wasn't supposed to be in here, but I couldn't care less. They had a dumb reason for keeping me out as well. No one was foolish enough to break into a castle even if this wing was less protected than the rest. I didn't enjoy people telling me what to do all the time! Even if I was to marry the prince, who, by the way, was twelve and I was fourteen. It wasn't fair. Just because Father wanted more power. Like Henry's fight to become the king of England wasn't good enough.

So I was stuck here until I died. I might as well get a look around my prison. Father went back to London, leaving me with Margret. She was great, don't get me wrong, but she was too excitable. Even having a conversation with her was a lot of work. How was I supposed to live here? Forever? How was I supposed to marry the prince? He was childish. Margret said he would grow out of it, but I doubted it. I wished Father would just let me grow up with Henry. But he was fourteen years older than me, and we were only half siblings, so why would he want to deal with me?

I walked down the empty hall, feet not making a sound as I went. It was so quiet, so empty. The only things here were me and the statues. That was kind of how I felt right now, empty, hollowed out, and under protected. I guess that's why I was so drawn to this place. It was me. I was tossed aside and taken for granted. No one really paid attention to me, just like this wing. It was like it was made for me, as a reminder that even though I was important, I wasn't as important as I wished to be.

I took a deep breath, stopping in the middle of the corridor. I closed my eyes. "I wish that someone would come save me. I wish that I could be free of all this."

Right before I opened my eyes, for a split second, I saw a boy with brown hair standing over another boy with blond hair in the middle of a forest. He was smiling and laughing at the boy on the ground. There was a girl, peeking out from behind the trees. She looked angry at the boy laughing. She was—

A loud cough made me open my eyes. "Hello?" I called out. *Yes, Charlotte, call out in the empty hallway in the least protected wing of the castle. You are very smart.* Sometimes my inner voice was really mean to me. I took a step forward, my dress swishing against the floor as I did. *Damnit! I hate these stupid things!* I picked up the poufy pink fabric and took another step. Silence. Perfect.

I started making my way quietly down the hall. As I neared the end, I heard a clink coming from the last statue. I took another deep breath. This time, instead of embracing the room, I accepted the fact that the person behind the statue might be trying to kill me.

I looked around quickly for something I might be able to use to hit him over the head with. One of the statues had a sword loose. I wiggled it free as fast but quietly as I possibly could, not wanting that person to hear what I was doing. I wasn't expecting it to be that heavy. I almost lost it, but I managed to keep it from hitting the ground.

I couldn't hold both my dress and the sword, so I hoped the person couldn't hear it swishing against the floor. I neared the statue, lifting the sword above my head. When I turned the corner, I went to swing down, but I stopped.

"You? What are you doing here?" In front of me was the boy from the market. My hands were still above my head, sword in position.

"I . . . um . . . maybe you could . . . a . . . put that down? I-I kind of like having my head." He nervously chuckled.

"Um, yeah . . . right . . . Sorry." I dropped my arms, resting the sword on the wall.

"To answer your question . . . I um . . . I didn't think I would actually see you . . . I um . . ." He paused, letting out a deep breath. "How about I try again? When I saw you that first day at the market, I thought you were the most beautiful girl I had ever seen, and I knew that I needed to see you again, so I went back every day, hoping to see you, and I did. But I knew I only had one more day, so I had to find an excuse to talk to you. I never thought I would see you again, but a few days ago, I caught a glimpse of you on the castle wall and I knew. I know how that sounds but—"

"Princess! Princess! Where are you?" Margret yelled, cutting him off.

His eyes went wide. "Yo-You're the princess? I-I-I-I am so sorry!" He bowed his head and went to run off, but I stopped him.

"I'm not the princess yet, I never want to be the princess! Please don't leave," I pleaded. "I know what you're talking about. I feel it to."

He lifted his head, eyes shining and smile wide. "You do? Really?"

"Yes." I smiled back. "Please wait here. I'll be back soon."

He nodded, and I ran down the hall. I rounded the corner, smacking right into Margret. We both lost our balance and fell. "Margret? What is it? Did something happen?" I asked, standing up and brushing off my dress.

"Yes, Miss Charlotte. I'm so sorry to bother you. I do know how you love your time alone. It is just that there is an intruder in the castle. He used this way, and I know how much you love your walks through this wing."

"I . . . um . . . know."

"What? Did he hurt you?" she exclaimed. Her plump cheeks flushed red, fists clinching.

"No, no!" I exclaimed. "It's the boy from the market. He's here in the castle."

"What?" Her face lightened. "The cute one? That speaks English?"

"No, the other one." My tone was neutral. I hoped my face was too or it would ruin the joke.

Her head tilted to the side, one eye closing slightly like she was glaring at me. "Where is he? We need to get him out of here before they catch him."

"This way."

1486

"He wants to meet with you tonight!" Margret squeaked, running into my room without knocking, I might add.

It had been about seven months since the boy from the market snuck into the castle. His name was Kaleb, and he was the sweetest boy I had ever met. We met about once a week outside the castle. Margret played the messenger, and you would think, after seven months, she would stop getting so excited every time he wanted to meet. But every time was like the first time.

"You do know you don't have to run in squeaking every time. One of these days, someone is going to hear you." I sighed, standing up.

I was sitting at my desk. It had a giant mirror mounted onto the back of it, leaning on the wall. I kept a brush, my journal, a quill and ink, as well as foundation with rosewater on it. I thought that I should put more stuff because it looked so bare, but I had no idea what else would look at home there.

My bed was pushed up against the left wall that had large posts on each corner. I supposed I could take the extra blanket from the foot of the bed, but that would just go on my chair. The table beside my bed had an oil lamp on it. I could move it or I could just get another one. Yes, that was what I should do.

"No one will hear me, miss. No one is around." She scrunched up her face like she was upset with the accusation. "He says to meet him at the benches and that you'll know what that means." She smiled before bowing and backing out the door.

I smiled too. He wasn't talking about real benches; he was talking about the trees. A while ago, on one of our walks, we walked down a path to a beautiful patch in the forest where there was a circle of trees. In the middle was high grass and flowers, too many different types to name. He said that it would be a perfect place for benches, and we could sit for hours there and no one would find us. Ever since then, our spot had been the benches.

Time to get ready.

***

"Kaleb? Kaleb?" I whispered harshly. It was almost midnight. I should have been getting back to the castle, not just meeting him. "Kaleb, this isn't funny." I moved to the middle of the field, holding my lantern, my dress pulling the grass to the ground. I felt it brush my ankles as it bounced back into place. It was a good thing I had the sense to wear a light green dress, or it would be stained. "Come on. This isn't a joke! Come out!"

"You're right. This isn't funny." I jumped. It wasn't Kaleb's voice. This wasn't good. "What's wrong, sweetheart? Did your man leave you alone out here?"

I turned around slowly, dropping my lantern to my side. The man was standing in the shadows of the trees. I could tell he had a crooked smile by the moonlight hitting his teeth.

"Well, don't worry about him"—he paused and took a step forward into the light—". . . I can take care of you." The man was older, my brother's age probably. He had curly brown hair that went pass to his shoulders, a pale face, and crooked yellow teeth. He was dressed in all black.

It took all the willpower I had not to gag. I know better. Although it wasn't something I liked to admit, I came across guys like that a lot. The ones who liked to take advantage of pretty girls late at night. "Could you walk me home? I don't think he's coming." I learned that you have to play with them. Make them think you didn't know what they were talking about. I'd confused a few of them so much, they didn't realise I was walking them to the castle until we were there.

"Oh, honey, we both know that's not what I'm talking about." He got over to me in a matter of seconds. Before I could even scream, he had a hand on my mouth and the other on my right arm. The next thing I knew, I was lying on the ground with him on top of me, my lantern flying from my hand. I flailed around, trying to break free, but he was too strong. He had me pinned.

"Hey! What are you doing?" It was Kaleb.

"None of your business," the guy said with his eyes locked on me. He had his right arm pinning my left arm and covering my mouth. His left hand was squeezing my right arm so tightly I would probably have bruises for weeks. "Now get lost. Give me and my girl some time alone." His breath stunk of old fish and rotten eggs.

"Get off of her!" I can't see him but his voice sounded like it was right—

The guy flew backward, like he was yanked off by a bear. I scrambled to my feet, my right foot catching my dress, causing it to rip. I barely noticed. Where did Kaleb go? Where did the guy go? What the hell was going on?

I heard a scream coming from the darkness in the trees. I looked around for the lantern, but in the struggle, it went out, and the moon retreated behind clouds. I was alone in the complete darkness. There was another scream. *Please, not Kaleb. Please.* I heard one last scream and rustling leaves. Someone, or thing, was coming right at me. *Please, be Kaleb. Please.*

"Come on, we have to go! Run!"

Kaleb came running out of the trees and grabbed my hand. I let him pull me out of the clearing, and through the path. Once we were out, we stopped to catch our breath, and I finally got a good look at him. His face was bleeding. I wasn't entirely sure where from. There seemed to be a number of gashes all over his face. "Kaleb, you're bleeding! What happened in there?"

"I'll explain later. For now, we have to get you back the castle. Come on quickly!" He grabbed my right arm gently, but it still caused me to flinch. "Are you okay? Did he hurt you?"

"He had me pinned. He gripped my arm so tightly." I rolled up the sleeve of my dress, revealing a hand print wrapped around my wrist.

Kaleb took my hand and kissed all the way around my wrist until I was giggling instead of wincing. "How's that? Do you feel better?" he asked, wrapping his arms around me.

"Much." I leaned onto his chest. His heart was beating slowly even though we just ran half way to the castle. My heart was still pounding so fast, I thought it might fly right out of my chest. I didn't understand how he never seemed to be out of energy or breath.

"I'm so sorry I was late," he whispered into my hair before kissing the top of my head.

"It's okay. You were here when it mattered."

"I promise I'll never be late again, and I swear to you, I will never ever let anyone hurt you. I love you."

"I love you too." I kissed his collarbone and snuggled back into his chest. I never wanted him to let me go. I wanted to stay like that forever. I wanted nothing more than to be with him for eternity. I couldn't believe how lucky I was to have found him.

"We should get you back to the castle. Someone probably noticed that you're missing." Kaleb pulled away slightly.

"I doubt it, but I agree. It's probably best that I get back soon. I've had enough excitement for one night, but you're coming with me. I don't want to be alone tonight."

"I won't leave your side. I promise." He linked his arm with mine and walked with me to the castle.

I went in alone and met him in the left wing, so I could lead him to my room. I knew the guard schedule like the back of my hand, so I knew which way to take him. Once we got to my room, I took off my overdress and slipped into bed next to him. It was the best night's sleep I had ever had.

1487

My half-brother was throwing a ball to celebrate his second year as king of England. That meant I got to go home! He said he was going to have one every year from then on until the day he died. That meant I was going to get to leave Scotland for two weeks every year!

Margret and I were in my room, unpacking. I was so excited! I finally got to meet Henry's wife. I was home. I got to see Mother and Father, and I didn't have to be trapped in the wretched castle anymore. The only downside was that I didn't get to see Kaleb for two weeks. I tried to push the thought to the back of my head. That was a good thing for me. I couldn't let Kaleb ruin it for me. As much as I missed him, I mustn't let it bring me down.

"Miss Charlotte, Henry wishes to see you before the ball," one of this castle's many servant girls said, knocking on the door of the room.

"Yes, of course. Margret, can you finish up here, I'll be back soon." She nodded and I smiled. "Thank you." I turned to the girl. "Lead the way."

She bowed. "Yes, miss."

"There's no need for that." I smiled. "I am a guest in your home. Please call me Char. All my friends do."

She quickly turned away as I approached, gasping. That happened a lot. I hated the formality of "Miss Charlotte" so I tried to get them to call me Char. Margret just started doing it. She thought that if anyone else heard her, she would get into a lot of trouble. Now, she decided she'd call me Char when no one was around. I agreed that that would be best.

The girl said nothing and retreated from the doorway. "Well, that's a new one." I chuckled. "I will see you at the ball."

I caught up with the girl halfway down the corridor. She kept her head straight, not looking at me once. Her brown hair was tied up but it was still longer than mine. It came down to at the middle of her back. It swished from side to side as she moved. Her gown didn't have a cage like mine, so the fabric wasn't held up at all. It was cream in colour and dragged along the ground.

"What's your name?" I asked trying to start up a conversation. Her shoulders tensed, and she said nothing. "Why will you not speak to me?"

"My name is not important. I must take you to the king and then I must leave." She veered left at the corner and disappeared down the next hall. I mean she literally disappeared into thin air. Where did I go now? I had no idea where Henry was! Was this a joke? I'd never been in this castle before, how was I supposed to find my way to his office? Maybe I shouldn't have pushed her so hard...

I kept walking down the hall the girl disappeared from. At the end, there was a door slightly opened. I could hear Henry's hushed voice on the other side. As I neared the door, I started to hear parts of a conversation.

"...belongs to us not," Henry said.

"Sir, it needn't matter. Everyone believes the chest to be at the bottom of the sea. If we find it, no one will know it is the 'cursed' treasure. It would help us with the fairs of our war." I didn't recognize the voice, but he must be a nobleman. The way he spoke was impressive.

"Okay. I shall sanction a mission to search the sea where *Mayfly* was last seen. Fly no flags. The last thing we need is Italy against us." I wasn't supposed to hear that. *I'm going to pretend like I didn't hear that and walk away now. Oh, Henry, what did you just get yourself in to?*

***

I'd been avoiding my brother since my first night here. I still couldn't figure out why that girl brought me to see him if he was busy. I hadn't seen her since then. Maybe she didn't actually work here. But then how would she know where the king's office was? And why did she want me to hear just that part of the conversation? None of it made any sense.

Tonight was the night of the ball. Margret and I were standing off to the side as the adults danced. Unfortunately, my brother decided to invite my future husband to that event. That meant at some point I was going to be forced to dance with him. I wished Kaleb were here to dance with. We had been together almost two years, and we had yet to have a dance. We only met at night, and by then, the music had stopped.

It was loud here, not I-can't-hear-myself-think loud but the-music-is-playing-and-people-are-talking kind of loud. It was a nice change to the loneliness of the castle. It put a smile on my face.

I watched as couples danced, the women being spun and the men watching their women like they were the most precious thing in the world. Everyone was smiling and laughing and having a good time. I couldn't wait for that to be me, but it never would be. Soon, I would have to stop meeting with Kaleb, and I would be forced to marry the prince. I would never be the happy woman dancing with the man she loves. I would be the princess and then the queen.

"My princess, would you care to dance?" *Great.*

"Of course, my prince." I faked a smile. James took my hand and led me to the centre of the floor.

I didn't want to dance. I wasn't in a dancing mood, well, at least not in a dancing mood with him. All I wanted to do was curl up in my bed and go to sleep. I was heading back to Scotland in a few days. I would get to see Kaleb. Maybe I would ask him to dance or make him dance with me.

"Charlotte?"

"Hum? Yes, sorry, my prince. I must have got lost in thought. You were saying?" I'd gotten very good at faking a smile. He didn't even question my thoughts.

"I was saying that you look very beautiful tonight." He smiled.

"Thank you."

"Excuse me, would you mind if I cut in for a dance?" It couldn't be. But it was. When I looked over I saw Kaleb standing beside me, smiling. My heart skipped a beat, and my smile became genuine. He came. He found a way into the castle and he came just to ask me to dance. I couldn't believe that he did this! How did he do this?

"Who are you?"

"James, this is an old friend of mine, Kaleb. I've known him for as long as I can remember. Would you mind cutting our dance short? I would really like to catch up."

"Not at all. I will find you later so we can finish." He smiled. "Good to meet you, Kaleb." He retreated.

He wasn't coming back. His father forced him to dance with me. I didn't even care. "What are you doing here?" I exclaimed. "How'd you even get in here?"

"It's not important. All that matters is that I'm here, and I travelled all this way for a dance. Would you care to satisfy me?" He smiled, his blue eyes sparkling in the dim lighting.

"I would love to."

August 14, 1488

I can't marry the prince. I love Kaleb, I don't love James, and I can't justify marrying someone I don't love. I told my father. He was *not* happy with me. He said that if I don't marry James, I won't be a part of the Stanley house. I don't care. I don't want to be part of the Stanley house if I can't marry the man I love. I'm running away.

I don't know what came over me. I just felt this overwhelming need to tell Father. I was sitting in the square with Margret, talking about what a beautiful day it was, and I felt this wave of guilt. I'm going along with my father's plan of marrying James while I'm in love with someone else. It's not fair to Kaleb, and it's not fair to James, and it certainly wasn't fair to me. So I decided that I must tell Father that I can't marry him.

Kaleb and I have plans to meet here at the benches. He should be here any second now.

Any second he will come through the trees and sit with me. I will tell him that I'm free, that I am able to be with him. We will run away together, and everything will be okay.

At least I hope it will be. I just gave up my family to run away with a peasant. I've never known anything but being nobility. What if I can't live like a peasant? What if Kaleb and I don't work out? How am I supposed to live alone as something I have never been before?

"Char?"

"Kaleb." I smiled standing up. I left my journal on the bag holding all of the things I needed. "I have to tell you something."

He was standing on the far side of the trees in the dark. "What is it, my Clover?" Clover was his nickname for me. He called me that for the first time over a year ago. We were on one of our walks, and we passed a patch of clovers. He told me that although clovers are common, if I found one with four leaves, it was considered very lucky, and I should hold onto it. Then he said I was his four-leaf clover. That whenever I was around, he felt like the luckiest man in the world.

"I told my father about you. I told him I can't marry James. I told him I love you."

"What did he say?"

That wasn't the reaction I was expecting. "Kaleb, I'm free. We can run away together. We can be together."

"Stupid." His voice sounded different, angry almost.

"What?"

"Why would you ever think I wanted to run away with you? I barely like you. All this time I've been waiting, and I can't even get what I want." He stepped into the patch of moonlight peeking through the trees. He didn't look the same, he looked scary. His eyes, normally sparkling, were icy. His smile turned to a snarl.

"Kaleb, what are you talking about?" I took a step back, and he took one forward. "Stop. You're scaring me."

"Good." He jumped me.

***

Everything hurt. I didn't know how long I lay there, but I couldn't get up. Every inch of me was on fire. Every inch of me was broken. I couldn't believe this. Three years and there was never any sign that he didn't love me. He snuck into two castles just to see me, he saved me for the guy who tried to rape me, and he never let me feel anything but loved. How did this happen?

"Are you okay?"

I looked up to see a boy standing over me. He looked about my age with brown hair. He almost looked familiar. I just couldn't place from where. "Who are you?" My voice came out shakier than I would have liked.

"I'm Pan. Who are you?" the boy asked.

"I don't know anymore." I felt a hot tear roll down my left cheek.

"Can I help you?" He sat down beside me. "Is there anything I can do?"

"Not unless you can take away the pain burning a hole through my chest." I tried to laugh, but I ended up coughing up blood. Kaleb didn't just beat me, he broke me. Although the pain in my bones was strong, the pain in my heart was too much too bear.

"What if I told you I know of a place where you will never grow old? A place that can heal any injury."

"Can you take me to it?"

He smiled a genuine smile. "I can."

***

"You never did tell me what your name is," Pan said. He was helping me stay upright with his arm around my waist, and I had my arm around his shoulder. We were standing on the sand of a beach surrounded by trees.

"Clover." I didn't know why I said that, but it felt right.

"Well, Clover, welcome. I'll introduce you to Zylan. I think you two will get along, and then she'll help you get all fixed up."

"Thank you for everything."

"Anything I could do to help."

He closed his eyes. The next thing I knew, I was standing in the middle of a clearing with a girl pointing an arrow at Pan's head. "Who's this? Kidnap someone else I see." The girl was crouched in a tree. Her hair was long and brown; her eyes were blue and unblinking. She was wearing something over them. It looked strange. She was wearing pants and a tight shirt. I'd never seen a girl dress like that before. She looked familiar too. Where had I seen her?

"Zylan, this is Clover. She's really badly hurt, and I would like it if you could help her." Pan looked sad. I wondered why she seemed to hate him.

She unpinned her arrow and stuck it in the case on her back then she slung her bow around her shoulder. I blinked, and she was standing in front of me, examining me. "What happened to you?" she asked, her angry eyes filling with pity.

"I got beat up."

She nodded to Pan. "I'll take her from here." He moved out of the way, so she could support me. "I'm guessing you've realised magic is real now." She smiled.

"It took me by surprise." I chuckled, ending in a harsh cough.

"Well, this will too."

Again with the blinking and being in a new location. Then we were standing in a river that flowed from a waterfall in the middle of a cave. "How is this—" I cut off when I realised she was standing in front of me, not helping me stand straight. "This is . . . Wow."

"I know. So Clover right?" I nodded. "How about I show you a little bit of The Island before we head back to my camp?"

"Can you teach me how to do that thing?" I asked.

"What th—oh you mean"—she disappeared—"this thing." I turned to see her standing on a rock, completely dry.

"Yes, that thing." I giggled.

"I can try, but first we have to get you more practical clothes. You can't go trudging around the forest looking like that."

Zylan held out her hand, helping me out of the water. I looked down at myself. I was still in the clothes I was wearing when I went to meet Kaleb, a black cageless dress. When I went to meet him, the dress wasn't ripped, and it didn't have blood all over it. Right then, however, it did.

"Sounds like a plan to me. I never want to wear this thing again."

"You never have to." She waved her hand, and I was wearing the same thing as her, except my shirt was red and hers was purple.

"Red's my favourite colour." I smiled, looking down.

"Huh, I pegged you for a blue lover. That's the colour I was going for. I guess The Island knew." She smiled and held out her hand. "Come on. I'll show you your new home. I know you'll love it. It already loves you."

1518

It was August 14. That meant Pan would be bringing someone new to The Island tonight. Zylan, Elena, and I were staking out Pan's camp to see who the new guy was. We kind of picked up a pattern when Pan brought Matt and then Elena. It looked like every ten years, on August 14, he brought a new kid here. Since he brought Elena last time, that means he would be bringing a boy this time.

"I bet he's cute." Elena giggled.

"You think everyone is cute," Zylan shot back.

"Well, have you seen Pan bring someone ugly yet?"

"You," Zylan and I said together.

"You guys are mean!"

"You know we're joking. Now shut up before Matt and Ace hear us!" I whispered.

We were joking. She was gorgeous. She had the pale complexion that everyone would kill for, long chocolate brown hair, and warm hazel eyes. Over the last ten years, we'd all become really close, but sometimes, I thought, she felt like the outsider, which was why she always got a little hurt every time Zylan and I ganged up on her like that. We met thirty years ago today, and we had been friends just as long. As close as we were with Elena, the closer we were with each other.

"Fine."

Zylan motioned us to move away from her position and go up. Our best vantage point was the trees. From there, we could see the whole camp, but the boys wouldn't see us, not that they paid much attention anyways.

We were all dressed in murky green tank tops that cut at mid-bellybutton and baggy green and brown pants, pulled up to our shirts. I never knew what I was missing, wearing dresses all the time until I started to feel the freedom of pants and showing a little skin. It was quite an amazing feeling really.

Once I'd found a good tree to climb, I settled myself at the top and waited. Pan returned with the new kid about twenty minutes later. Elena was right; he was cute. His face made him look young, but his body looked like he could have been a twenty-five-year old blacksmith. His arms had bulging muscles emphasized by the fact that his shirt was so tight. It looked like his left eyebrow was pierced along with the right side of his lip. I could see a little bit of a tattoo peeking out from under the collar of his shirt. He was a troublemaker, no doubt about it.

"You might as well come down and say hello, girls," Pan said.

How did he always know? We didn't make any noise. We were here half an hour before he came back, how did he know? He wasn't even facing us! His back was against Zylan and Elena and I were out of his sight!

"Who's this?" Zylan asked, appearing in front of the new boy. He blinked, probably caught off guard by the fact that she just appeared and because of what she was wearing. "Where are you from?"

"Zylan, give the boy a chance to settle in before we go asking a million questions." I appeared beside her. The boy blinked again.

"She only asked two. No need to go exaggerating things, Clover." Elena appeared on the other side of Zylan.

"Thank you, Elena."

"Can everyone do that?" the boy asked.

"No." Matt rolled his eyes. "These four like to show off with it though."

"Yeah. I can't really do it either. One time, I almost did, but I almost impaled myself with a branch in the process. I've been uneasy about trying again," Ace added with a chuckle.

"Can someone teach me how to do that?"

"Don't ask Pan. He's an awful teacher." Ace laughed.

"Can someone answer *my* questions?" Zylan exclaimed, rolling her eyes.

"I'm Justin, I'm from Sweden."

1520

I hear a scream. I wonder who it is. I hope it's not Kaleb. He just saved me. There's another scream. Please don't be Kaleb. It sounds horrible. There's tearing cloth, breaking branches, and the occasional scream. I wish I could do something. I wish I could do anything, but I'm frozen. How could I let this happen? Kaleb might die in there because he was trying to protect me.

I hear another scream. This time, it's cut short, and something comes running toward me. It's Kaleb! But he doesn't look the same. His ears are pointed and his teeth are raiser sharp. He doesn't slow down when he nears me. He just jumps and lands on top of me.

I feel a heat rip through my body as his teeth sink into my neck. I try to let out a scream, but there's nothing. Not a sound. All I can hear is the sound of his growl, all I can feel is his teeth tearing me—

***

"Clover! Clover, wake up!"

My eyes flew open, and I gasped for air. I felt the side of my neck. There was nothing there. It was just a dream. I was on The Island. I wasn't in Scotland. I felt tears burning my cheeks as they rolled off and hit the dirt.

I must have fallen asleep practicing. Pan and I had been meeting once or twice a week since I got here. He'd been helping me feel powerful again. Kaleb took too much from me that night. Pan was helping me get it back. But it wasn't Pan who woke me up, it was Justin.

"What are—"

"Pan sent me to tell you he couldn't make your meeting. I found you tossing and screaming. Are you okay?"

"No, I'm really not." The tears burned hotter.

"Come here," he said, holding his arms open.

I leaned against him, and he held me while I cried into his shoulder. He played with my hair and tried to calm me down. We sat there for a while, while he talked and tried to make me laugh. Maybe he wasn't such a bad guy. Maybe it could work.

Chapter 8

This Isn't Real

Zylan

"Ze, he's back," Aurora says, pulling my book out of my hands.

In the town square there are little circle and wooden tables are set up around the perimeter. They're normally for the grownups to sit when they get tired, but after dark, all the grownups are putting their children to bed and no one is around. Cristoforo, Marco, Aurora, and I always come here to hang out. We have an oil lamp set up in the centre of the table, so we can see each other and I can read.

"I know. Can I have my book back? Please?" I sigh, holding out my hands.

She's talking about the boy who lurks in the darkness. After Wendy's funeral, I saw him every single night. Well, not saw, sensed. His presence is always around after dark. My friends think it's weird, the fact that this random guy follows me around and I don't find it creepy. When I first sensed someone watching me, I freaked out, but after a couple days, I could sense he wouldn't hurt me.

Mother says I have a gift. The ability to sense a person's intention is one I got from her. After Wendy's death, I started to get these weird feelings pouring off a person every time they walked by. One time, a man walked by, and I could feel pure rage flying off him. I ignored it, thinking I was just imagining it, but later that week, I found out he killed his wife and child before killing himself. After that, I never ignore another feeling again, so when the boy showed up, I knew he wouldn't hurt me. I feel like he's more of a guardian angel sent by God to make sure what happened to Wendy doesn't happen to me.

"How could you know?" she exclaims, throwing her arms in the air as she does. Great, she lost my page. *"You haven't looked up from that book once! And you claim to be almost blind!"*

"I told you," I say calmly. "I get this feeling when he's around. Now can I please have my book back?" I reach across the table to grab it, but she pulls it farther away from me.

"Guys, back me up here!"

"Just give her back the book," Cris mumbles, picking at his nails. I can always count on him to back me up. Well, almost always.

"Marco!" She glares at him.

"The guy isn't following you around. If she doesn't think it's a problem, leave it alone."

Aurora looks like both of them just told her, her entire family is dead and she's dying of consumption. "Fine!" she yells, throwing my book on the table, then she storms away.

***

"I'm telling you! The world isn't flat. The only reason everyone believes that is because maps are flat. If someone invented a spherical form of a map, then people would believe it's round."

My friends think it's hysterical when I talk about my beliefs. Like, hell yeah, I think dragons are flying around the mountains in Tibet; and that people can start fires without trying; and that somewhere out there, there is a place where magic is a normal thing, and people aren't burned at the stake for practicing. Of course, that's not possible for them. They're logical, well, to a point.

"Then why is it that the ships who get close to the edge never return?" Cris asks. This is one of the few topics he refuses to back me up.

"Maybe there is another land, one where it is okay to be different. Maybe they like it better, so they decide never to return home to start over."

Laughter erupts from them. We are sitting in our normal spot, or at least I am. The other three are rolling around on the ground, laughing at me. I refuse to let it bother me. So what if they don't believe? It's what I need to believe. I just return to my book and let them get it out of their systems.

They always think it's weird that I read so much. Only men and royalty are supposed to be able to read, but Father taught me after Nathan died.

Nathan was my older brother, a lot older. When I was ten, he was twenty. He died at sea the night before my eleventh birthday. Father blamed himself for getting him into sailing in the first place. He had lost his only son, so he decided to teach me how to read before we moved from London, England, to Genoa, Italy. It was much easier to learn Italian when I could read the words I was trying to say. So as weird as they think it is, I don't care.

I can sense the mystery boy watching. I know he believes me. I know he has magic I know that if he came over right now, my friends would believe me. But he won't come over, not until I really need him to. When I need him, I know he will come.

"Okay. Let us just say we believe you. How long would it take to get to this mystery place?" Cris asks, trying to get back on his seat.

"I do not know. However long it takes. Does it look like I have any sailing experience? Because I do not."

"Why have you never told your father of your beliefs?"

"I have."

***

"I do not want to hear it, Zylan. Those kids are a bad influence on you! I do not want you spending any more time with them. For god's sake! Look at you! You look like you belong in a whorehouse! I'm not having another incident!" Mother screams.

"Maybe I do! Because I can't do anything right! You hate me, my friends think I'm crazy, and Father isn't here to back me up. You never wanted kids anyways. Now I'm the only one left, so I might as well run off to a whorehouse, so you'll never have to see me again! You'll get what you always wanted. No kids." I push past her and run to my room, locking the door behind me, so she can't yell at me anymore. I can't believe she brought that up. It wasn't even my fault. But how could he be the one to blame when I dressed the way I do?

I'm so sick and tired of being the bad kid. I'm so sick and tired of Mother always judging me. I'm so sick and tired of everything. "I wish that someone will take me far away from this wretched place, so I can be free of all this. I know you're out there watching. If you hear this . . . please take me away to wherever you come from and prove to me that I'm not crazy," I say out my window.

But the boy never came. I sat at my window all night, waiting for something, I'm not sure what. Maybe I am crazy, maybe the boy doesn't care, and maybe all my theories are just that, theories. I wipe the tears sliding down my cheeks as I sit.

There's a bench in front of my window with a long cushion and two small pillows on both ends. It's push right up against the wall. The way my room is set up is like a box, but where the window is, the wall is pushed out, so there is an indent as thick as the bench. Whenever I sit here, I lean on the left wall and watch the world around my window.

My house is at the top of a hill, overlooking the ocean, so I can see the beauty the world possessed. Whenever I feel alone or unwanted, I look out this window and remember the world is a big place. Just because I'm having a bad day today doesn't mean it will always be like this.

Tonight, I fall asleep on the bench and dream of the boy. I finally see his face: pale skin, bright green eyes, brown hair. He wears a light green vest over a black long-sleeved shirt with the sleeves pushed up to his elbow. His pants are a black and his boots are brown. He smiles at me as he stands outside my window.

"Please, come in," I say, smiling back.

"I wish I could stay, but I cannot." He's British. The very familiar accent is music to my ears. It reminds me of home, of when I was happy. "I just needed to tell you that you are not crazy. Everyone here is just too stubborn to see it. I need you to know that you will be okay. I will always be here if you really need me. I promise you that I will never ever let anyone hurt you." He holds up his right hand, his pinkie finger outstretched. I lock mine with his. "I'm sorry but I have to go. I will be back tomorrow. Good night, beautiful. Sleep tight." He kisses my forehead before he goes.

"Have a safe trip, my angel," I whisper into the night.

When I wake up to the morning light pouring into my room, I smile. Even if it was just a dream, it makes me feel like everything will be okay. I know the second I open my eyes that, no matter what happens today, I will be okay. So I watch as the sun peeks over the horizon and shines its light over the ocean. I push away the memory of why I was upset last night.

***

I'm so tired of these godforsaken dreams. After what happened in Pan's tree house, I remember every dream I have in great detail. I almost wish I forgot them like I used to.

Three days he's been gone, and he still manages to fuck with my head. Pan is the bad guy. He killed my parents. These dreams couldn't have happened, yet they feel like memories. They have some truths: yes, I had an older brother; yes, I moved from England to Italy; yes, I had some out-there ideas, which were all proven true when I got here; and yes, my dad did teach me everything I know. But I never sensed him watching me, my friends never laughed and called me crazy, and I never fought with my mom.

I don't know why he's doing this, but I wish he would stop with the mind games. I'm tired of remembering my dreams. I'm tired of sleeping, and believe me, I see the irony in that.

"Island to Zylan. Snap out of it," Clover says, waving her hand in front of my face. I blink twice, trying to focus.

"Come on, Ze. What's going on with you? Everyone can tell you're off," Ty says, taking a seat across the fire from me.

"I'm fine. I'm just tired." I pull my blanket tighter around me. It's a chilly night even with the blazing fire in the centre of our mini-circle on the edge of camp and away from everyone else. "I haven't been sleeping well lately."

"We all know you don't sleep. Come on, Ze. We know you better than anyone. What's going on?" Ace wraps his arm around my waist and pulls me closer to him.

"I'm telling the truth. I'm used to sleeping a couple hours then waking up from a dreamless sleep all fine and dandy. But the last few nights I've been sleeping longer then waking up to weird dreams. I'm not used to it. It's throwing me off a little. Thank you for your concern, but I promise I'm okay." I smile and give Ace a quick kiss on the cheek before dropping my blanket and standing up. "Alright, everyone. I've warmed up a little bit now. How about that food?"

"Finally," Hunter says, standing up on the other side of camp.

"Who said you could eat?" I raise my left arm and drop it, forcing him to sit back down. "Now stay until everyone else eats."

"That's not fair!"

"You're right. We still have to hear your voice." I close my left hand into a fist and twist. He tries to say something, but his voice is gone. "Much better. Now"—I flick my right wrist and food appears on a long table—d "who's ready to eat?"

We used to do this once every couple of weeks. The whole island would get together, and we would have a meal. We would sit in our little groups and enjoy ourselves. There was no feud, and there was no fighting. We just sat together and had fun.

I figured we should do it more often now that we were together all the time. Tonight's our trial night. Other than Hunter's sarcasm, we might actually get through this night incident free.

Once everyone, including myself, has food, I let Hunter up and give him his voice back.

"You're a bitch, you know that, right?" he says as he passes me.

"Yes, but I'm a powerful bitch, and you would do well to remember that." I smile sarcastically and sit back down. "Speaking of bitches, where the hell is Elena?"

"Too scared to face me." Clover smiles and takes a bite out of her roast beef.

"You wish." Elena appears behind Clover and gives her a nasty look. "I was trying to find Pan since none of you seem to care. I lost track of time."

"Why are you looking for Pan? Your true love is standing over there."

"For the love of god, Clover. Stop with the Hunter jokes. I'm tired of it."

"And I'm tired of you staring at every boy you see, including mine, just to make Hunt jealous. I'll stop when you stop."

"One, I don't stare at boys to make him jealous. Two, I don't stare at boys in general. And three, if I did stare at Justin, maybe it's because I FOUND OUT FOUR DAYS AGO THAT YOU'VE BEEN WITH HIM FOR 430 FUCKING YEARS."

I'm going to have to break this up. I sigh and set my plate down on the log beside me. Ace puts his hand on arm and gives me a look that says, "I can't believe they're still doing this, and I'm sorry you have to deal with it." I shrug with a weak smile.

"DON'T START—"

I stand up and toss my arms in different directions. Clover and Elena fly in different directions across camp until they hit a tree.

"Okay," I say calmly. "I'm tired of you two fighting. I think we all are. So I'm going to put you both down and then the three of us are going to take a walk and work this out."

"Fine," Elena and Clover mumble.

"Okay," I say lowering my arms. "Now let's go."

"Remind me not to piss her off," Tyler whispers to Justin.

"Ty, you always piss me off. But you make me laugh sometimes, so I keep you around."

"Love you too, Ze," he says with a smile, a laugh, and a fake kiss. I shoot him a smile and a wink back.

"I'll be back. Ace, please make sure no one kills anyone while I'm gone." I bend down and kiss him on the cheek.

"Can I throw people into trees too?" he asks with a hint of sarcastic excitement.

"Of course, you can." I smile as Clover and Elena join our little circle.

"Yay." He rubs his hands together, putting a devilish smile on his face. I roll my eyes and laugh.

"Come on you two." I turn toward the forest. "Elena right, Clover left. No talking till we get where we're going."

After five minutes of walking in complete silence, I stop in the middle of the closest clearing. "Okay. Fight it out."

The both look at me like I'm crazy. "What?"

"Look, I have my own issues I'm trying to work out, but I'm not taking it out on the two of you. Whatever is going on, I don't want to hear about it. I'm tired of you two getting into it then expecting me to listen to both sides and help you reach a middle ground. You need to learn how to get over your own issues. So"—I wave my hands and a bo staff appears in their hands—"you are going to talk and try to hit each other. I'll be here if things get out of hand."

They look at each other then back at the bo staff in their hand. "Nope. I'm not doing it," Elena drops her staff.

Clover takes one more look at hers then drops it as well. "I'm sorry."

"Me too."

"Good." I smile and hug my best friends.

"Thanks, Ze," Clover says.

"That is what I am here for. Now come on. We have a meal we have to finish, if Ty hasn't eaten the whole table yet."

"You mean Hunter. Like Pan said, no one can out-eat Hunter." Clover laughs as we start to walk.

"Well, we'll actually never know . . . Justin and Hunter never actually had that eat off remember," Elena points out.

"We should do that when we get back. We should have Ty and Ace join too." I laugh. "I bet Ace wins."

"You're only saying that 'cause you love him." Clover rolls her eyes.

"No, I'm saying that cause to him it's eating. To Hunter, Justin, and Tyler, it's a competition. If they want to win, they're not going to focus on digesting their food and will eventually puke it back up and not be able to eat any more."

"Well, we won't know until we put them against each other. I think Ty's going to win."

"Ou, El's got a crush on Ty!" Clover teases.

"Maybe a little one," she confesses.

"What!" Clover and I scream.

"Shush!" El hisses. "We're almost back at camp."

Clover and I stop in our tracks. "We're not going back to camp until we hear about this!" I exclaim. "How could you not tell us?" When I see the look on her face I stop. "Scratch that . . ."

"That what I thought." She laughs. "I mean the first time in camp, I thought he was cute. I mean how could you not?" Clover and I nod in agreement. "We kind of hooked up a few times, but it never really went anywhere."

Clover gasps. "Oh my god!"

When they see I didn't freak out at the news, they look at me crocked. "What? You're forgetting Ty and I are best friends. I already knew that."

"He promised not to tell anyone!"

"He probably figured you'd tell me eventually. Don't be mad at him. He was excited. He really liked you at the time."

"He told you that?" she blushes.

"Is there something you don't understand about the term 'best friends'? Yes, of course, he told me that, bimbo." I roll my eyes. "But that was a long time ago. I don't want to get your hopes up." Mostly because I know he really likes Willow, and last he told me, they're seeing each other now.

"It doesn't matter anyways. It's a tiny, tiny crush. I like him, but I don't think I'd actually want to see him in that way."

Clover rolls her eyes. I know what she's thinking. She's always picking on Elena about Hunter. Elena wanted to get us off her back by telling us about her "tiny, tiny" crush, so we would get off her back, but it backfired when she realized how close I was with him. Clover and I both know she still loves Hunter, and that pretending is easier than dealing with the problem head on. I understand that so I don't push, but Clover, she keeps trying to get Elena to admit it to herself.

Under normal circumstances, Clover would have said something, but right now, she bites her tongue and leaves it at an eye roll because she knows that I will kill her if they start fighting again.

"Why did you roll your eyes?" Elena's face starts turning red.

"I didn't! Zylan, did you see me roll my eyes?"

"Nope. El, you must have imagined it. Not that I blame you. She does roll her eyes a lot." I laugh.

"That's true." Elena laughs as well.

"Alright. If you two are done, we should get back to camp now before the boys eat all of our food."

Elena and I nod. It takes a few minutes to get back to camp from where we stopped. We spend the whole time laughing and talking in a way that hasn't happened in forever.

I stop them right before the entrance to camp. "We need to start talking like this again. We're going to plan a day where we just talk all day."

"Agreed."

I smile. "Alright. Let's get this competition started!"

The three of us push past the branches in our way. Everyone's still sitting in their groups, talking and laughing. It's just like it used to be. This is how it's supposed to be: no fighting, no yelling, no Pan. This is perfect.

"Took you guys long enough," Justin says as he stands up to meet Clover.

"No need to get anxious, J. They were only gone twenty minutes." Ace laughs, also standing to meet me.

"The only anxious one was Ty, waiting to see if you send him flying into a tree for making googly eyes at your girl," Hunter yells from across camp. He's sitting by himself next a tree.

"I do not! And even if I *did*, it's because I didn't know they've been together for . . ."—Ty pauses, trying to figure out if we told him how long, which we didn't—"however long they were together."

"Hey! Don't copy my explanation!" El exclaims. "That's your doing?" she asks Ace, looking back at Hunter. Ace nods with a smile.

"What did he do?" I ask with a laugh.

"He breathed." Ace shrugs and wraps his arms around me. "I figured you would want to come back to a smile." He kisses the top of my head.

I smile up at him. "How thoughtful of you."

"All right, lovebirds. Can we get to the reason we rushed back here?" Clover asks.

"Right. Ace, you have to let Hunter go. We're going to do an eat-off with the four of you."

"Finally!" Justin yells. "I will destroy all of you. Let's do this!"

"Hun, we talked about this. There will be no more 'I will destroy you' talk, remember?"

"Sorry," he mumbles under him breath, rolling his eyes slightly. Luckily Clover didn't see it, or I'd be breaking up another fight.

I step away from Ace and flick my wrist, so the empty table is full of food again. "Okay, Ace, let Hunter up."

"He doesn't have to." Hunter stands up and brushes himself off. "I was sitting there of my own free will." His eyes flicker over to Elena for a quick second then back to me. "Ace's magic sucks."

I chuckle to myself. He waited till El walked back into camp so that she would smile at his timeout. He's been trying to make it up to her since Lydia. I thought he gave up two hundred years ago, but every once in a while, he does something that makes me think he's still trying.

"I tried my best." I turn to smile at Ace.

"She really did." He smiles back. "Alright. Are we ready to do this?"

"Hell yeah!" Justin yells again.

"Babe, seriously. Chill."

"Sorry," he mumbles again.

"Could you guys hang on a second? Elena, Clover, and I never got to eat, and someone"—I glare at Ty—"ate my food."

"What are you looking at me for? Ace did it!"

"No, he didn't. He knows I'd hurt him."

"It's true. You never fuck with Ze and her food."

"Dude, I thought we were friends. Why didn't you warn me?"

"Like Hunt said. If she beats you up, it's not petty." He shoots Ty an innocent smile.

"I hate to break it to you, Ace, but that fact that you didn't warn him so she'd kick his ass is petty," Clover says, walking over to the food. Elena nods in agreement as she joins her.

"Yeah. If you want Tyler beaten up, you're going to have to do it yourself."

Ty's eyes go wide. "Hey, hey now. Everyone has made googly eyes at Ze at some point during their time here. Are you going to beat up all of them?"

"Chill, man. I'm messing with you. Let's eat, okay?" Ace walks over and bumps him on the shoulder, harder than he should have.

Ty rubs his arm. "Sure, man."

Ace isn't as bulky as Tyler, but that doesn't stop Ty from shrinking slightly. Ace is third oldest here. He's got eighty years on Ty and could take him down in less than a second even though Tyler's better at magic. No one here could take Ace in a fight and win except Pan or me, of course. If Ace threatens someone, they shrink whether their taller or bigger or both. No one would take him on.

"Alright! Let's get this show on the road," I say.

"I still don't understand that saying," Clover says, scooping the last bit of food onto her plate.

"It relates to the circus because they're constantly moving," Brian says. "The circus host would tell everyone to pack up, so they could 'get the show on the road.'"

"It's rude to eavesdrop, Brian," Clover says, rolling her eyes.

Brian starts to say something, but I raise my hand to stop it. "We're not doing this right now. Clover, we're in the middle of camp where everyone can hear us. Shut up, sit down, and watch the show. You four"—I point to Justin, Ace, Tyler, and Hunter—"behind the table let's do this."

"Yes, ma'am." Hunter salutes sarcastically.

"Call me ma'am again, and I will end your life. Don't test me."

He stays silent as he walks behind the table.

"Alright, eat as much as you can. If you puke, you lose. If you stop eating for longer than a minute, you lose. Go."

Elena

1505

I heard the loud sounds of crashing and banging coming from outside my room. *What could possibly be so important? The sun was not even up yet.* I groaned, throwing the sheets off of me. "What is going on out here?" I asked, poking my head out the door. I was in a nightgown, and it would be wrong of me to be seen in anything other than my full dress, so I could not leave.

No one answered me. That meant I was going to have to get dressed to find out what was going on out there. But I did not feel that it is worth it. The noises had stopped, and I was sure that I could sleep now.

I closed the door. My room was once again pitch-black. It was much easier to get to the door than it was to get to the bed. My hallway was lit by oil lanterns and candles, but my room was lit by nothing. Walking to the door, there was a sliver of light peeking in from the crack under my door. I lost that light walking away.

I felt my way slowly over to the bed. I managed to hop back in without injuring myself. As soon as I closed my eyes, the noise started again. I could not have been the only one in this house to have heard that! Why was no one telling Caroline to keep it down? I did not want to get up again. I did not want to get dressed. I did not want to start my day when the sun had yet to start hers.

"What is all that noise?" my mother yelled from just outside my door.

Thank goodness, I do not have to get up.

"Can you get Elena up? I need her to help me with this."
Perfect.

Caroline always had these foolish ideas in the middle of the night. I wondered what it was this time. Last time, she claimed she cracked the code to time travel and all she needed was the whole town's supply of pots. If it were not for the power my family had in this town, she would have been burned at the stake ages ago, and my life would be a lot quieter.

"No. Go back to sleep. You can finish this idea of yours tomorrow when the sun is east."

"But, Momma, this has to be done in the dark. The sun will try and take it away from me." I could hear her voice waver. She was holding back tears.

"How about tomorrow night? As soon as the sun sets, we will all help you." Mother's voice softened.

"Okay." Her voice perked up again. She was probably smiling.

"Let's get you back to bed." Finally, I could get back to bed myself.

***

"Did you hear that racket last night?"

"How could I not? Caroline woke up the whole street last night!"

Two girls sitting at the table three down from me had been talking about my sister for the last ten minutes. I knew better than anyone how she could be, but it was not her fault. People did not understand that. She had been that way for as long as I could remember.

"There's something not right about that girl. She should not be allowed to wander the streets."

I tried not to listen, but it was so hard. They were talking about my little sister. She was only nine. She did not understand that she could not run around doing things like that in the middle of the night. One day, she would learn, and people would stop talking about her like she was possessed by the devil.

"They don't let her leave alone," the blonde-haired one dropped her voice and leaned closer to her brown-haired friend. "I heard a group of people talking. They said if she goes out alone"—her voice dropped more, and I had to strain to hear her—"they're going to send her back where she belongs."

The brown-haired girl clapped her hands over her mouth. "But she's just a little girl!" The other girl shushed her, so she lowered her voice. "You don't think they would actually . . . you know . . . kill her."

"I have no idea I hope not."

They would. No one said something they did not mean. If Caroline went out on her own, someone would kill her. My parents knew this. That was why we never let her leave on her own, or left her home alone. My older sister, Delilah, was looking after her today. Tomorrow, my older brother, Angelo, would look after her. The day after, I would. The day after that, my younger brother, Jonathan, would. And we repeat. We had been since the first threat four years ago.

"Elena! I'm so sorry I'm late. My father wouldn't let me leave." My boyfriend, Tyler, came running up the street. Our families were very good friends, so we had known each other for as long as I could remember. As we grew up, we became closer and closer, and our parents thought we would be a perfect match. They were right.

I smiled and stood up. "It is no problem. I have been enjoying the sun. I do not get out enough."

"You have to stop talking like that! Everyone already thinks you're a bore! Have a little bit of fun. Soon you'll be old, and you wouldn't be able to have fun."

"I'll have plenty of time to have fun when I'm dead. There is that better?" I tried to be proper, I tried not to be rude, I tried to be a good girl, but he was such a bad influence.

"That might be true, but you won't be having fun with me." He winked and pulled me toward him.

"Tyler! Stop. People are here." I giggled.

"Come on. Let's go for a walk." He held out his arm. I took it, and we headed in the direction he came running from.

We had been together three years, since I was ten and he was twelve. He made me really happy. He was a really sweet guy, and he never failed to make me smile or laugh. He had these warm hazel eyes that could make a person's heart melt, and the brightest smile I had ever seen. His black hair was kept short and out of his eyes. He and his father were blacksmiths, so unlike a lot of men around here, he did not grow out his hair. Although he was only fourteen, he did have good muscle tone from working with his dad after he finished school. His face was more defined than most boys his age with his sharp jawline and cheekbone.

"Why are you staring at me?"

"I cannot help it."

"Can't. You can't help it."

I stopped walking. "Why do you always do this? You know I can't help it. It was the way I was raised. I have always talked like this. Why are you just now trying to change it?"

He turned his face away from me. "Sometimes it makes me feel like you talk like that just to make the people around you feel less important, like they aren't as proper as you."

"That is not—that isn't true! Honestly, it isn't. It's just that I've been like this my whole life. It is—It's hard to change that." I gently turned his head to face me. "I promise you, I will try. I'm sorry."

"Thank you." He gave me a weak smile.

1506

She got out. No one knew when, no one knew how. She got out, and we hadn't been able to find her for hours. Mother was crying uncontrollably ever since we noticed she was gone. We left Jonathan to comfort her and the rest of us went searching everywhere she could have gone.

How could this have happened? We were all home. We were all sitting together while she was in bed. She had been sick for days. How did she even get out of bed? What if someone saw her?

Oh god, Caroline, why would you do this? What idea could have gotten you out of the house this close to dark?

Mother sent me right over to Tyler's house. She told me to ask them to help. They knew the way she was, and Mother knew they would help. So Tyler and I were searching the woods behind my house.

We moved last year because Caroline kept waking up the neighbours, and they asked us to leave. We gladly did. There was a house on the outside of town no one was using. It was property of the town, and they were happy to get rid of it. They think it was cursed because of the family that lived in it last.

It was almost thirty years ago. One kid disappeared at sea, and the mother lost her mind after losing her son and husband the same way. Plus she lost another son to sickness five years before that. Apparently, he disappeared as well. When the two daughters went to check on her, let's just say there was a good reason why no one wanted to live in that house. The whole thing gave me the creeps, but I got used to it after a while.

"Caroline!" Tyler yelled. "Car! Where are you?"

"Car, please come home! We're all worried about you! Let us help you with your idea!" Nothing. "Maybe if we split up, we can cover more ground," I suggested when we hit a break in the path.

"I don't like that idea. There's a lot of forest to cover, and I don't want you to be alone, especially in the dark."

"How about we walk five minutes out, and if there's nothing, we meet back here. If there's a trail, we'll call out. Sound good?"

He hesitated for a second but nodded. "Fine, but any sign of trouble, come get me." He kissed my cheek before turning down the left side of the path.

I watched as his lantern faded away until there was only a slight glimmer of light showing me where he was going. I took a deep breath before walking down my side of the path. I held my lantern as far out as I could reach, trying to illuminate as much of the forest as I could.

It was creepier at night. It was creepy enough that I tried to avoid it during the day, but at night? I could feel the chill running up my spine with every step I took deeper into the forest. Every leaf that rustled, every branch that cracked under my feet made me jump. Maybe Tyler was right. We should have stayed together.

I took another deep breath and continued forward. I counted four and a half minutes. I thought I should head back.

I stopped. I heard whimpering coming from down the hill on my right. I swung my light around. At the bottom of the hill, I saw Caroline. "Car! Car, are you okay!" I called. "Tyler! Tyler! I found her!" I yelled as loud as I could before I made my way down the hill. My foot caught a loose root and I lost my balance. The next thing I knew, I was lying beside Caroline with my whole body burning.

I tried to push myself up but a sharp pain in my right arm prevented me from doing so. I let out a sharp breath and used my left arm this time. I managed to get myself up. With my left ankle throbbing, I walked over to Caroline.

"Car, are you okay?" My voice came out as a whisper as I kneeled down beside her.

"Elena? Elena, I hurt everywhere. I can't move." Her voice was shaky. She was crying.

My lantern broke on the fall down the hill. It was hard to see but the moon did give me enough light to see she was hurt bad, really bad. "What happened?" Her injuries were definitely not from a fall down the hill. I could see the footprints of the people who attacked her. The people who attacked a ten-year old girl.

"I had it this time, I know I did. But they stopped me. They said I didn't belong here, they said I needed to go back to where I belong." She coughed, blood flying from her mouth.

"Who? Who're they?"

"I . . . I don't know. They covered their faces. They came so fast."

"You're going to be okay. Tyler is coming, and he will bring help." That was a lie. I had no idea if he heard me, or if she would make it long enough for him to realise I was trapped here.

"I'm tired. I think . . . I . . . might . . ." Her eyes closed.

"Car, Car! Come on. You have to stay awake." I slapped her cheek lightly. "Come on. You'll be okay if you just wake up," I whispered. I felt tears rolling down my cheeks. "Come on, Caroline, just wake up."

"No, she won't."

I jumped up and turned around, ignoring the pain in my ankle. "Who are you?"

"Peter. Peter Pan." A boy with brown hair and green eyes stepped into the moonlight.

"Peter Pan isn't real. He's just a story."

"Oh, but I am real. And your sister won't make it if you don't let me take her. I can promise you that I will keep her safe. I can give her a long happy life away from the people that did this to her. If she stays here, she will die."

"You can't be real. Magic isn't real."

"We don't have time for this. Do you want her to live or not?"

My tears flow faster as I choked out words, "Promise me she will be okay."

"I promise you. She will be just fine. I have to take her now though." The boy stepped closer.

I wanted to believe him, but every inch of me was telling me I was a fool. I took a deep breath, ignoring every screaming thought in my head. I kneeled back beside my sister. "Everything is going to be okay. Caroline, I love you. Safe travels." I leaned down and kissed her forehead, tears landing on her face. "Okay, take her."

"Good luck, Elena."

"How—" Everything went black.

***

"Elena! Elena!"

I could hear Tyler's voice, but I had no idea where it was coming from. Everything was black. My memory was fuzzy. I found Caroline, but something happened. Someone took her. Who was it? Why did they take her?

"Elena, come on. Wake up! I can't lose you! Please wake up."

Tyler? I tried to speak, but my throat burned. I tried to open my eyes, but my eyelids were so heavy. "Ty," I managed to whisper.

"Oh, thank god! Elena, are you okay?"

"I . . ."

"Don't talk. It's okay I'll get you home." I felt his arms slide under my knees and my back. "Come on. Let's get you home."

August 14, 1508

It's been two years since we lost Caroline. It's been really hard. Mother has been a mess the whole time. She never leaves the house, she doesn't eat much, and she doesn't get out of bed really. I can't remember the last time I saw her smile or laugh or do anything other than cry. Father tried for a while, but he gave up and left, left the four of us to help her.

I think she feels guilty because she never wanted Caroline. She only wanted four kids. After my little brother was born, she planned to stop. Caroline was an unplanned, unwanted accident, and Mother can't live with the fact that she treated her differently from the rest of us, and now she's gone.

It's not mother's fault she ran off. That's just the way that Caroline was. We all know that, she just can't accept it. Now the rest of us have to deal with it.

I take a lot of walks through the woods. Sometimes, if I'm really quiet, I can still hear the sound of her laugh, the sound of her feet hitting the path as she runs, and the sound of her panting as she drops to the ground. But when I open my eyes, I know it's not real. It's my imagination trying to remember her, trying to hold onto her like I should have that night.

I don't remember much. I think I saw a boy. He said something about taking her somewhere, and I let him. I don't know why. I don't remember what he looked like, I don't remember what he said his name was, but I think he said my name. It hurts to remember. I don't want to remember, but sometimes, I dream about it. When I wake up, I'm sweating, crying, and screaming. Delilah always comes in to calm me down, but I'm not sure how much longer she's going to do that. She's almost twenty now. She should be living with Robert, her husband, not taking care of Jonathan, Angelo, and me although Angelo may be leaving soon as well.

Soon the house will be emptying out. Maybe this place really is cursed. Maybe the spirit of the mother still lingers, maybe she is the reason Caroline ran out, and maybe she wants all mothers to suffer like she did. I just want to leave. I want to run away and never look back. I want someone to save me and take me somewhere better than here. Somewhere I can be free. Somewhere I can be someone better than myself.

"Tyler, what are we doing here? I'm tired. It's late, and it's dark. I have to go check on Mother."

"Trust me, please." He smiled, leading me farther away from town. I sighed and let him pull me away. "So I . . . sorry. I'm a little nervous. I-I'm . . . Okay, wow! I'm a blubbering idiot apparently. Hold on. Just give me a minute."

"Tyler, what are you doing?" I sighed stopping this time. "I'm not in the mood for any of your games."

"I'm not playing any games. Come on." He pulled me farther. "We're almost there."

"Almost where? Come on! We're been walking for twenty minutes. Where are you taking me?"

"Here." We stopped on the edge of a dock. I smiled. "You remember?" His smile brightened when he looked over at me.

"Of course. This is where we met."

I was two. I don't even know how I remember, but I do. My parents had brought me here to learn how to swim. I had been terrified, and I was not happy to be standing on this dock.

Apparently, my parents weren't the only ones with this idea, or they planned to meet at the dock, because Tyler's parents were with him at the same time.

"I can't believe you remember that." His smile widened.

"How could I not? You're the only reason I got in the water. I was scared!" I giggled.

"You didn't look it."

"I had to put on a brave face! You were laughing at me!" I laughed. "So what is it that we're doing here?"

"I've had the biggest crush on you since I was six years old. It took me double those years to work up the nerve to ask you to be with me. And now it's taken triple those years to ask for your hand." He dropped down to one knee. "Elena, I love you so much. I can't imagine my life without you. Will you please do me the honour of being my wife, of dealing with me for the rest of our lives?"

I felt tears rolling down my checks. "Of course. I will! I love you too!"

He stood up and threw his arms around me. "Oh thank god! I couldn't handle a no. Here, I made this for you." He pulled away and handed me a small golden ring.

I laughed through my tears and took it from him. "I can't believe you were worried."

"I hate to break this moment, love—Oh, wait. No, I don't."

Tyler and I looked over to see a dock full of pirates. He stepped in front of me. "What do you want?"

"You see that, lads? 'e's tryin' to pertect 'er. Kill 'em," the pirate in front said, rubbing his hook for a hand like he was cleaning it.

"Run. Go get help. I'm not going to let them hurt you."

"Tyler, you can't do this on your own."

"Elena, run!" he yelled, pushing me away.

I did as he said. I shouldn't, I knew I shouldn't run. He had nothing to protect himself with. He wasn't going to make it out alive. But I ran anyways. I ran and I ran and I ran until I reached the town. "Pirates! Pirates!" I dropped to my knees screaming. "There are pirates at the docks!"

The men, all of them, grabbed their tools and ran. They ran back in the direction. I should have stayed. He won't make it. I felt the tears rolling down my checks, burning a hole in my soul. He was my everything. How would I live without him? I opened my hand and stare at the ring. I didn't even get a chance to wear it.

"Are you okay?" I looked up to see a boy with brown hair and green eyes looking down at me. He looked familiar. From where?

"No, I just lost everything. They'll never make it in time."

"Can I help you?" the boy asks, sitting in front of me.

"Can you take me away? Can you help me be free?" I tried to hold back my tears.

The boy smiled. "I know just the place."

***

"What is this place?" The boy brought me to an island in the middle of the North Sea. There was no one on it, well, as far as I could tell. All I could see was sand and trees.

"Home." He smiled, admiring the beauty in front of him.

"Who are you?"

"Pan."

"Peter Pan? Is this Neverland?" I exclaimed. I mean I'd heard stories about him, but I never believed them.

"I prefer Pan."

"Pan it is then."

"Take my hand. I'm going to introduce you to Zylan and Clover."

I did. The next thing I knew, I was standing in the middle of a circle of trees. There were two girls, one with long brown hair and the other with short blonde hair, sitting on the forest floor.

They looked over. "August 14. You were right," the blonde haired one said.

"Ha! Told you!" They stood up. "I'm Zylan, this is Clover. We will be your hostesses for the rest of your now immortal life." The brown-haired girl, Zylan, said with a smile.

They were dressed like boys. Why were they dressed like boys? They both wore baggie black pants and a tight white strapped shirt.

"Why is she staring?" Clover whispered.

"Remember how I was wearing boy clothes when we met? Remember your reaction?" Zylan whispered back. "I think she's taken off guard."

Clover looked down. "Oh no! We forgot to change!" She waved her hands quickly, and they matched me. We all wore a light pink dress that drags along the floor.

"Why were you dressed like boys? Why are you now dressed like I am?"

"Trust me. Once you've lived here long enough, you'll realise how impractical dresses really are." Zylan smiled and waved her hands. Now she was back in her pervious outfit. "Much better."

"Can you teach me how to do that?"

"We can, but for now"—this time the hand waving landed me in their outfit—"you're going to want to wear this."

I couldn't even get a protest out. She was right. That was much more comfortable than a dress and corset. "This is great! So now we can start?"

"I like her."

"You'll do great here."

"I'll leave you girls to it," Pan said. I forgot he was here, and by the look on their faces, Clover and Zylan forgot too.

1698

It was August 14 again. It was time for another boy to come. There were twelve boys at the moment. For the most part, they were pretty cute, and for the most part, pretty good. Ace and

Justin didn't really pay attention to us, so two of the hottest were off the table. Plus, Noah and Adam were very obviously not into girls, even though they tried. It wasn't a good experience. I was looking for someone who was into girls and looking for a good-times-no-feelings kind of thing. I hoped this guy would help me forget. None of the other ones could.

Clover, Zylan, and I were doing our annual stakeout of Pan's camp. Even though there were twelve of us now, it was still our thing. We always snuck out just before nine, giving us plenty of time to find the camp and get settled in. I don't know why we bothered hiding. Pan always knew we were there, and he always told us to come down and meet the boy. I guess it was all part of the tradition.

This time it was freezing though. It was never really cold here. Sometimes, it was chilly, but today it was freezing. We all, even the guys, had bulky coats and warm pants on. I just hoped we never had to wear them again.

We were set up in our normal vantage points: Zylan, centre; Clover, right; me, left. Pan should be showing up any second now with the new boy, all confused and dazed from transporting across the island. It was always funny watching them catch their ground. The first time was always the worst. It almost made it worth the cold.

"Everyone say hello to Hunter." Pan didn't pop in. He walked in. He walked in with a boy with black hair and hazel eyes. A boy whose face I could never forget, would never forget. I grabbed the chain around my neck. It couldn't be.

"Tyler?" I appeared in front of him. "But . . ."

His eyes widened. "Elena . . . I knew it was you. I knew I would see you again."

Zylan and Clover appeared beside me. "Elena? Are you okay?"

I ignored them. "This can't be real. You can't be real."

"I am. I really am real." His eyes welled up with tears. He wrapped his arms around me. "I thought my brain was tricking me. I never thought I would get to hold you again."

"Neither did I. I'm so sorry I left you at the docks. I'm so sorry for everything."

"You two know each other? How?"

"Zylan, Clover, this is my boyfriend, Tyler," I said, pulling away.

"Fiancé actually, and I prefer Hunter," he corrected. I wondered why he changed it. I wondered how he survived. "I'm so happy I have you back." He kissed my forehead. "I'm never losing you again."

***

"Wait, let me get this straight. He was your boyfriend of six years, he proposed to you the night you were attacked by pirates, and you thought he was dead. Now he's here on the island 190 years later?"

I just finished explaining my relationship with Ty—Hunter. "It's unbelievable. Trust me, I know. I don't understand how it happened either. I thought I lost him. I thought I was never going to see him again. That's the only reason I left with Pan. I can't believe this."

"At least you can ask him what happened! I would give anything to know what happened . . ." Clover trailed off and dropped her head.

"So would I. You should go talk to him." Zylan smiled. "We'll meet you back at camp."

I smiled back. "Thank you. And please don't tell anyone. It's not fair that I'm the only one who got a loved one back. Just, please, keep this between us."

"Worry not. Your secret is safe with us." Clover lifted her head, smiling again. I wondered what happened to her, what answers she wished she had. I hoped she found them one day.

I hoped everyone here found the answers they were looking for. All of us had so much unfinished business.

1700

"Hunter? Hunter?" I called out. It was still so weird, calling him that. I thought after two years I might get used to it, but I really couldn't.

We were supposed to meet an hour ago. He had been late a few times, but not this late. What could he possibly be doing? I wandered around the paths around our meeting place for a while, but I gave up. I should head back to camp. Maybe I had the wrong day.

Camp wasn't that far from our meeting spot, so I decided to walk instead of popping back in. It would give me time to think, much needed time to think. We were apart for so long, it was almost like starting a new relationship. Maybe it wasn't working out. Maybe I should just call it quits before I fell too hard again.

I pushed my way through a patch of branches to find Lydia straddling Hunter's lap. He was running his hand through her hair, and she was gigging.

"Hunter?" I could feel my heart pounding.

"Elena? What are—" Lydia cut off when Hunter threw her of his lap and stood up. Her eyes went wide like she just realized what was going on. "Oh my god, Elena. I'm so sorry I had—"

I raised my hand, cutting her off. "Please leave."

She swallowed, stood up, and ran off.

"Elena—"

"You lying bastard. I don't want to hear anything you have to say." I felt tears coming to my eyes, but I pushed them back. "I hope you have a good life, and I hope she makes you happy. I hope they all make you happy, if that's what you think you need. I never want to see you again, but that's not going to happen, so I'll settle for you never speaking to me again." I kept my voice calm as I ripped the chain I'd been holding on to for 192 years off my neck. "I didn't want to let this go. I didn't want to let Tyler go. He didn't leave my mind once, but I guess he forgot about me." I dropped the chain holding the ring he gave me on the docks. "I was hoping you would be him, but you're not Tyler, and I'm tired of pretending like you are. Goodbye, Hunter." I turned around and walked away. He didn't even try to stop me. I broke into a run.

I thought I could hear him talking to me, but there was no way it was possible, especially the words that I thought I was hearing.

"Elena, I'm so sorry. I should have been there for you. I should have tried harder to find you. I should have known you were alive. I should have looked for you." There was a long pause. "I was never good enough for you." Another pause. "I won't let this go. One day, I will win you back. And on the day, you will have this ring, and I will have my happiness back. I will never let you go again."

I wished the words were true, but I knew I must have made them up in my head.

Chapter 9

Spatula

Zylan

Father returns home today. I can't wait to see him. With everything that's been happening with Mother, I need him home. I need him to take my side, he always takes my side. So I sit on the rafters in the kitchen and wait for him to walk through the door, so I can hug him.

When I'm trying to avoid Mother, I find places she'll never think to look. One day while I was looking for something to eat, I heard her coming down the hall, so I needed to find a place to hide. I jumped onto the countertop and pulled myself onto the wooden rafters that hold up our house. Mother passed underneath me and walked right out the door. Now whenever I wait for Father to come home but don't want to get into a screaming match with my mother, I sit up here.

Any second now, my father will push open that door, and everything will go back to normal. Mother won't be mad, I won't be sad, and Father will understand.

The sun is starting to set when the door handle starts to turn. I jump off the rafter onto the counter, ignoring the sharp pain that shoots through my ankle. Then I hop off the counter and run to the door. When it swings open, Father is standing in the doorframe, holding a bag in his left hand and another in his right slung over his shoulder.

He smiles when he sees me. "Zylan," he says, dropping his bags.

"Father," I say, smiling back before running up to him and giving him a hug.

"How have you been?"

"The fighting has been getting worse, but I can handle it. I am so glad you are home."

"So am I. So am I."

He pulls away and says he is going to talk with Mother. I nod and watch as he disappears around the corner. I hadn't noticed before, but he's limping. It was not too noticeable, just enough to show he's in pain. He normally stood tall and proud, like he's royalty, but he's hunched over with his head down. Although he's forty-two, normally, he could pass for at least thirty. But right now, he looks ten years older than he is. Something happened while he was sailing, something bad.

Every other time he had come home from a trip, he was happy. He loves sailing, but he loves being home so much more. But the way he looked when he walked through the door made it seem like he doesn't love either anymore.

I think about trying to get him to talk about it. I always talk to him about my problems, so it's his turn to talk to me. I figure I'll just wait for him to be done with Mother, and then I'll talk to him. So I go to my room and wait, but he didn't come out that night, and when I woke up in the morning, he was gone.

***

This time when Father came home, he went straight to bed. Mother is screaming at me some more about how a lady is supposed to behave. I'm so sick of hearing about the way

I'm supposed to act. She doesn't listen to me. She never listens to me. It makes me so mad. "A lady should dress properly! A lady should be home before dark! A lady should HAVE RESPECT FOR MEN!"

"WELL, THEN CLEARLY I'M NOT A LADY! I'M SO SICK OF YOU TELLING ME EVERYTHING I DO WRONG! I'M DONE!" I don't know where that came from, but I'm not sorry I said it.

I start to walk away when a chair hits the wall beside my head. "DON'T YOU DARE WALK AWAY FROM ME!"

I stop and whirl around. "Or what?" I ask, stepping forward. "You'll beat me? You'll drown me? No, it has to be something different than the way my siblings died. Maybe you'll find a pirate and steal his gun. How's that sound, Mother? You going to shoot me?"

She goes to open her mouth when there's a bang at the door. I sense rage flowing off of him like a wave of air. I know she feels it too, that's why she's looking at me the way she is. She knows that something bad is going to happen as soon as she opens the door, and she's sorry about the way she's been treating me.

"Momma, don't open it," I whisper.

"Go get your father up."

"Momma . . ."

"I know, sweetheart. I love you too. I'm so sorry for everything. Now go."

I run down the hall to get Father. When we come back, the door is wide open, and Mother is gone. Father orders me to go to his room and lock the door behind me. I don't listen to him. At first I poke my head out their bedroom door in hope of seeing something. Then I hear someone coming, so I lock the door and run under the bed. Shortly after that, Mother comes running in. She gets shot, and I cry into her shoulder.

"I'm so sorry, Momma." I whisper as tears start pouring out of my eyes. "I love you, Momma. Please don't be gone."

That's when I sense him. *Sure enough, when I look up, I see
the boy from my dream, the boy watching me.*

*"Is my father okay?" I ask. I feel the tears building up in
my eyes, but I try to hold them in.*

*The boy kneels down and looks me in the eyes. "I'm so
sorry, but I don't know. I promised him that I would keep you
safe, so we need to leave now." He holds out his hand to help
me up, but I kiss my mother's forehead and slide her off my
lap before I take it. "I'm Jacob, by the way. Jacob Pan."*

"Zylan," is all I can make myself say.

*Once we're out of the house, he picks me up and carries
me. I feel safe. I always knew he would be there when I needed
him, and here he is. I end up falling asleep in his arms as he
takes me to wherever we're going. When we get there, I don't
want to let go. I hold on as tight as I can before I hear the
arguing. The two voices are so similar. I can't tell who's who.*

"Who's this? Where's Jaden?"

*"This is Zylan. On my way to get Jaden, I saw her family
being attacked by pirates, and if I hadn't grabbed her, she
would have been dead."*

*"She's not a child, Jacob. She can take care of herself.
What about Jaden? Who's going to protect him? What if he
dies tonight because you got her instead? You should have just
done what you were told."*

*"So what? Just because Zylan's seventeen instead of seven,
she didn't need my help? You weren't there. You didn't see it. I
did, and I'm not going to apologize for saving her."*

*"Fine. You want to help her? Do it from The Island, not
from here."*

***

My eyes flutter open. I can't believe this is still happening.
It's been a week and my dreams won't stop. They keep getting
more and more outrageous.

Hiding from Mother? I would never do that. We were so close. I told her everything. She would never yell at me the way she did in those dreams, no matter what I did. Plus, I would never say those nasty things to her. She was my mother, and I loved her.

Pan rescuing me? Ha! He killed them and kidnaped me. I hate these dreams. I hope he never comes back and these dreams stop.

I'm so caught up in my annoyance that I don't notice Ace isn't in bed. I blink a couple times and reach over his side of the bed for my glasses. They're not there.

"Ace?"

"Looking for these?" His blurry figure walks toward the bed from the dresser. I can see his left hand has something in it, so I just assume it's my glasses.

"If that's what I think it is, then yes." He hands them to me. "There you are." I smile and laugh a little once they're on my face.

"You looked so peaceful. I didn't want to wake you." He sits down next to me.

"Thanks, but next time, get me up." I kiss his cheek before hopping out of bed and walking over to the dresser.

I moved in here a week ago, right when the stupid dreams started. But I have to say, I really missed having a real bed and pillows and kitchen and everything I didn't have while living in the woods. Ace did such a good job making this tree house. It makes me happy.

He made it two stories, and the only way in is through the tree. He hollowed it out, making a small door at the foot of the tree with a staircase leading to the hatch in the centre of the living room. In the living room, there are two long benches facing each other, and a smaller one just in front of the doorway to the kitchen. All the benches have soft cushions and three small pillows leaning on the back. The room is about thirty meters wide, fifteen meters long, and three meters tall. The left and right walls have two square windows, two by two, in exactly the same place.

The kitchen has the same dimensions. The east wall has four tall cabinets with nothing in them yet, and the south wall has a gas stove in between a break in wooden counter top. The west wall has a continuation of the counter and three small cabinets hanging off the wall. In the middle of the ceiling, there is a string hanging down, so we can pull the latter to our bedroom down.

Our room is thirty by thirty by three meters. A bed is on the south side with a night stand on the left and right sides of it. On the night stand is a book and an oil lamp. A dresser is pushed onto the west wall, and the window is on the east wall. The window is set up exactly like the one from my house back home. The wall is pushed out slightly, and a bench is underneath of a window, so I can sit and watch the sun rise and set like I used to.

I change into a blue shirt and a black skirt. I pull my hair out of my face, leaving one strand down, so I can tie the rest up. As soon as I'm done, I make my way down the latter to find Ace in front of the stove.

"Something smells really good," I observe, walking over. It smells like a bakery, when it has just finished baking bread mixed with a hint of sweetness. "What's cooking?"

"Pancakes!" he exclaims with a wide smile.

When I walk over, I see a pan over a small fire with dough bubbling on it. Next to the stove is a jar of syrup that looks to have been freshly collected. "Ah, so that's where you disappeared to this morning. Syrup collecting."

"Only the best syrup on the island!"

"Why are you so excited this morning?" I laugh slightly.

"Because I'm with you." He smiles, wrapping his left arm around my waist and kissing the top of my head.

I smile, not able to do anything else. He's honestly the sweetest guy on the planet, and he makes me so happy whenever we're together. I don't know what I would do without him.

"What can I do to help?"

"Absolutely nothing." He kisses the top of my head again. "Just go sit in the living room and relax. I should be done in a couple of minutes."

I shrug and start to walk in that direction when a small rock flies through the window and lands just beside the latter. Ace and I look at each other before slowly walking over to the window. Clover and Justin are standing outside, holding a handful of pebbles each.

"What do you want?" Ace asks.

"To come up. Is that alright with you?" Justin yells back.

"There's a door you know?" I state sarcastically.

"We wanted to make sure we weren't interrupting anything, you know . . ." Clover smirks, trailing off.

I roll my eyes. "Whatever. Just come up."

"Elena and Tyler are right behind us too," Justin says as I make my way to the living room.

"Leave the hatch open then. Ace is making pancakes. Have you eaten yet?" I ask, pulling the hatch open.

"I have not. I'm so glad too. Ace makes the best pancakes," Tyler says, popping his head through the hatch as soon as I open it, giving me a heart attack in the process.

"I thought you were behind them," I hiss, holding my heart.

"When have I ever passed up an opportunity to scare the shit out of you?" He smiles and gives me a quick hug before running into the kitchen.

"Remember that when I get my revenge!" I call after him.

He looks at me and fakes a shiver. I roll my eyes and whip a couch pillow at him. He ducks at the last second, so it hits Ace in the back of his head. Tyler snuffs a laugh as Ace turns around to glare at us.

"Enough, children."

"I am ten years older than you. Tyler is the child here."

I turn my attention back to the hatch to help Elena up. "Sounds like we missed all the fun." Elena pouts. "Why do I always miss out on all the fun?"

I help Clover up. "Because you suck the fun out of everything," she whispers as she passes Elena and heads to the kitchen as well.

Elena takes a page out of my book and tries to whip the pillow at Clover. Another failed pillow throw, which hits Ace in the back of the head. This time, Tyler bursts out laughing when Ace turns around to glare at us, apron around his waist and spatula in hand.

"If one more pillow hits me in the back, I swear to god, I'll—"

"Spank us with the spatula?" Justin suggests, poking his head through the hatch.

I choke on a laugh while Tyler hits the ground clutching his stomach. Clover leans on the counter for support, Elena uses the couch, and Ace's glare at us deepens before he joins us laughing.

"Actually, no. I'm going to make you eat it." He turns back around to focus on the pancakes.

I help Justin up. "Someone's feisty this morning," he whispers as he crouches down to close the hatch.

"'Cause you crashed my perfect morning with my perfect fiancé and I got two pillows whipped at my head in the span of a minute. Now if you'll shut up, I'm going to finish making you all breakfast."

"Okay," Justin mouths as he takes a seat on the couch.

I chuckle and plop down on the couch across from him. Elena and Tyler join me, and Clover joins Justin.

"Right, guys. Pick the couch with all three of its pillows to sit on." I laugh.

"Well, you could always throw them over here." Clover grins.

"You are absolutely correct." I grin back.

There are seven pillows left, more than enough for the five of us to throw a pillow each. Clover and I stand up and grab the pillow behind us. Justin looks at us with warning in his eyes. I shrug and mouths, "Come on."

Tyler and Elena grab a pillow each as well. Justin finally rolls his eyes and stands up. He grabs his pillow from the smaller couch. I use the fingers on my left hand to count to three. Once I get to three, all of throw our pillows at Ace.

He takes a deep breath then turns around slowly, holding five spatulas. "Alright. Who wants to go first?"

Clover, Elena, Tyler, and I have the same idea. We each grab Justin by a limb and throw him onto the kitchen floor. When he stands up, he brushes himself off and looks at Ace. "Give me two of those."

Ace drops one and hands Justin two. "One," Ace starts.

"Two," Justin continues.

"Three," they finish together as they lunge forward.

"Shit! Run!" I yell, and we scatter.

I dive for a hatch on the floor. I'm so glad I didn't put the rug back on top, making it easy for me to get it open. I take a look behind me to find Ace and Tyler squaring off. Both ready to jump forward if the other moves. Elena and Clover are dodging Justin. No one will notice if I climb down the hatch and disappear, so that's what I do.

Once I'm sure I'm out of sight, I stop running and catch my breath. I'm not much of a runner. I never have been. Normally, I would just pop myself into a new location, but it's kind of unfair, considering the only one who can do magic properly is Ty. They can only find me if they know exactly where I am, which they never do, so they'll pop up all over The Island looking for me.

I stay away from my usual spots, hoping they won't think to look in Pan's tree house for me. I want to find out where he went and why he decided to go now. A whole damn week he's gone, and he doesn't tell a damn person where the fuck he's going, not even his best friend.

When I finally make it up the ladder of his tree house and reach for the front door, a shock vibrates through my whole body, knocking me off my feet. "Damnit, Pan. Even when you're not here, you manage to be a bastard." I stand up and brush myself off. I stand half a meter from the door and put my hand as close to the door as I can without feeling a shock.

Normally, with magic, it's about believing you can do something so much that you can actually do it, but Pan's magic is different. He uses objects to bind his magic. I have to find what he used in order to reverse his paranoia.

I close my eyes, putting both hands on the invisible barrier and take a deep breath. I focus on tracking the source of the spell to its origin. I see Pan grab the paper I dropped before walking over to him. He goes to set it on his desk when another sheet of paper drops to the floor. It must have been attached. How did I not notice?

Pan reads through it before crumpling it up, setting it on fire, and throwing it out the window. He paces around the room for a while before he takes a deep breath. He walks over to his nightstand and pulls out a silver chain. That chain was mine. Father gave it to me on my twelfth birthday, and I never took it off. I thought I lost it that night, but he's had it the whole time. I feel my blood boiling in anger, but I try to block it out.

He holds my necklace in his hands and closes his eyes. He opens his eyes and drops the chain on top of the nightstand. Then he starts packing. That bastard stole my necklace and used it to keep me out of his stupid tree house.

"Ze?" Tyler's voice snaps me back to reality.

"What?" I ask, shaking my head.

"Ace almost got me, so I disappeared to find you. I never would have guessed you'd be here."

"Yeah. I was trying to see if he left any clue of where he was going, but he locked down his place. I was just about to break in. Want to be my partner in crime?"

"Any other time I'd say yes." He laughs. "But Pan will kill me if he finds out I was in there without permission, especially if I was in there with you. Come on. We should go. I'd rather Ace didn't kill me for being alone with you."

I laugh. "He's all talk. He's not much of a fighter. The only reason he would actually kill you is if you made a move on me, which we both know you'd never do."

He smiles. "Well, apparently, no one else knows. Willow still refuses to see me because she thinks I'm in love with you." He rolls his eyes.

"That would be ridiculous." I laugh. I hope it sounded genuine. "So you lied to me? Last I heard the two of you were on the go."

"We were for about a week. She saw the two of us talking a while back and jumped to conclusions."

I roll my eyes. "Well, ever since El and Hunt, all the girls were super paranoid. I guess Willow still is. But you're right. We should get back to save Clover and Elena. They can't be doing so good right now."

He nods. "Ready?" He holds out his hand.

"Ready." I take it.

When we're standing in my living room, I see Clover duck away from Justin, leaving her foot in place, so he falls. I let go of Tyler's hand and laugh. Clover runs over and hides behind me as Justin gets to his feet. "Take her instead!" she yells, pushing me forward.

I snort. "Fat chance." I stop Justin in his tracks as he moves toward me. Tyler does the same as Ace moves his attention away from Elena and toward him.

"I'm a lover not a fighter. Can we stop this now?" Ty asks.

"Let me out and we'll see," Ace says.

"Nope. You have to promise to stop, or you can stay there all day."

"Fine. I promise," Justin says.

I let him out of my hold and turn to Ace. "Please stop."

"Fine, fine. But no more throwing pillows at me." Tyler lets him out but moves back when he takes a step toward him.

"Okay. Everyone out," I say, waving to the hatch on the floor.

"What? We didn't get any pancakes!" Justin exclaims, pouting.

Clover smacks him on the shoulder. "You weren't supposed to get any pancakes. Come on. We're leaving." She shoves Elena toward the hatch which Tyler is opening.

"Fine." Justin follows, protesting silently. "But you owe me pancakes."

"Okay Justin, whatever you say." Ace rolls his eyes.

The four of them make their way out through the hatch. Once they're gone, I lock it behind them and turn back to Ace. He smiles as I walk over to him.

"Finally, some alone time," he says, wrapping his arms around me.

"Well, maybe if you woke me up to go syrup hunting, we would have had more alone time." I smile up at him.

"You're right, as per usual, but I wanted to let you sleep. You looked so peaceful and cute." He smiles back as he lets go. "Now come on. I took the last of the pancakes off before our pillow versus spatula fight."

I take his hand, and we walk to the kitchen. I jump up onto the counter beside the stove and wait as Ace moves the pancakes from the pan onto the plate and drowns them in syrup. He hands me the plate with a smile. "You know me so well." I giggle.

"That's because I love you."

"I love you too." I smile and put my plate beside me on the counter, grabbing his hand before he has the chance to move away. I wrap my leg around his hips and pull him against me.

"We have pancakes to eat. They're probably already cold," Ace says, even though I know full well that he doesn't give a damn about those pancakes right now.

I grab his shirt with one hand, pulling him toward me and use the other hand to play with his hair because I know he loves it. Once he's close enough that I can kiss him, I do, moving the hand from his shirt to his hair as well. When I'm satisfied that he doesn't remember that he made pancakes, I pull just out of his reach. "Still hungry?"

"No." He grabs my waist and yanks me against him, crashing his lips into mine. He wasn't always like this. Sometimes I had to work him up a bit before he would attack me with kisses like this one.

He wraps his arms around my lower back and lifts me off the counter. "Up . . . stairs?" I ask between kisses.

"Not . . . a . . . chance."

He carries me over to the living room and drops me onto the couch, not breaking the kiss for a second. He positions himself on top of me. My legs still wrapped around him, and my hands still tangled in his hair.

He pulls away from my lips, leaving kisses all along my jawbone, down my neck, and along my collarbone, and moving to the other side. I keep my fingers tangled in his hair as I let little hums escape my lips.

Ace keeps kissing along my neck until he finds my favourite spot, causing a moan to escape me this time. I feel him smirk into my neck before he begins to nibble at it and drive me crazy. I shift my weight and use my hips to flip him over onto the ground. I land with my knees on each side of his hips and my hands beside his head.

"Ouch," he says with a chuckle.

"It's your own fault. You damn well know what that does to me." I smile.

"I do." He smirks again.

"Oh, you keep that smirk plastered on your face because it's my turn now." My smile deepens as he closes his eyes.

"Oh, I will."

"Okay," I say, jumping up and skipping up away from him.

He appears in front of me and grabs my hands. "Oh no. Not this time. We have nowhere to be, and no one to bother us." He wraps his arms around my waist. "You are all mine today. No more interruptions." He leans down and kisses me gently this time.

"I wasn't going to stop. It's just, in the living room, anyone can pop in, but I've charmed our bedroom to be apparition proof. Shall we?"

"Yes, please." He releases me from his death grip and follows me upstairs.

"Now"—I jump into his arms—"are you ready?"

He slams me up against the nearest wall and starts back at my neck. He pauses at my ear. "Darling, I'm always ready for you," he whispers, causing shivers up my spine.

"Then by all means, go right ahead."

Pan

1478

I was standing on the cliff, trying to figure out what to do. She hated me. She wouldn't come near me, and I didn't know why. What could I have possibly done to her? How could she hate me this much? I showed her this spot, I kept her from jumping off this cliff, and I saved her from those pirates. What did I do wrong? Every time it looked like we were making progress, it got worse. Nothing ever worked.

Don't think about it. One day she'll realize everything you did for her. She will come around with time.

So I tried not to think about it. The sun was high in the sky. Judging by my shadow, it was about midday. I saw the ship that had been sail around The Island since we got here. I didn't know why, and I didn't really want to ask. I thought it could be the same ship that attacked Zylan, but how could I know for sure?

It looked different this time. I think it was sailing away. Why now? Why not any other time? Today was the tenth year. It couldn't be a coincidence.

Follow them. You want to get your mind of Zylan. Find out what they're doing.

But do I really trust Zylan alone?

You're thinking about her. Stop that.

Maybe I could check on her village. See how everything is going.

That's thinking about her!

Shut up! I'm not listening anymore.

You just told yourself to shut up.

Okay, we're done now. I'm leaving. I'm going to check on her old friends. See if everything is okay.

***

I saw Zylan's friend, Aurora, standing on the docks, talking to a boy. She was trying to hold it together as she spoke.

"The last captain to hold that chest was my best friend's father. They weren't supposed to come back. He was supposed to take it right to Turkey. No one knows why he came back, but if they hadn't, we wouldn't have been attacked, and my best friend would still be alive.

"They ransacked the village, looking for anyone on the crew. They killed them all and their families. They burned her house to the ground, and no one was ever found."

"I am very sorry for your loss, miss," the boy said.

Aurora couldn't hold it in anymore. She cried harder. Her voice was so muffled, I could barely hear her. "It's my fault! It's all my fault. I should have just let her be. I shouldn't have been so mad about the boy! I lost my best friend because I was too stupid to just let her be." The boy looked confused, so she tried to collect herself before continuing. "There was this boy. I used to see him hanging around her all the time. Whenever I pointed him out, she would always just smile and say, 'I know,' which was weird because she's basically blind. She would always say, 'I can sense him. Don't worry. I'll be fine.' I got so tired of hearing it. I stopped wanting to spend time with her. I cancelled on her the night of the attack. She shouldn't have been at home. She should have been with us. On her birthday too." Aurora sniffled.

"I saw the boy that night. He was looking for her. I'm guessing, but he heard us instead. I was making fun of her, and he came up to us. He said magic was real. I thought he was just as crazy as her, but he showed me. He showed the three of us. I hope he got to her. I hope he rescued her like she always believed he would."

Aurora stopped. Her eyes went wide, and she slapped her hand over her mouth. She probably just realized how crazy that sounded. The boy tried to get her to say more. He believed her. I could see it in his eyes, but she ran off.

I wished I could help her. But I looked exactly the same as I did ten years ago. All I would do was drove her mad. I'd ruined her enough.

The boy looked over at me. It was like he knew I was who she was talking about. He was looking at me like he had known me all his life. It looked like he was going to come talk to me, but instead, he boarded the ship, taking the cursed treasure.

***

I snuck on board of the *Mayfly*. If the village people were correct, and I believed they were, the pirates would attack this ship. If they wanted this treasure, they couldn't get it. It would be nothing but bad news if they did.

As it drew close to dark, I heard them yell, "Below deck." The pirates were here. I stayed hidden until the chaos. I slipped out of my hiding spot to find the boy from the docks. He was young, meaning the captain would keep him away from the fighting. He would probably be in the captain's quarters; I just have to find it. Wandering around wouldn't help. It was probably a good time for some magic.

I reappeared, finding the boy mentally cursing himself for not doing anything. "You're doing something. You're guarding the chest."

He jumped up, sword in hand. "You? How did you get in here?"

I arched an eyebrow. "Have you ever heard of a thing called magic, boy?"

"Yes. Do not call me boy. You are just a boy yourself."

I chuckled. "I'm older than I look, eighteen years older to be exact. Why are you in here? Why are you not fighting with the others?"

"Why should I tell you? You are one of them, a pirate."

"I can assure you that I'm not. I'm Pan. I followed this ship from the island I live on." A lie, but it would sound bad if I told him I was hiding out on his ship.

"Pan? As in Peter Pan? I thought that they were all just stories, saving dying kids and bring them to Neverland. You are real?"

My brother? Had what he was been doing been getting around? Should I correct him? No. If he believed I was Peter, maybe he'd trust me.

"Yes, but please call me Pan. I insist."

"I am Jason."

I opened my mouth to say something else, but a hook-handed pirate came into the room. I knew this pirate. He was the one I saw standing over Zylan's father. He must have replaced the hand Zylan's mother took with a hook. That was what I would call him.

I went back to Zylan's village that night, thinking about taking her home. Her father was gone and her mother was dead. She had nothing to go back to. When I was there, I ran into the pirates. I took their treasure and brought it back into town. I didn't think he would be very happy to see me . . .

"Well, Jason, it's nice to meet yee. Where be me treasure?" he asked, flashing a smile.

"It is not your treasure. It is a chest that was meant for Turkey."

"Me mistake. Where's te chest?"

"You are not getting it."

"Ah, so it be here." He grinned. "That's all I need know." The grin deepened.

Damnit, Jason! He mentally yells at himself so loud, I could hear it.

"Calm down. He's not getting the chest," I said, stepping into Hook's view.

"You again," he snarled.

"Hello, Hook. I see Zylan's mother really did a number to that hand of yours. If you wish to keep both, I suggest you may want to leave. I wouldn't want to be the one to take it from you." My smile mimicked his.

"I won't be leavin' without me treasure." He ground his teeth.

"Very well." I pulled out my sword. "Try to take it."

Hook drew his sword and we fought. He was good, especially for someone who probably hadn't practiced in ten years. Peter probably put them there to torture me and Zylan. If she saw the ship, she was going to lose it. She couldn't know that they were around.

"Ace! Where are you?" a random guy yelled, running into the room.

I tried to keep Hook's attention on me. If he wasn't paying attention to them, hopefully, he wouldn't find the treasure under the floor boards.

"Here!"

"Captain told us to abandon ship. We are to bring the chest onto a row boat and get back to shore."

That got Hook's attention. I managed a shot to his left shoulder, a really good shot, causing him to bleed. He didn't seem to notice at all. He ducked out of my reach and dug his hook into the guy's shoulder. The guy let out a cry of pain.

"Show me te chest or I kill 'em." Hook pointed his sword at Jason's throat.

"Okay! Okay!" the man exclaimed. "It is not here. Captain used this room as a diversion. It is one floor below."

"Let's go." Hook pulled his hook out of him and put his sword at his back.

As soon as they disappeared, I ran over. "Where is the actual chest? We need to get it to my island where it will be safe." I knew where it was; it was just a formality to ask.

He hesitated but only for a second. "It is under the desk. We have to hurry. David is not that good at lying. He'll be back up here any minute."

***

"This is Neverland?" Jason asked.

We each had a handle of the chest, standing on the beach—a small patch of sand surrounded by trees as far as we can see.

"You could say that."

"So what now?" he asked. "When can I go home? Can I even go home?"

"We have to bury this deep in the forest. As for home . . . you can stay here and never grow old, or you can return home. But because you have stepped foot on this island . . . you will not have much time." My head dropped as I finished, mostly out of guilt for lying. It was so lonely here. I just wanted someone who would actually talk to me.

"Let us get this buried."

I looked up and grinned. "Good choice! I know the perfect place."

1479

"You're so stupid! I haven't eaten in days! That's the first deer I've seen in a year! Why do you insist on ruining my hunt! And my life."

I had to pretend the words didn't hurt, so I laughed. I didn't know why. I just laughed.

"What do you want Pan?" she asked with a sigh.

"Zylan, I'd like you to meet Ace," I said, waving him out of the trees.

He made the connection. I could see it in his eyes. I couldn't let him tell her. She could never know.

"What kind of name is Ace? Who named you? A retard? Or your cripple friend?"

"I named myself. Pan said I could change my name and leave the past behind me," he said through his teeth.

"So the former then." She whirled to face me. "You didn't let me do that! Why did he get to do it?"

"You didn't give me the chance!"

"So what? That's not on the welcome sign? Oh, wait. There is no welcome sign because you kidnap people!"

"I tried to save you!"

"By bring me here? That's a shit job!"

"Fine!" With that, I disappeared. I just went into the trees. I still needed to talk to Ace.

"Look what you did now. He's not bad guy. What's wrong with you?"

"So much you can't even begin to understand!" And then it was her turn to disappear. I didn't understand why she wouldn't talk to me, why she wouldn't let me help her.

"Great. Why couldn't someone have taught me that when I got here. Now I have to find my way back to camp . . . again. A year and I still get lost. Great job, Jason. Great job." He sighed.

"Ace." I was leaning on a tree just in front of him.

"Jesus Christ, Pan! Why do you do that?" he exclaimed, holding his chest.

"I figured you wouldn't want to walk back to camp, but if I was wrong . . . " I paused, standing up straight.

"You weren't wrong!"

I grin. "I figured." The grin didn't last long. I had to get to the real reason I stuck around. "You recognized her name, didn't you?"

"I did."

I walked over and put my hand on his shoulder. "Promise me you'll pretend not to. Promise me you won't tell her anything about what happened on the ship, or that you were in Genoa. She can't know that the ship that attacked you was the same one that attacked her town. Promise me you won't say anything please."

"I promise."

***

I should probably check on Ace's family. He had been here awhile, and I could tell he missed home. If I could tell him that everything was okay, maybe he would feel better about leaving. I discovered this neat trick for finding out what was going on on earth while I was on Neverland. In the centre of the island, there was a lake. The water there was so pure, it allowed for a link between us and them. It was how I found out about Zylan's mother taking Hook's hand. Now I could use it to see Ace's family because Neverland and The Island are exact mirror images.

I sat in front of the pond, put the palm of my hand on the water, and thought of Ace's mom. He'd told me so much about her, I felt like I knew her. Nothing came up. That was strange. Maybe if I went back a little bit?

I went back a year and swallow. The reason there was nothing was because she was dead. She killed herself. I was watching her do it now.

After she got the news of Ace's disappearance, she lost it. Her two daughters went over to see how she was doing. She was delusional. She was screaming and crying. They were trying to help her, but they couldn't. They should have run, and I should have brought Ace home.

His mom ran at her daughters and killed them both. Once she snapped out of it and realized what she had done, she killed herself. None of that would have happened if I had let Ace go home. I ruined his family.

1488

It was exactly ten years from the last time. This time when they headed out, I considered not following them, but Zylan still wasn't happy. I thought maybe I'd run into a girl that she would get along with. If that happened, great. If not, maybe she and Ace would eventually get along, but I wasn't sure I liked the idea of that.

So I headed out as well. Now I was standing off to the side in a town's square. There were two girls sitting off to the other side. It looked like one was royalty and the other was her servant girl. The noble girl wasn't acting like a typically one. She was actually conversing with her servant and treating her like a human. In fact, the servant girl actually addressed her by her name, Charlotte.

"For the millionth time, Margret, call me Char or at least Charlotte. I thought we were passed this," she said.

That was *not* normal. I had a feeling she and Zylan would get along well. She was perfect; all I needed was a reason she would want to leave. The reason didn't take long to present itself. She was supposed to marry Prince James, but she was in love with a peasant.

If her father were to find out, he would disown her. That was what I needed. That was exactly what was going to happen. I planted a seed in her mind, *Tell your father you love Kaleb, and you can't marry the prince. It wouldn't be fair to either of them.* All I needed to do then was find the peasant.

***

It wasn't hard. I asked around at a few places, the third had someone named Kaleb that worked with them. He lived with a big family on the edge of town. I found it easily; their house was huge. If I didn't know any better, I would believe he was noble as well. There must be a lot of them to live in a place like this.

"Kaleb! Come play with us!" There were two young boys and three young girls playing in the front yard. Lucky me too. I didn't have to go hunting for him. He was going to come right out.

I heard no one respond but the five children nodded their heads and continued playing. Five minutes later, a giant wolf with brown fur came out the front door. The five kids all ran and jumped on him. My eyes went wide. What kind of children would jump on a wolf? It could hurt or even kill them.

Instead of doing anything, it just fell over and let them jump around on it. "Kaleb, you're supposed to fight us!" one girl whined.

The wolf jumped up and started snarling. The kids screamed and ran, hiding from it. *The wolf is Kaleb.* I'd heard about men that could turn into animals, but never did I imagine I would see one. *Does Charlotte know?*

He gave them a couple minutes to hide and then ran after them. It didn't take very long to round them up either. *I think this is a bad idea, I should go.*

***

I found Charlotte after dark in the middle of a field. I wanted to see how it went now that she was free to be with him. I was glad I left the house when I did. Kaleb probably would have been able to sniff me out and that wouldn't have been good. I was happy I could help her be free.

She was sitting on the grass with a bag and her journal. She was writing something in it when a voice made her look up. "Char?"

"Kaleb." She smiled, standing up. She left her journal on the bag next to her. "I have to tell you something."

He was standing on the far side of the trees, in the dark. "What is it, my Clover?" That was a weird nickname for someone.

"I told my father about you. I told him I can't marry James. I told him I love you."

"What did he say?"

That wasn't the reaction I was expecting. I didn't think she was expecting it either. *Oh no. Did I screw up? Could I have accidently planted the thought without realizing?*

"Kaleb, I'm free. We can run away together. We can be together."

"Stupid." His voice was almost like a snarl. There was no way this was the same guy who played with those children earlier today. I messed up. I should have stayed away.

"What?"

"Why would you ever think I wanted to run away with you? I barely like you. All this time I've been waiting and I can't even get what I want." He stepped into the patch of moonlight peeking through the trees. His face didn't look human. His eyes were black, his hands were turned to claws, and his face had morphed slightly. She probably couldn't tell, and if she could, she would ignore what she couldn't understand.

"Kaleb, what are you talking about?" Charlotte took a step back, and he took one forward. "Stop. You're scaring me."

"Good." He jumped her.

***

I watched as he hurt her. There was nothing I could do even with my magic. I was no match for a werewolf. His claws tore at her dress, and his teeth sunk into her flesh. If I didn't help her, she was going to turn into one of them.

I stepped out of my hiding place and walked over to her. "Are you okay?"

"Who are you?" Her voice was shaky. I couldn't blame her. She must have been terrified.

"I'm Pan. Who are you?"

"I don't know anymore."

I felt my chest clench. I did this to her.

"Can I help you?" I sat down beside her. "Is there anything I can do?"

"Not unless you can take away the pain burning a hole through my chest." She tried to laugh, but blood ended up coming up.

"What if I told you I know of a place where you will never grow old? A place that can heal any injury."

"Can you take me to it?"

I smiled. I could fix this. I would fix this. "I can."

***

"You never did tell me what your name is," I said. Yes, I already knew it, but I was giving her the same opportunity as Ace to change it.

I was helping her stay upright with my arm around her waist and her arm around my shoulder.

"Clover."

"Well, Clover, welcome. I'll introduce you to Zylan. I think you two will get along, and then she'll help you get all fixed up."

"Thank you for everything."

"Anything I could do to help."

I closed my eyes, not because I had to anymore, but because it killed me to see what I did to her. When I opened my eyes, we were in Zylan's camp. She was in a tree with an arrow pointed at my head. How did she always know I was coming? "Who's this? Kidnap someone else I see."

"Zylan, this is Clover. She's really badly hurt, and I would like it if you could help her." I dropped my eyes. Any other day, I would have said something back, but today, I deserved it.

She unpinned her arrow and stuck it in the case on her back then she slung her bow around her shoulder. In a blink of an eye, she was standing in front of Clover, examining her.

"What happened to you?" she asked.

"I got beat up."

Zylan nodded to me. "I'll take her from here."

I moved out of the way so she could support her. "I'm guessing you've realised magic is real now." She smiled.

"It took me by surprise." Clover chuckled, ending in a harsh cough.

"Well, this will too." And they were gone.

1495

I'd been too afraid to check up on Kaleb. Actually, it was more like ashamed. Before I checked on the present, I looked way back. I saw how they were together. He would have done anything for her, and I messed up. I took all of that away from her without even trying. I should have just left well enough alone. I should have found someone else.

With a deep breath and shaking hands, I reached into the water. I had to know, even though I didn't want to, I needed to do this. There was no present Kaleb, exactly why I'd been so reluctant. I forced myself to go back.

He was a werewolf. The family he was living with was his pack. He told them what he did to Clover. He went back to them crying. He couldn't understand why he did that. His pack couldn't stand for it, and they used him as an example.

He let them tie him up and take turns tearing pieces out of him. He didn't let out a cry until the very end. The last thing he ever said was, "I'm so sorry, my Clover."

I did that all because I wanted Zylan to have a friend. How could she like me if I couldn't even find a reason to like myself?

1508

I followed the ship again. I decided, after Clover, I was never going to wander off on my own. I was only taking people that needed saving from the pirates. I wasn't ruining anymore lives.

The pirates docked in England, the same town that Ace grew up in. It made me cringe to be in the same town Ace's mother killed herself, but I couldn't think about that. I was here to rescue someone.

Hook docked really late this year. It was pitched black on the ocean, and now there was only a slight glimmer of light on the docks. I was standing on a sail, out of view, when we finally docked. I could hear the voices of two people below. I was guessing the pirates heard them too because they weren't making a sound.

"Almost where? Come on! We're been walking for twenty minutes. Where are you taking me?" It was a girl's voice.

"Here." I saw the figures of a young man and woman as they approached the edge of the dock. "You remember?"

"Of course! This is where we met." *You picked the wrong day to do this my friend.*

"I can't believe you remember that."

"How could I not? You're the only reason I got in the water. I was scared!" The girl giggled.

"You didn't look it."

"I had to put on a brave face! You were laughing at me!" Now the boy laughed. "So what is that we're doing here?"

"I've had the biggest crush on you since I was six years old. It took me double those years to work up the nerve to ask you to be with me. And now it's taken triple those years to ask for your hand." He dropped down to one knee. "Elena, I love you so much. I can't imagine my life without you. Will you please do me the honour of being my wife, of dealing with me for the rest of our lives?"

The girl, Elena, looked like she was crying. "Of course, I will! I love you too!"

He stood up and threw his arms around her. "Oh thank god. I couldn't handle a no. Here, I made this for you." He pulled away and handed her something, I was guessing it was a ring.

I could tell Hook was getting irritated. He waved his crew members forward. He wasn't waiting for them to leave. This was my opportunity to rescue someone that actually needed saving.

"I can't believe you were worried."

"I hate to break this moment, love, oh wait no I don't."

They looked over at Hook and his whole crew. The boy stepped in front of Elena. "What do you want?"

"You see that lads? 'e's tryin' to pertect 'er. Kill 'em," Hook said, rubbing his hook. He always picked the worst times to clean it.

"Run. Go get help. I'm not going to let them hurt you."

"Tyler, you can't do this on your own."

"Elena, run!" he yelled, pushing her away.

She did what he asked. She ran and didn't look back. I waited to see what Hook decided to do with him before I went off to find her.

"Ain't that a beautiful sight, mates! 'e's cryin'!" Hook laughed. "Take 'em aboard. We're gonna 'ave fun with 'em. And find the girl. We can't 'ave 'er ruinin' 'r fun t'night."

The first two pirates behind Hook walked toward Tyler with their swords forward. He could try and fight, but there was little point. They'd just kill him instead of taking him hostage.

He didn't struggle. He let them pull him on board without a fight. *I'll find you again, my love. I promise I will see you again.* His thoughts echoed in my head. Maybe one day they would meet again, but it wouldn't be for a long time. Luckily, where he was going, and where I was hoping Elena will let me take her. They had all the time in the world.

I left the ship to find Elena. When I appeared in town, I got there just in time to see her collapse on the ground screaming.

"Pirates! Pirates! There are pirates at the docks!"

All the men grabbed their tools and run. By the time I'd made my way over to her, everyone was gone. She was kneeling on the ground, crying. In her hand she was holding the small object Tyler handed to her. I was right about it being a ring. In fact, it was a beautiful golden ring with a pattern on it. He must have spent a long time working on it.

"Are you okay?" I asked.

She looked up at me with tear-stained cheeks and bloodshot eyes.

"No, I just lost everything. They'll never make it in time."

"Can I help you?" I sat down in front of her.

"Can you take me away? Can you help me be free?" I could see her trying to hold back tears.

I smiled. "I know just the place."

***

"What is this place?"

"Home." I smiled.

"Who are you?"

"Pan."

"Peter Pan? Is this Neverland?" she exclaimed.

My brother had really made a name for himself. I could tell her the truth, but then I would have to tell Ace as well. He'd spent the last thirty years believing I was Peter. He would never trust me again.

"I prefer Pan."

"Pan it is then."

"Take my hand. I'm going to introduce you to Zylan and Clover."

As soon as she did, we were standing in the middle of Zylan's camp. She and Clover were sitting in the middle.

They looked over. "August 14. You were right," Clover said.

"Ha! Told you!" They stood up. "I'm Zylan. This is Clover. We will be your hostesses for the rest of your now immortal life." I'd never seen Zylan smile like that. Well, except for one time, but that was a long time ago.

They were both wearing baggie black pants and a tight white shirt. I found it so adorable how they always match. Elena didn't seem to understand why they were dressed like that.

"Why is she staring?" Clover whispered.

"Remember how I was wearing boy clothes when we met? Remember your reaction?" Zylan whispered back. "I think she's taken off guard."

Clover looked down. "Oh no! We forgot to change!" She waved her hands quickly, and they then matched Elena. Zylan did *not* look impressed. I almost forgot how she looked in a dress.

"Why were you dressed like boys? Why are you now dressed like I am?"

"Trust me. Once you've lived here long enough, you'll realise how impractical dresses really are." Zylan smiled and waved her hands. Now she was back in her previous outfit. "Much better."

"Can you teach me how to do that?"

"We can, but for now"—that time the hand waving landed Elena in Clover and Zylan's outfit—"you're going to want to wear this."

She looked surprised. "This is great! So now we can start?"

"I like her."

"You'll do great here."

"I'll leave you girls to it," I said.

By the looks on their faces, they forgot I was there.

Chapter 10

Did It Happen This Way?

Zylan

It's August 14, 1469. I'm standing on the top of the cliff watching the breeze pull the trees from side to side. I hear a wolf howl from somewhere in the forest. I see the birds flying around, above the trees. If this is the last thing I'll ever see, I could deal with that. I take a few steps forward, so I'm standing right on the edge. I close my eyes and take a deep breath before I take a step forward. I expect to fall, but I don't. Instead I open my eyes to see Pan standing in front of me.

I've been trying so hard to avoid him since he brought me to this place. I can't face him, not after what he did to my parents. Just because he thinks I didn't see him do it, doesn't mean that I wasn't hiding under that bed. I saw his boots; I know he did it. But he acts as if he rescued me. He brought me blankets, set up a camp for me, made me dinner.

"Why?" I ask him. "Just let me die please."

"Why would I do that? I didn't save you from that pirate so that you could jump off a cliff," he says. Pirate? He's the one that did it. Isn't he? I saw the boots but not the face . . . maybe he didn't do it. "Come here, I want to show you something."

He leads me over to a part of the cliff wall that is covered in vines. He waves his hand in front of it, and it reveals a cave. The sunlight hits the mist, and an array of colours fill the air. Purple dances across the cave's ceiling, red floats over to the left side, orange slides across the cave floor, and some deep blue hovers centimetres above the water. The right side has a waterfall pouring out of a large crack in the wall. I walk in farther finding large rocks, spaced perfectly for a person to walk through. Although the cliff is gray, the inside of the cave is brown. Not a gross poo-coloured brown, but a warm, light-coloured brown. All the way around the cave wall, there are torches two meters above the ground lighting the room as Pan waves the vines back into place.

"It's beautiful," I whisper.

"This is where I come when I need to think. It makes me appreciate life." He walks over to one of the smaller rocks and sits down. I follow and sit on the one next to him. I feel like there's something wrong. I feel like my mind is playing tricks on me. I want to believe that pirates actually killed my parents and he didn't.

***

Later that night, I follow him to his camp. He sits down in front of a small fire and lights a candle. He sits there for a long time staring at it before closing his eyes and blowing out the candle. As soon as the light from the candle is out, I remember. He saved me. He brought me to Neverland, and someone else sent us here. He used to watch me, protect me. I spent the last year hating someone who's done nothing but try to save me.

***

"I'm going to meet Pan. I'll be back in a few hours," Clover yells from the other side of camp. We set up on the far east side

of the Island, away from Ace and Pan. Our camp is a circle about forty meters wide. Set up in the middle is a fire pit, my bed on the right side, hers on the left.

"Okay," I say, pretending to do something. I don't trust him, not after he killed my parents. I don't want to tell Clover that, so I just follow her to her lessons and make sure he doesn't hurt her like he hurt me.

Once she's out of sight, I grab my bow and a few arrows then head out after her. They always meet in the same spot, a ten-minute walk west of camp, in a small clearing. When I get there, she has her back facing me and sword pointed at Pan.

I hide behind a tree and watch the lesson. Clover swings right, Pan blocks left then flips his wrist and strikes to her left. She blocks quickly and tries to flick her wrist the same way to strike the top of his head. He raises his left hand just in time for his sword to block the blow. Then he makes a wide circle—causing her to lose her sword—and pokes the tip of his blade into her throat.

"You've been practicing." He smiles lowering his weapon.

"I have." She smiles back. Then faster than I thought was possible, she reaches forward with her right hand, grabbing his sword hand. She steps forward bringing her left elbow around to meet his face. That takes him by surprise so he lets go of his sword, allowing her to pull it away from him. Finally, she spins around and presses the blade into his throat.

He's still smiling like he's really impressed. "Well done!" he exclaims clapping his hands.

"Thank you!" She smiles pulling the sword back then flipping it around so he can take it back. "Thank you for agreeing to teach me in the first place, and saving me. I'm really glad I met you."

His smile grows. "You know what? I'm really glad I met you too."

Maybe he's not such a bad person after all.

***

I am so tired of these goddamn dreams. Pan is *not* a good guy. I don't understand why I'm still having these stupid dreams. He's been gone for almost two weeks. How the hell is he still able to get into my damn head?

"Zylan!" Clover yells snapping me back to reality.

"Yup, hi, sorry." Clover, Elena, and I decided we wanted to have a girls' day. We've been sitting on the cliff wall for hours just talking. We chose the cliff because it has these plants that, when crushed and mixed with the water from the waterfall, make you tell the truth.

"Can you answer my question now?" Elena asks.

"Yes . . . What was your question?"

"Have you ever considered giving Tyler a shot?"

Clover and I both look at her confused. I thought I didn't hear her ask the question, but judging by Clover's reaction, she just asked if she could ask a question. "You do realise she's been with Ace, basically her whole time on this island, right? Tyler came long after they were together." I nod in agreement.

"Oh please, like you two never fought. Answer the question honestly, not that you could lie right now, but you could, not tell the whole truth." She chuckles.

"Oh, come on. I'm not entertaining you."

"Now I'm curious." Clover shifts so she is sitting next to Elena. "You have to answer. It's now my question as well."

"Fine, fine. I'm going to tell you something, and if either of you tell anyone, I will kill you. Very slowly. Very painfully. Promise me."

"Promise!" they exclaim together.

"Now spill!"

I lean in really close and start whispering. "Me and Tyler have this agreement. Whenever Ace and I get in a fight and break up . . . Ty and I . . . don't do anything because he's my best friend. Weirdos." I chuckle.

"You really had us going for a second there." Elena laughs. "But that wasn't my question. Have you, ever considered, hooking up with Tyler while you and Ace were on a break?"

"Yes. Every time, I mean have you seen him? But he's my best guy friend, and I love Ace. I would never, ever, do something to screw either of those things up. But there was this one time . . ."

Elena and Clover gasp. "Oh my god! Saint Zylan, what did you do?"

I take a deep breath. "This time I'm serious. If you tell anyone, I will kill you."

The nod excitedly. "Not a soul, promise."

"It was a couple hundred years ago. Ace and I got into a huge fight about telling everyone. I couldn't see why it was so important to him. I mean it's not like I was purposely keeping it a secret. I just didn't want to go around making out, and whatever, in public. If anybody had asked, I would have told them, but no one ever did. I didn't see the point of everyone knowing our business. But he got so mad.

"You guys have seen how close me and Ty are. We've participated in the occasional light flirting, that's just the way we are. Ace accused me of cheating with him, which I would never do. Then I got mad, I thought he knew me better than that. We had been together for two-and-a-half centuries, but apparently, that didn't matter. So I told him that it was over. I didn't want to be with someone who didn't trust me and then I walked away.

"I was wandering around trying to keep myself from crying, not paying attention to anything, and I bumped into Ty. He said he'd been looking for me. It was the second Sunday of the month which meant we were supposed to meet up and have our monthly chat. Naturally, I apologized and asked if we could do it tomorrow because I wasn't feeling good.

"When he saw the look on my face, he said no and then he hugged me. He didn't ask if I was okay or what was wrong or if he could do anything or how he could help. He just hugged me and let me cry. We stood there for a long time. I don't know exactly how long.

"Once I finally stopped crying, he pulled away and wiped the tears from my eyes. He took my hand and wrapped his arm through mine. 'Come on, we're going to get your mind off things,' he said leading me to our usual meeting place. He got us a blanket and laid it down so we could look up at the stars and talk. We did a lot of talking that night, about a lot of things.

"I was talking about my life before the Island when I felt this overwhelming desire to sneak a glance at him. So I looked over, and he was looking at me with his beautiful brown eyes." I take a deep breath remembering every second of the moment. "I have never wanted to kiss someone more in my life. We both kind of moved in for it, at least I thought he did. But he turned his head back to the sky and continued our conversation."

Clover and Elena sit there like statues for about a minute until Clover manages to find the right words. "So, after that moment, you guys never talked about it. You never were like 'oh hey, Ty, I think I kind of like you, how do you feel about me?' You just left that moment hanging in the air and went on?"

"What else was I supposed to do, C? I went in for it, and he moved, then a couple days later, Ace apologized and we got back together. He's all I've known for almost five hundred years, and I'm not about to throw that away on some maybe situation, which I have already been rejected for."

"That was over two hundred years ago! You said you were crying. Maybe he felt like he would be using you if he let it go any further. Ty is one of the best guys I know, if he thought, even for a second, that he would be taking advantage of you, he would have stopped himself."

Clover nods her head in agreement. "You know it's true, Ze."

"Well, it's too little, too late. That moment is long over, and Ace and I are very happy together. I want it to work between us. Now, Elena's turn. Speaking of Tyler's, do you ever miss Hunter? From before, when he was Tyler?"

"I wish I could say no. Every time I look at him, I see my Tyler and then I see Lydia straddling him and I want to strangle him. Sometimes I wish I had stayed with him." She sighs and looks down. "Sometimes I wish he was still my Tyler."

"Did you ever figure out why he calls himself Hunter now? I know a lot of us changed our names, but why Hunter?" Clover asks.

"It probably has something to do with the fact that he's a man slut. He probably hunted girls. Now it's Clover's turn."

"Urg. All right, ask away."

"Have you ever been in love with anyone other than Justin?"

"Yes. Once. Before I got here. I wish I could say I hate him, and I hope he died a slow and painful death. But he was my first love, and I could never hate him. I thought, maybe one day I would learn to hate him or forget him. No such luck." She sighs and looks off toward the skyline.

"I can relate to that one." The words come out of my mouth without me realising I said them.

"What? Who did you love that you wish you could hate?" Elena and Clover both snap their heads to stare at me.

"Jacob." I can feel the confused look on my face. I don't know why I said that.

"Who the hell is Jacob?" they say together.

"Pan."

"What the fuck! Zylan, are you on drugs? Well, I know you're on truth drugs, but did you have anything else?"

"I've been having these weird dreams since Pan tried to show me the truth about my life. Ever since they started, I feel like I loved him, but that can't be possible because I remember him killing my parents. But these dreams are telling me that he saved me from pirates."

"There's no way he killed your parents. He's in love with you. It's written all over his face every time he looks at you. There's this look of longing and sadness in his eyes whenever he sees you," Clover says.

"It's true. Clover and I have actually talked about it before. It's why we couldn't understand why you hated him."

"Well, I never actually saw the person who did it. All I saw were boots . . . I've always felt like there was something wrong with that memory, but whenever I try to search deeper into the memory, it hurts." I sigh. "Wow, these truth herbs don't fuck around."

"Tell me about it." Clover scratches her head. "So, what are you going to do about this? I mean Pan isn't here to tell you the truth, and even if he was, you wouldn't believe him."

I look down over the cliff wall. "I have no idea. I keep thinking I don't want him here and wishing he won't ever come back and that he'll die a slow and painful death, but now . . . I wish he would come back. I need to know what's going on with my head, and even though I don't trust him, I think he's the only one that can give me the answers I need to move on with my life."

"What if you find out what really happened and you realise you never loved Pan?" Elena asks.

"What if I find out I did? Ace and I have had about eight lifetimes together. What if I find out I was secretly in love with Pan the whole time? I don't want to know." I stand up and brush myself off. "I don't want to do this anymore."

"Fine. Run and hide from it, but that's not going to change the fact that you feel this way now." Clover stands up as well.

Elena sighs. "Well, if we're all standing up now." She pushes herself to her feet then her eyes go wide. "Okay, don't panic but there is a giant wolf standing behind you guys."

Clover and I turn around slowly. Once we see the familiar brown furred and blue-eyed wolf, we let out a sigh of relief. "El, it's Clover's wolf. The one that follows her around all the time. You've seen him before, calm down."

"Oh." She sighs in relief as well. "We should name it. We can't just call it Clover's wolf."

"You're right . . ." Clover stares at it.

After a minute of her staring at it and not saying anything, I put my hand on her shoulder. "C, are you okay?"

She shakes her head and snaps out of it. "Yeah . . . I just feel like I . . . I don't know. Its eyes remind me of someone I used to know." She pauses. "Let's call him Jamie."

"How do you know it's a him?" Elena asks coming to stand next to us.

"I don't know . . . I just have this feeling. We could always follow him around until he has to pee and find out."

I think the wolf laughed. He closed his eyes, bowed his head, and—I swear to God—I heard him snort. This wolf wasn't a normal wolf. I've known that since the first time I saw him. He follows Clover around all the time. He attacked Pan one time in the middle of one of their training sessions, and he understands what we're saying.

Clover smiles. "At least Jamie appreciates my humor."

"That's because he's obsessed with you. Why? One of the world's great mysteries." Elena rolls her eyes.

"At least someone's obsessed with me. You have no one."

The wolf and I roll our eyes at the face Elena makes. "All right, I think he and I are thinking the same thing when I say do *not* start. This was a bonding day, not a fighting day." I turn to the wolf—I can't call him Jamie, for some reason it doesn't feel right. "Okay, so today is supposed to be a girls' day. If Clover's right and you are a boy, which I think you are too, can you watch her from the bottom of the cliff. I promise she's safe."

He bows his head and walks away.

"Hear that, Elena? You can't push me off the cliff now. I'm safe." Clover laughs.

"Shit, there go my day's plan. Whatever will I do now?"

"Come back to camp," Tyler says as he appears behind us.

The three of us scream and clutch our hearts. "Ty! What the fuck?" I yell. "Stop doing that!"

"But why?" he whines. "It's so much fun!" He smiles.

"This better be important. It's girls' day." Clover crosses her arms.

"So tough for someone who was screaming like a baby less than ten seconds ago." Tyler laughs.

"Oh, you want to see tough?" I ask. I lift my right hand, raising Tyler off the ground, above our heads. Then I move him so he's dangling over the cliff.

"Okay, okay! You made your point!"

"Did I?" I drop my hand slightly; he falls a couple inches.

"Yes! Yes! Put me down!"

"Well, if you insist." I push my hand down to the ground and he falls all the way, screaming his head off the whole way down. I pull my hand up at the last second so he's hovering a foot above the ground. I leave him there for a couple seconds before letting him fall that last foot.

"All right, you made your point. Bring him back up here." Now it's Ace's turn to scare the shit out of us. We turn to find him and Justin leaning on the cliff.

"When did you get here?" Elena asks.

"While Tyler was dangling over the cliff. We came to tell you that Pan's back at camp."

"Girls' day is being postponed," I say. "All right, let's go back to camp."

The three boys disappear first, and before I can follow them, El and C grab my arms and keep me planted. "I know that you think your happy with Ace, but I would just like to point out that the smile you have on your face when you see Tyler is way bigger than the one you get when you see Ace."

"That's why I couldn't believe you were with Ace when you first told me. I always thought it was Tyler."

"I know that you guys think you know what's best for me, but I am so happy with Ace. We're engaged. We're going to have a big wedding with all our friends, and I'm going to spend the rest of my eternal life with him, like I've been doing the last 496 years."

They sigh. "Fine but between Pan, Ace, and Tyler, your life is a hell of a lot more complicated than you would like to admit. I think that you should tell Ace about your memory problem and talk about this together."

"Yeah, now that Pan's back, you're going to have to stop running from your problems."

I sigh. "I know, but that's not a problem for today. We can figure all this out tomorrow morning."

"All right, let's go see where Pan's been all this time."

Justin

1517

He wouldn't stop coughing. "Enok, come on, buddy, you're going to be okay, just breathe." My little brother had been sick for months now. He was only five, and we had no idea what was going on with him. No one could help us.

He kept coughing. I didn't know what to do. I didn't know how much longer he was going to keep going through this. I didn't know when he was going to get better. I didn't know if he was even going to get better.

"Enok, please be okay."

"He's not going to make it much longer."

I jumped up and turned around. Standing in front of me was a boy about my height. He had light brown hair and a pale face. His clothes were green and brown. He looked like he just stepped out of the forest.

"Who are you? Why are you here? What do you want?"

"I'm Peter, Peter Pan, I'm here to save your brother. I want to take him to Neverland with me. He will be safe there. He can have a good life there."

"You're crazy! Peter Pan is just a story. This is the real world, the real world where my brother is dying."

I looked back at him. He was lying on my bed with his eyes shut. His breathing was shallow, and he had a dry cough that acted up every few minutes. He was pale, very pale. It was hard to look at him. It was even harder to hear him struggling for air.

"I'm not a story. I can help him. You just have to let me take him to Neverland. We don't have much time."

"You're not Peter Pan! Leave!" I yelled at the boy. "Let me spend my last moments with my brother in peace!"

"I can't do that. I need to take him." The boy stepped toward me.

"You can't do that." I blocked his path.

"Good luck, Justin. I wish you the best next year." His tongue turned from Swedish to English.

"What is that supposed to mean?" I responded back in English. The boy was taken off guard.

"Interesting." He waved his hand in front of my face before I could answer. Everything went black as I fell to the floor.

1518

"No way you're going to do it!"

"You're the one who told me to do it. If you want to back out, I'll take your money either way." The kids in the village didn't think I could do it. None of them ever think I could do it. But I always did, and they always had to pay. The parents around here didn't like me very much. I didn't do anything except get into trouble, really. That was how I made my living.

Both my parents died three years ago. I had to take care of my two little sisters and three—well it was three, now it was two—younger brothers. I was the oldest. I had to drop everything and take care of them. I was only fourteen, the only thing I was good at—the only thing I was still good at—was taking risks, doing things no one else wanted to do.

"Fine, do it then."

I took a deep breath. *You can do this, one bite, that's all it's going to take.* I picked up the tiny red pepper and examined it. All I had to do is swallow one bite and I would get ten thalers for it.

One of the boys in the village was talking about how it was the hottest pepper in the world. His father had it imported from India. He was going on and on about how no one can stand one bite of it, so obviously, I had to take a bite out of it. All the kids in the village wanted in on this bet. In total I would have enough to buy us a good dinner and still have leftovers.

"Okay, here it goes." I took another deep breath and brought the pepper to my mouth. One more breath and I took the bite. At first it wasn't bad. After a few seconds, my mouth started to tingle. After twenty seconds, my mouth felt like it was on fire. I couldn't show it; I only got the money if I didn't react. "All right, pay up!"

They all moaned, handing over their coins. Once I had all my coins in hand, I calmly made my way home where there was a cup full of fresh milk I could gobble down.

After my parents died, I took overlooking after everyone. Once my younger sister reached fourteen, she started helping out too. If what I was doing could seriously hurt me, she always patched me up and made sure everything was in place to help me feel better. She had been helping out for a year and a half now and it was a lot easier for me.

We were pretty close, closer than the rest of my siblings. The three of them were a lot younger, from ten to six. They all whined about how the other kids had more money and less chores. We were the poorest family here, and still we were better off than everyone in the neighbouring village. They didn't understand that Kachina and I were doing the best we could to keep them fed and clothed with a roof over their heads.

I wanted nothing more than to be free of this responsibility, to have some help from a real adult, to be as ignorant as the three of them. I wished I could stomp my feet and yell and cry about how unfair the world is, but I didn't have that luxury and I didn't have the time.

I wanted to do that three years ago when my parents died. I wanted to do it last year when Enok got sick and disappeared. I wanted to do that when no one found him. But I couldn't, and I still couldn't, not until the only person I have to take care of was myself.

"Justin! Hurry up! The milk is going to spoil!" Kachina yelled as I approached the front door. She was standing on our porch with the cup in her hand.

"I'm coming! I'm coming!" The burning in my mouth was starting to become manageable, but the sweat dripping down my face wasn't from the mid-July sun.

She didn't wait at the door. She met me half way down the street. "My god! What have you done to yourself?" she exclaimed, shoving the cup in my face. "Don't answer that, just drink!"

We lived on a farm. Mother and Father moved us here from Birmingham when I was five. They said that life here would be easier. It probably would have been if they hadn't both been murdered.

Living on a farm had made life more manageable though. While I was making money off the kids, Kachina is making money off the adults. We had three cows and twenty chickens. We sold fresh jars of milk for one thaler each and a dozen eggs for two thalers.

"Kachina, relax! I'm fine. My mouth even stopped burning." I took the cup and had a sip. "Here, take this while I finish." I handed her the money, and she retreated with a glare.

Once she was clear out of view, I finished the cup in three gulps. I let a sigh escape my lips. That was the best cup of milk I had ever had, and I would never take another one for granted. My mouth stopped burning, and breathing didn't pierce a hole in my lungs anymore. *Whoever first milked a cow, I thank you for it. Whoever found out milk cures a burning mouth, I thank you for sharing that knowledge with the world!*

The sun beat down on me as I finished my walk to the front door, but the sweat was starting to retreat. Soon it would be dark and time to count our earnings for the day as well as time for me to do the risky stuff of my own free will.

***

"You have to, I dared you!"

Four friends and I were crouched behind the trees of the dock. Strom just dared me to sneak aboard a pirate ship. *A pirate ship!* "If I'm caught, they'll kill me, no question about it. What if I die? I have four people to take care of!"

"You won't die! You're the sneakiest person I know. Besides, most of the pirates are off the ship, all you have to do is crawl in and crawl out. If you do, I'll give you ten thalers, each of us will," Hemming said.

"Fine." Forty thalers was too much to refuse; I had to.

I moved from my position, moving silently toward the ship. It was scary looking—dark blue with black sails. The front holds a dragon, mouth open, and it was larger than any ship I had even seen—if I was caught, they definitely wouldn't show mercy. I swallowed my worries and kept moving. I had to do this.

With every step, I could feel my heart pounding in my ears. I'd never been more scared to carry out a dare.

I stuck to the shadows, out of the moonlight and away from the lanterns. They couldn't see me, they couldn't hear me, I couldn't leave a trace. All it would take was ten seconds in and ten seconds out.

I stopped once I reached the dock. I crouched behind one of the polls and looked for a way on. The back looked like it had a gap between two decks; I could sneak on there. I snuck along the dock to the back. The ship didn't look very deep in the water. It was a big ship, you would think it would have hit the sand, but it was tied right up to the dock.

The boat looked like it was in the water a long time, getting to the gap could be an issue if it was too slippery. I looked around to make sure no one could see me before grabbing hold of the rope keeping the boat secure. I used the rope to get to the ship, and from there I had to climb a short distance up the slimy wall.

Ten seconds in, ten seconds out, I told myself at the gap. I took a deep breath and crawled in.

One. The lighting was dim.

Two. The creaking was creepy.

Three. The walls were light brown with pictures hanging.

Four. I felt a chill up my spine as it creaked.

Five. I turned to leave but a hand grabbed my shoulder.

Six. I swallowed.

Seven. "You shouldn't be here."

Eight. English, try, and remember English.

Nine. "I was just leaving."

Ten. "Not anymore."

Dead.

***

"I found 'em lurkin' at the gap. Thought 'e could look 'round an' leave," the pirate that caught me said, handing me over to the captain.

We were at the back of the ship by the wheel. The captain stood in front of me as I was forced to kneel at his feet. He was tall, with black hair and blue eyes. His face was pale and neutral. He studied me. "Lock 'em up. Ware 'em down."

So I wasn't dead. They were going to try and make me part of the crew. A boy, about my age, with black hair and brown eyes grabbed my arms, pulled me to my feet, and dragged me down the stairs. All the pirates on board were standing off to the side, watching me get pushed to the cells.

It was a huge ship. It took five minutes just to get to the bulge. From there the boy pushed me to the very back and into one of the two cells. He turned to leave. "Wait! How long have you been here?"

"Ten years today," the boy said over his shoulder.

"How old were you? Seven? Eight?"

"Eighteen, you can't grow old where we're going. No one grows old where we're going."

"That's impossible! What are you talking about?"

The boy walked back to my cell. "I thought it was impossible too. But here I am, twenty-eight, still lookin' eighteen. Captain says they've been sailin' 'round an island for the last fifty years waitin' to get their treasure. We only sail out every ten years, meaning I was at the wrong place at the wrong time . . ." He looked off like he was remembering that night. He quickly blinked and shook his head. "'Nough 'bout me. Get comfy, newbie, you're in for a long life." He started walking off again.

"Wait! What's your name?"

"Tyler."

"What happened to you? Why are you like this?"

"I lost my world and I'm never getting her back."

***

The water was ice-cold. I couldn't feel parts of my body. I couldn't get warm. I'd been down here almost an hour. The ship wasn't moving yet, which meant I still had a chance to get out of here and get my forty thalers.

One of the crewmembers came down while I was looking for a way out, so I had to stop and I was too afraid to continue my search. I had only just resumed looking five minutes ago. The bars were too close together to squeeze through, and although I knew how to pick a lock, there was nothing here to pick a lock with. I decided to find where the leak was coming from. I find that, and I could swim out.

"There's an easier way out."

I jumped up and turned toward the cell door. It was wide open, and there was a boy with brown hair and green eyes standing on the other side. He looked familiar, but I couldn't place him.

"Who are you? Is this a trick?"

"No. I'm not a part of this crew. I'm Pan, and I'm here to rescue you. Unless you don't want my help."

"How do I know you are who you say you are?"

"You don't, but you should trust me. I can take you away, to a place where you will not grow old, where you can be with people your age with no responsibilities. Or I can leave you here to be a pirate for the rest of your life."

"Take me." I didn't know what came over me. I had four people to take care of. I should be staying. I should be trying to get back to them. But I couldn't do it anymore. I couldn't be strong for them anymore. "Take me to this place."

"Come, we need to move quickly."

The boy led me up the stairs. The ship was a maze. At every turn, there were two different ways. Finally, we made it back to the gap I came in. "What now?"

"Jump!" he yelled pushing me off the ledge.

***

"You might as well come down and say hello, girls," Pan said.

What was he talking about? I saw two boys sitting in front of a fire. They both nodded and said hello. Where were the girls?

"Who's this?" a girl with long brown hair asked appearing in front of me. I blinked. How did she do that? Where did she come from? Why was she wearing pants? She was showing a lot of skin . . . what kind of place was this? "Where are you from?"

"Zylan, give the boy a chance to settle in before we go asking a million questions." Another girl appeared. She had short blonde hair, just past her shoulders. She was wearing the same thing as the other girl. Why?

"She only asked two, no need to go overexaggerating things, Clover." Yet another girl appeared. She had long brown hair as well, but a different shade.

"Thank you, Elena."

"Can everyone do that?" I asked.

"No." One of the boys rolled his eyes. "These four like to show off with it, though."

"Yeah, I can't really do it either . . . one time I almost did, but I almost impaled myself with a branch in the process. I've been uneasy about trying again," the other boy added.

"Can someone teach me how to do that?"

"Don't ask Pan. He's an awful teacher."

"Can someone answer my questions?" the girl standing in front of me—Zylan I guessed—exclaimed, rolling her eyes.

"I'm Justin, I'm from Sweden." I smiled.

"Why do you speak perfect English? And why do you have an English accent?" the blonde girl—Clover—asked.

"I was born in Birmingham, I moved to Sweden when I was five, and my parents continued to speak English until they died three years ago."

The three girls frowned. "Sorry, we're done now," they all said and disappeared.

"Seriously, someone has to teach me that."

"Ask Zylan. She's the reason the other two can do that. I'm Ace, and that's Matt." Ace stood up and walked over to me. "Nice to meet you, Justin. I can help you if you need anything."

1520

"Justin, I need you to find Clover. We were supposed to have a lesson, but something just came up," Pan said appearing in front of me.

"Enough! Enough with the heart attacks! Why do you always insist on doing that?" Every time I jumped out of my skin, and every time he laughed and didn't listen. This time he didn't laugh.

"Sorry, just please go find her. She should be around centre island." He disappeared after that. What could be so important that he didn't laugh?

"Yes, sir," I said to an empty space. I chuckled to myself and headed out.

Pan had been meeting with Clover to teach her to use a sword. I could have done that, but she avoided me. I've tried talking to her and I've tried making an effort to spend time with her, but it was like she couldn't get away from me fast enough. One time she actually ran away from me, like sprinted away.

I didn't know what I did wrong. I didn't know if it was something I did or maybe the reason she was here. But she wouldn't even give me a chance. She wouldn't let me show her I could help her. I wished she would.

I walked in the direction of the centre of the island. It wasn't a big place, but it took a fair amount of time to get from one side to the other. I was walking from southeast. Hopefully I didn't have to wander around looking for her. And I hoped she didn't run away this time.

I walked quickly through the trees. There weren't really paths. There were some breaks; but mostly I had to push my way through branches, step over roots, and move around groups of trees. I approached centre island in about ten minutes. I was looking for a clearing, big enough for them to practice.

I heard screaming coming from the west. I ran over, branches scraping me, probably leaving cuts all along my arms and chest. I ignored it, running faster. I came to a small clearing maybe twenty meters wide. Clover was lying off to the side, tossing. She let out another scream.

"Clover! Clover, wake up!" I shook her awake.

Her eyes flew open. She looked around, tears filling her eyes. "What are—"

"Pan sent me to tell you he couldn't make your meeting. I found you tossing and screaming. Are you okay?"

"No, I'm really not."

"Come here." I sat down opening my arms. I pulled her toward me.

She leaned against me and cried. I sat there and helped her calm down. I played with her hair and tried to distract her. Maybe I was right. It wasn't me; it was what happened to her. Hopefully this proved I wanted to help her, I wanted to protect her.

1580

I finally wore her down. I finally got her to give me a chance. Ace said he would help me, and he did. We had plans to meet in ten minutes. I showed up an hour ago to set up, and I still wasn't ready yet! I was going to try and stall her; maybe I could get Ace to distract her.

"Ace, bud, if you can hear me, keep Clover out for twenty more minutes," I whispered into the wind. It worked before. All you had to do was say the name of the person you were trying to reach and then the message. We learned that when we were talking about Zylan and Clover, and they heard everything because we said their names first. They weren't happy with us. Let's just say, we've never made that mistake again.

I think he heard me. I finished setting up after fifteen minutes, and five minutes later, Clover walked into the small clearing. I scrambled to my feet. "Hi."

She paid no attention to me. She just looked around at the scene. "I've never been here before. How did you find it?" She looked at me now. "You did all of this?" She raised her eyebrow.

She was referring to the picnic I spent an hour and a half setting up. No, it didn't have to take that long. I just needed it to be perfect. I set up the blanket with the basket open. I pulled out all the food and set it up in the perfect order for eating. I asked Pan to get some things for me, and he jumped at the chance. It was kind of weird actually. He's never nice, to anyone . . .

I blushed. "If I only have one shot, why not make it count?"

She walked over and sat down; I followed. "So, Justin, you have a lot of tattoos. What do they all mean?"

I looked down at my arms. "I have no idea. People dared me to get them, and I had to in order to provide for my family. We had nothing."

"Can you tell me your story?"

"Where do I start?"

"We have lots of time. How about you start at the beginning?" She reached for a piece of bread.

"Well, it all started when I was fourteen . . ."

Chapter 11

Take Me to Neverland

Pan

Fun fact about my journey to Neverland—I got lost coming back. See it's really easy to get from the sky to the ground. It's a whole different story trying to get back. My boat is enchanted to fly for me. I figured it wouldn't be a problem, and it wasn't. That was until I realized, my magic only works when I'm on the same plain as the Island. Once I got to Neverland, I started to get weaker and weaker until I couldn't even get food. I just kind of sailed around the ocean in a tiny wooden boat with a couple days' worth of food and drinking water. Once I realized I had no idea how to get back, I started to ration everything.

After almost two weeks, I had almost lost hope of finding my way back until I saw the all-too-familiar pirate ship. Somehow my boat managed to find its way home without me guiding it. When I landed on shore, the first thing I did was imagine myself a chicken dinner. Once that was out of the way, and I was refreshed, I made my way back to camp. Boy was I surprised to find out what I missed, and I wasn't I happy about it.

Shortly after my arrival, Ace, Justin, Clover, Elena, Tyler, and Zylan made their way into camp with a lot of questions. None of which I wanted to answer, so I did what I always do: disappear.

Now I find myself sitting on the cliff with my feet hanging off the edge. How am I supposed to get Zylan to come to Neverland with me if she's engaged? She won't want to leave, especially with me.

I let out a frustrated groan and lay back. "Nothing ever works out for me!" I rub my forehead trying to soothe my throbbing head. What do I do now? I promised Wendy I would come back. I promised myself I would bring Zylan back to her sister.

"What's not working out for you?" I peek one eye open to find Zylan standing over me.

"For someone who wants me to leave them alone, you seem to enjoy my company." I sigh sitting up.

"Well, you ran off without answering anyone's questions, and since I was in charge, I'm supposed to get the answers out of you." She sits down beside me and looks out toward the horizon, covered in fog. "You stole my getaway spot," she says after a minute.

"You don't remember, do you?" I ask looking over at her.

"Remember what?" She keeps her eyes dead ahead, like if she looks at me, her eyes will start to burn.

"Never mind." I shake my head. She won't believe me if I tell her, so there's no point in trying.

"Where did you go?"

"Neverland."

"So this isn't Neverland?"

"No."

We sit there for at least ten minutes staring off into the distance. There's no wind today, no birds chirping, no sun shining. There's nothing but silence surrounding us. And we just sit there, both of us trying to find something to say. Anything would be better than the silence. Or so I thought.

"You know, I spent 543 years trying to avoid you, mostly successful. But in the last month I've talked to you more than I have in all the years I've been here. Sometimes I think I can handle it, seeing you all the time I mean, but I can't."

"So then why are you here? Talking to me? You could have sent someone else to get me to talk."

"Because as much as I want to hate you, I can't shake this feeling that something's wrong. Something in my head is throwing me off, like everything I thought I knew is wrong. And the only reason I feel like that is because of what happened in your tree house. It's like my memories are trying to change, and it hurts. A lot. Whenever I try to think about it, I get this sharp pain that shoots through my head. I want you to help me." She rubs her temples like she's thinking about a memory right now.

"I thought you didn't trust me."

"I didn't. Now I think I have to."

I tell her everything I know. I can tell by the look on her face that she believes me. But I can also tell by the look on her face that she doesn't want to. Then she just disappears, leaving me by myself on top of the cliff, extremely confused.

"Let's go," Zylan says reappearing next to me ten minutes later. She changed into a red shirt and black pants. I'm pretty sure that means she's ready for anything.

"What?"

"Take me to Neverland."

"Are you sure? It's a long trip. I was gone for two weeks."

"Well, we won't be, there and back. Two days, tops."

I can't tell her I don't know how to get back. She needs to know what happened to her, what happened with us. I need her to stop hating me and the only way to do that is this way. I swallow my initial protest and nod. "Okay, I'll get the boat set up. We'll make this as fast as possible."

"Okay, Captain, what do we need?" She smiles.

***

"There it is," I say as we approach.

I couldn't see Neverland until it was basically right in front of me. The trees are hidden under a thick blanket of fog. The only light around us is coming from the oil lamp at the front of the boat.

When the boat hits the shore, I pull out the rope, tying it around a small stake and stick it into the ground.

As soon as we step foot on Neverland, Wendy bounces out of the forest. "I knew you were—" she cuts off as soon as she sees Zylan.

They stare at each other, like neither one believes the other is standing in front of them. Neither of them blinking for fear the other will just disappear. Both of them look like they want to say something but can't find the right words. Finally, Zylan takes a step forward, tears filling up in her eyes. "Wendy?"

"Zylan," Wendy whispers, tears are filling her eyes as well.

They both take several slow steps toward each other before sprinting across the sand. They meet in the middle throwing their arms around each other. They wobble slightly, almost losing their balance from the momentum of the run. They stay like that for a minute, crying into each other's shoulders whispering about how much they missed each other.

I give them their time, standing there awkwardly, rocking back and forth. I know I shouldn't be annoyed with this delay, but I am. I need Zylan to stop hating me, and the only way that's going to happen is if Peter shows her the truth.

Finally, they pull away. "Jacob said you were alive. I didn't want to believe it. I mean I did, but I didn't want to get my hopes up. You look so different." Wendy smiles quickly wiping the tears from under her eyes.

"I can't believe you're alive. I thought for sure Robert had killed you. It tore me apart, seeing you like that, in the ally. Oh my god, I missed you so much." She hugs Wendy one last time before pulling away.

"You have more important things to think about right now. Like your memories. I know for a fact, there is no way Jacob killed Mother and Father. Trust me." Wendy looks over her sister's shoulder and smiles at me. "He would never do anything to hurt you, in fact, quite the opposite, he—"

"Wendy! Can you take us to Peter please?" I interrupt. That is definitely not what I need her to know right now.

She frowns, rolling her eyes. "Fine." Once I get closer to her, she drops her voice. "She's going to find out as soon as Peter fixes her. You might as well just tell her."

"She's engaged."

"Ja—"

I raise my hand cutting her off. "Let's just get this over with."

***

"I was going to ask where you disappeared to, but I'm guessing she—" Peter waves his hands in Zylan's direction, "—is the answer."

"Fix it." I can't make myself say anymore through my clenched jaw.

Peter is standing on the pathway leading up the cliff. He has his arms crossed over his chest, feet shoulder width apart, planted firmly to the ground. He always stands like that when he feels threatened; he tries to make himself look bigger, fearless. "I told you before you left, *she* is the only one that can fix her memories."

Zylan is too busy looking back and forth between the two of us to hear a word he said. So I ask the question she should have asked. "How is she supposed to do that? Only the one who casted the curse can lift it."

"Unless part of the curse was how to undo it," Zylan says, eyes still jumping between Peter and I.

"Wow, smart girl, no wonder you—"

"Peter. Fix it." I cut him off. It's like everyone is lining up to tell her how I feel about her.

"Jacob. I can't. But I can tell you how she can."

"She has a name, and she can hear you," Zylan says sarcastically rolling her eyes. "Don't tell *him* how *I* can fix it. Tell *me* how *I* can fix it. Does douchebaggary run in the family?"

"He got it from Father," Peter and I say at the same time, then glare at each other.

"You want to know how to fix it? Kiss him." Then he just disappears, leaving us both speechless and confused.

Clover

Zylan came up to me with a bag and told me that I was in charge until she came back. When I asked where she was going, all she said was that something happened with Pan and she needed to get answers, so she's leaving for a day, two tops, and I'm supposed to make sure that nothing happens while she's gone. Then, before she disappeared, she told me not to tell Ace and that she would explain when she got back. I mean, I know Elena and I were basically forcing her to talk to Pan, but she never listens to us. Now, out of the blue, she finally decides to listen? Why does she need to leave the Island to get her answers? I wish she would have talk to Ace first, that way I wouldn't have to lie to him, but she didn't.

So, I've been avoiding Ace for three hours. I'm a terrible liar, and she knows that! Why would she tell me? Right now, I have Justin distracting him on the other side of the island. The less I have to see him, the easier it will be to deal with, and hopeful by the time he figures out something is up, Zylan will return to explain. I told everyone else that Pan and Zylan were going to be away for a bit, so I'm in charge until they get back, and if they had any problems they're supposed to come to me. I got a lot of "yeah whatever's."

We're all hanging out in the main camp in our groups chatting away. Most of our group is missing due to Zylan and Pan being off the Island and Justin and Ace on the other side of it. Tyler, Elena, and I are sitting awkwardly off to the side not sure what to talk about. Tyler's not really a good friend of mine; he just hangs out with Justin, Ace, and Zylan. The only time we really talk is when all of us are together.

Although Elena and I are getting along again, we really struggle talking without Zylan, unless we're talking about her, which we can't do with Tyler sitting with us because he'll just tell her.

"I think I'm going to go hang out with Hunt, it'll be less awkward," Tyler says standing up.

Elena and I let out a breath. "Well, if you think so," I say.

He nods and walks across camp and sits next to Hunter. They start chatting instantly.

"That was seriously awkward." Elena laughs.

I roll my shoulders. "Tell me about it. We should never hang out with him without Ze, J, or Ace."

Elena opens her mouth to say something when I hear a branch move and a twig snap. Normally I would have ignored it. We live in the forest. If I jumped every time a branch moved, I'd always be on edge, but today there was no wind and everyone was in camp except Justin and Ace, but I knew they wouldn't come to camp all day. I just had a feeling that someone else was out there.

"Did you hear that?" I whisper to Elena, cutting her off.

"I did . . . why do you look like that?"

"Like what?"

"Like you're going to check if there's someone out there? It's just a tree."

"There's no win—" I get cut off by a scream.

Camilla is sitting on a log on the other side of camp. She's really skittish, so normally I wouldn't pay any attention, but when I look over I see a sword in the middle of her chest and blood dripping out of her mouth. Her eyes go wide and then blank. I just watched the life drain out of a person. I never thought that would happen, not since I got here.

When the sword gets pulled out of her, she drops, revealing a pirate standing behind her. He has yellow teeth and a crooked smile. His face is covered in dirt, and his clothes are torn. I'm surprised there's enough fabric to cover all of him. He's fat and ugly, uglier than anyone I've ever seen before.

That's when the others start to box us in. There are at least fifty pirates piling in around us, coming in from all directions. All of us are slowly processing what is going on and are starting to get to our feet. But not before a couple pirates get to us first. I see Romeo, Gia, and Brian fall before I jump into action. I rip my sword out of its holster just in time to see one guy running toward me with his sword above his head, screaming. Wow that's stupid. I leave my right foot planted where it is but move my left leg so all my weight is on it. I leave my sword in his path, crossing my left hand across my chest as an extra block just in case I miss. But I don't. He skewers himself. He's dead, next.

I kick the lifeless body of the pirate off my sword. The next one is a little smarter. He even put up a little bit of a fight. He swings to my left. I block, right hand tipping the sword downward, causing a loud clanking sound to echo throughout the camp. There's a lot of that sound right now. He tries to regroup, but I don't let him. I bring my sword hand around my head, my left hand meeting it just before I strike, slicing him diagonally, from his left shoulder to his right hip. He's dead, next.

This one's as dumb as the first one. He tries cutting me in half, right down the centre, head to toe. I block above my head on a slight angle, right hand angling the sword downward, my left hand supporting the back edge. I push the back edge to my right, my left arm quickly brushing my right, before I cut him in half instead. He's very dead, next.

An arrow flies by my head. My eyes follow it until it lodges itself into a pirate about to stab me in the back. My sword is blocking my left side, and my left hand is up from the momentum of my last swing. I roll my wrist as my left leg swings around me. As I thrust my sword into the guy's gut, I twist all my body weight onto my left leg. Finally, as I pull my sword out, I kick him to the ground landing in dragon stance—all weight on my right, left leg straight, left arm parallel to leg, sword arm above my head. He's dead too, next.

The next pirate to attack is one-handed with a left hook. He's much better than the rest of these amateurs. It's almost hard to keep up. My right side is completely open to his attack. He thrusts forward to just below my ribs. I get my sword around just in time to block. I swing my left foot around so it's planted just beside his right foot. Then I swing my right foot around so we're back to back. My head follows the direction of my elbow as I try to catch him off guard by hitting him in the back of the head. He blocks. I rotate my wrist letting the hilt of the sword readjust in my hand, hoping to catch him as I do, pulling my left leg around. Unfortunately, I miss and pull my right leg back. Then we circle each other for a while. Neither one of us breaking eye contact or messing a step.

"You're good, little girl." His voice is deep, almost sexy. He's tall with slick back black hair and a little bit of scruff along his jawline and above his lip. He has pale skin, not ghostly or sickening, but the kind of pale the Irish are. The black surrounding his pale face works for him. He has bright blue eyes. If he wasn't trying to kill me, I might consider him hot, for an old man.

"I'm not as young as I look, Grandpa."

He swings to the top of my head, but I'm faster. I block then whip my arm around leaving his arm too far to block my next strike. I cut his cheek and pull back, left side facing him, sword above my head, left hand in front of me ready to block. He wipes his cheek with the back of his sword hand. "Huh, that be the way yee want to play it?" He strikes to my right so I block, but before I can retaliate, he circles his wrist and my blade flies from my hands. Then he backs me up until I hit a tree. The tip of his sword rests on the space between my collarbone. "'Nough a this nonsense, girl. *Where's Jason?*"

"I don't know any Jasons. Maybe you have the wrong island. Sorry you had to kill all these people just to learn you are in the wrong place. Better luck next time, Granny."

His eyes flare with anger. "I watched Jacob bring him here. I saw them step foot on the beach. Don't tell me, I have the wrong island you stupid little bitch." *I wonder why he changed his speech.* His jaw is clenched as he pushes the sword deeper into my skin.

"Look, asshole, I don't know any Jacobs or any Jasons. You think they're here? Be my guest looking for them. But if you call me a bitch one more time, *I will end you.*"

He snorts. "How? If you haven't noticed—" he smirks pushing the tip farther until I feel a sliver of blood drip down my neck, "—I'm the one with the weapon."

"Yeah, but I'm the one with the mad skills Ace, Pan, and Justin taught me."

"Where is this Ace you speak of?"

"I don't know. I have him on the other side of the island so that I won't tell him that his fiancé, my best friend, left here with one of his best friends, who she might be in love with, to do god knows what! Try checking there!" I didn't realize how mad I am about the situation until the words slipped out of my mouth.

He looks at me sideways. "I'm not here to listen to your friend's relationship problems. I'm here to find my treasure. *Now take me to Ace.*"

"I thought you were looking for Jason. I can see the old age is already starting to go to your head." He sets his jaw and pushes forward a little more. "Okay! Okay! I'll take you—wait he's right there."

The one-handed pirate looks over in the direction of my out stretched arm. He loosens his death grip on the blade long enough for me to disarm him. I snake my right hand around the blade over his hand, using my left hand to make sure I don't slice my neck with the sword. Next, I spin around elbowing him in the face and pull the sword out of his grip. I end up with both hands on the hilt of his sword pressing it into his neck, just like Pan taught me when I first got here. "Well, this is an unfortunate turn of events. But you should know you're not the only one with a weapon."

"You mean that hook?" I snort. "Useless, just like cell phones."

He looks at me sideways, again. "What the hell is a cell phone? You know what? Never mind, I don't want to know. But you might want to look behind you."

"I'm not as stupid as you. I'm not going to fall for that."

"Fine, but you're going to feel something in about ten seconds."

"One . . . two . . . three . . . four . . . five . . . six . . . seven . . ." Sure enough a sword wraps around my neck. "You're three seconds early . . . would you mind coming back when I get to ten?"

I twist my head to see the look on his face. He actually looks like he's going to do it. "Are you stupid, Ratman? Don't actually do it."

"Sorry," the guy whispers in my ear.

Wow this guy really is dumb, dumber than a stump. "Take us to Ace."

Zylan

"He's probably lying. I mean it's probably true, but there's has to be another way. Spells have loopholes . . ." and that's just part of it. Ever since Peter disappeared, he's been rambling on like this. I don't know how much more of this I can take.

"Pan," I try to cut in, but he keeps going. "Pan," I say a little louder, still rambling. "JACOB!" I scream.

He blinks like I caught him off guard. Before I can second-guess my decision, I grab his face and pull him toward me. His lips are hard against mine, at first. But they begin to soften, his hands moving from his sides to my hair, as soon as they do all the memories that I had from that night begin to fade away until I'm only left with what really happened. I did know he was there all that time. I did believe in magic before I saw it for myself. My friends did think I was crazy. Mother and I did use to fight all the time. Jacob really did save me. And I really do feel like an asshole.

I pull away. "I-I-I'm so sorry. I had no idea. You saved and I treated you like the bad guy. I—"

He kisses me again. This time, there's no hesitation. This is what he wants, and what Pan wants, Pan gets. And as much as I hate to admit it . . . I want this too. My hands move from his cheeks to around the back of his neck, moving closer. His hands moving from my hair to my waist, pulling me against him. Neither one of us want to break this kiss.

I forget about everything. I forget about Ace. I forget about our engagement. I forget about the Island. All I know is how right this is. I want this. I've wanted this since I was fourteen, since I first felt him watching me.

But when we break apart, I realize how much damage this could do to my relationship. I cheated on Ace. Even if he forgave me, I would never forgive myself. I spent 543 years hating Jacob for what I thought he did. But now I'm standing at the front of the cliff, with my arms wrapped around my fiancé's best friend, after I made out with him. I pull all the way away from him, jumping back.

I can't believe I did this. I can't believe I hurt Ace like this.

"I—"

"Jacob, come with me if you want to find out what happened." I hear a woman's voice float through the air. When I look behind me, there is a woman with a long white nightgown and brown hair.

"Mother?" he whispers.

"Yes, my little angel. Follow me."

Tyler

1556

Another black eye that needed no explanation. Father
had been drinking again. Mother would not stop him. She
was too afraid. How could someone blame her? I would
rather Father took it out on me than her. I hated it when he
hurt her.

I kept telling her we should run, but she would not hear
it. She could not fathom the idea of running from the man
she swore to love unconditionally. She could not see what it
was doing to me. She could not see that what he was doing
was wrong.

Even though Father beat my older brother, Tyler, almost
to death, Mother refused to see that he was wrong. It
happened when I was eight; Tyler was ten. I remembered
running into his room, screaming at Father to stop. He did,
long enough to toss me aside like a bug.

When he finally left Tyler, he was almost dead. His
breathing was so shallow I could barely here it, but he took
my hand and told me it was all going to be okay. His exact

words were, "Joseph, it is all right. I am not afraid. I know everything will work out the way it was meant to."

The next day, he was gone. I always figured that Father took him out and buried him in the backyard. He told Mother that Tyler ran away and that it was her fault he did it, then he beat her and she took it. I always hoped that he really did run away, so that one day, I would see him again. I knew it was foolish of me, but he was my brother.

That was eight years ago, and still, Father was a monster that destroyed everything in his path. He did not care who he hurt; he did not care about anything but his precious bottle. If anyone stood in the way of that . . .

Today I told him I thought he had a few too many drinks. I thought he was going to smash his bottle over my head. Instead he punched me in the face and told me, "You ought ta learn your place, boy. No son a mine be tellin' me I had too much. I had just 'nough." Then he punched me again.

I had to leave. I needed to get out of this town, this country if I had to. I must leave, but I must convince Mother to leave with me. I would not leave without her. We must leave to survive. Father would not take much more of me. I was afraid I must find refuge far, far away from him.

***

"I must beg your pardon, miss. I did not see you there." I held my hand out to help the girl I just knocked over. I was so caught up in my thoughts. I was not paying much attention to where I was going. The next thing I knew I had bumped into someone, and they were knocked to the ground.

"It is quite all right, sir. I believe we both were not paying much attention." She stood and brushed off her dress.

When she looked up, I was struck for words. Her beauty is overpowering. She stood a foot below me. Her skin was pale, her hair is black, pulled away from her face, her eyes sparkling green. She stood in front of me smiling, her lips plump and pink.

"Sir, are you all right?" she asked after a minute.

"Yes, yes. I apologize, it is just . . ." I looked away shyly. "You are very beautiful."

She giggled. "I bet you say that to all the girls you bump into in the streets."

"I can assure you, you are the very first." I bowed. "Joseph, and you are?"

"Late. Maybe I will see you again, Joseph." She curtseyed and then disappeared into the crowd.

Who is that girl? I need to know her.

***

"You're late!" Father stumbled to the door as I walked in. He was about to swing at me; instead, he doubled over and vomited onto the floor. "Tula! Tula! Clean this up then get me another drink."

You have had way too much already. I rolled my eyes as he passed out into the fresh vomit he just tried to get rid of. I stepped over his sleeping body and walked to my room. We needed to get out of here. We could not stay with this monster anymore. I hoped Mother would be able to see that.

Upstairs, I walked into my room, the first door on the right. I walked three steps and collapsed onto my bed. My room was rather small. I had room for a wardrobe, bed, nightstand, desk, and chair. The wardrobe was on the right wall, pushed into the back corner. The bed was in the centre of the back wall with the nightstand on the left side. The desk and chair were pushed into the left corner of the front wall, right beside my window. There was almost no room to move around. Most of the time, I had to crawl over my bed to get something.

I grabbed the book off the nightstand, but before I got a chance to open it, Mother burst into my room. "How could you let him lay there like that?" she yelled.

"He tried to punch me, again. I was five minutes late. Does that earn me a beating?" I questioned dropping the book beside me.

"Does your father deserve to be left lying on the floor in a puddle of vomit?" she asked, ignoring my question as she always did when I ask her that.

"Yes, I believe he does."

The look on Mother's face was awful. She had the same look on her face that I had every time Father stumbled home after a long night of drinking. She looked like *I* was the bad guy, even after everything Father had done. She still looked at me like I was a horrible child. She thought that I should worship him just because he was my father, but I believed that no parent should be worshipped unless they deserved it. My father deserved nothing but awful things.

She did not say a word. She just turned around and walked out. I needed to leave. She would always take Father's side. I would not be able to save her; she would not let me.

* * *

"You again?" The unnamed girl from the street was here again. This time when I bumped into her, she stayed on her feet. "Are you following me?"

"I assure you I am not. Are you following me?"

"No, sir!"

"What are you doing out here this late at night? It is not safe. There are many bad people out and about tonight."

"I was supposed to see a friend, but I believe she stood me up." I saw an outline of the girl's figure looking around.

Tonight was very dark. The moon and the stars were hiding behind cloud. Sometimes our village officials would come around just before dark and light the oil lamps around the street, but tonight, I believed, they decided not to. Normally that was a sign, something would happen, something bad. The worst kind of people lurk in the cover of night fall.

"Allow me to walk you home. You never know what is lurking out there."

"How do I know you are not a 'lurker,' as you say?"

"You do not, but if you will take my word, I promise you that I am not."

"All right, I will allow you to walk me home." I could barely see her, but I thought she smiled, which made me smile.

"Will you allow me your name this time?" I asked holding my arm out for her to grab. She took it but said nothing. "All right, how about you tell me how you knew it was me? I could not even see you."

"I have really good vision."

"Why will you not tell me your name?"

"Because, in my culture, your name is sacred, only the people closest to you are supposed to know it."

I paused and turned to face her. Moonlight peeked through the clouds now. "So you will never tell me?"

"Maybe I will eventually." She smiled and turned away.

"Wait! I thought I was walking you home."

"I can assure you, I can take care of myself." With that, she disappeared into the darkness and I lost track of her.

1557

I needed to see her again. There was something about her that just made me need to see her. I should have left a long time ago. The beatings were getting worse, but this girl was keeping me here. I did not know why.

It was dark right now. The streets were basically empty. Tonight, the town officials had lit the lanterns so the criminals were staying away. I walked alone kicking the rock in front of me. I watched as it skipped three times and stopped, then skip three times and stopped. I kept watching it until it got lost under the dress of the woman in front of me.

"Sorry m—you? Are you sure you are not following me?"

The mystery girl was standing in front of me smiling. "I knew!"

"You knew what?"

"Nothing, do not mind." She giggled and started to walk off.

"Why do you keep doing this? Why will you not tell me your name? Why do you always run off without answering me? I am tired of this game!"

She did not turn back. I watched as she ran farther and farther, her black hair down and swishing back and forth as she went. *I need to know her. I will know her.*

* * *

The lights were out again. I should be home by now, but I still could not face them. Mother still could not see that he was a monster; she could not see that he ruined everything he touched. In her eyes, I was the bad son, and I needed to be taught my place. The only one that needed teaching was Father. I hoped someone at a nearby tavern would teach him a lesson the next time he tried to start a fight. I hoped they taught him so well that he never, ever returned home.

I walked along the empty streets. There was moonlight tonight, so I could see down the road. I loved walking at night. Everything was so quiet. The chaos of the day had come to an end, and the peace of the night was all that remains.

I knew that night was when bad people come out to do bad things, but that did not make the night bad. These people took advantage of its darkness, but the night was not always dark. Like tonight, the moon was high in the sky shinning its light over the town.

A scream broke me out of my admiration. It came from the alley I had just passed.

Keep walking. Do not get yourself into unnecessary trouble.

Ignoring the voice inside my head, I turned around. When I looked down the alley, I saw a girl. She was lying on her back with a huge man on top of her. He had one hand over her mouth and the other ripping open her dress. She was flailing around trying to hit the man on her, with no effect.

"Hey!" I yelled running up the alley. When I got close, I realized, it was not just a girl; it was her, my mystery girl.

The man looked over. "Get lost, kid."

"Get off her first."

The man looked me up and down then laughed. "What are you going to do about it?"

I knew I did not look scary. The man kneeling over my mystery girl was twice my size, muscle wise, but he was about my height. He could probably throw me into the next town without breaking a sweat. But at least he would be paying attention to me and not her.

I took a deep breath and rolled my shoulders. "This." I threw myself forward without thinking. I knocked the man off her and jumped to my feet. He tried to take a swing, but I jumped back. Another swing and I ducked.

Fighting was like a good dance, one person led and the other followed. The leader always got tired first. I had spent most of my life dodging punches. All I had to do was tier him out enough that I could run. This was the one situation where I was glad Father beat me. If this man hit me, at least I knew I could take a punch.

I let him back me onto a wall. This time when I ducked, his fist landed on a brick wall. He let out a cry of pain. This was my chance. I flew past him and grabbed the girl's hand before running out of the alleyway. We kept running until we could not go any longer. By then, we had long since lost the big man.

"Thank you, thank you so much." She threw her arms around me.

When she pulled away, I could see the damage he had done. Her light pink dress was ripped in four different places, with spots of blood staining the front. Her under dressing was pulled out, so the four holes reveal skin. She had dry tearstains on her cheeks, and her hair was half up, half clinging to her. There was a cut on her eyebrow, and her lip was bleeding.

I removed my jacket and gave it to her. "Here, you look cold."

With shaky hands, she took it and wrapped it around her like a blanket. "Thank you." She turned to walk away.

"Wait, this time, please allow me to walk you all the way home."

She nodded. "I would like that very much."

I held out my arm for her to take. "Lead the way." This time I did not push her to tell me her name, but she finally did.

"Azaline. My name is Azaline."

I smiled at her. "Well, Azaline, it is a pleasure to finally make your acquaintance."

***

Azaline. I loved her name. I could not get it out of my head.

I had not seen her since I walked her home after the incident. It had been about three weeks and I was dying to see her again. She was the only reason I was still here. Father had been getting worse and I should be long gone but I could not leave without saying goodbye. I could not leave without seeing her one more time.

I had been wandering around the dark streets for weeks, hoping that she would be out. I had yet to have any luck. Wherever she was, she was not coming out. I did not blame her, either. If I was her, and that happened to me, I would not wander about after dark.

Tonight was the same as all the other nights. I sat on a bench on the street we first met, and I waited awhile. When she did not show up, I would move on to wandering the park, then the streets around her house, and every place we had ever run into each other.

My time at the bench was coming to an end when I saw a figure moving toward me. It was too dark to make out, but it looked like a woman. Could it be her? I did not stand up. I waited until I could see a face. "Azaline." I smiled. It was her.

"How long have you been here?" she asked, smiling back.

"Not long," I lie.

"I know you are lying." She giggled. "Come, let us walk. I have not been able to get out of my house until now."

I stood and offered my arm. She took it, and we walked. I led her toward the park. "How are you doing?"

"I am just fine, thank you for asking. I have been thinking about you a lot. I really wanted to thank you for saving me, but I have not been able to find the right words."

"What was wrong with those words? Just the fact that you thought about me was quite enough. I am honoured."

"You are rather strange. I like it."

"I like you." I stopped walking and turned to face her.

"I like you as well." I leaned down toward her. She met me halfway. *I have been dying to do this since the day I met you.*

"Me too," she said with a smile. I thought I said that in my head, but I guess not.

1558

"You cannot go out tonight. Father will be out late, and he expects you to help me with dinner. He wants it on the table by the time he gets back." Mother still did not understand. Father was a drunken fool that deserved nothing, not a dinner on the table after a whole night of drinking and especially not her.

"I do not care what he wants. Azaline and I have had these plans for weeks now, plans that I have told you about, *a lot*. You cannot make me help you because I refuse to help him. I am leaving now. Goodbye, Mother."

"You will regret this!" she yelled as I walked out the door.

"The only thing I regret is not doing this sooner," I yelled over my shoulder, closing the door behind me.

Halfway down the street, I bumped into Azaline. "A year and a half later, and you still want to bump into me." She laughed.

"I am so sorry. There is so much in my brain I sometimes do not pay attention." I held out my hand to her. "Shall we get going?"

"I would like that every much." She smiled. I love her smile; it lit up her face even on the darkest of nights.

"I have set up everything. I hope you like it."

"If it is with you, I will love it, like I always do."

I led her to the park. In the centre of the grass, I had a blanket and a basket. I asked favours from many of my friends, and it worked. I got them to play for us. When we stepped on the grass, the music started. "I hope you enjoy the music."

"I love it."

Her smile was wide. She had her hair down, coming to a stop at her midback. Her dress was light blue and dragging along the ground; it highlighted her eyes. She was the most beautiful thing I had ever seen in my life.

I love you.

"I love you too."

"I . . . I did not realise I said that out loud."

"You did n—" she shook her head and giggled. "Well, it happens to the best of us. Shall we eat?"

"I thought you would never ask."

So we ate. My friends played their music throughout the whole dinner. After we finished, she asked if we could go somewhere alone. I suggested a walk, but she had something else planned. She took me back to her home, where we were all alone. I was not expecting her to open up to me so quickly. I was not expecting our amazing night together. I loved her so much words could not even put it into perspective. She was so amazing. She was the most perfect woman I had ever met.

***

The door opened as I approached Azaline's home. I expected to see her—she always knew when I was there, even if we had no plans to meet—but instead I was met by her father. I did not believe that he liked me. Every time I saw him, he had his arms crossed with a disapproving look on his face. Today was no different, except that he was standing in front of the door.

"I don't want you around anymore. I want you to stay away from my daughter."

"Sir, what—"

"Don't come back." He turned around and slammed the door.

What could I have possibly done?

I stood there, in front of her house, staring, hoping to catch a glimmer of Azaline. I saw her face pop up on the glass, only for a second. She had fresh tears in her eyes. This was not what she wanted. Her father just did not like me, and because of that, I would never get to see her again.

She took a breath, leaving fog on the glass. With a shaking finger, she traced the number eight. She wiped it away and moved from the window.

"I will see you then, my love. Eight at the park," I whispered as I walked away.

***

"We need to get rid of him. They are offering good money, if we give him to them. This could solve everything." Father was trying to corrupt Mother. He wanted me gone, and he was going to sell me. To whom? I had no idea, but I was getting out of here. At eight, I was going to ask Azaline to marry me so we could run away together.

I snuck quietly back to my room, cracked open the window, and headed out. There were vines growing up the side of my house, so I used those to climb down. The sun had not yet set—the mid-August sun normally set just after eight—so I had to move quickly in case they decided to check on me. It took about ten minutes, at a steady pace, to get to the park.

There were still people walking around, so I blended in. If my parents came looking for me, it would not be too hard to escape them. I moved to the other side of the grass, toward the hill. If I needed an escape, the trees would cover me. I watched all the people once I was seated at the top of the hill.

Everyone looked so happy. There were children laughing and playing catch. Their parents were watching them as they walked around chatting. I could not wait for that to be me. I loved children, and I wanted so desperately to a better father than my own. I hoped, one day, to be one of the fathers here, watching my children as they enjoyed life. My children would never know the abuse I was exposed to. Never.

"Joseph?" I heard from behind me.

"Azaline." I stood up and turned around, a smile plastered on my face. I was free of my parents now. I had nothing keeping me from running away and spending my life with the woman I love. I did not think anything could take this smile off my face, but as soon as I saw the look on Azaline's, the smile dropped and I was not sure anything would bring it back.

"I am so sorry about my father. I should never have told him. I should have kept it to myself. I have to tell you something." She was crying. Her eyes were puffy and red.

"Wait. Before you do, I must tell you something. My parents intend to give me up. I overheard them talking about selling me to someone. I have no idea who they were talking about, but whoever it is, cannot be good. I know your father does not like me much, but all I have ever wanted is someone like you." I got down on one knee. "I have no ring. In fact, I have nothing, but all I need is you. Azaline, will you please marry me? Will you please run away with me?"

"Joseph, I cannot. I have a life here, I have friends. My father would die if he lost me. I could not live with myself if I left. Please understand. I never wanted to hurt you and I do love you, but I cannot do this. I cannot leave."

She pulled her hand out of mine and walked away. I let her walk away. I let her leave me, kneeling there, crying like an idiot. How could I let myself believe someone like her could have loved me? How could I have been such a fool? I wiped my eyes and stood.

She left without telling me what she thought she had to. I should have let her speak first. She was probably going to end us. I probably could have saved myself the humiliation. I wished I had never bumped into her. I wished I was never born.

"Joseph! Where have you been? Your father and I have been looking for you everywhere!"

"Sorry, Mother, I was out for a walk. Let us get this over with. To whom am I being sold to? I am ready to go. I am ready to leave you and Father."

She did not try to tell me I was mistaken. She led me away from the park. We headed to the very edge of town, to the docks. I was being sold to pirates. *Great. This day cannot get any worse.*

* * *

"Welcome to the crew, boy," the captain said. He was leaning on the wheel in front of me. Mother and Father left me on the ship and collected their money. I would never see them again, and I did not care. I would never see any of my town's people again.

"When can I start?" I wanted to forget as soon as possible.

"We got an egger one, boys!" The crew laughed. "In ten years, the next time we port. Until then, Hunt, show 'em the quarters."

Ten years? There is no way that we would sail around for ten years before we port next.

A boy, Hunt, I assumed, waved me to follow him. I followed him down a staircase. They had a nice ship, very big. Most pirate ships that I had seen were small; they could not have fit more than thirty people. This one, I was guessing, could fit eighty, easily.

"Admiring the ship?" Hunt asked.

"It is nice."

"Well, better get used to it. You're gonna be on it a long, long time, mate. Round here, we don't age. Guess how old I am."

"Seventeen, eighteen?" *What is he talking about?*

"Sixty-eight. Where we're goin' no one grows old. Don't believe me? That fine, you will. This is your room, you'll be livin' with me for a long time, get comfortable." With that, he left and I was alone.

"You're not alone. I'm right here."

I jumped up, compressing a scream. "Who are you?"

"Pan. I'm here to rescue you unless you want to be a pirate for the rest of time. You are?"

I did not think about it. I did not want to be myself anymore. "Tyler. I have nothing left, to rescue me would be torture." I looked down at my feet. I was tired of this life.

"I'm not taking you back there. I live on an island where you will be free to do whatever you please. There are ten of us, you would make eleven. If you choose to stay here, I won't stop you, but this life is not one you want. Trust me."

"Take me there."

Pan smiled. "Will do."

* * *

"Guys, this is Tyler." The four boys sitting around a fire waved. "Come on out, girls, say hello."

"Hey," a girl with long dark brown hair said appearing in front of me. She looked familiar. She had the same face as someone, but I could not place it.

"What she said," two other girls said appearing beside the first one.

I just stared at the first girl. Why did she look so familiar? Why could I not place her face? "Yes, we wear boy clothes, get over it." She rolled her eyes and walked over to the fire. The blonde one followed her.

"Don't mind them. We just get the staring a lot, and I think she's getting sick of it. But can you blame us for this? I mean dresses are so uncomfortable," the other brown-haired girl said.

"Yeah!" the first girl waved her hand.

I blinked, and I was dressed up in a pure white wedding dress, fully equipped with corset and veil. Everyone burst out laughing, even me.

"I will have you know. I was not staring because of your clothes. I was staring because you are very beautiful."

"AWE!" the three of them yelled.

"That is so damn cute! Zylan get him out of that dress!" It was gone. Zylan. That was a strange name, kind of like Azaline . . .

"Damn, we got a smooth one on the loose," a blonde-haired boy said with a laugh.

"Don't make fun of him. He's going to be the only one gettin' any. You guys are boring," the blonde-haired girl said. Zylan and the other girl burst out laughing then the three of them disappeared.

"What does she mean 'gettin' any'?" I asked.

"Something you've never done before," a black-haired boy said. All the boys laughed.

***

"Please do not put me in another dress," I said after bumping into Zylan. "I am sorry." I offer my hand to help her up.

It had been a week since I arrived on the Island. I walked around the forest for most of the day trying to learn where everything was so I wouldn't get lost. It was just after sunset when I walked through a patch of trees right into Zylan. It reminded me of my first encounter with Azaline.

She chuckled. "I accept your apology. But it seems like I owe you an apology as well. I shouldn't have put you in that dress. It was childish of me. I promise it won't happen again." She accepted my out stretched hand and stood.

"Thank you. You are correct about the comfort of dresses. I would not wish to wear them either." I smiled. "What are doing out so late?"

"I could ask you the same question. I've always loved the nighttime. I come to this clearing to watch the stars as much as I can."

I looked up at the sky. It was very beautiful here. I could see why she would like this spot. "I am trying to learn the forest as best I can. It is very confusing here. I can see why you like this spot, not a lot of the clearings have an opening like this one. I used to love watching the stars back home."

"Care to join me? I wouldn't mind the company." She smiled. She had a beautiful smile, a familiar smile.

"I would very much enjoy that."

"Good." Her smile widened as she flicked her wrist. A blanket appeared on the ground at our feet.

"Could you teach me that?"

"I could. Would you mind waiting till tomorrow? The stars are calling me." She laid down on the blanket.

"Tomorrow sounds perfect." I smiled and lay down beside her.

We talked most of the night. There was never an awkward or silent moment. I had never spoken to someone like this, not even Azaline. Zylan was amazing. She was funny and outgoing. She was different and I loved it.

"It's getting late. Would you like me to take you back to camp?" she asked.

I did not, but I figured she must have been tired. "Would you mind?"

"Not at all." She smiled and took my hand. I never wanted to let it go; it felt so right. A second later, I was standing outside my camp, and I hesitated letting go of her hand when she did not drop mine.

"We should do that again," I said as I found the willpower to let go.

"How about next week? Same time, same place."

"That sounds perfect to me." I walked back into camp with a smile that lasted all night.

Chapter 12

More Questions Than Answers

Clover

The two pirates push me forward with the tip of their swords poking into my back. They walk me through the camp. I have to step over dead bodies as I go, mostly pirates but a few of us. The fighting stopped almost as soon as the pirates trapped me, so I walk in silence. I step over Trixie and Azalea, then Phoenix and Quincy. I count nine of us dead in total. Wide, blank eyes, white skin, blood still pouring out freshly cut wounds. The rest of us are being tied to trees. Some are seriously injured—they're being left lying on the ground—while others have only a few scratches.

I see Elena being pushed out of camp kicking and screaming some nasty words at the guy doing the pushing. She has one pirate in front of her and another holding a sword to her neck. Ten seconds later, Hunter comes running from the other side of camp with his sword above his head. Stupid! First thing you learn about sword fighting is never, ever, leave yourself open for an attack like that.

The guy holding Elena turns just enough to block the attack to his head and drive his heel into her knee. She cries out in pain before getting grabbed by the pirate in front of her. Now she's being held the same way but facing the fight.

The first pirate swings his sword around pushing Hunter's sword toward the ground. They both step back to regroup. Then Hunter makes another mistake and attacks first, aiming to the pirate's left side. The pirate blocks, flicking his wrist quickly, causing Hunter to lose his sword. Dumbass.

He takes a step back putting his hands up in fighting position. The pirate smirks like he thinks he won, but Hunter's a lot better with his hands—or at least that's the rumour, I wouldn't know. The pirate strikes to his left, but he ducks moving around the pirate, right in front of Elena. The pirate standing behind her take the sword away from her neck for a split second using the hilt to whack Hunter on the back of the head.

Elena tries to warn him, but it's too late. He lands face-first in the dirt and doesn't get up. She tries to break free of the pirate's grip, launching herself forward to Hunter's side, but she ends up getting cut slightly by the blade instead. Then she gets a nice whack on the head as well, and the two pirates grab hold of each arm and drag her unconscious body out of camp.

"What are you going to do to her?" I ask.

"Nothing you need to concern yourself with, love," the hook-handed pirate says. "Now walk faster." He pushes his sword into my back a little more, not enough to break the skin but enough to cause me to flinch.

"Or what? You gonna kill me? Go for it, then you won't find Ace, and all your pirates died for no reason. Fuck you, I'll walk however slow I want to walk."

He makes a weird sound, almost like a growl before releasing the pressure on my back. *Damn fucking right you piece of shit.* About five minutes into the walk, I realize that I should probably pick up the pace. I mean, I really don't want to be alone with these guys for longer than I have to, plus Justin and Ace can definitely take these two—or at least Ratman. I think that's what he's called anyways. I mean it makes sense; he kind of has a rat face. His hair is flying up in all different directions. His eyebrows are pretty bushy, his eyes have a slight squint, and his face is chubby, like he has cheese stuffed in his cheeks.

As we walk, I feel my heart pounding. I wouldn't be surprised if they heard it. I don't know why it was beating so fast. I wasn't scared. I wasn't pushing myself. I wasn't doing anything that would require my heart to beat this fast.

I was right about someone hearing it though. Well, something at least. Whenever I'm in distress or my heartbeat is faster than normal, James comes out of nowhere.

Now, he comes tearing through the trees and jumps at Hook. He doesn't even look fazed. He tosses his sword to Ratman before taking on Jamie. The fight doesn't last very long. I wish I could say it went in my favour, but it looks like Hook Hand has fought a few large wolves in his time. I can't see what he does because Jamie is on top of him, but after a minute, he falls on his side with a whimper.

"Thank you for trying," I whisper under my breath as the pirates push me to keep moving. He opens his eyes and tries to lift his head. He looks at me with such sad eyes. I just want to run back to him and curl up next to him. He was just trying to protect me, and now I don't even know if he's going to live. When this was all over, I want to find him and thank him, properly.

When I told Justin to distract Ace, he said he would keep him in the tree house, so that's where I lead the pirates. I make sure to step on a branch as we approach the entrance. The pirates think nothing of it, but I know Ace heard it. He's always alert and ready for battle, no matter how unlikely an attack was to happen.

Sure enough, we don't make it to the entrance. Ace comes charging out of the door at the foot of the tree, followed by Justin. Somehow, I end up on the ground while the fight breaks out. I take this opportunity to get out the restraints holding my wrists together. I watch Justin get a few shots on Ratman but receive some as well. He has a gash on his left arm, a scratch on his right cheek, and a cut on his right leg. He doesn't flinch though; he fights through it. Just as he is about to disarm the pirate, Hook Hand brings his sword down on his back. Justin's eyes go wide and he falls to his knees. Then he falls all the way to the ground, just like Hunter did.

"No!" I scream running toward him. I drop to my knees beside him and roll him over, resting his head on my lap.

He smiles at me, a little bit of blood dripping down the side of his mouth. "Hey, don't cry. I'm okay, I'll be fine." He reaches up to wipe the tears off my cheeks. "Don't worry about me. I refuse to die before our wedding." He tries to laugh but ends up coughing up blood.

I smile through the tears. "I refuse to let you die before our wedding. I waited my whole life for this, 540 years. I'm not letting you get off this easy."

He smiles again. "I love you."

"I love you too." I kiss his forehead, before his head rolls to the left.

Pan

I follow Mother up to the top of the cliff. She stands on the edge looking out over the horizon. She looks just like the last time I saw her. Her skin is slightly tanned, green eyes sparkling, light brown hair falling down to her midback. I stand back a little bit and wait for her to say something. But she just stands there for a few minutes. Zylan is standing beside me with her arms crossed, tapping her foot. I don't blame her. If this had nothing to do with me, I'd be doing the same thing.

Finally, Mother takes a deep breath and turns to face us. "I'm sure you have a lot of questions, but I'm not sure I can answer all of them. What I can tell you is what really happened that night you ended up in Neverland." Another deep breath. "When I was younger, I . . . did some pretty stupid things. One of them was really bad. I ended up being haunted some pretty bad things. But then, when I met your father and had you, boys, I figured out a way to banish the presence so I could raise you both.

"Everything was so prefect until I got sick. I hadn't told your father what I did, so he had no idea what I was doing . . . The sicker I got, the worse the presence was. After a few months, it became strong enough to possess your father."

"What does this have to do with him ending up in Neverland? Your back story is of little interest to me, and by the look on his face, him too." I turn to look at Zylan, who looks as annoyed as she sounds. But she's right, all I really want to know is how I got here in the first place.

"I was getting there . . . Anyways, the night you and Peter planned to escape, the night I died, the presence was particularly agitated and lost control. The last thing you remember before waking up was your father choking you out, yes?" I nod. "Well, it wasn't him. That's why you ended up in Neverland. You were killed by something supernatural, so you were sent to this place for a second chance.

"The reason Peter sent you away was because, by saving Zylan, you strayed from the path. The way to your second chance. Peter didn't want to mess up his own, but at the same time didn't want you to die, so he sent you to Neverland's mirror."

"Why didn't he just tell me? Why keep that a secret?"

"Either way you wouldn't have listened. It was foretold." She weakly smiles. "You, my angel, were destined for something different than your brother. You were destined for love, and he was destined for rebirth. I'm so sorry."

"What the fuck is that supposed to mean?" Zylan moves forward. "You're saying, you didn't tell him that he could have a second chance because some guy thousands of years ago spit out some crap about twins who died. One could live again, but the other chooses a girl. Not to mention, your dumbass is the one that got them killed in the first place. What kind of piece of shit mother are you? Don't you know that you're supposed to protect your children? Or did they not teach you that in asshole parent school?"

"I don't know who you think you are, but this isn't about you. This is between me and my son." The soft tone in Mother's voice has disappeared, and there is venom present behind her words. She looks almost as angry as she sounds. Her eyes are narrow and glaring at Zylan—like if she stares hard enough she'll burst into flames—her cheeks are red, and her jaw is clenched.

"No, she's right. I didn't deserve not knowing, and Peter and I didn't deserve to die because of *your* mistake. What was this prophecy that you didn't want to tell me?"

Mother's eyes start to well up with tears. She swallows and blinks them away. When she tries to say something, nothing comes out. She scrunches her nose in confusion but tries again. That doesn't work either. Her eyes go really wide before she drops to her knees and starts to draw something in the dirt. Then, in the blink of an eye, she disappears, leaving me speechless and confused for the second time today.

Zylan

Pan is standing frozen, mouth slightly open. I walk over to where she dropped to the ground. Written in the sand is HE'S COMI. I'm guessing she got cut off before she could finish with the NG, or she's a terrible parent and really stupid. I roll my eye. When I look up, Jacob still hasn't moved; I can't blame him. If that was me, I'd be traumatized not to mention that encounter must have really ruined his memory of his mother. I can definitely relate to that one right now.

I walk back over to him and put my hand on his shoulder. "Pan," I say softly. He still doesn't move. "Jacob? Are you okay?"

He blinks slowly and moves his eyes to look at me. "No."

I move in front of him, putting my hands on his cheeks. "Knowing this doesn't change anything. I'm so sorry I hated you all those years and blamed you for everything and never tried to figure out the truth. Thank you for saving my life, thank you for watching out for me, thank you for everything." I pull him toward me and give him a hug. He hugs me back, taking a deep breath. "Are you okay now?"

He chuckles slowly. "Not really, but I'm getting there. I'm glad you were here for this. I wouldn't have been able to do that alone." He pulls away and gives me a weak smile. "Come on, we should probably go find Wendy."

"You're probably right." I smile. "Thank you, for saving her all those years ago. I'm glad someone finally heard my prays after—" I stop short. I feel all the air in my lungs being sucked out. I hear the echoes of screams and swords clashing. I see fire clouding my vision. All I can smell is blood. Something's happening on the Island, something very bad. "We need to get back to the Island. Now."

"Zylan, I didn't tell you something. . . I don't know how to get back . . . It's a miracle I made it back last time and that took two weeks. . ."

"We don't have time for that." I grab his hand and picture my home with Ace.

When I open my eyes, I'm standing on the sand of the beach in front of the tree. He's not here. I don't know how I know but I do. I almost don't even look around, but something told me I should. Good thing I did.

"Jacob! It's Justin! He's bad we need to get him to the waterfall now."

Jacob runs over and picks him up, tossing him over his shoulder. "I've got him. You go back to camp and see what's going on over there."

Before I can argue, he's gone. I take a deep breath to collect myself before appearing back at camp. It's not camp anymore, it's a war zone. There are dead bodies everywhere, people missing limbs, people crying. I shouldn't have left. I never should have left.

"Zylan! Zylan we need your help!" Iris yells running over. She looks horrible. Her short blonde hair, normally well looked after, is knotted and flying in different directions. Her face has cuts and dirt everywhere. Her shirt is ripped open exposing a plain white bra also smudged with dirt. Her skirt is torn at the side—she probably did that herself, to give her more room to move.

"What happened?"

"We were attacked, a bunch of pirates. They killed nine of us and took eight that I know of. But no one's seen Ace, Justin, or Clover. It doesn't look good." She turns around and motions me to follow her.

"Who's the worst of the injured?"

"Eli's missing a leg, Edward lost a hand, Shawn's eye is gone, Delilah lost a few fingers, and there's no sign of Ivana, nose. Oh, and Finn, he's missing an arm, three toes, and a part of his shoulder. It doesn't look good for any of them, especially Finn."

"Who's looking after them?"

"Noel, she's over here." Iris leads me to the other side of the camp. She wasn't kidding. It doesn't look like any of them are going to make it. They probably wouldn't if it weren't for the waterfall.

"Move, I've got this." I step into view, and Noel whirls on me.

"To hell you do!" She screams. "Where the hell were you when the pirates attacked? Not here! You can't waltz in here and expect everyone to get out of your way!"

"I know I deserved that, and I know you're pissed, but if you don't get out of my way, they're all going to die, and unlike the last nine deaths, these six will be on you. You can yell at me all you want once everyone is fine. Until then, shut up and get the hell out of my way." As pissed as she might be right now, I know she doesn't want to listen, but at the same time she knows I'm right so she moves. "Thank you." I stand in the middle of the badly injured. "How many of you can reach me while I'm standing here?" Everyone. Perfect. "Don't move I'm going to help you guys." A second later, I'm standing in the pond part of the waterfall. The six of them float on their backs for a minute before they realize they've left camp.

"What the—" Finn starts until he realizes he has his arm, all his toes, and the missing piece of his other shoulder back. "Zylan, I don't know if I've ever told you this, but I love you, you are a goddess!"

"Agreed!" Shawn chimes in, poking at his eye making sure it's real. "How did you know this was here?"

"My guardian angel showed me a long time ago." I smile. "Okay, come on, cripples, let's get moving. You guys aren't the only injured people on the island."

***

Two hours later, we finally got everyone patched up and whole again. The next part was calming down the boys out for blood. Out of all of them Troy had the most reason to be angry, but he let the others lead the charge. And they did a pretty good job. By the end of it they had Pan on board for a raid. I was the one that talked them out of it. As much as I wanted to lead the attack myself, it was a bad idea. The waterfall healed everyone, but part of the process is sleep. But god forbid, I suggest that. Now everyone's screaming at each other, trying to get their point across but not listening to anyone else.

How did this happen? Five hundred and forty-three years I've been on this island and *nothing* has ever happened. Yes, we've had scrapes and bruises, but the reason half these people are here is because they almost died, myself included. This was supposed to be their second chance, saving grace, no one expected something like this.

"You're right. They should rest, but you know better than anyone they're not going to." Jacob joins me on the rock I'm sitting on.

"What do you mean I know better than anyone?"

"Oh please, you're telling me that the second they all fell asleep, you weren't going to try and raid the ship yourself?"

"Okay you caught me. Are you going to try and stop me?"

"No. I'm coming with you. This is all my fault, and I'm not going to lose anyone else, but at the same time I know I won't be able stop you."

"Good." I smile. "You're learning."

He chuckles. "So what are we going to do about them?"

"I don't know. Can't you just put them to sleep like you did with me?"

"It doesn't last very long . . . but I can."

"It's better than nothing."

"Okay, I'll take care of this, you get everything ready."

"You're not leaving without me," Justin walks up beside us. "Don't say I can't because Clover thinks I'm dead, and I will tell everyone what you're doing if you don't take me with you."

"Okay, fine, be ready to leave in five."

***

Five minutes later, Justin, Pan, and I are standing at the edge of the camp, weapons ready. "Zylan, I'm going to need your help to knock everyone out," Pan whispers. He looks tired. He's trying to hid it, but I see it. There are bags under his eye, his normally red cheeks, the colour of snow. He's drained, but he doesn't want to show it.

The camp is feeling pretty empty. With nine of us dead and ten of us missing, there's thirty-seven of us left. That means he has to knock thirty-four people out for at least four hours. It would be hard to do this even if he wasn't feeling weak. I shouldn't have pushed him to go back to Neverland. I should have given him time to recover.

"What do I have to do?" I keep my voice low. The thirty-four of them that are left are all sitting in the centre of camp, huddled around the fire, not saying a word. They're all scared, angry, and really sad. I should have protected them; they all came here for a second chance.

"Give me your hand." I do.

Pan closes his eyes. I feel tingly, like when my leg falls asleep and I try to wake it up. But unlike my sleeping leg, the tingling moves throughout my entire body. I can feel the power flowing through me. I can feel it as it flows through Pan too. It's like it hasn't even left me. I can see him picturing the thirty-four fall. After the third one falls in his head, they're all asleep.

"They're all asleep," I say. His eyes fly open, and his hand leaves mine, our connection breaking. I wonder if that's supposed to happen.

"But I was . . ." He shakes head, like the thoughts running through his head aren't important enough to bring up. "Okay, let's go."

"So what's the plan? We can't just poof onto the ship, so how do we get on?" Justin asks.

"We're going to 'poof' to the edge of the island. Then we will talk about a plan." Pan says, still unfocused.

***

"So let me get this straight. You want to walk to the ship, underwater . . ." Justin is standing with his mouth slightly open. He thinks that we're crazy.

"Yes, it's easy! All you have to do is relax. It's all going be fine, okay?" I try to calm him down. "I'll go first, then you, then Pan if you start freaking out, we'll just send you to the surface. Does that sound okay?"

"Yeah, okay, I'm trusting you guys. Please don't kill me, again."

I cringe. It's my fault he almost died. I should have never left the Island. I should have just left good enough alone.

Then we wouldn't have to rescue ten people, and nine of us wouldn't be dead. We would all be, mostly, happy and alive.

"Well, let's get on with it!" Pan exclaims.

I walk into the ice-cold water, taking a deep breath before it swallows me. The spell Pan and I are casting surrounds me like a bubble, well, a half bubble or a third of a bubble I guess. It'll be completed as soon as Pan's in the water. It allows us to stick to the sand, breathe, and see in front of us. Although a slow method of transportation, it's the most practical. The pirates can't see us coming or will they expect anyone to come from beneath them.

The ship is anchored about a hundred meters off the shore. The pressure from the water makes, what should be a two-minute walk, about ten. Once we get to the anchor, I wave Justin to grab hold. What we didn't tell him is that in order to get to the surface, we have to 'pop' the bubble. Once he has hold, Pan and I release the spell, and he floats up to the top—okay, more like flails to the top, but he gets there just the same.

"Thank you so very much for your warning. It was very kind of you," Justin hisses as soon as our heads come above the water.

"Yell at us later, we have people to save," I say, studying the boat.

It's been in the water so long, it's a wonder how the thing floats. It's so worn down with algae stuck to the ship wall almost all the way up. It will be way too slippery to climb, even with all the cracks in it. I grab hold of the anchor chain and pull myself out of the water. Justin and Pan wait until I'm at the top before following.

"Ladies first," Pan says sarcastically.

"Then you should go first."

"You both should have gone first, hurry up!" I whisper, crouched on the edge of the gap.

I can sense Justin and Pan glare at me before Justin finally grabs the chain and pulls himself up. "That was rude," he whispers once he's at the top.

"And here I was, thinking we lived in a time where women are equal." I turn away from him and crawl into the ship. There are two pirates sitting at a table bickering. They're supposed to be guarding the gap. Lucky for me, they're so caught up in conversation; they don't even see me. I jump down from the ledge, silently, and tiptoe over to the "guards." All it takes is one smack of their heads together, and they're out like a light.

Pan and Justin walk in as I'm collecting the weapons. "Not bad, for a lady eh?" I shoot them a dirty look.

"I—"

"Shut up, let's go." I turn toward the empty staircase. Time to find our people.

***

I stop Justin and Pan at the top of the stairs leading to the bilge. That's Pan's best guess as to where they'll be held, considering how many people he's rescued from the cells of the ship. He swears they won't use them until they're weaker. I hope he's right. No one deserves that. Absolutely no one. "I'll go see if they're there. Wait here and stand guard." Justin looks like he wants to object. I don't blame him. I want to see Ace just as bad as he wants to see Clover, but he knows this is a better idea.

"Hurry please," he says.

Hunter

1508

"Elena, run!" I yelled pushing her away. This was the last time I was going to see her. The last time I was going to see her beautiful long brown hair. The last time I was going to watch her move gracefully along the ground like she was a cheetah. The last time I would see her smile was when I gave her that ring. I closed my eyes and faced the pirates again.

"Ain't that a beautiful sight, mates! 'e's cryin'!" The leader laughed. "Take 'em aboard. We're gonna 'ave fun with 'em. And find his girl, we can't 'ave 'er ruinin' 'r fun t'night."

The first two pirates, behind the leader, walked toward me. They were smiling, revealing rotten teeth, some wooden. They had their swords forward. I could try and fight, but there was no point. They would just kill me instead of taking me hostage. Maybe then I could have a chance to escape and get back to her. I could get back to my Elena.

I didn't struggle. I let them pull me on board without a fight. *I'll find you again, my love. I promise I will see you again.*

***

The pirates locked me in the cell before making their way to the village with the rest of the crew. They haven't caught Elena yet; I could feel it in my soul. She was going to be okay, and I was going to find her, if not in this life then the next.

I was on the bottom deck at the back. There were two cells side by side.

I should have taken Mother's advice. I should have waited. But I wanted it to be our anniversary. I wanted it to be at the place we met. I should have just waited . . . I shouldn't have made it so difficult.

I needed to find a way out. I needed to find Elena. There was a leak, which meant there was a hole. I just had to find it, and I could get out. It would work. I knew it would.

I looked for where the water was deepest, that was the most likely spot for the hole. Unfortunately, the water looked evenly flat, in this cell. The other cell on the other hand, was drowning in water. That was probably why they put me in this one. I couldn't get out. I would be stuck here until I died. I wouldn't make it out.

1518

Ten years and I hadn't aged a day. Ten years I'd been on this ship. Ten years I'd been alone. Apparently, we got to leave today. Hook said they got a letter saying they could only leave every ten years. Why? I had no clue, but this had been going on since 1468. All they needed was treasure, and they were free. Every ten years, until we find the treasure, we would get one night on earth to do whatever we wanted.

Well, not we yet. They still thought I would try and run away, so Hook would be keeping a close eye on me while the crew went loose. Even if I could escape . . . it had been ten years. Elena had probably forgotten me. She was probably married to someone else. She probably had kids by now. I had nothing to go back to. What was the point?

Next time we land, they would let me off. Next time, I would be free to move on like she probably had. Next time, I could forget.

A bell rung through the whole ship. That had never happened before. I was sitting in my quarters. Should I go see what was going on?

"Someone snuck on board, come on let's go!" Mark, another boy about my age—well, he looked about eighteen as well—exclaimed running into our room. Everyone had a bunk mate; mine was really annoying, that was probably why he was mine.

"I'm comin', I'm comin'."

                                            ***

"I found 'em lurkin' at the gap. Though 'e could look 'round an' leave," Tommy said to Cap'ain.

The boy was kneeling in front of him looking up. I remembered being in his place with no hope of ever getting out. I swallowed and pushed the thought aside. I couldn't think of the past. I had to think about now.

"Lock 'em up. Ware 'em down."

I walked forward and pulled him to his feet. My crew watched the boy as I dragged him to the bulge.

After a five-minute walk, we made it to the cells. I shuddered slightly as I push the boy into the cell and locked the door. Ten years ago, that was me. I turned to leave. "Wait! How long have you been here?"

"Ten years today," I said over my shoulder.

"How old were you? Seven? Eight?"

"Eighteen, you can't grow old where we're going. No one grows old where we're going."

"That's impossible! What are you talking about?"

I walked back to the cell. "I thought it was impossible too. But here I am, twenty-eight, still lookin' eighteen. Captain says they've been sailin' 'round an island for the last fifty years waitin' to get their treasure. We only sail out every ten years, meaning I was at the wrong place at the wrong time . . ." Elena running away from the docks flashed through my brain. I blinked and shook it off. "'Nough 'bout me. Get comfy, newbie, you're in for a long life." I started walking off again.

"Wait! What's your name?"

"Tyler."

"What happened to you? Why are you like this?"

"I lost my world, and I'm never getting her back."

***

Mark wanted to go with me to see the new guy, but Cap'ain wouldn't let him. He snuck down after me. Good thing too because new guy escaped right after. Hook thought he did it. Good for me, not so much for him. Actually, really good for me, I no longer had an annoying roommate. I had the place all to myself.

If Mark hadn't been so curious, I would be the one that walked the plank. I'd be the one that was shark food. Maybe I should have taken the fall, but I kind of want to keep living. I could feel that Elena was still alive. I just wanted to see her one more time, even if she didn't remember me, even if it was from a distance.

1528

They were letting me go today. I had to go under supervision, but I could go. I didn't know what I was going to do . . . probably get drunk and try to forget. By the time we landed in England again, she would probably be long dead so I had to get over this soon. I couldn't do it anymore. I couldn't.

"Cheer up, man! There are lotsa girls that would kill to get a piece a ya," Jamie said.

"It's not 'bout 'em. Just wanna forget, you know?"

"These girls'll help ya. Trust me. Happy huntin'."

With that the boardwalk went down and we were off to create chaos. 'Bout damn time too. Time to forget.

***

The local pub was full of drunken men and woman. It was loud and rowdy. My crew was hitting on the really drunk girls who still wouldn't go for them. It was fun to watch. I sat at the back table, staying out of the way and laughing.

The girl at the bar kept bringing me drinks. I didn't want to keep drinking them, but I couldn't stop myself. The more I drunk, the more I wanted to show up my crewmates. I wanted to show them how easy it would be for me to get a girl. I wanted to be a part of the crew. I was tired of being the "newbie."

I stood up and walked over to Rich. He did pretty good for himself. He wasn't an ugly guy, like most of the crew on the ship. In fact, he had a girl on his lap now. "Aye! 'ere 'e is! We were just talkin' 'bout ya. Cordelia, this be our handsome new member, perfect for your sister." His grin deepened turning to a smirk.

"You're right! He's very handsome. Elena! Come here."

My heart stopped. I couldn't do this, it was still too soon. I wasn't ready to move on.

"Cordie, I told you not to try and set me up with one of your drunk pi—oh, hello. I'm Elisa." The girl smiled at me. I thought her sister said Elena . . . I was clearly not over it.

"I'm Tyler." I smiled back at her.

"What's a handsome guy like you doin' in a place like this?" she asked with a giggle. She was beautiful. She had long black hair, bright green eyes, and pale skin. Her dress was a deep red, dragging along the floor.

"Lookin' for a beautiful girl such as yourself to spend some time with."

Elisa blushed. "Well, I'm not one for hanging out with pirates. You have to make it worth my while."

So that was exactly what I did. We snuck off, had a good time, and while she was sleeping, I took off back to the ship, never to see her again.

Did I feel bad? No. I forgot about Elena. It was just for a little while, but I still forgot. For one time in the last twenty years, I didn't miss her. I didn't think about her, nothing. I had a good time with someone I'd never see again. I was starting to like this pirate thing. Maybe next time, I could get a few more.

1568

One more week till we leave the island. One more week until I forget about Elena again. She'd been slipping farther and farther away with every dock. So far, every time we land, I got double the girls as last time. 1528, one. 1538, two. 1548, four. 1558, eight.

I doubt very much that I would get sixteen this time, and even if I did, I doubt very much that I'd be able to . . . deliver. Eight was hard, sixteen? Not happening. But it was still a good time.

The guys started calling me Hunter. I think I liked it. It worked, I do hunt. I think I was going to hold on to it.

I was sitting on the wall of the ship. I liked to come up here sometimes. I liked to look at the island we sail around. It was beautiful. I hoped that one day I'd be able to step foot on it.

I didn't understand why we couldn't just dock and live there. I mean we circle it, so why couldn't we just dock on it? I asked once. Hook was very, very unhappy with me . . . he threw a letter in my face and told me to get out of his sight. The letter said:

Dear pirate,

Hello, I bet you're wondering why you're trapped sailing around this island. Well, the answer to that is my brother. Well, you too, but mostly him. You attacked a village where the girl he loved lived. He decided to save her life instead of sticking to the plan. If you hadn't attacked, I would still have my brother and the girl would be long dead, so really I guess it is your fault.

Anyways, I write to you now to explain how to escape. Every ten years, the island you circle will touch down on earth and you will be able to search for your treasure. Once you have it, you will be free to, once again, bring chaos.

Also, in case you're wondering, you won't be able to get into the island, not while my brother and that stupid girl are there. If they ever leave, that will be your one shot to land.

Much love,
Your Curser.

Clearly the guy who wrote that was messed up . . . if I was his brother, I would leave too. So while the people living on the island got dry land, we got to sail, lost forever.

This place taunted me. I could jump ship and swim to land, but I wouldn't be able to stay. I wouldn't even be able to touch it. So I was stuck looking at it from a distance. Sometimes, I saw people come to the edge. They sat on the sand and looked out onto the water. Sometimes they even went for a swim. But me? I just had to watch, just like I was now.

Cap'ain decided to anchor today, so I'd been staring at the beach for almost two hours. No one had come out yet, but I hoped they did. I liked to see people that looked my age; no one here did. Cap'ain looked about twenty-five, thirty at most, but the rest look like they were in their forties or fifties. Mark was as close as it got to my age, but he was long dead, and those kids from 1518 and last time were close too but they got out and I didn't. Maybe next time we could get a new kid; that would be great.

I was about to get up and go below deck when I saw *her*. It was Elena, standing on the beach with two girls. I knew it was her. I could never forget her face. I could never forget the way she stood, the way she laughed, the way she smiled. I knew it was her. I knew I would see her again.

I stood up, grabbing the rope latter beside me. I used it to keep me balanced as I try to get a closer look.

"Hunt, man, what're you doin'? You're gonna fall, come down." It was Tommy's hand on my shoulder.

"It's her. I know it is."

"Hunt, come down. I can't see."

I jumped down and looked at him. "It's her I know—" when I looked back no one was there. "But I swear I saw her! She was . . . right . . ." I sighed. I thought I was over it. I guess sixteen might be a good plan next week.

1698

One hundred and ninety years today. We were due to touch down in about ten minutes. I couldn't wait to feel my feet hit land. I just wanted off this ship and freedom into the world. I hoped we found this damn treasure soon. I couldn't handle much more of this sailing thing.

The guys were killing me. I didn't know how much longer I could go without trying to jump ship. I wanted out. I wanted off. I wanted freedom. I'd almost completely move on. I hadn't thought about Elena in forever, mostly because I knew she was long dead. The only way I was seeing her again was in death, so it might as well be sooner rather than later.

Ten minutes passed, then twenty, then thirty. The air was getting colder. It was August where could we be that was so cold, and why were we not moving? I grabbed a coat off the back of my desk chair and made my way to Hook.

He was standing on the back of the deck facing the water. It was frozen. We weren't moving because we couldn't. We were stuck in the middle of ice, meaning our one night on land, we were stuck on the sea.

"Sorry, Hunt, we're stuck. We gotta wait till next time."

"Then I'm going to bed. Later, Cap'ain."

It was a sign. I was done with this. I was done walking these halls over and over and over again. I was tired of seeing the same people day after day after fucking day. I was so tired of being alive. I was ready and willing to die now. I was ready to see Elena again.

"Oh, Tyler, you won't see her if you die. She's very much alive."

I spun around. "Who are you? Why can you hear what I'm thinking?"

"You know what? I've been doing this a long time and *no one* has ever asked me that. Not one person. But to answer your first question,

I'm Pan. I live on that island you are so fascinated with. There are twenty-four of us in fact. If you join me, poof twenty-five. What do you say?"

"How did you get on here? Why did you call me Tyler? No one calls me Tyler. My name is Hunter now."

"'Twenty questions' hasn't been invented yet, and for your information you're supposed to play it with a girl so you can ask her if she's square or not." The boy laughed at himself and ignored my questions.

"What are you talking about?"

"There you go again! Oh, if only you could see the future." He laughed again. "Well, are you coming or not? I'm not sticking around much longer."

"You've only answered one of my questions. What are you doing here? Better yet, why are you here?"

"To rescue you of course. I can hear the thoughts of people who want to die. I don't want you to die, and I know someone else who wouldn't want you to die. So what do you say? Are you coming or not?"

"Who?"

"Elena of course. Who else? Now come on, I'm running out of patience."

"That's impossible. It's been 190 years. She's long dead, why are you trying to trick me?"

"I'm not! You should be long dead too, but here you are very much alive and annoying. If you don't leave with me now, you will never see her again."

I hesitated, but only for a second. Who would make this up? "Okay, let's go."

***

We were standing on the beach. I'd been dreaming about standing on this beach for as long as I could remember. "Thank you."

"Come on, let's go meet the group."

He led me through the trees from one side of the island to the other. Since he said we were "almost there," it was twenty minutes, a walk over a river, and then another ten minutes.

"If this is your idea of 'almost there,' you have no sense of direction!"

"Yeah, I know. That's why I normally just poof into camp from the beach, but I haven't had enough exercise lately so I wanted to walk."

"Are you fucking joking right now? Are you actually serious right now? You're an asshole."

"Trust me, it'll be worth it once you walk in." We passed through a patch of moonlight, so I could see the smirk plastered on his face.

I rolled my eyes but stayed quiet. He was just going to give me a sarcastic answer if I said anything else. From this point, it was another five minutes before we walked into his camp. There were twelve boys sitting on the ground by a fire.

"Everyone say hello to Hunter." *So he does listen sometimes . . .* No one looked up; it was like they didn't even notice I was there.

"Tyler?" I knew that voice. I remembered her face. She still looked the same. "But . . ."

I remembered the time I saw her and those two girls. I thought my brain was tricking me, but I was right, she was alive. "Elena . . . I knew it was you . . . I knew I would see you again."

"Elena? Are you okay?" The two girls she was with on the beach appeared beside her. They looked worried about her.

She ignored them, keeping her eyes locked on me. "This can't be real. You can't be real."

"I am. I really am real." I felt my eyes welling up with tears. I threw my arms around her and pulled her toward me. She still smelled like the vanilla she used to, but now it was mixed with trees. She was exactly the same. "I thought my brain was tricking me. I never thought I would get to hold you again."

"Neither did I. I'm so sorry I left you at the docks. I'm so sorry for everything."

"You two know each other? How?"

"Zylan, Clover, this is my boyfriend, Tyler," she said pulling away.

The name didn't sound right. I wasn't the same person I was the last time we saw each other . . . "Fiancé actually, and I prefer Hunter," I corrected. I hoped she could understand. "I'm so happy I have you back." I kissed her forehead. "I'm never losing you again." *You have to forget your pirate ways. You can't lose her again.*

***

"You froze them? Really? Then what was the whole 'everyone say hello to Hunter' business about?"

This guy was literally insane. I didn't understand what his deal was or did I understand why everyone seemed to be so attached to him.

"I figured you would want to say hello to Elena without twelve guys staring at you. I said that for Elena, Zylan, and Clover. Don't worry, they won't tell anyone. You'll still be able to fool around with no attachments if you chose to do so." I opened my mouth to argue. "Let me stop you right there. You were a pirate for 190 years. You can't just change that overnight. Now you will be on dry land with twelve girls and you are free to do whatever you like. But if you do, just remember Elena hasn't forgotten about you. The whole time she's been here, she's been trying to forget but she can't. I know you did. All I'm saying is you have to get a feel for each other again. Maybe instead of picking up where you left off, you should start at the beginning." He disappeared.

"You're crazy!" I yelled into the empty space.

Is he though? My inner voice was a pain in the ass.

"Yes. He is crazy. I finally got her back. Why would I mess that up?"

Because you've been a part for 190 years. You moved on, you almost forgot about her. It's not like you can change who you are. It wouldn't be your fault.

I pushed my voice down. "This is not the time to be thinking about that. I won't go back to my pirate ways. I will be the guy that Elena remembers."

Then why are you sticking with Hunter?

I couldn't answer that question, and deep down, I knew that until I could. I didn't deserve her or anyone for that matter. I should have told her, but instead I let my ego get in the way and I screwed up in every possible way.

***

I found myself wandering around the Island looking for something to do. Elena was busy doing something with Zylan and Clover. I was so happy to be back with her, but sometimes it was hard to relax. Sometimes I found myself waking up in the morning, wishing I was still on the ship.

No one really talked to me. Justin remembered me, even after 180 years. I guess it was hard to forget the guy who dragged you down to the cells and left you there to become a pirate. Tyler also remembered me. He felt bad for leaving me there all alone. I didn't resent him for it, but I tried to keep my distance because his name just reminds me of the person I once was.

All I wanted was to fit in somewhere. I never belonged on the ship, but at least I had people to talk to, people who would listen. All I had here was a few guys who didn't really like me or want to be bothered with me.

I needed something to distract me, and I knew just the thing.

Some girl had been throwing herself at me since day one. Maybe she could occupy some of my time, so I didn't go mad waiting for Elena to finish whatever it was that she was doing.

1700

I looked at the gold ring in my hand. I remembered the day I made this. I remembered how nervous but excited I was that I was going to spend the rest of my life with the woman I loved the most. I remembered my heart pounding in my throat as I got on one knee and asked her to marry me. I remembered the tears in her eyes as she said yes. I remembered my heart breaking as I watched her run for town, just as I felt my heart breaking as I stood here and watched her run now.

I should have listened to Pan. I should have told her what happened to me. I should have begged her to give me another chance. We should have started over.

Two hundred and four years ago, I realized that this girl was going to be the girl I married. I swore to myself that I would protect her and love her the way that she deserved. But I didn't do that. I broke her heart. She trusted me with it, but I couldn't be the man she needed me to be, and I destroyed it.

I felt tears pouring out of my eyes. "Elena, I'm so sorry. I should have been there for you. I should have tried harder to find you. I should have known you were alive. I should have looked for you." My voice traveled quietly though the wind.

I messed up. She never forgot me, but I forgot her. "I was never good enough for you."

I curled my fingers around the ring. "I won't let this go. One day, I will win you back, and on that day, you will have this ring, and I will have my happiness back. I will never let you go again."

Chapter 13

I Can't Do This

Clover

Great. Pirate prisoners. What a way to go. They took ten of us, nine of us are girls—big surprise there—but I can't figure out why they wanted Ace or why they call him Jason. We're in cells in the bilge of the ship. For a guy who seems like a pretty smart guy, Captain Hook Hand had really poor planning.

The bilge of a ship is the most prone to leaks, making it the easiest place to escape from. We're all lying in a small puddle of water, meaning there is a leak. We just have to find the hole and make it bigger so we can escape. I know that seems a little complicated considering we all have some form of magic, but I already tried opening the door, but my magic isn't working. I've tried making the door disappear, clicking the lock, swinging it open. Nothing's working . . . I don't understand why.

I'm waiting for everyone to wake up. Apparently, we were too much of a pain in the ass to keep conscious while transporting us to the ship, so they knocked everyone out.

I'm not too sure why they decided to keep me awake and walk me through the ship, but I did get a good look at it, so I'm not complaining.

I'm sitting against the wall where it meets the cell bars. The rest of the girls are scattered around the cell, some just lying in the water, and some are propped up against the wall, heads hanging low. Why did this happen? Today of all days?

Maybe the pirates saw Pan leaving the island and thought this would be the perfect time to strike. Maybe they got sick of sailing around and decided to try and claim the land. No, they would have stayed on land if that were the case. And what about this treasure? Five hundred and twenty-three years and I've never seen any treasure anywhere on the Island, why come looking here?

"Clover?" Elena sits up, slowly, looking around, eyes half closed. "What? Where are we?"

"Do you not remember the pirates?"

"Damn. I was hoping that was a dream . . . how long was I out?" She rubs her temples with the palm of her hands and yawns.

"About three hours . . . I think." I want to say longer because—I know it hasn't been but—it feels like it's been days. "I figured out a way off the ship, but we have to wait for everyone to wake up . . . We're sinking the ship."

"Sounds like a plan to me. I don't want to become these gross ass pirates' 'play thing.'" She gags. "I'd rather die."

"Yeah, I know what you mean. I'd kill myself before I'd let anyone of those dirty pirates touch me."

Elena sighs and looks through the bars. "Why did this happen?"

"From what I can gather, they're looking for treasure. The guy with the hook, I'm pretty sure he's the captain, was looking for a guy named Jason . . . I told him there was no one by that name here. Then Ace came up and he demanded him . . . I think, he thinks, Ace is Jason and he has the treasure."

She rolls her eyes. "Why couldn't they have just asked nicely. It's not like any of us need that treasure nor did we need to die or get kidnapped or injured."

"Sometimes you can be really stupid, you know that right? They're fucking pirates. If they asked nicely, they might as well just be sailors." I roll my eyes. "It doesn't matter what happened up to this point. All that matters is getting out of here. We can't do that if you say something stupid and get yourself killed, do you understand?"

"Why are you such an asshole?"

"I was left in charge when this happened while one of my best friends left the Island with Pan and told me not to tell her fiancé, and I watched *my* fiancé die right in front of me because I lead the pirates right to him. I feel like this is all my fault, and the only way I'm going to forgive myself is if I can save everyone now. That is why I'm being such an ass."

Elena doesn't say anything. She just stands up and walks over to me. "Oh my god, Clover. I'm so sorry." Then she kneels down and hugs me. I lose it.

"It's all my fault," I cry into her shoulder. "It's all my fault."

"Shush, shush, no it's not. It's the fault of no one but the pirates that did this. You can't blame yourself because you couldn't have known this would happen. None of us could have," she whispers stroking my hair. "It's not your fault."

"Thank you," I whisper pulling back. I wipe the tears from my cheeks and give her a half-assed smile.

"Anytime." She smiles. "What are best friends for?"

"Clover?" Everyone starts to wake up. I'm glad I got my meltdown out of the way before this. It's up to me and Elena to get everyone out of here. I can't have them seeing me like that. I need more than anything to focus. We're getting out of here. I quickly stand up and wipe my eyes. I need to keep it together.

"Hey, is everyone okay?" I ask as they rub their eyes and start to realize where they are.

"Where are we?" Willow asks. She uses the wall to help her stand up.

"On the pirates' ship, but we won't be for long, I have a plan."

"We're all ears," Ryan says as she rolls her neck side to side.

"So this cell is a little flooded, which means there's a hole somewhere that we can make bigger so we can swim to shore. Everyone here does know how to swim right?"

They all nod their heads. I kind of figured because almost everyone here lived off the coast of the ocean. Pan must have followed these pirates from the Island every ten years and saved someone from them, ever since Zylan.

"All right, everyone, search. The faster we find this the faster we can get out of here," Elena says.

The cell has a bunch of wooden table tops, chairs, desks, and buckets. They must be trying to use them to slow the leak or at least try to hide it. The faster we get them out of the way, the easier it'll be to narrow down where the hole is.

"I think I see it!" Willow exclaims, drawing our attention to right side of the pile.

"Yeah, it's here," Jasmine confirms, moving the table top to reveal a large crack.

"You would think that they would have put the hole under the middle of the pile because it's harder to get to," Olive says.

"Maybe they were trying to throw us off." Lydia shrugs.

"Or they're stupid," Elena says.

"Either way, let's get cracking," Faye says crouching down.

"We can't leave without Ace!" I exclaim.

"To hell we can't. What if they don't throw him in here? What if they just torture the information out of him then toss him overboard? We can't wait. We have to go before they come to take one of us!" Jasmine throws back.

"Fine. You guys work on the hole. I'm not leaving without Ace."

"Neither am I." Ryan, Willow, and Elena say.

The other five girls roll their eyes and start chipping away at the hole.

"What's going on here? I thought we taught you better . . . no man left behind, remember?"

Everyone's heads whip toward the cell bars. "Zylan?" I ask. "How—"

"We don't have time for that. Come on let's go." She waves her hand. The lock clicks, and the door swings open. How come she could do it but I couldn't? "Clover?" She calls after everyone passes. "I'm so sorry. If I had known, I wouldn't have left you in charge. I wouldn't have left. I can't imagine how you feel."

"You're right. You can't. You didn't watch the love of your life die in front of you because your best friend left and told you to not to let her fiancé find out."

"Justin's not dead . . . he's here. In fact . . ." she trails off and steps out of the way.

"Clover," Justin says. He's standing at the foot of the stairs on the other side of the ship. Between us are a dozen barrels, half-dozen polls, and a bunch of random crap scattered everywhere.

"Justin? I . . . saw you . . . oh, my god." I run over to him, somehow avoiding every obstacle in my way. I jump into his arms, wrapping my arms and legs around him. He holds me like that for almost a minute as I cry into his shoulder. "I saw you die. How did this happen?"

"Zylan found me, and Pan brought me to the waterfall. You thought you could get rid of me that easily?" He laughs, but I can hear the shakiness of his voice. He was scared. He still is, and I don't blame him.

"I thought I was never going to see you again." He puts me down.

"Baby, I'm right here. I promised you I was never going to leave you, and I never break a promise. I love you." He kisses my cheek. "But we have to go. I have to rescue my best friend." He smiles.

"Let's go do that. Hey, Zylan? I'm so—"

"Don't you dare apologize. I deserved that. I shouldn't have left."

"No, you didn't. You just wanted answers, I would have done the same."

"I'm still sorry." She hugs me before we run upstairs.

***

Apparently, they snuck onto the ship. I mean it wouldn't be hard . . . Pan and Zylan both have magic; that's the easy part. The hard part is getting to Ace. According to Zylan, there are five guards outside the captain's quarters, and it looks like there are six more inside, plus the captain himself. It's not going to be easy to get in nor will it be easy to get him out.

Zylan and Pan are trying to come up with a plan now. A week ago, she would have been screaming at him for disagreeing and then do whatever she wanted anyways. She never told anyone why she didn't like him, but everyone could tell there was something off. At our weekly dinners, she would spend her time on the opposite side of the camp not looking in his direction, even though he would be staring at her pretty intensely the whole time.

But now . . . she's listening to everything he's saying, nodding, smiling, shaking her head. She's even standing right next to him. Something changed when they left, and I'm dying to know what she found out about her memories. I shouldn't care because of the situation we're all in, but I do.

"No we can't just poof in there. We can only see the outline of shapes through the door, if we get in there and they're all staring at us. No way are we getting out of there let alone Ace!" Zylan interjects.

"So how do we get in there?" Ryan asks.

"We fight our way in."

With that everyone agrees. Zylan, Justin, and Pan are the only ones with weapons, so we have to get some more. Pan suggests taking the weapons off of the guards at the front. The five of them have two swords, each making ten, and there are nine of us. The only problem is, *actually* getting them. While the rest of them are bickering, I see Zylan slip away. She slides her bow off her shoulder and takes out five arrows.

It not going to work. She can't hit five guys at the same time she's going to blow it. But she angles the bow parallel to the ground and fires. It hits all of the guys in the heart, and they drop. Problem solved. It was easy . . . almost too easy . . .

It doesn't make any sense. Why would the captain put us in a cell easy to escape from but leave Ace in a room with eleven guards? Unless . . . they wanted us to escape. This trap is but who for . . .?

"Wait! Don't—"

Zylan

Clover screams, but it's too late. Jacob's already swinging the door open.

The door is booby-trapped. It releases four arrows all aiming at Ace's heart, but Jacob waves his hand and they all fall to the ground. It feels like I haven't seen Ace in days. He's all beaten up and bruised. They must have been trying to get information out of him. His wrists are tied to the chair. His eyebrow is split open causing blood to drip down around his eye. His lip is cut and also bleeding. His eye is black, and it looks like his nose is broken. What could they possibly want from him?

I let out a sharp breath of air before pulling my own arrows out of place. I send one in the direction of Ace. It lodges itself in the left arm of the chair, cutting through his restraints. My next arrow flies past his ear, landing in the pirate about to stab him. Ace manages to get his other arm free and grab the dead pirate's sword.

Just as I'm about to send an arrow into a pirate taking a swing at Clover, I sense *him*. The pirate from the memories. The one who killed my mother.

I look around, scanning the room. Then I see him, a one-handed pirate. I know it's him because his evil smile deepens as soon as he sees me. He's standing by the window on the back wall. My dad tried to teach me all the ship lingo, but I never really listened so I'm not sure of the actually terms. From what I gather, this is definitely the captains' quarters. It's the biggest room on the ship, with a huge desk about a meter from the wall of windows. It's covered in maps, books, papers, knickknacks, and a bunch of other things I'm not familiar with. The walls are lined with cabinets, and there are artifacts scattered all over the room.

How is this possible? It's been 543 years. He should be long dead. There's no way he lived this long . . . then again I shouldn't have lived this long either. But I was rescued. There's absolutely no way that this guy was rescued and brought here unless . . . Peter must have done this.

"Zylan!" Jacob screams snapping me out of it. Just in time too.

I use the arrow I had already set up and release it into the chest of the pirate coming at me from the left. He drops, and I return my attention to the man at the window. I should shoot him. I have the opportunity to. But I get this overwhelming feeling that I have to talk to him.

I get across the room in about five seconds. Somewhere along the way, I got another arrow in my bow and have it pointed at the pirate. "You know who I am?" I ask, trying to keep my voice from wavering.

"You be the reason I got no treasure," he says plainly.

I look at him sideways. "I'm sorry, what? You killed my whole family and 'you be the reason I got no treasure' is all you have to say? That's it?"

"You want me to apologize, love? I'm a pirate, I don't care."

I take a deep breath in and out. "Then I'm not sorry for this." I pull back and release the arrow. But instead of it hitting the one-handed pirate, it hits a tree. I'm back on the Island, along with everyone else. They look as confused as I feel. "What happened?"

"We got Ace back. I couldn't stand to see anyone else fall, so I got us out of there." Jacob says making his way over to me. He's smiling like he did something good, but it drops as soon as he sees my face.

"I ALMOST KILLED HIM! WHY WOULD YOU DO THAT? THREE MORE FUCKING SECONDS!" I scream at him. But my voice drops. "You couldn't have waited three more seconds?" I feel the tears pouring out of my eyes.

"Zylan . . ." his eyes fill with guilt. He wants to apologize, but he's not sure how. "I'm—"

"Save it." With that I'm gone. I don't know where I wanted to go, but I end up on the cliff.

The sun has set. The sky is pitched black, not a star in sight and no sign of the moon. The fog from this morning is thicker. I should have felt this. I should have known something bad was going to happen today. There's never any fog here; it's always sunny. I should have known.

This morning when I woke up, Clover, Elena, and I were having a good time. I was smiling; everything was normal. I knew where I stood with Clover. I knew Pan couldn't be trusted. I knew that my life wasn't normal, but I was simple. "I wish I could go back to this morning. I wish I never left with Pan. I wish I never kissed him. But most of all I wish . . . I didn't like it, that I didn't love him, that he let me die back in my village, with my family."

I drop down on my knees and cry. Until two weeks ago I hadn't shed a tear in hundreds of years. Lately I can't keep myself together. To think, if Willow and Iris hadn't seen Klaus and Hunter, none of this would have happened. I never would have spent all that time with Pan, and I never would have had a reason to question everything I remembered.

Ever since Neverland I only remember what actually happened . . . none of the stuff Peter stuck in my head. I can't remember why I hated Jacob all those years; all I remember is how much I loved him. Not loved. Love. I'm in love with him, ever since that first night I felt him watching. How am I supposed to carry on with Ace now that I know the truth?

I remember everything. Five hundred and forty-six years' worth of memories with Jacob came flooding back, and I can't think of anything else. Not even the memories I have with Ace. Yesterday I could have told you the exact moment we first kissed—year, month, day, hour, minute, second. Now I can't even remember the year.

Everything is a mess. How am I supposed to marry Ace? How am I supposed to look at him when all I can think about is that kiss with Pan? I can't do this. Not anymore.

I look up at the sky and wrap my hand around the ring Ace gave me. Put it on a necklace before I left for Neverland with Pan. Every year for ten years, I wanted to jump. Could I do it now? Only one way to find out. I wipe the tears from under my eyes and push myself up to standing. I don't think I told my legs to move, but I find myself with my toes hanging over the edge. One more step and—

"Not again. Please don't do this," Jacob says.

"I can't do it anymore. Jacob, if you ever loved me, please just let me go."

"I can't do that. Zylan, I can't let you jump, I still love you."

I turn around slowly. "Please don't. Please, please, please don't say that. You can't love me. You know that, I know that. Just let me take one more step, you'll forget all about me."

"No, I won't," he whispers, tears welling up in his eyes. "I need you, even if that means you have to hate me again."

"What are you— Pan? Why is it so dark? When I left, it was sun up . . ."

"You don't remember?" His eyes fill with worry. "Zylan . . . there was an attack. We were off the island for a bit and pirates attacked the camp."

"What!" I exclaim. "Is everyone okay? Why can't I remember?"

His face drops. "I think you better hear it from someone else. Come on let's go back to camp."

"But I want you to tell me. Pan, what happened?" Something doesn't feel right. How could I be missing a whole day? It couldn't have been worse than the day my parents died, and I didn't forget about that . . . "Wait, I can't remember how they died. Pan, I can't remember how I got here. What's happening to me?" I feel tears pouring down my face. I know they died; I know something really bad happened, but how did it happen?

"Come on, let me take you home. Ace is probably really worried about you."

"I—" I can't remember why he would be worried about me . . . Who is he to me?

***

"Zylan! Are you okay?" a boy with blonde hair and blue eyes exclaims running over to me. His face is bruised a bloody; someone should take him to the waterfall. I search my memory. . . Ace, his name is Ace. "What happened? Why did you just disappear like that?"

"I . . ." I can't find the right words. I remember him slightly. I know he means something to me. I can feel it. I just don't know why I can't remember what that something is.

"Ace, give her some space. She doesn't remember anything that happened today. She barley remembers anything," Pan says making his way up behind me.

Everyone stops what they're doing and looks at us. All the faces are familiar. I remember Clover and Elena; we've been best friends since they came to the Island. I see Tyler and Hunter staring at me. I know Tyler and I were—are— friends. I fixed his arm a couple weeks ago. I remember Hunter's a jerk who thinks he can do whatever he wants because he was a pirate for almost two hundred years. Justin is standing with Clover. He's the only one not looking at me; he's looking at her. That boy is so in love with her. I'm so happy they're getting married.

Wait. I'm getting married too. There's a gold ring on my necklace. Ace . . . Ace asked me to marry him the same day Justin asked Clover. I remember.

My parents died August 14, 1468, after a pirate ship attacked our village. Pan found me crying over my mom's body. I remember. I remember everything except for today.

"Zylan?" Ace asks softly. "Are you okay?"

"I don't know . . . I'm starting to remember everything but today."

He pulls me toward him into a hug. "Come on, let's get you home." He pulls away.

I nod. Everyone is still staring. This must be my fault, something I did today caused this. Ace wraps his arm around my shoulder and leads me out of camp. I see Clover, Elena, Tyler, and Justin stand up out of the corner of my eye. They follow us to the tree house Ace and I have been living in for two weeks.

***

"What's the last thing you remember?" Clover asks once we're seated.

Ace brings me a cup of tea and then sits beside me. "We were talking when Ty showed up, followed by you guys. Pan just came back from wherever he went and you guys wanted me to talk to him. I didn't want to, but you forced me to. I found him sitting on the cliff wall and then it was pitched black. The sky I mean."

"You came back to camp and told me you were leaving the Island and you needed me to keep Ace occupied. You said you needed answers, and Pan was the only on that could give them to you. You didn't want anyone to know you were gone. About an hour or two after you left, pirates attacked. They were looking for someone named Jason—thanks for the fake name by the way, Ace. I had no clue who that was, but

I mentioned Ace and the pirate made me take him to him." Clover pauses and looks at Ace to continue from his point of view.

"The pirate disarmed me and took us to the ship. We both thought Justin was dead, so we were a little bit too shocked to fight. The two pirates knocked me out and took me to the captain's room. They beat me for information about the treasure Pan and I brought here my first day. I told them I didn't know where it was. Pan took it somewhere only he would know where to look—somewhere no one would find it. They didn't believe me. They set up a trap, knowing how easy it would be for the girls to escape. They wanted to ambush you. But Hook didn't anticipate you, Pan, and Justin showing up as well."

"You and Pan got back just in time to save my life. You planned to sneak on the ship by yourself, but Pan talked you down. I told you there was no way you were going without me, and we came up with a plan. Once we were on board you knocked out the guards and took their weapons. We found the girls trying to break out themselves. We headed up to the main deck and came up with a plan to get Ace out."

"From there you snuck away and shot all the guard in front of the door—very impressive by the way. We were going in when Clover realised it was a trap. It was too late, and the door swinging open released four arrows aimed at Ace. Pan saved his life, but there was a battle. I lost track of you . . . did any of you see?" The boys shake their heads. "Well, anyways, Pan got us all out, but you didn't seem happy about it. You screamed at him. Something about you almost killing someone."

"You disappeared before any of us got the chance to ask what happened," Ace says.

"You guys always get to have all the fun." Tyler pouts

I take a sip of my tea, ignoring him. "So me and Pan leaving the Island has something to do with the pirate's attack. I need to talk to him." I try to stand, but Ace pulls me back.

"There's a reason you don't remember today. If Pan thought it was a good idea to tell you what happened, he would have done it on the cliff. Right now, I think the best thing to do is just get some sleep. Maybe it was just too traumatic and your brain shut it out. Sleep tonight and we'll talk to Pan tomorrow."

"I agree. I'll go talk to Pan now and we'll try to figure it out." Clover smiles and stands up. "Get some sleep, we'll talk tomorrow."

"I'll go with her," Elena says standing up as well.

"I need—"

"Nope, we're going to bed." Ace stands, grabs my tea out of my hands, and picks me up. "Good night, you guys." He smiles and carries me to the kitchen. He pulls down the latter and flips me over his shoulder.

"Hey!" I exclaim. "I'm not a toy that you can just throw me around!"

"If I put you down, you have to come to bed."

All I can see is his butt, but I can tell he's laughing. "Fine! Put me down!"

He puts me on my feet and smiles. I've seen him smile a million times; something about this time feels different. Everything feels different now. Something inside me is screaming that this is wrong, that I should be trying to figure things out.

"Come on, let's go to bed."

"First, let's get you to the waterfall."

Ace pauses. It's like he forgot he is bruised and bloody. "That's probably a good idea." He smiles and takes my hand.

Pan

1518

I snuck on board again. Apparently, I did a much better job than the boy standing in front of Hook right now. He was the kind of trouble maker that didn't think he would ever get caught. This must have been a harsh reality check for him.

"I found 'em lurkin' at the gap. Though 'e could look 'round an' leave," the pirate that caught him said, handing him over to Hook. He got pushed to his knees.

I stayed up in the sails like normal; the dumb pirates never looked up. The boy was at the back of the ship by the wheel. He looked like he was keeping it together fine, but his mind was running all over the place. "Lock 'em up. Ware 'em down."

A look of relief flooded his face. He thought he would have a chance to escape before they leave port. I might have to help him with that. Another boy, with black hair and brown eyes, grabbed his arms, pulled him to his feet, and dragged him down the stairs. I recognised him, Tyler. I guessed they decided to keep him around.

All the pirates on the ship were standing on deck, watching him. I was going to have to be creative about getting down to the cells, and I was going to have to do it fast. *I'll just go down there and hide behind something. I just have to wait for Tyler to leave the boy, and I'll get him then.*

It didn't take much to hide from Tyler. He wasn't very attentive. I made it down before them, so I hid behind a barrel. When they came down, the boy was pushed right into a cell. Tyler turned to leave.

***

The boy had another visitor about two minutes after Tyler left. I'd been waiting for an hour to make sure no one else comes. The boy was very entertaining to watch. He tried to squeeze through the bars, then he tried finding something to pick the lock, and now he was looking for the hole that the water was leaking in from. I thought I'd save him from the realization that the leak was in the cell next to him.

I stepped out of my hiding place and walked over to the bars. "There's an easier way out." I waved my hand, and the door swung open.

He jumped up and turned toward me. A look of confusion crossed over his face.

"Who are you? Is this a trick?"

"No. I'm not a part of this crew. I'm Pan, and I'm here to rescue you. Unless you don't want my help."

"How do I know you are who you say you are?"

"You don't, but you should trust me. I can take you away, to a place where you will not grow old, where you can be with people your age with no responsibilities. Or I can leave you here to be a pirate for the rest of your life."

"Take me." He paused. "Take me to this place."

"Come, we need to move quickly."

I led him up the stairs. The ship was a maze; even though I snuck through it all the time, I still got lost. At every turn, there were two different ways. Finally, we made it to the gap. I assumed this was where the boy came in from; he seemed to find it familiar. "What now?"

"Jump!" I yelled pushing him off the ledge.

***

"You might as well come down and say hello, girls," I said. I could feel Zylan's presence surrounding the camp. I had a feeling this would become a reoccurring thing.

He was confused. I didn't blame him. He could only see two boys, Ace and Matt, sitting in front of a fire.

"Who's this?" Zylan asked appearing in front of him. He looked confused. "Where are you from?"

"Zylan, give the boy a chance to settle in before we go asking a million questions." Clover appeared beside her. They were still wearing the same thing, and it was still adorable.

"She only asked two. No need to go overexaggerating things, Clover." Now it was Elena's turn, and she was matching with them. I loved these girls; they were so cute.

"Thank you, Elena."

"Can everyone do that?" Justin asked.

"No." Matt rolled his eyes. "These four like to show off with it, though."

"Yeah, I can't really do it either . . . one time I almost did, but I almost impaled myself with a branch in the process. I've been uneasy about trying again," Ace added with a chuckle.

"Can someone teach me how to do that?"

"Don't ask Pan. He's an awful teacher."

"Can someone answer my questions?" Zylan exclaimed, rolling her eyes. She wasn't really mad; she just wanted attention.

"I'm Justin, I'm from Sweden." He smiled.

"Why do you speak perfect English? And why do you have an English accent?" Clover asked.

"I was born in Birmingham. I moved to Sweden when I was five, and my parents continued to speak English until they died three years ago."

The three girls frowned. "Sorry, we're done now." They all said and disappeared.

"Seriously, someone has to teach me that."

"Ask Zylan. She's the reason the other two can do that. I'm Ace, and that's Matt." He stood up and walked over to Justin. "Nice to meet you, Justin. I can help you if you need anything. I know how confusing this island can be, and Pan over here sucks at being a guide."

"Hey, buddy, watch it," I warned. I tried to make it sound threatening, but Ace just laughed. He knew I wouldn't do anything.

1520

I messed up. I should have brought him home, to his family. When I put my hands into the water this time, I saw head stones, four of them. Two people were standing in front of them. They say JUSTIN, ENOK, GUDMUND, and MELINA. They thought Justin was dead, and because I took him, two of his little siblings died.

They didn't have enough money, and no one would help them. I did that. I should have just brought him home. I should have brought all of them home.

I was supposed to meet Clover for our sword lesson. I couldn't do that now. I had to cancel or postpone. I remembered Ace telling me Justin had a fancy on her. Maybe if I could get them together, I could forgive myself for ruining both their lives.

I just needed to find him and tell him to cancel for me. Maybe if they spent some time together, it would help. I closed my eyes. I just had to picture him and then—

"Justin, I need you to find Clover. We were supposed to have a lesson, but something just came up," I said appearing in front of him.

"Enough! Enough with the heart attacks! Why do you always insist on doing that?" I knew I should laugh. I always laughed, but today I couldn't do it."

"Sorry, just please go find her. She should be around centre island." I knew I threw him off, but I didn't care. I couldn't laugh right now.

"Yes, sir," I heard him say as I made my disappearance.

1558

It was still light out. We landed close to a village, so we got there during the day. I followed Hook around for most of it. He ran into a man desperate for drinking money. Hook said if the man brought him back someone he could use as a crew member, he would give him money.

They laughed when they got back on board. They weren't actually expecting to get a crew member from a poor drunk man, but that was what made this time so strange. This was the worst one yet. A few of the boys I'd taken to the Island have had run-ins with Hook, but never had I seen a parent sell their child to the ship for money. What kind of parent could do that?

The boy just stood there and watched his parents walk off the ship. He was pretty beat-up; his father was probably just like mine. I could spot an abuse victim from a mile away.

"Welcome to the crew, boy," Hook said. He was leaning on the wheel in front of the boy. Hook didn't look like he normally did; he almost looked like he pitied the boy for having parents like that.

"When can I start?" He wanted out of his life. This time I'd be rescuing someone who needed it, someone who had nothing left. I could help him start over.

"We got an egger one, boys!" The crew laughed. "In ten years, the next time we port. Until then, Hunt, show 'em the quarters."

Ten years? There is no way that we would sail around for ten years before we port next. He had no idea what he was getting himself into.

Hunt—the same boy whose name was Tyler, they must have given him a nickname—waved the boy to follow him. The boy followed him down a staircase. I made a mental note to check up on Tyler's years on the ship when I got back to the Island.

It was fun to sneak around here now. I had a pretty good feel for the place. I knew exactly where they were going to take the new guy. Luckily, I had a few minutes before they got to Tyler's room, so I had time to find a hiding spot.

"Admiring the ship?" Tyler asked. They were walking up the hall I was hiding in.

"It is nice."

"Well, better get used to it, you're gonna be on it a long, long time, mate. 'Round here, we don't age. Guess how old I am."

"Seventeen, eighteen?"

"Sixty-eight. Where we're goin' no one grows old. Don't believe me? That's fine, you will. This is your room, you'll be livin' with me for a long time, get comfortable." With that he left, and the boy sighed. He thought he was alone.

"You're not alone, I'm right here." I stepped out of my hiding spot.

He jumped up, compressing a scream. "Who are you?"

"Pan. I'm here to rescue you, unless you want to be a pirate for the rest of time. You are?"

"Tyler." *Hum, interesting, the same name as the boy he would have been roommates with. I wonder if it's his real name, or if it's just a name that came to him.* "I have nothing left, to rescue me would be torture." He looked down at his feet.

I am tired of this life.

"I'm not taking you back there. I live on an island where you will be free to do whatever you please. There are ten of us, you would make eleven. If you choose to stay here, I won't stop you, but this life is not one you want. Trust me."

"Take me there."

I smiled. "Will do."

***

"Where are we?" Tyler asked. We were standing on the beach I bring all the new kids to.

"Home." I gave the same response I did with Elena, mostly because it was home for me but partly because I had no clue where we actually were. "Ready to meet everyone? Well, mostly everyone."

He shrugged looking around. I grabbed his shoulder and thought of camp. Ace, Matt, Noah, and Justin were sitting around a fire in the centre of camp. Tyler took a step back. Transporting was hard to get used to, but he took to it pretty well.

"Wow. That is amazing!"

I snorted. He would change his mind soon. "Guys, this is Tyler." The four of them wave. "Come on out, girls, say hello."

"Hey," Zylan said appearing in front of him. He blinked.

"What she said," Clover and Elena said appearing on either side of her.

Tyler doesn't blink this time. He just stares at them. "Yes, we wear boy clothes, get over it." Zylan rolled her eyes and walked over to the fire; Clover followed her.

"Don't mind them, we just get the staring a lot, and I think she's getting sick of it. But can you blame us for this? I mean dresses are so uncomfortable," Elena said.

"Yeah!" Zylan waved her hand. In the blink of an eye, Tyler was dressed up in a pure white wedding dress, fully equipped with corset and veil. Everyone burst out laughing, even Tyler himself.

"I will have you know, I was not staring because of your clothes. I was staring because you are very beautiful."

"AWE!" the three of them yelled.

"That is so cute! Zylan, get him out of that dress!" It was gone.

"Damn, we got a smooth one on the loose," Ace said with a laugh.

"Don't make fun of him. He's going to be the only one gettin' any. You guys are boring," Clover said. Zylan and Elena burst out laughing then the three of them disappear.

"What does she mean 'gettin' any'?" Tyler asked. Now it was the guys turn to laugh.

"Something you've never done before," Matt said.

***

How could I have messed up this bad again? He had a son. The night he was sold to Hook, his girlfriend was going to tell him she was pregnant. That was why her father was so angry with her and him. She looked familiar, but I couldn't place it. As I watched her story unfold, I tried to place her face.

That day when she went home, her father had calmed down and realised that Tyler was probably the best thing for Azaline. She tried to find him. She went back to the park, wandered around all night, and then finally went to his house. His parents didn't tell her what really happened; they said he ran away.

She was terrified she was going to have to raise the baby alone, but she never got the chance. During the child's birth, she died. The baby barely survived, but it did. Azaline's father couldn't take the pain, so he gave the bay to the church.

I should have taken him home. I couldn't believe I did this again.

1698

We ended up in the middle of nowhere. The ship couldn't even sail out because the water is frozen. It was finally time to rescue Elena's old boyfriend or fiancé if being engaged for two seconds counted. I didn't know if I could trust him. He'd been a pirate so long. What if he didn't take to the Island well?

I got on board just in time to find Tyler talking to Hook. "Sorry, Hunt, we're stuck. We gotta wait till next time."

I finally figured out why they called him Hunt. He spent so much time trying to forget about Elena that he hunted girls. He did pretty well for himself too. He forgot about her for a while, but I knew she never forgot him. I hoped she didn't take this too hard. Maybe I shouldn't do this . . .

"Then I'm going to bed, later, Cap'ain."

I got to my hiding spot by his room before he reached the hall. I heard him coming the second he stepped down the stairs. He was thinking about Elena and how much he wanted to see her. *All right, maybe this will be okay.*

"Oh, Tyler, you won't see her if you die. She's very much alive."

He spun around looking for where my voice was coming from. He did a full three-sixty before he saw me. "Who are you? Why can you hear what I'm thinking?"

"You know what? I've been doing this a long time and no one has ever asked me that. Not one person. But to answer your first question, I'm Pan. I live on that island you are so fascinated with. There are twenty-four of us in fact. If you join me, poof twenty-five. So what do you say?"

"How did you get on here? Why did you call me Tyler? No one calls me Tyler. My name is Hunter now."

"Twenty questions haven't been invented yet, and for your information, you're supposed to play it with a girl so you can ask her if she's square or not." I laughed at myself. Sometimes when I was having a bad day, I peeped into the future of the world for a good laugh. I wasn't sure I liked where the world was heading, but I didn't have to deal with it, so I found it hilarious to watch.

"What are you talking about?"

"There you go again! Oh, if only you could see the future." I laughed again. "Well, are you coming or not? I'm not sticking around much longer."

"You've only answered one of my questions. What are you doing here? Better yet, why are you here?"

"To rescue you of course. I can hear the thoughts of people who want to die. I don't want you to die, and I know someone else who wouldn't want you to die. So what do you say? Are you coming or not?" A lie but whatever.

"Who?"

"Elena of course. Who else? Now come on, I'm running out of patience."

"That's impossible. It's been 190 years. She's long dead. Why are you trying to trick me?"

"I'm not! You should be long dead too, but here you are very much alive and annoying. If you don't leave with me now, you will never see her again."

He hesitated for a second. "Okay, let's go."

***

We were standing on the beach. He looked at all the trees, soaking it all in. "Thank you." I was freezing my butt off, and this guy was just looking around like he'd never seen land before.

"Come on, let's go meet the group."

I didn't really want to rescue him, and I was cold so I decided to walk, hopefully to keep warm. I led him through the trees from one side of the Island to the other. He kept asking me how far we were, so I kept saying we were almost there. I should have left him on the ship.

"If this is your idea of 'almost there,' you have no sense of direction!"

"Yeah, I know. That's why I normally just poof into camp from the beach, but I haven't had enough exercise lately, so I wanted to walk."

"Are you fucking joking right now? Are you actually serious right now? You're an asshole." He was the one that was soaking in the scenery; he should enjoy this walk and stop complaining.

"Trust me, it'll be worth it once you walk in." Hopefully he was serious about wanting to see Elena because she was going to be there. Maybe I should let them have the reunion as just them. I decided to freeze all the boys and give them a chance to catch up.

I saw him roll his eyes but stay quiet. He knew I was just going to give him a sarcastic answer if he said anything else. I didn't like him. I should have just left him there.

From this point, it was another five minutes before we walked into camp. The twelve boys were huddled around the fire keeping warm. I froze them as we walked in. "Everyone say hello to Hunter."

"Tyler?" He recognised her voice. When he looked into her eyes, I saw it. I saw his love for her. He had it buried for a long time now, but it all came to a surface. "But . . ."

"Elena . . . I knew it was you . . . I knew I would see you again."

"Elena? Are you okay?" Zylan asked appearing beside her, Clover following closely behind. They never broke from their pattern; Zylan always went first. It was a big-enough change that they were worried.

"This can't be real. You can't be real." Elena ignored them.

"I am. I really am real." His eyes started welling up with tears. He threw his arms around her, almost hitting me—and Zylan—in the face and pulled her toward him. "I thought my brain was tricking me. I never thought I would get to hold you again."

"Neither did I. I'm so sorry I left you at the docks. I'm so sorry for everything." She blinks away tears.

"You two know each other? How?"

"Zylan, Clover, this is my boyfriend, Tyler," she said pulling away.

He flinched slightly. Elena didn't seem to notice. His name didn't sound right to him anymore. "Fiancé actually, and I prefer Hunter," he corrected. I hoped she could understand that he changed. I hoped she didn't get her heart broken again; she had been through so much already. "I'm so happy I have you back." He kissed her forehead. "I'm never losing you again." *You have to forget your pirate ways. You can't lose her again.*

That's going to be harder than you think, my friend.

***

"You froze them? Really? Then what was the whole 'everyone say hello to Hunter' business about?"

He thought I was insane. I probably was, but I was right about this. He did *not* want that reunion in front of twelve guys. I would have frozen Zylan and Clover as well, but I really wanted to see her and she would have known something was wrong if Clover didn't follow her. Elena probably wouldn't have noticed at first, but after things calmed down, she would have been suspicious.

"I figured you would want to say hello to Elena without twelve guys staring at you. I said that for Elena, Zylan, and Clover. Don't worry they won't tell anyone, you'll still be able to fool around with no attachments if you chose to do so." He opened his mouth to argue. "Let me stop you right there. You were a pirate for a 490 years, you can't just change that. Now you will be on dry land with twelve girls and you a free to do whatever you like." *But it better not be with Zylan.* "But if you do, just remember Elena hasn't forgotten about you. The whole time she's been here, she's been trying to forget, but she can't. I know you did. All I'm saying is you have to get a feel for each other again. Maybe instead of picking up where you left off, you should start at the beginning."

Then I disappeared into the woods. I wanted to see how his internal war was going to play out. It was times like this I was happy to hear thoughts.

"You're crazy!" he yelled into the empty space.

Is he though?

"Yes. He is crazy. I finally got her back, why would I mess that up?"

Because you've been a part for 190 years. You moved on. You almost forgot about her. It's not like you can change who you are; it wouldn't be your fault.

"This is not the time to be thinking about that. I won't go back to my pirate ways. I will be the guy that Elena remembers."

Than why are you sticking with Hunter?

"I guess we'll find out soon," I whispered to myself.

***

With Hunter being around, it reminded me I never checked up on Elena's family after she got here. Another reason I should have just left him on that damn ship, just like I should have brought Elena home.

Her mom lost it after she left. She disappeared. They looked for her everywhere. Her family was broken apart again. All because I took her away.

Her mother was found five years later; no one knew how she ended up six towns over, face down in a lake. However it happened, it was my fault. I ruined everything I touched.

I messed up again, and I didn't find out until 190 years later. I should have left Hunter on the stupid ship with those stupid pirates. I hated him, almost as much as I hated myself.

Chapter 14

I'm Sorry

Pan

I can't believe I did that to her, again. I changed her memories, of me, of Neverland, of everything. She doesn't remember leaving with me to go to Neverland; she doesn't remember sensing me as I watched her all those years. She doesn't remember anything Peter planted in her head. So now she doesn't hate me, but I changed all her memories of loving me. She doesn't remember seeing Wendy again or the fact that I have a twin. Unfortunately, I didn't know what to replace her day with—I couldn't think—so she's missing all of that day. She doesn't remember finding Justin, going to the boat, rescuing Ace, none of it. I can't imagine what she's going through, what she's thinking, but anything is better than what she was thinking up on that cliff. I couldn't stand to watch her drive herself crazy again. I'm not good for her, I know that. She belongs with Ace; he makes her happier than I ever could. I would rather see her happy with him than live the rest of her life a mess trying to figure everything out.

I need her at 100 percent. Any chance we have of keeping this treasure safe rests with everyone staying focused.

"What did you do to her?" Clover asks. I almost got to sleep, but she and Elena burst through the door and shook me awake. "She doesn't remember leaving with you. What happened while she was gone, being on the ship with the pirates, or what happened after she screamed at you and disappeared? She's missing an entire day. Why would you do that? What happened while you were gone?"

"I . . ." I don't know where to start, let alone, if I should tell them. I rub my eyes and sit up. "Look, this isn't the time for this . . ."

"I don't give a shit if you think this isn't the time for it. The last thing she remembers is all of us trying to get her to talk to you. She's freaking out, Pan. She thinks it's her fault the pirates attacked, but she's not sure why. You need to fix this," Elena says.

"I can't, however she's feeling now. It'll be ten times worse if she remembers. Trust me on this on. If you're really her friends, you'll leave it alone."

"We *are* her best friends which is why we can't stand seeing her like this. Pan, you have to fix this." They sit down on the edge of the bed. "I know how you feel about her . . . how can you watch her suffer?"

"How . . . Never mind, it's probably really obvious, everyone seems to know." I put my head in my hands and let out a sigh. "Look, Clover, Elena, it might not seem like it now, but I'm doing this because of how I feel. She almost jumped, again. I couldn't watch her destroy herself like that."

"What happened while you guys were gone? What broke her so bad?" Elena asks.

"Do you guys really want to know?"

"Yes," they say together.

"Fine, give me your hands."

***

"You want to know how to fix it? Kiss him."

"He's probably lying, I mean it's probably true, but there has to be another way. Spells have loopholes. I don't know what kind of loopholes but . . ." I don't even know what I'm saying anymore. There are just words pouring out of my mouth.

I'm not even sure all of them are making sense. Zylan's not going to do that, she can't do that.

"JACOB!" she screams. I blink. Before I know what's happening, she grabs my face and pulls me toward her. My lips are hard against hers. But as soon as I realize what's happening, they begin to soften, my hands moving from my sides to her hair.

She pulls away. "I-I-I'm so sorry. I had no idea. You saved and I treated you like the bad guy. I—"

I kiss her again. This time, there's no hesitation. This is what I want; this is what I've wanted for 546 years. Scratch that, this is what I need. Her hands move from my cheeks to around the back of my neck, moving closer. I move my hands from her hair to hair waist, pulling her against me. Neither one of us want to break this kiss.

She jumps away from me. "I—"

"Jacob, come with me if you want to find out what happened." I hear a woman's voice float through the air, a woman's voice I will never forget. When I look behind Zylan, there she is.

"Mother?" I whisper.

"Yes, my little angel. Follow me."

***

I stand there frozen, mouth slightly open. I had so many memories with this woman, and now I know it was all a lie . . . everything I knew just got ripped apart . . . what am I supposed to do now?

"Jacob? Are you okay?"

I blink slowly and look at her. "No."

She moves in front of me, putting her hands on my cheeks. "Knowing this doesn't change anything. I'm so sorry I hated you all those years and blamed you for everything and never tried to figure out the truth. Thank you for saving my life, thank you for watching out for me, thank you for everything." She pulls me toward her and gives me a hug. I hug her back, taking a deep breath. "Are you okay now?"

I chuckle slowly. Even with my world falling apart, she still manages to make me smile. "Not really, but I'm getting there. I'm glad you were here for this. I wouldn't have been able to do that alone." *I pull away and give her a weak smile.* "Come on, we should probably go find Wendy."

"You're probably right." *She smiles.* "Thank you, for saving her all those years ago. I'm glad someone finally heard my prayers after—" *she stops short. Her eyes go wide and she gasps for air.* "We need to get back to the Island. Now."

"Zylan, I didn't tell you something . . . I don't know how to get back . . . It's a miracle I made it back last time and that took two weeks . . ."

"We don't have time for that." *She grabs my hand.*

Seconds later, I'm standing on the sand of the beach in front of her tree house with Ace. No one's around. Zylan disappears from my sight. I assume she's looking for Ace.

How did she just poof here? It took me weeks to find my way home . . . she shouldn't have been able to do that . . . could I have done that?

***

Justin, Zylan, and I are standing at the edge of the camp, weapons ready. "Zylan, I'm going to need your help to knock everyone out," *I whisper.*

The camp is almost completely empty. With nine of us dead and ten of us missing, there's thirty-seven of us left. That means I have to knock thirty-four people out for at least four hours. It would be hard to do this even if I wasn't feeling weak. I spent two weeks sailing blindly with almost no food, and before I could get any rest, Zylan dragged me back there.

"What do I have to do?" *she keeps her voice low. The thirty-four of us that are left are all sitting in the centre of camp, huddled around the fire, not saying a word.*

"Give me your hand." *She does.*

I close my eyes and pull power from her. I imagine it flowing through her, to her fingertips, and to me. I feel a rush of power wash over me. I picture all the people falling asleep, one at a time.

"They're all asleep," Zylan says ripping me from my train of thought.

"But I was . . ." I trail off as I open my eyes. They are all asleep . . . but I was only at three . . . how is that possible?

I shake it off; there is no time for this. "Okay, let's go."

"So what's the plan? We can't just poof onto the ship so how do we get on?" Justin asks.

"We're going to 'poof' to the edge of the island. Then we will talk about a plan."

***

I watch her. Hook is in here, and if she sees him . . . I need to make sure she's not going to do anything stupid. Just as she's about to send an arrow into a pirate taking a swing at Clover, she stops dead and drops her arms, arrow still set up.

Zylan turns around and finds Hook standing in the back corner. She stands there frozen in place, with a pirate coming at her from the left.

"Zylan!" I scream, snapping her out of it. Just in time too.

She uses the arrow she has and shoots it into the chest of the pirate. He drops, and she returns her attention to the man at the window.

She walks across the room, not looking around, not stopping for anything, in about five seconds. At about three second she pulled out an arrow, set it up in her bow, and has it pointed at Hook. "You know who I am?" she asks, voice wavering slightly. I don't pay attention to the rest I need to get us out of there.

I see a pirate walking toward Justin out of the corner of my eye. I try to shove him to Neverland, but it doesn't work. He doesn't budge.

Hook has his other pirates start to flood the room. If we don't get out of here now, we're all going to die. I can't let that happen, so I focus all my energy into getting my people out of there.

"What happened?" Zylan asks looking around.

"We got Ace back. I couldn't stand to watch see anyone else fall, so I got us out of there." I say making my way over to her. I smile until I see her face. Eyes narrow, eyebrows scrunched together, face so red it looks like she's going to explode.

"I ALMOST KILLED HIM! WHY WOULD YOU DO THAT? THREE MORE FUCKING SECONDS!" She screams at me. Her voice drops to a whisper as she finishes. "You couldn't have waited three more seconds?" She starts to cry.

"I . . ." I can't believe I hurt her again. I should have waited three more seconds. I should have let her end this. I feel my own eyes tearing up. "I'm—"

"Save it." With that she's gone.

I know where she is. The same place I always go when I feel like she's feeling right now. I try to picture myself standing on the cliff, but I used all my energy on getting us out of there. It looks like I'm going to have to walk.

I need to move quickly. The last time I saw her on the cliff feeling like this, she went to jump. I can't let that happen. No matter what I have to do, I can't let her jump off that cliff. I break into a run once the gray wall is in sight.

I find her just in time to see her walking toward the edge of the cliff. I run faster.

"Not again. Please don't do this," I say as her toes curl over the edge.

"I can't do it anymore. Jacob, if you ever loved me, please just let me go."

"I can't do that. Zylan, I can't let you jump, I love you."

She turns around slowly. "Please don't. Please, please, please don't say that. You can't love me. You know that, I know that. Just let me take one more step, you'll forget all about me."

"No, I won't," I whisper, tears welling up in my eyes. "I need you, even if that means you have to hate me again." I muster up all the power I have left and even pull power from the island. I have to do this . . . even if it kills me.

"What are you—Pan? Why is it so dark? When I left, it was sunup . . ." I feel weak. It takes everything in me to stay upright. The skyline blurs slightly. I can barely hear what she's saying, and standing is taking all the energy I have. I can't let her see me waver. I have to stay strong.

"You don't remember?" I can't believe I did this. "Zylan . . . there was an attack. We were off the island for a bit, and pirates attacked the camp."

"What!" She exclaims. "Is everyone okay? Why can't I remember?"

I drop my head. "I think you better hear it from someone else. Come on, let's go back to camp."

"But I want you to tell me, Pan, what happened?" She bows her head, eyes scanning left and right. She's trying to remember something, something I took away from her. "Wait, I can't remember how they died. Pan, I can't remember how I got here. What's happening to me?" She starts to cry; the tears roll down her cheeks, but she doesn't make a sound.

"Come on, let me take you home. Ace is probably really worried about you."

"I—" I can't remember why he would be worried about me . . . Who is he to me?

Her thoughts echo in my head. Oh no, what have I done?

***

They let go of my hands. "You . . . all those years and you never said a thing . . ." Clover trails off.

"How could I? She never gave me the chance . . . now do you see why I can't fix this? Whatever she's doing now will be nothing compared to what she was going to do."

"She's going to figure out the truth eventually . . . she's not one to let things go," Elena says.

"I know, but for now, I need all of you at 100 percent. You get that right?"

"Yeah, but I still don't like this. You need to figure out what to replace her day with. She won't be at 100 percent until then."

"That's the problem. In order to do that, not only do I have to replace going to Neverland but all her thoughts after that. She can't know she ever felt something for me, and I have a feeling a lot of her thoughts from that day were about me. And it has to be at exactly the same time."

"How did you do it before? I mean, she remembers the 543 years she was on the Island, but she doesn't remember you watching her. How did you do that?"

"I piggybacked onto Peter's curse. The memories he gave her were still present. I just pulled them forward. The only thing I changed was the day Hook attacked her village. The rest of her major memories, I wasn't a part of, so I didn't have to change anything there. But I can't do that here. That day is too fresh in her mind. She'll remember every thought, and I can't figure out how to change them." I sigh, rubbing my eyes with the palm of my hands. How could I let this happen?

"So let us help you. Just because you brought us here doesn't mean you alone are responsible for all of us. This isn't all about you. It's about all of us as a whole. Zylan is part of that whole, and we won't be able to do this without her. So let us help you, help her, help us," Clover says.

"Okay, let's brainstorm." I force a smile.

All they want to do is help their best friend, but neither of them would be in this mess if it weren't for me. I can't believe what I did to Clover. I should have just let her be happy with Kaleb. I can't believe I took Elena away from Tyler—Hunter—that night on the docks. I should have read Peter's letter. None of us would be in this mess. They both could have been happy. They all could have been happy.

***

It's been a few days since the attack. I'm pretty sure that the only reason they choose that day to attack is because I was gone. If that wasn't the case, there's no reason they haven't tried again. Everyone is really on edge, figuring that they can attack again at any time. No one's sleeping, no one's laughing, no one's talking.

I want to do something, get rid of the pirates myself, but I can't think of a practical way to do that. Peter made it impossible for me to get rid of them. Honestly the only way to do this is kill them and I can't kill them all, even with my magic . . .

"Pan? We can't go on like this. I heard everyone planning to go back onto the ship . . . I think we should do it." I hadn't noticed Zylan standing in front of me.

"I agree, but we need a plan. I can't lose anyone else."

"I'll get everyone together. Let's plan." She smiles and disappears a second later.

***

"I know that it's been a rough few days, and I know you want to go over there swinging and shooting without a plan. We've already lost nine of us. I don't know about you, but I don't want to watch anyone else fall. We *need* to go in with a united front. As much as you want them all to pay, you need to think of your own life over killing all of them."

Zylan managed to get everyone together in a few minutes. That meant I had to make up my speech basically on the spot. I think it could have been better had I of had more time. It doesn't seem to have really gotten to them. They all look depressed, like it's not even worth it to try and fight. All the faces looking at me right now are the same as the day I rescued most of them.

"Nothing will get accomplished if we all die," Zylan adds.

"Then what's the plan?" Willow asks.

"We need to attack from every angle, at the same time. This means from inside the ship and out. A group of us will start from the bottom of ship where the bilge is. The rest will have to scale the ship wall. The only way this is going to work is if we all attack at the *exact* same time."

"How are you deciding the groups?" Hunter asks, crossing his arms. Of course, out of all the people here, he was the one that had to be a dick.

"Does it matter to you?" Zylan shoots back. Not rude, but her tone isn't friendly either.

"Yeah, it does. I don't want to scale the ship's wall. It's gross and slippery. Trust me, I know, I was there the longest."

"Fine, stay here. If you don't want to scale the fucking wall, keep your foot up your ass and stay the hell out of my way. Anyone else that has a problem with scaling the wall then you can stay here too." She crosses her arms and shoots Hunter a dirty look.

With that his posture shrinks and he takes a step back. He didn't expect that reaction; he just . . . always has to act like an ass. He clearly wasn't planning on sticking around here. He probably just wanted to be part of the group on the inside. He was going to be, but now . . . I don't think Zylan would let that happen.

I want the people I trust most on the inside with me. Ace, Zylan, Clover, Justin, Elena, Tyler, and Hunter. I think I'll try and get Ace to talk her into it. Plus, we also really need Hunter because he knows the ship the best.

No one else had any objections, so we broke up the teams. They wanted to head out tonight, but Zylan talked them into waiting a couple days for everyone to get their strength up. We—at least—need one good night sleep before we can even think about heading into battle. So off everyone went.

Chapter 15

The Truth

Zylan

"Zylan, can I talk to you for a minute?" Pan asks coming up to me.

I smile. "Sure, what's this about?"

I'm sitting on a rock off to the side of camp. Everyone has been acting weird toward me since the attack. I don't blame them, at all. But it's kind of lonely. I'm not used to this, having everyone avoid me. I'm always the one people talk to when they're upset or worried. I can feel the fear in the air, but most of it is directed at me. I wasn't here to protect them when they needed me and now I can't even remember why I left. They hate me. They will until they know the truth, and so will I.

"Sorry I've been avoiding you. I didn't know how to tell you what happened when we were gone . . . I talked to Clover and Elena. They helped me come up with a way to restore your memories so I don't have to tell you." He sends me a shy smile. "I'm sorry for what you've been going through the last couple of days, but I'm going to help you now."

"How?" I try to conceal my worry. I do want to know what happened, but I also don't. There is so much wrong with this situation.

"Just follow me, they need to help." He stands up and offers me his hand. I take it.

***

When I look up, I see the boy from my dreams, the one who's been watching over me since Wendy died.

"Is my father okay?"

The boy kneels down and looks me in the eyes. "I'm so sorry, but I don't know. I promised him that I would keep you safe so we need to leave now." He holds out his hand to help me up, but I kiss my mother's forehead and slide her off my lap before I take it. "I'm Jacob by the way. Jacob Pan."

"Zylan."

***

"Pan . . . is your name Jacob?" I ask.

His eyes go wide. "Shush!" he exclaims pulling me away from camp. We walk for five minutes before he stops. "You remember?"

"I remember the day the pirates attacked. You found me cling to my mom. You introduced yourself as Jacob . . . was that real?"

"Yes. Do you remember anything else?"

"I knew you for a really long time. You used to watch over me. I could sense you watching me every night. One night I even had a dream about you . . . you used to protect me, make sure I was okay." I pause trying to remember more. "That's it. There's nothing from the day the Island was attacked."

He looks down, as if looking for something to say. "Okay . . . that's good. Um, let's go find Clover and Elena. We'll get you back to normal." He starts to walk away.

"Pan, wait. I'm not going anywhere until you tell me what happened. I don't want my memories back until you soften the blow. Where did we go? Why did we go there?"

"Neverland. We got your memories fixed." He sits down on a log and covers his face with his hands. "I'm so sorry, Zylan. I can't lie to you anymore. I shouldn't have wiped your memories. I should have just talked you down. I just couldn't watch you try to jump again."

"What? You're not making any sense!"

"Here." He moves one hand from his face and waves it.

At first, I don't understand. At first, he just looks like an idiot. But then I feel a sharp pain in my head. I wince but don't make a commotion. Then the pain grows. I sit down holding my head. Then the pain explodes. I scream and fall over.

Everything comes flooding back. Our kiss, my love for him, Wendy being alive, finding Justin, having everyone yell at me, how much I hurt Ace, almost killing my parent's killer. I messed up. That's why I was on the cliff. That's why Jacob did this.

"Zylan! Zylan!" He's kneeling next to me.

I try breathing again. Nice and slow, in and out. "I'm okay, I'm okay. I have a problem though." I push myself up, trying to sit. Jacob helps me lean on a tree and stay balanced.

"What's wrong?" His eyes fill with worry.

"Your logic. Why would you take away my memories just to give them back?" I laugh weakly.

"You scared me! You were going to jump off that cliff, and I couldn't stand to watch that. I had to do something fast, and the only thing I could think of was making you forget what happened. The last thing I wanted to do was violate you like that again, but there was nothing I could do." He looks down covering his face again. "I messed up. I'm so sorry. I don't blame you if you hate me now."

"I couldn't hate you again, not even if I tried. We've been through way too much for that." I chuckle.

"All right, I'll hate myself enough for the both of us." He laughs as well.

"Don't. Now help me up. I want to go talk to Clover and Elena."

"I think you should rest a minute, they can wait."

"Fine, I'll just help myself." I pull myself off the tree. I start to stand when Jacob stops me.

"Fine, fine. Have it your way stubborn, little girl."

"Hey! I'm only eight years younger than you!"

"I meant that you're small." He says it with a straight face, but I can see him cracking as he helps me up.

"From the rumours, I'm not the only small one here." I smirk and turn away.

"Hey now, that wasn't very nice!" he exclaims running after me.

"Neither was erasing my memories, so you know what? Suck it up, old man."

He puts his hands up. "I surrender."

***

"Thank God he told you! I was going crazy keeping this from you!" Clover exclaims throwing her arms around me.

Elena goes next. "He gave you back everything right? Like you know he's in love with you and all that right?"

"Yes, thanks for that." Jacob rolls his eyes.

"Hey, I don't blame you. I'm loveable!" I smirk.

This is all so weird. I hated him for something he didn't do. After almost 545 years, I find out I was really in love with him, but I'm getting married; and now Jacob, Clover, Elena, and I are all laughing like there isn't a giant magenta elephant in the room . . . this whole thing is so messed up it's like it's not even real.

"We need to figure out what we're going to tell everyone. I can't deal with them looking at me the way they are. They need to know what happened without having to explain everything. I'm the reason they're all here, and I'm part of the reason nine of us died . . . they have a right to know."

"Part of your story is mine, and I'm not quite sure I'm ready to let this out. Can we just tell them half the story?"

"Jacob, you've kept this secret long enough. It's time to let it go," Clover says.

"Fine we'll talk to them together. But we're not telling them everything. Some stuff shouldn't be said . . ." Jacob looks at me. We all know what he's talking about, and none of us would have said anything about it anyways.

We planned what to say; what was the most important stuff and what could be left for another time. All we need right now is to rebuild the trust.

***

Clover gathered the crowd while Jacob and I went over how we're going to break this up. We decided it would be better if I introduced, but he started. So we're standing in front of them as they stare at us with blank faces.

"Okay, everyone, it's time to tell you the truth. I got my memories back, and I need to come clean with all of you. I know that you aren't very happy with me right now, but no one feels worse than me. I let you guys down. I should have been here, but I was off the Island with Pan."

"The first thing you should know is that I'm not Peter Pan, and this isn't Neverland. My name is Jacob. I have a twin brother named Peter, and he lives on Neverland. We got into a fight 543 years ago and sent me here. The reason for this fight was Zylan. I was on my way to save a child named Jaden, but I saw her village being attacked by pirates. The same pirates that now sail around our island.

"I rescued Zylan from the captain, but that was against Neverland's rules. Peter sent me here. He cursed Zylan to not remember what really happened that night, along with the pirates. The reason they attacked while Zylan and I weren't here was because they're looking for a treasure chest. One we can't let them get to. Ace and I brought it here 533 years ago to keep it out of their hands, and after just recently reading a letter from my brother, that was the right thing to do.

"If these pirates get the treasure, they will be reintroduced to the world, and it won't be good, for anyone."

"The reason we left the Island was to go to Neverland, so I could find out what really happened that night. Little gaps in my memory were driving me crazy. Jacob told me the truth about his brother and said the only way to fix these gaps was to go to Neverland and get Peter to reverse it.

"The reason I forgot what happened the day of the attack was because Jacob wiped my memories. I was so overwhelmed with the flooding memories and the belief that the attack was my fault, I tried to kill myself. He thought that if I didn't remember, I would be better off.

"I'm so sorry I let you guys down and my actions were ridiculously selfish. I hope that you can all forgive me one day, forgive both of us. We want to make this right, anyway that we can."

"We're sorry," Jacob and I finish together, unplanned but kind of nice.

Ace runs over to me and gives me a hug. I hurt him so much, and he doesn't even know it. His best friend lied to him for 533 years, and he still pats him on the shoulder and says thank you.

They all forgave us. They all hugged us and told us they understood, even Hunter had nothing to say. They didn't ask any more questions, push me for information about what happened the night of the attack on my village, or even ask about Neverland. They just went about their activities. The life of the Island was restored, and I can feel the energy start to change.

I missed my ability to sense things; now that I have it back, I'm never going to take it for granted again. Everything is back to normal. Now that we're all on good terms, we're finally ready for a united front. We're finally ready to rid the world of those nasty pirates. I can finally kill the man who ruined my life.

***

That night was amazing. Everyone finally knew the truth or at least most of it. We were all on the same page for the first time since we all stepped foot on this island. We were finally united.

Jacob started a bonfire in the centre of camp. All night we sat around it laughing and enjoying ourselves. He played his flute, and Tyler sang. He admitted he dabbled in singing before he came to the Island so naturally we all forced him too. He was good. Really good.

We danced as well. We haven't done that in forever. We were all happy. This could very well be our last night together. None of us said that, but I know we were all thinking it. We spent it together, enjoying ourselves, and it was the best night I ever had on the Island.

We told stories about our time leading up to our first day here. We found out there was a connection between almost all of us—well, the main group of us at least. Elena, Justin, Ace, Tyler, and I all had a sibling that almost died and went missing. Justin, Hunter, Elena, Tyler, Ace, and I all had an encounter with the pirates the day of being brought here— Hunter obviously more so. Clover was the odd one out though.

After a long time talking, we decided we needed sleep before our attack. We all stayed in camp together, even Jacob.

I should be sleeping now, but I can't make myself. I have way too much bouncing around in my head to even shut my eyes. Ace has been passed out snoring for, I want to say, an hour, but it's probably only been ten minutes. I slide out from under his arm, careful not to wake him. He stirs slightly but just rolls over and continues sleeping.

I sit up. Almost everyone is peacefully sleeping in pairs. Even Hunter and Elena are cuddled up to each other. I smile. They were pretty close last night; they even talked about how they met and their time together. I haven't seen her that happy since the day he got here.

"Zylan?" Jacob asks. He's sitting on a log in front of the burn-out fire pit.

"You should be sleeping," I say standing up.

"So should you."

"Fair point. Couldn't sleep?" I ask walking over to him.

"Yeah." He pauses and looks off into the distance. "Can we talk? We haven't really had a chance yet."

I nod. "Come on, let's not wake anyone up." I stand up and walk to the edge of camp. I pause before I push through the branches. He didn't follow me. He's still sitting on the log staring at me. "Come on!" I whisper waving him forward.

He sighs and stands up. "I'm coming, I'm coming."

"What do you want to talk about?" I ask as he holds the branches out of the way for me.

"Everything. There are things I haven't told you, things I haven't thought about in hundreds of years. I'm not a good guy. I've done horrible things, and I can't hold on to them anymore. I just can't."

"Cliff?" I ask. I have no idea what he's going on about, but I think he deserves for me to listen before I judge him for his choices.

He nods and takes my hand. When we rematerialize, we're standing in the all-too-familiar setting of the cliff. It's a clear night, not a cloud in the sky. We're looking at a full moon with all the stars present. There's a warm breeze blowing east. It's a beautiful night, maybe the last one some of us will see. We sit down at the edge of the cliff and let our feet hang over. He doesn't waste any time.

"I lied to Ace his first day here. I told him if he went home he wouldn't have long with his family. I lied to Clover. I'm the reason she's here. I cursed Kaleb. I watched him beat her up and leave her for dead. He loved her so much. He would have done anything for her, and I ruined that. I saw Elena and Tyler—well, Hunter now—on the docks the night he asked her to marry him. I could have saved them both, but I choose to save Elena. I knew Hunter was on the ship all those years. I could have easily saved him, but I choose not to. The only reason I rescued him in 1698 was because the Island landed in the middle of nowhere and the ship never docked. I would have left him there forever. This could have all so easily been avoided if I wasn't trying so hard to get you to stop hating me. I messed up so many lives because of this.

"Sometimes, when I disappear for long period of times, it is because I'm checking on the families of the people I've 'rescued.' Ace's mom killed herself and his two sisters because she couldn't handle the loss of him. Kaleb was a werewolf in a pack before Clover. The pack found out what he did to her, and they killed him. He let them too. He was so broken that he let his family rip him to pieces. His last words were, 'I'm so sorry, my Clover.' Elena's mom wasn't functioning even before Elena went messing. When I took her, her mom lost it. She disappeared. They found her five years later, washed up in a lake six towns over. Hunter was so heartbroken after losing Elena. He joined the crew. He didn't care who he hurt, he didn't care what village was ransacked. You know why they call him Hunter? He hunted girls. Every time they docked, the crew made beats on how many girls he could get. He used girls to forget his pain, the pain of losing his whole world. I took that away from him. Justin's family struggled.

Justin was taking care of all his siblings. With him gone, they struggled with money. They didn't all make it and that's my fault. And Tyler, his girlfriend was pregnant. He had a son he doesn't even know about, a son that grew up without parents. She died during child birth and he was left at a church. That little boy grew up with no parents because of me. It was all my fault."

Tyler's story struck a nerve I thought I had buried a long time ago. I don't know what to say to that. I can't defend what he's done, but I can't say it was the wrong thing to do. Clover was definitely not something he should have done. Same with Hunter, he should have rescued them together. But the rest wasn't his fault. He couldn't have possibly foreseen the reaction of their families. All of us would have been long dead without him.

"I'm not going to defend what you did to Clover or Hunter. That wasn't right. But Ace made his own choice, Elena begged you to take her, she told me herself. What happened to their families was *not* your fault. You rescued Justin from the same fate as Hunter and you made Clover happy again. You can blame yourself for all of this, or you can accept the fact that you can't change the past. I'm not going to speak for all of us, but personally I'm glad you brought me here. I got to have a long life here, with people I love more than I thought I ever could." I look over at him. He has tears streaming down his face. "Jacob, look at me. Jacob, please. I know you're beating yourself up about this, but you can't do that right now."

He turns toward me. His normally sparkling green eyes are swollen, red, and filled with sorrow. "Why are you being so nice to me? You hated me for so long with fake memories, how can you sit here and know this and not hate me?"

"He didn't just change my memories from that night. He changed all the memories I ever had of you. You won me over so many times over the last 546 years. Peter took away all of that. I don't hate you because I never have. I hated what

I thought you did. I got 546 years' worth of memories back, memories of loving you, feeling safe around you, waiting for you to visit me. Even when I thought you killed my parents, there were times where I forgot about that, times where I thought you were a good guy and wanted to believe my brain was playing tricks on me." I put my hand over his. "Jacob, as much bad as you think you've done, you've done more good. Look at how happy everyone was before the pirate attack. We were getting along, everything was good. And so are you. Don't forget that." I pause and wait for him to say something.

We sit there for a long time. Long enough to watch the moon start to move across the sky. Long enough for the sun to start peeking over the horizon. Neither of us say a word; we just sit there and take in our surroundings.

"Zylan, can I ask you something?"

"Go ahead."

"When we kissed, what was it like for you?"

I laugh. "Really? That's what you've been sitting here staring off into space thinking about?"

"I've been thinking about it since it happened." Jacob pauses. "I just want to know if there could ever be a chance for us . . ." He keeps his eyes straight ahead as he trails off.

"I—Jacob I can't do that, not right now. You have to understand that I do love you, but Peter took so much away from me. I forgot about it. I didn't know that I did, love you I mean. I moved on with my life, and I think that you should too. There is a girl out there that would kill to have someone like you, and it kills me to tell you I can't be that girl, at least not right now. I'm sorry."

I can feel my heart breaking as the words leave my mouth. You have no idea how much I want to reach over and tell him that's a lie. You have no idea how badly I wanted to tell him there's a chance. But I couldn't.

He looks down. "Thank you."

"For—" he's gone.

***

When I get back to camp, everyone is waking up, and Jacob is nowhere to be found. I just can't win. In the last week I've hurt every single person that I love. After all of this, I have to take time to myself, a lot of time.

"Ze, where'd you go?" Ace asks. He's sitting on a log.

"A walk. I needed to clear my head. Sorry I should have woken you up." I force a smile and sit beside him.

He smiles back at me. "It's all right. I really needed that sleep." He puts his arm around me and kisses the top of my head. "Is everything okay with you? I know it's been a rough few days, especially for you."

I lean my head on his shoulder. "Yeah, I'm okay. But after today, after we win, I'm going to need some serious time to myself."

"I get that."

"Could we talk for a few minutes? There's some stuff I need to tell you and there's no right time, but I feel like I need to tell you before we do this."

"Sure, we can—"

"Is everyone ready? I got us a nice breakfast. We can't go in hungry." Jacob appears in the middle of camp, interrupting Ace.

"Yeah? Where is it then?" Hunter's back. I was wondering how long it would take him to get back to normal. Now I know.

Jacob waves his hand. This isn't breakfast. It's a feast. When we waved his hand, the fire pit disappeared and got replaced by a long table. On it is fruits, vegetables, pancakes, waffles, syrup, bacon, ham, eggs—of all kinds—toast, peanut butter, a wide assortment of jams, forty-five plates stacked, and much more.

"You didn't get this. You poofed it, cheater," Clover says.

"Where do you think it comes from? There are some very angry twenty-first century people with no breakfast and no table."

I laugh. "Is everyone done with sarcasm, or should he send it back?"

I'm answered by an attack at the table.

"It can wait till after breakfast, go ahead." I smile and wave Ace toward the table. He smiles back and heads over.

I wait until everyone has food before I go up. By the time I get there, Hunter and Justin are going for seconds, but there's still a lot left. I grab a plate then waffles with syrup— way more than I need—and chocolate-dipped strawberries, along with two slices of ham and one piece of bacon. It's the best meal I've ever had.

Once everyone is finished, Ace and I make our escape. I pop up in a clearing on the far side of the Island and hope that we won't be interrupted. There is so much he needs to know, and I have no idea how I'm going to say any of it.

"Okay, what's going on, Ze?" Ace asks leading me to a log so we can sit.

"Jacob and I didn't tell everyone the whole story. Only Elena and Clover know, not because I told them, but because they confronted him." I add seeing a hurt look appear on his face.

"So what's the whole story?" The look is still there, but not as prominent.

I take a deep breath and tell him everything. The three years leading to Jacob rescuing me, going to Neverland, the kiss, and all the feelings that came rushing back. Once I started, it just kept coming. When I finally finished, I could feel the tears pouring out of my eyes.

"I'm so sorry. The last thing I ever wanted to do was hurt you, but I had to tell you because you needed to know why I was giving this back to you." I unclip the silver chain around my neck and hand it to him.

He looks at the chain in his hand and closes his eyes, a single tear rolling down his cheek. "I understand," he says and stands up. "You need time to yourself so you can figure out what you're feeling. I don't like it, but I understand." He leans down and kisses the top of my head. "I understand." He whispers again and disappears.

The second I'm alone I break down. I know I needed to do it, but I hated myself for it. I wish that things were different.

***

When I get back to the camp, some of the boys are sharpening swords. Some of them are practicing with each other; some are helping the girls.

Most of the girls shoot arrows. We're a lot stealthier than the boys, so it's easy for us to be long distance. While the boys are running in like a herd of elephants, we can sneak up onto the sails and be the eyes.

Each of us has twenty-four arrows in our cases. Hopefully it will be enough. The boys that are helping us are sharpening the arrows.

Because Clover, Elena, and I are going into the ship, we also have swords, just in case we run out of arrows.

By the time we're all ready to move, it's 7:00 AM. The sky is bloodred as the sun moves higher and higher east. There are dark clouds moving west over the Island as well. If I learned anything from all my years of reading . . . those dark clouds are a sign that we should wait one more day.

"What are you looking at?" Clover asks as she and Elena sneak up beside me.

"Those clouds don't look good . . ."

They look up. "No, they don't, but the sun is still peeking over the horizon. That's a good sign. Don't think about the weather. Everything is going to be okay."

"I guess we'll see."

Chapter 16

The Attack

Zylan

They haven't anchored the ship since the day they attacked. I'm guessing they're expecting us to retaliate—a fair assessment—and they think it'll be harder to get on board if they're moving. It won't be harder, especially with the amount of us that can do magic.

Jacob has us all on the beach. He thinks it's actually better that they're sailing. They won't be expecting us to come at them from underwater. If they're sailing, they can't see us coming at all. All we have to do is wait for them to cross our path. The ship doesn't move very fast; we won't miss it.

He wants the girls to go first. We're quieter, so he thinks it will be easier for us to get in position than the boys. Especially because most of the guys are way angrier than us. They won't be able to hold long enough for a joint attack if they go first. So that's the plan.

Lydia and Noel lead the group; and Clover, Elena, and I are trailing behind. We're using the same method as Jacob, Justin, and I. It's the easiest and least detectable.

The ship always sails the same distance away from the Island—as far away as it can get—about a hundred meters from shore. All we have to do is walk that far and wait.

As my head disappears under the water, I notice the clouds rolling over this side of the Island. I push all my bad feelings down. I can't let this throw me off. At least we'll have dark coverage; I just hope it's enough.

The girls have all gathered at our meeting spot, when I see the bottom of the ship heading toward us. It's going to be a really tight squeeze. They look about five minutes out; the boys might not all make it here on time. They better move their butts faster.

Jacob and I combined our magic to keep everyone under. That's forty-five people we're keeping planted to the sea floor and breathing. It's starting to wear me out. I bet he's struggling as well; he's used a lot of magic the last few days, and it can't be easy for him.

Only half the boys have joined us, and the ship is almost right on top of us. There's no way Jacob and I will be able to keep everyone under long enough for the ship to go around the Island again. *Come on, Zylan, think. Can you get them here faster?* Maybe if I wasn't feeling weak, I could pull them forward. *Do what Jacob did to make everyone pass out. Use someone else's energy on top of your own.*

I grab Clover's hand. She looks at me funny, but I ignore her. I close my eyes and imagine pulling everyone toward me. I keep my eyes closed until Clover shakes my arm. They're all here, just in time too. The ship is right above us.

I nod to Jacob, and we release them. This time Justin doesn't flail to the top; he's graceful just like the rest of us. Once everyone's up, we all fan out to our positions. Jacob, Ace, Clover, Elena, Hunter, Justin, Tyler, and I are at the very back. The eight of us are looking for the hole the girls dug when they were trying to escape. Everyone else is climbing up the ship wall.

They must have patched the hole up. We go all the way around the back and underneath, but we can't find it.

"What now? We can't cancel everyone's gone," Justin says. We all come together right at the back.

"Why don't we just poof in?" Hunter asks.

"I have something sarcastic to say to that, but he's right. We have no other option." I can't believe I'm agreeing with him.

"What if there's someone there?" Ace asks.

"Fair point, but we don't really have a choice. I don't see why someone would be though. They have no prisoners or anything," Clover adds.

"The reason they're sailing is because they're expecting something. They know the bilge is the most vulnerable part of the ship, someone will be there." Jacob's argument is fair, but again we don't really have a choice.

"I know these guys. I was part of the crew for 190 years. Trust me when I say they're really not that smart. If there's someone there, they're probably sleeping."

Everything that's brought up has an argument to it. We're running out of time for this. I'm just going to pop in. If there's someone there, I'll shoot them before they can do anything about it.

While everyone is distracted, I disappear in the cells. I stay very quiet as I peek through the bars. Hunter was right, the person that's supposed to be watching is passed out in a chair. I take my bow off my shoulder, grab an arrow out of my case, and set it. I aim for the centre of the guy's head. He won't suffer, it'll be over quick. I send the shot then appear back in the water. They didn't even notice I was gone.

"It's taken care of, come on let's go." I don't stay long enough for anyone to yell at me.

They appear in the cells shortly after I do. "You shouldn't have done it on your own. What if there had been more than one?" Clover asks.

"You saw me take out five at the same time. Now come on, the others won't wait much longer. Do you want to be the reason this all goes to shit? Because I don't." She rolls her eyes at me but says nothing else.

"Come on." Jacob waves the cell door open.

We pull out our weapons and walk toward the stairs, past the dead pirate. *I'm sorry it had to be this way.* We move up the stairs as quickly as possible. From the stairs, Hunter takes point. Jacob, Justin, and I found our way around eventually; but we have to do it quickly, which is the only reason I agreed to let Hunter come along. I hang at the back, just in case someone pops out of their room at the wrong time. Jacob does the same.

Right at the top of the stairs there's a wall. Hunter turns right and pauses in front of the first door. He takes a slow breath and continues walking.

"That was his old room," Jacob whispers to me.

I nod. This must be really hard for him, coming back here after all this time. He was with these people for a really, really long time. They were really close at one point, now he's going to have to fight them. I would not want to be him right now. I can't imagine what he's thinking.

Once we're at a steady pace, Jacob and I flip around so we're facing the hall instead of the group. We walk slowly to the end of the hall and pause as Hunter looks around the corner. I'm guessing it's all clear because he starts moving. Just as Jacob and I are turning the corner, two pirates come out of a room at the end of the hall.

We duck around the corner as fast as possible so they don't see us. We pause kneeling down. We have to wait for them to come so they don't have time to yell for anyone. They round the corner in thirty seconds. I shoot the first guy between the eyes as Jacob stabs the second centre chest.

"We can't leave them in the hallway, we're going to have to hide them," I whisper grabbing one guy's arms.

"It's going to slow us down. Where do you suggest we put them?"

"The cells." I drop the guy's arms. Instead I put my hands on the two pirate's chests and picture the cells. They're gone in seconds. "Come on, we need to catch up." I pull another arrow out of my case to arm myself then stand up.

When we look up, they're gone. They must not have noticed us stop so they have no one guarding their back. *Damn it!*

"Relax. They can't have gotten that far. I know the ship well enough to find them on this floor. It's just the next we have a problem with."

"Lead the way." We stay back to back in case we have another run in, but there's nothing. Around the next corner we can either go straight or turn left. He goes to the left, but I stop him. "You're sure it's this way?"

"Positive. Trust me."

I let go of his arm. "I do."

At the end of the hall we catch up to the rest of them. They had absolutely no clue that we lost them. We're going to keep it that way.

Hunter turns right and heads directly to the end of this hall. The staircase is right in front of us, but he passes it. "Hunt, man you missed the stairs. Are you sure you know what you're doing?" Tyler says.

"You were on this ship once too. Did I not take you from the second staircase?"

"Dude, that was forever ago. How should I know?"

"Stop bickering and start moving your asses. We're lucky we only ran into two guys. If we continue like this, everyone will be out of their rooms," I whisper.

"Two gu—"

"Later."

We're silent again. In the middle of the hallway, there's another staircase. This one Hunter goes up. At the top of the stairs, it's one long hallway. This one has obstacles everywhere. There are plants and broken bottles and random chairs scattered all around us. Jacob and I have face forward, so I really, really hope no one comes up the stairs.

When we finally make it past all the junk, to the end of the hall, we do a zigzag to the next hall. This one is completely bare of everything; it's almost creepier. The walls are grey, the lighting is scarce, and the silence is intense.

Luckily this hall is short, and the next one we turn left down is full of objects again. Hunter stops in the middle of the hall in front of a huge bookshelf and scratches his head. "There was a door here. This is the only way up the back of the ship."

"The door is probably still here. Why don't we just move this?" Elena says.

"It's going to be loud," he shoots back sarcastically. *Oh no, here we go.*

"Rumour is that's how you like it," she says under her breath, rolling her eyes. Clover and I seem to be the only ones that heard it because we slap our hands over our mouths and the boys look at us weird. They were getting along just fine; there was a part of me that was kind of hoping it worked out—a part of me I hate, but a part of me nonetheless—but they have a lot more work to do before that can be a possibility.

"Okay, everyone out of the way," I say pushing through. I put my hands on the shelf and picture the cells again. Once it's gone, the door is visible.

I let Hunter take point again. He pushes the door open and doesn't acknowledge me at all. *You are very welcome, asshole.* I roll my eyes.

"Play nice, the pirates are the enemy today," Jacob says coming up behind me.

"Stop listening to my thoughts, I have private things up there." I glare at him. I'm scared I'm going to start thinking about something I don't want him to know and then it'll just be awkward.

"I can only really hear them if they're directed at someone or really strong, so if you don't think about anything powerful, I won't see it." He smiles. Actually it's more like a smirk.

"You little shit." Now he's got me thinking about the first time I saw him. When I was sitting in my room writing in my journal, looking out over the lake. He came to my window and told me I wasn't crazy, that everyone else was just blind.

He smiles slightly. He knows exactly what I'm thinking about, but this time he says nothing about it. "Come on."

"I'm going, relax." I walk through the door. The rest of the group hasn't made it to the top yet.

I take a deep breath. It's almost time. I feel the anxiety building up. I try not to worry about it. It's all going to work out. One way or the other, we're never going to have to see the pirate again and that's all that I care about.

At the top of the stairs is a small gap underneath the wheel. There's a small wall between us and the deck crew. It's the perfect hiding spot for us. I push past everyone to the front. The signal we all discussed was an arrow to the centre sail. As soon as I shoot it, the girls will know they can start firing off the deck crew and the boys will come over the wall.

I pull the string back, take a deep breath, aim at the centre mass, and release. The second my arrow hits the post, arrows start flying from all directions. Also, I was right about the boys coming over like a herd of elephants. They come over screaming. *Idiots.*

Jacob gives me a look. *Sue me.* I shrug and move into battle. I want a high vantage point so I can keep an eye out for Hook Hand. He's not out here yet, but he won't stay hidden for long. I make my way up to the wheel having to shoot three guys coming at me with swords.

I have my bow set up just in case someone needs my help and I can see everyone. I watch for anyone who seems to be struggling. I see Dylan on the other side of the deck. He strikes the pirate left, then right, then left again. The pirate seems tired of blocking; he swings his sword around, throwing Dylan's out of his hand. The pirate takes his right leg, sweeping it behind Dylan's left and knocks him to the ground. Before the pirate has the chance to strike, I send an arrow into the back of his head. Dylan scrambles to his feet, grabs his sword, and heads back into battle.

Out of the corner of my eye, I see Vlad surrounded by five pirates. I set up to take one of them out, but Vlad does a full three-sixty and takes the head off all of them. *That was really impressive.* It's like he can feel me watching because he turns around and winks at me before moving back into a fight.

Then I see Hunter. . . *Why are you even alive? Seriously, what is the point of your existence?* He's flailing his sword around in front of a pirate about to lose his patience. *What are you doing? You're going to get yourself killed!* He circles and circles and circles his sword. When he finally puts his sword on guard, he's in the most ridiculous stance I have ever seen in my life, and the pirate just knocks his sword out of his hand.

Do I really want to save him? He kind of did it to himself. . . It didn't matter anyways. Elena snuck up behind the pirate and took his head off. Hunter tries to say something, but she stops him. I can't make out what she's saying exactly, but it looks like "hurt me again, that's what's going to happen to you." He swallows and nods, then grabs his sword and returns to fighting.

More of the crew is starting to flood the deck. There are a lot of people and not a lot of space. Some of them are starting to climb the sails. I try to shoot as many as I can down, but it's not enough. Ryan fell, along with Tara, Faye, and Unique. The boys are doing about the same—Luke, Eli, Matt, Damon, and Edward are lying dead on the deck.

I can't see Ace or Jacob anywhere. They probably went down to the quarters. If they get to the crew before they can get up here, we have less to do up here. Risky but smart, I hope they're okay.

There's still no sign of the captain. Where could he be? There's no way he would leave his crew to fight this while he's hiding out somewhere. What could possibly be keeping him away from his crew?

We can't keep fighting like this; we're losing too many people. I have to find Ace and Jacob. We have to start tying up the crew, we can't lose everyone.

A pirate comes at me while I'm heading down the stairs. His sword is above his head, blocking his vision. I reach for an arrow, this is my last one. I release it into the centre of the pirate's chest and continue on.

I drop my bow and arrow case. It's useless now; it will only restrict my movements. I pull my sword out of the holster on my left hip. I manage to get to the second deck without a run in with anyone. Navigating the second deck is slightly challenging. I kind of remember where Hunter took us, but this ship is a maze.

I turn left at the door and make my way down the messy hallway. Then I turn right at the creepy clear hallway. Then there's the zigzag and another messy hall is on my right. If I remember right, the stairs are at the end of that hall.

I don't run into any pirates while I'm walking. I feel like I should have; something isn't right. The ship holds at least a hundred pirates. I saw maybe forty on the deck, and we've taken out about twenty-five—give or take—up to fight on the deck. That leaves about thirty-five unaccounted for. There's no way that thirty-five pirates would be hanging out down here, with the ruckus that's going on up the stairs.

At the end of the cluttered hall, I see the stairs. About halfway down, I hear Ace's voice. "Pan! I have my end. How are you doing?" he yells.

"All tied up over here too!" His voice is closer.

At the bottom of the stairs, Jacob is wrapping a rope around the hands and feet of a knocked-out pirate. I put away my sword. "How many were there?" I ask, causing him to jump and let out a tiny squeak.

"How do you do that?" He holds his heart taking a deep breath. "You're like a cat!"

"If one more person compares me to a cat, I will kill them. Can you answer my question—how many pirates did you tie up?"

"Twenty, why?"

"There are at least fifteen of them missing, including the captain. Something's not right."

"Ace! Let's go we gotta get back up there." He turns back to me. "Go back up there and start tying them up. We need to get answers, and killing them all won't get us anywhere."

I nod and head back up. This time is easier. I think I have it memorized now. It takes me about two minutes to get up to the top deck. At the top of the stairs, I get jumped by a pirate.

As we tumble down the stairs, I feel a burning sensation down my chest, I ignore it. At the bottom, he lands on top of me, with his hands around my neck. My arms are pinned behind my back. I can feel the dagger strapped to my back. If I can wiggle it out fast enough, I might have a chance. I ignore the pain in my left arm. It might be broken, but I can't worry about that right now.

The guy on top of me pushes down harder with every struggle I make. I can feel my lungs struggling for air as I get my arm loose. He's not paying any attention to that, so he doesn't try to block as I dig the dagger into his left side. He lets out a whaling screech, jumps up, rips the dagger out of his side, throwing it into the wall, then he tears his sword from his holster. I do the same and prepare myself.

He swings at my left side, *predicable.* I block, scooping above our heads and down to my right. I take my right leg and kick him backward. As he stumbles, I swing my sword down to the top of his head. Despite his stumbles, he blocks, swinging my sword out of my hand.

He smiles like he won, but this fight won't be over until he's dead. He swings at my left side again. This time I duck out of his reach and tackle him. He hits the stairs, losing his sword in the process. Now the fight is fair.

He gets his feet on my hips and kicks me off. When I hit the wall, my left arm explodes with pain. *This is not the time to crap out on me. Ignore it and move on.* I ready myself for another attack. He lunges at me. I dive out of the way and roll to my feet. The pirate ran himself into the wall. I use his disorientation to slam his head back into the wall. He crumbles to the floor. I won.

Ace and Jacob come running around the corner to find me standing over the pirate. "Took you guys long enough." I laugh.

They're staring at me like they can't believe I'm still standing. I look down and see why. My shirt was ripped open exposing a huge gash running down my chest; both my arms have scrapes and bruises all over them, plus my left arm looks . . . bad. "Are you okay?"

"We don't have time for that. Hook Hand is still missing, and we're still losing people. Let's go."

I don't wait for them to protest. I grab my sword off the ground and my dagger out of the wall, and I leave them standing at the bottom of the stairs. On the top deck, the fight isn't going so well. Finn, Dixie, Jasmine, and Shawn joined the rest of our dead on the deck floor.

Out of the corner of my eye, I see Chad lose his sword. I grab my dagger and whip it across the deck, into the pirate's head, but it's too late. He already had his sword lodged in Chad's gut. I run over as he hits the deck.

He looks up at me and laughs. "I've had a long-enough life. I'm ready to see my family and friends again. It's all good." Then he just dies. *Okay then.* I grab my dagger out of the guy's head and wipe it on his shirt, before putting it back in its case.

I count fifteen dead. That's way too many. I need to stop this. I have to do something and I have to do it fast. *Think, Zylan. What can you do?* Magic. Magic has to work.

I hear sounds of screaming and clinking and yelling. I have to block them all out. If this is going to work, I'm going to need all the energy I have with no distractions. I close my eyes and concentrate on the ropes. I picture them grabbing hold of the pirates and dragging them to the closest sail.

When I hear the cheers, I open my eyes. The girls are starting to make their way down the sails when four of the guys attack the pirates. "Stop!" I scream. They jolt back, flying across the deck. I didn't mean to do that . . .

"Why? They attacked us! We need revenge!" Conner yells from the back of the crowd.

"Look I know you're all pissed off. I am too, but we can't kill them like this. It's cowardice, but we're sure as hell not going to let them go and continue fighting. We've lost too many people to these pirates, and we're not going to lose anymore." I pause taking a deep breath. "I've been counting crew members, and there are fifteen unaccounted for, at least. We need these people alive to answer our questions. We will get justice, but it will have to wait."

"Zylan's right. We can't lose any more people. We can't let them win by killing us all," Jacob says walking over to me.

We're standing at the front of the ship, where the deck is raised slightly. From here I can see everything. The fifteen of our dead, lying on the deck with blank faces, the thirty-something dead pirates, the remaining thirty of us—minus Jacob and I—beat up and exhausted, and the twenty pirates tied to the sails, struggling to get free.

"They're not going to tell us anything! What's the point?" Cole yells.

"The point is we're not savages. Some of these people have been part of this crew for the same about of time I've been alive. That's 560 years. The only person to blame for these attacks is the captain, and he's not here. They'll—"

"Cap'ain would never leave us to fight while he hides! You're lying to your own people! You must have already killed him!" One pirate spits at me.

"You're lying to yourself," I shoot back. "We've checked just about everywhere. He's left you to die while him and fourteen others are hiding somewhere on this ship. Tell us where and this won't be painful."

The pirate says nothing. "Don't you see? He doesn't care about you! He's using you to distract us while he's safe."

"There's a secret hiding spot under the deck of Cap's room. It's got 'nough space for fifteen," the pirate on the post closest to me says. The rest of the crew starts screaming and hissing at him. "What? He left us! We have to send off our brothers because of him!"

"No! It's because of them! They killed almost forty of us and you just threw Cap into the fire!"

While the pirates bicker with each other I sneak off. Hook Hand's quarters is at the very back. If he's there, there will be nowhere for him to run. If he's there, I can finally kill him.

As my hand touches the door handle, I take a deep breath. This is it. This will finally be over. I push the door open and draw my sword. At the back of the room, I see something on the wall. I don't know why it caught my attention, but it did.

I walk over to it. The room is a mess. This guy seriously needs to clean all of this shit up. There are papers thrown all over the floor, ink is spilt all over the desk, maps are pulled out of their slots and laid out everywhere, and his dresser is wide open with clothes falling out of it.

After manoeuvring to the back of the room, I find what I had been drawn to. There's a golden dagger dug into the wall.

"Zylan, why haven't you checked under the desk?" I turn to see everyone standing in the doorway.

I look back and pull the dagger out of the wall. The note in my hand has three words scribbled onto it.

Your too late

I don't know what's worse, the fact that he's on the Island, looking for the treasure, or the fact that he used the wrong you're . . .

Chapter 17

The Damage

Zylan

I have no clue how he got to the Island without anyone seeing him. I also have no clue how he knew we were coming. Everyone was below the water before I saw the ship. It's really dark right now. There's no way he could have seen us coming under water. How could this have happened?

We left right away. We took our people and brought them back to the Island. As soon as this is over, we're going to have a huge funeral where we can all mourn. We lay everyone down on the beach and split into teams. Clover, Ace, Elena, Tyler, Hunter, Justin, Jacob, and I stick together. Everyone else is in groups of six.

Lydia's group takes the east, Conner's takes north, Brandi's takes west, and Noah's takes south. Our group takes centre island because that's where Jacob says the chest is. Everyone has a lot of ground to cover, and we can't let them get the chest.

"Watch each other's backs. This will all be over soon," I say before we separate.

My group heads straight down the beach, into the centre of the forest. I stay at the back, letting Clover and Elena take the lead.

I watch everyone as we walk. Clover and Elena have been getting along surprisingly well. Hunter is getting along with the boys lately. He has a habit of making people want to kill him, but he's been pretty good the last couple weeks. He and Tyler are walking together, whispering about something I can't hear. Every once in a while, he'll look up at Elena and watches as she talks to Clover. It would be cute if I didn't kind of want to kill him.

Ace, Justin, and Jacob are walking right in front of me. They also have their heads down whispering about something. Jacob doesn't seem to be participating in the conversation, but he's listening pretty intensely. Ace turns back to look at me and gives me a weak smile. I smile back. I was kind of hoping he would fall back and talk to me, but he waves Jacob to do it instead. I wish I had waited to talk to him until after all of this. "She needs you right now." He's trying to keep his voice low, but he's never really been any good at whispering.

"How's your arm? Can I help?" Jacob asks falling back to meet me.

I stop walking. "Take away the pain, I can't do it myself. I'll fix it when this is done." I wince as he grabs my left hand. My arm is covered in black bruises, and my elbow is out of place. He gently brushes his hand over my arm. The bruises disappear and the elbow realigns, but it won't last long. I'd say I have about five hours before I should go to the waterfall. "Thanks." I roll my shoulders, just to make sure the pain is gone.

"No problem." We start walking again. "How are you doing?"

"Probably as good as you are. Fifteen, on top of the nine before. How could this have happened? Better yet, why now? They've been sailing around for 543 years. Why have they just now decided to attack us? Why couldn't they have left us be?"

"Something my jerk brother did, probably. If I had known what he did to you, I would have fixed it a long time ago. I should have just read the damn letter instead of tossing it aside." He sighs. "I just want this done with. As soon as this is over, I'm getting rid of this cursed treasure, once and for all."

"I'm helping." I smile at him.

He doesn't smile back. "We should talk, once everything's done. Like really talk, not what happened on the cliff." I nod. "And I'm sorry for disappearing like that. Don't tell anyone but—" he lowers his voice "—I'm pretty sensitive."

I let out a hushed laugh. "Don't worry, your secret is safe with me."

"Promise?"

"Pinkie promise!" I giggle holding out my right pinkie to him.

He locks his with mine. "I trust you." This time he smiles.

I hear a branch crack to my right. "Guys, stop!" I whisper.

I pull my sword out of its holster and quietly make my way to where I heard the crack. The trees all have low hanging branches with lots of leaves and no visibility to the other side. I lean on one of the trees and wait to hear a voice.

After about thirty seconds, I hear a hushed voice I don't recognize. I wave everyone to surround the area. They look at me funny. It takes a few seconds for them to process what I'm telling them to do. Once they've clued in, they fan out. I wait about thirty seconds before I tumble through the trees. I catch my balance and look around, like I'm embarrassed. There are five pirates standing in front of me; Hook Hand isn't one of them. "Oops, that's embarrassing. I thought I was stumbling onto something important, you must be the fall guys."

I don't give them a chance to move. With the wave of my hand, they all hit the floor—asleep. I'm not a monster. My group moves in as soon as the last one hit the ground. "Girl, why didn't you just do that on the ship?" Clover asks, staring.

"Honestly? I never even thought about it, and I wanted them all dead. Now we need them alive."

"Why didn't you leave one awake then?" Hunter asks sarcastically.

"The same reason you're a dick, it's more fun." I shoot him a dirty look. "All right, smart mouth, tie 'em up. I got questions."

He returns the dirty look. "No."

"Fine." I shrug. "If you're not going to be helpful, you can join them in slumber." I wave my hand, and he joins his old crew on the ground.

"That was a little much, funny, but a little much," Elena says looking at him.

"Meh, I don't feel bad about it."

Jacob chuckles. He waves his hand and the five pirates, plus Hunter, are tied to a huge oak tree. "Figured you might be tired, thought I might help out."

I smile. "Much appreciated." I move in front of one of the pirates. His head is hanging down, his black hair covering his whole face. I slap his cheek a couple times before he jolts awake. He tries wiggling free before he realizes his whole body is wrapped in rope. "So now that you figured out fighting is useless, I'd like to ask you a couple questions. If you don't answer honestly . . . you're going to want to answer honestly."

"Do your worst, bitch," he spits at my face.

I wipe it from under my right eye, blinking a few times to make sure it didn't actually get into my eye. "Okay, have it your way." I move to hit him, but Ace grabs my arm.

"Let us do this—you, Clover, and Elena should keep moving. Find Hook before he finds the treasure. Please."

"Ace, I have to—"

"No, you have to find Hook. Please. Go, we can take care of this."

"Ace is right. Go, we got this. We'll catch up with you," Tyler says stepping up.

"But—"

"But nothing, come on, girl, we're losing daylight!" Clover exclaims grabbing my arm.

I wince slightly but ignore my pain. "What daylight? Huh? There's no sun."

"Stop using sarcasm to hide your feelings. Let's go," Elena snaps.

"Okay, okay. I'm coming." I turn back to Ace, shaking Clover off. "Thank you."

He gives me a weak smile and shrugs like it's nothing.

I feel like I should say something, tell him I love him or something, but I just told him I didn't know if I actually did. I feel this hole in my chest, growing. I can't explain why it's there, but it makes me feel like I should turn around and go back, that I should say something more. I try not to think about it. This isn't the time to be thinking about it. I need to focus.

"Island to Zylan, hello? Is anyone there?" Elena says waving her hand in front of my face.

"Sorry, what happened?"

"I asked how you're doing. I know we've all been through a lot, but you've been . . . I just want to see how everything's going."

"Well, in the last week, I've found out the following. One, the guy who I thought murdered my parents actually saved me from pirates. Two, I've actually been in love with the guy I thought I hated for 543 years for 546 years. Three, I can't marry the guy I actually remember loving for five hundred years because I'm in love with his best friend. Four, the pirate that actually killed my parents has been sailing around this island for 543 years, and I had no idea. Five, my whole life has been a lie."

Clover and Elena stop walking. "You're not going to marry Ace? Because of Pan? Are you going to tell him?" they ask together.

"Really? Out of all that, the only thing you hear is that I'm not going to marry him? Well, I already did and put yourself in my shoes. Think for a second that you have 546 years' worth of memories of loving someone and at the same time you have five hundred years' worth of memories of loving someone else. How can you, in good conscience, marry one of them without having time to think about both?" I raise my eyebrows at the silence. "That wasn't a rhetorical question."

"I agree. I think that you should 100 percent think about it, but don't call off the wedding just yet. You should talk to Ace again and explain that you just need a little time alone. He's one of the nicest guys ever. He'll wait for as long as you need, and you know that," Clover says after a minute of thinking.

"Six days ago you were trying to get me to do just this and now you've changed your mind?" I shake my head. "What if he waits, and he doesn't like the outcome?" I pause and look at my feet. "I mean, I've been with him for so long, but it almost feels like a lie?"

"What do you mean?"

"There were a whole ten years that I spent with Jacob alone on this island. He saved me every year on August 14. I would go up to the cliff and stare off into the distance. Then I would walk to the edge and try to jump. He stopped me every year. Despite how I treated him, ignored him, ran in the other direction whenever he got close. And every year on August 14, I would remember what really happened, how much I cared about him and how much he cared about me. But the next second, I couldn't remember any of it. If I had never lost my memories, I know 100 percent, I wouldn't be with Ace, so how can I marry him?"

"You can't."

I bow my head. This is *not* the time or the place we should be looking. "Come on, we have treasure we need to keep from pirates."

They nod and follow in silence.

The silence doesn't last very long. Up ahead we hear the yelling of—what I'm assuming to be—pirates. It has to be the captain this time, it has to be.

"Why are they so loud?" I whisper.

"They think we're all on the ship?" Elena suggests.

I shrug. "Makes this a whole lot easier." I wave them to move around the clearing and head up the trees.

This is where Jacob took me the first night I got here. It's a tiny clearing, almost exactly centre island. Surrounding it are large oak trees, with enough low hanging branches, it's easy to stay out of sight. I head up a tree that's tilted slightly, so I don't have to do any crazy manoeuvres to get up it.

This time I wait until I know for sure that Clover and Elena are ready to move in. While I wait, I look down at what's going on. The pirates are all surrounding a small hole in the ground. Three of them are digging while the hook handed and a ratlike pirate watch.

Just as I hear a clink and "got som'in' cap'ain," I see Elena and Clover's heads pop up. Hook Hand walks forward as the other three brush off the chest in the dirt.

"Clover, Elena, we need to move. We can't let them get that back to the ship. Follow my lead. When the coast is clear, grab the chest," I whisper into the wind. I see them nod before I jump down. "You found it? Great! I've been looking for it everywhere!" I walk toward the hole. "Thanks, I can take this out of the way for you." As I approach the chest, three pirates block the path. "Okay, okay, I get it. You want to make me work for it. Fine by me."

I don't give them a chance to arm themselves. Before they can blink, I have my sword out of my holster and covered in blood. I took off the first guy's head, half the second guy's, and sliced the chest of the third. "Okay, so that's done. I'm just going to ah . . . clean off my sword here 'cause it's a little gross." I wipe the blade on the third pirate's shirt. "So I'm just going to take this and—" as I reach down for the chest, a blade flies by my hand, lodging in the chest.

"You're not movin'." Hook Hand is leaning on a tree about ten meters in front of me.

"Feisty, under normal circumstances, I might actually like you. *But* I'm still holding a teeny, tiny grudge from you killing my parents 543 years ago. I know, I know! It's old news, but it still hurts. And—"

I pull my sword out of my holster and aim it at the ratlike man. He's been trying to sneak up on me since I started talking. "Tsk, tsk, tsk. Don't you know it's rude to try and kill someone in the middle of a conversation?" I turn back to the captain. "Did you send him to do that?" He shrugs, like he doesn't care about anyone but himself. All he wants is that damn treasure, and he doesn't care who dies in the process. "That's just rude! We were having a civilized conversation." I turn back to the rat pirate. I let him get close enough to me that I can slash my sword down his chest and allow him to join his brothers in the beyond.

When he drops, I turn back to Hook Hand. He genuinely looks a little sad watching the rat man hit the ground. He sighs and peels himself off the tree. "I actually liked 'em. Oh 'ell."

"It's just you and me, old man. What are you going to do about it?"

"What I shoulda done 'at night." He lungs at me, pulling out his sword.

I block his out stretched sword and spin around, leaving my left hand as a block and my sword above my head. I giggle. "Feisty again. If you want to kill me, you're going to have to catch me first."

I turn around and run out of the clearing. I duck behind one of the trees and wait for him to pass. After a few seconds, I start to think he's not coming, but eventually he rushes past me. I wait for about a minute to make sure he isn't coming back.

Once I'm convinced, I walk back into the clearing. Clover and Elena are already pulling the chest out of the ground. It's not very big, maybe fifty centimeters by twenty-five centimeters. I can't imagine why anyone would want this chest in the first place . . . it can't have more than two thousand dollars in it. It doesn't seem like it's worth the trouble.

"We need to get that somewhere safe. Let's take it to my house. There's a loose floor board in my room."

I kneel down beside them and study the chest. It has a weird-looking design on it. There's a snake wrapped all the way around the base and the seams. The lock is a massive snake skull that takes up the whole centre of it, and the handles have lion heads. I thought this was going from the English government to the Turkish government. There's no way in hell that they would send over something that looked like that.

"We've got this. You have a pirate that needs some serious killing," Clover says moving to one handle.

"It only takes two people to get this where it's gotta go. Seriously, kick that guy's ass. We won't let anyone get this." Elena grabs the other handle.

"Are you—"

"Get out of here!"

"Okay! Okay, I'm going."

I walk for ten minutes looking for Hook Man. I can't find any trace of him walking anywhere. The path leading away from the clearing has no sense of disturbance. Where could he have gone? I keep my sword out, just in case he decides to try and jump me.

Every once in a while, I'll kneel down and look for a boot print, a broken branch—anything that can show me where he went—but there's nothing. How can a guy who spent most of his life on a ship know how to cover his tracks this well? What is this guy's deal?

"Lookin' for me?" I look up and find him leaning on a tree just ahead of me. How did I not see him?

"You were the one looking for me." I stand up slowly.

He shrugs as if to say *not really*. He steps away from the tree and walks toward me. He doesn't have a weapon out, so I drop mine to my side. I'm still ready if he tries to attack, but it looks like he's just going to try and talk me to death.

"Look at you, you're all grown up and strong." His tone of voice changes. He stopped talking like a pirate and started talking like someone who actually knows grammar.

"I looked exactly like this when we met last."

He starts to circle me as if he's studying me. "No, you've changed. Back then, you wouldn't have stood up to me."

"You didn't even know me. We never even met. You just walked into the room."

He laughs. "You think that, but I had met you many of times before that."

"That's not possible." I got everything back. I would have remembered that. *What's the point of him lying?*

"Oh, my darling little girl, so naive. One day you will figure this all out. I hope I'm there to see it, but for now, I have a treasure to get, so I bid you goodbye, for now."

"Look, I have no clue what the hell you're talking about, but you're not getting that treasure. Not now, not ever."

"Your father . . . he would be so proud of you," he says, stopping in front of me.

"You know nothing about him," I say through my teeth. "I've had enough."

I swing my sword around to hit his left side. He blocks with his hook and rolls the blade over it—the sound makes me cringe—throwing it off to the side. I manage to keep hold of it, but it's a tight squeeze getting to above my head to block a downward strike from a sword that came out of nowhere. I swing my sword and come in for a strike to the side of the head with the hilt.

He blocks my arm and throws it away, coming in with a kick to my stomach. I spin to my right setting my guard up again. We circle each other, neither one of us wanting to make the first move. I wait for him to get tired. I might be angry, but I'm not going to let my emotions ruin my chances.

I don't have to wait long before he sends a strike to my right side. I sidestep, blocking then strike in retaliation. He blocks, circling, and sends my sword flying out of my hands. His next strike, I duck under his arm and move in close. From here, I knee strike the groin area, elbow strike the left side of his face, and punch him a couple times in the stomach.

He stumbles backward a little bit, hitting the ground. Unfortunately, I'm close enough that when he sweeps his leg, I hit the forest floor as well. My left arm explodes with pain again. I need to get this fixed really soon.

Before I get a chance to stand again, he's over me with his sword to my neck. "Don't move."

"Kill me, get it over with. You're not getting the treasure. You're never getting the treasure."

"I'm not going to kill you, that's the last thing I would ever want to do. I do, on the other hand, want to kill him." Before I can ask what he's talking about, he throws his sword to his left. When I look over I see Ace, standing twenty meters away. His sword is up, and he was running toward me. Hook Man's sword lodges itself in the left side of his chest.

"No!" I scream, sending the pirate into a tree. I try to get to my feet, I try to get to Ace, but someone is holding me back. I feel burning tears rolling down my cheeks. This can't be real, this can't be happening.

Ace hits the ground knees first, then falls to the side. He lies there, with open blank eyes, staring right at me. I can't get to him, the arms wrapped around me are pulling me away. I don't understand why they won't let me go to him.

"Zylan!" The voice feels so far away. "Zylan!" A little closer. "Zylan!" Right in my ear. "We have to go!" I recognize the voice now. Jacob has hold of me, trying to drag me away. That's when I see why, there are twenty pirates moving toward us.

"We can't leave him!" I scream trying to break away. The tears are burning my cheeks as they pour harder now. "I have to get him!"

"We'll come back! I promise you we can come back. But we're outnumbered. We have to run."

"We can't leave him!" I yell again. The pirates are getting closer now; they're almost at Ace. They don't deserve to be close to him . . . I don't deserve to be close to him.

"We will come back, I promise."

I lose the will to argue. I lose the will to move. I lose the will to stand. Jacob spins me around and tosses me over his shoulder.

I knew we should have waited. Why couldn't they have just listened to me?

Chapter 18

Aftermath

Zylan

We went back for Ace a few hours later. He wasn't there. All the pirates vanished into thin air. They must have taken Ace with them, but why?

No one wanted to do anything, so we put off the funerals for a couple days. None of us knew what to do nor were we in the mind frame to do it.

I keep walking around, expecting Ace to pop out from behind a tree and yell, "Got you!" but I know he won't. A lot of people are feeling the same way. We were all so close; we lost almost half the members of our family. How can we move on from any of this?

It's been three days, and today's the day we're doing the funeral. Jacob and I are digging up twenty-five holes. Neither one of us could, being ourselves, use magic; it just didn't seem right. Clover, Elena, Justin, Hunter, and Tyler are chiseling twenty-five head stones while Jacob and I dig.

I'm on my last hole when Elena comes up to me. She has tears in her eyes as she hands me a stone. "We thought you should do Ace's. None of us felt right doing it."

I feel my own tears come to my eyes as I take it. "Thank you," I whisper staring down at the gray headstone. It's rounded off at the top but flat at the bottom. I put it on the edge of the grave I need to finish. I'll do it as soon as I finish this.

With teary eyes, I finishing digging a grave that will remain empty forever.

***

I look down at the plain stone in my lap. I can't figure out what to write. Nothing I can come up with will do him justice. Nothing I could ever say would do him justice. The one-handed pirate killed him because of me. I wish he had killed me instead. I should have done something; I should have gotten up faster, I shouldn't have left him there. At least I would still have him if I had gotten to him.

Every time I try to put my knife to the stone, I lose my nerve. I can't write this, it's not right. I wasn't there when he needed me, but he was always there when I needed him. It's not fair. I should have been the one to die.

"Zylan?" Jacob is standing behind me, staring at the blank stone.

"Yeah?" I look back down at my lap.

"Everyone's almost ready. Can I help?" He sits down next to me.

"Here, I can't do this." I hand it to him and disappear to the cliff.

I sit with my legs hanging over the edge and look at the skyline. It's close to dark. The sky is bright orange, with specks of pink, red, and purple. They mix together, creating beauty so perfect I can't believe it's real. I sit there and stare over the Island until I lose track of time.

The trees are being pulled gently, side to side, by a light breeze. I hear the songs of different birds, the howls of wolves, and the cricking of crickets. It's peaceful here, it's like nothing else matters, all there is, is here and now. No yesterday and no tomorrow, only the beauty that the Island possesses.

"Zylan? Come on, the funeral is starting soon," Elena says from behind me.

"We're all waiting for you," Clover adds moving beside me.

"I don't deserve to go. I did this." I can't bring myself to look at them.

"No, you didn't, the pirates did it. I know you blame yourself, but you shouldn't. You deserve to mourn, just like the rest of us. You might be tough as nails, but you can't keep this bottled up. You have to grieve with the rest of us or you're going to explode." Elena puts her hand on my right shoulder.

"We love you, and we're not going to leave you here by yourself. If you don't go, neither of us are going to go." Clover sits down on my left and puts her hand over mine.

I feel tears rolling down my cheeks. None of this is right; none of this should be happening. Have I tried to figure out what happened over five hundred years ago, none of this would have happened. "I can't go. I can't look at everyone and speak like they want me to. I don't deserve to grieve or mourn. This is my fault, and I can't do this right now. I can't do this ever."

Clover and Elena look at each other. They think I don't notice as they have a hushed argument, but I do. Once they've finished, they sigh and disappear, leaving me to myself again.

"Zylan." Jacob sits down next to me. He doesn't say anything else; he just sits beside me with his left hand over my right as we watch the sun start move across the sky. He sits there in silence and listens to me cry. He moves closer so I can lean my head on his shoulder and then we just sit there, the only sound, coming from our tears hitting the ground.

***

"Why aren't you with them?" It's nightfall before I break the silence. I sit up, wiping my eyes.

"The same reason as you. I don't think I deserve to be there either. I did way too much to hurt them. I can't face them." He wipes his eyes as well.

"I kind of feel like we should have gone. Not for us, but for them. I've been thinking about it a lot actually. We should have gone to honour their lives." I shake my head.

"We're being kind of selfish right now, huh?"

I nod. "We're never going to be able to win."

He stands up and offers me his hand. "Let's go now, everyone will probably be gone. We can honour them on our own."

I take his hand, and we're standing behind all the chairs full of people in front of the graves.

"They're here, let's start," Clover says jumping to her feet. She waves us forward, into two chairs right at the front.

"You haven't started yet?"

"Of course not. How could we start without you two?" Elena jumps to her feet as well. "So now that we're all here, would anyone like to say a few words, about anyone?" And that's how it starts.

***

Everyone got up and said something about each one of the twenty-five. The whole thing took almost three hours. Jacob and I went last because we had known everyone the longest. When I stood in front of everyone, I couldn't find the right words to say. All I could think of was the first day I met all of them, so I told every story.

When Jacob got up, he talked about how well he knew all of them. He had the most to say about Ace. He couldn't get through the whole story without pausing to get control of his tears.

At the end, I stood up again and I said, "Every single person in a grave today was loved, is loved. We had so many amazing moments together, but it's time to let them move on. They will never, ever leave us because they're all right here in our hearts and memories. No matter what happened the last two weeks, nothing will ever change that.

"I miss every person that was taken from us, but I know them well enough to know, they wouldn't want us to be sad forever. They would want us to move forward, together. So that's what we have to do, move forward. We will never forget them.

"We've mourned their deaths, now it's time to celebrate their lives."

That's what we're doing now. Jacob poofed us up some great twenty-first century alcohol and we're celebrating. I have a huge glass bottle full of something really strong, and I'm sitting watching everyone. We have a huge bonfire burning in the centre of camp, with people dancing around it and singing.

I see Clover and Justin sitting off to the side watching as well. Justin has his arm around her, and she's leaning on his shoulder. They look happy together, and I'm glad. I hope their wedding goes amazing. It will bring a little bit of light to the darkness we've been facing lately.

I look around for Elena, but she and Hunter are missing. I hope that they start over this time. There are way too many broken hearts today; we can't have anymore, ever again.

Tyler is sitting with Willow whispering in her ear. She smiles wide and bumps him with her elbow. I feel a pang of jealousy, but I push it down. They look good together. I remember Ty and I talking about her. He's liked her since she got here in 1588. They've been on-again-off-again for about a hundred years now. I force myself to believe that I hope they go on again.

Jacob joins me on my log. He also has a huge bottle of something strong. It seems to be having the same effect on him as well; nothing.

"How are you doing?" he asks.

"Same as you. I don't think this is strong enough. It just tastes bad."

He chuckles. "Well, here's to hoping it knocks us on our asses." He holds his bottle out to mine.

"Here, here." I tap mine to his, and we drink.

"Do you think we'll ever be able to move forward from this?"

I look around at everyone sitting in their groups, drinking, laughing, enjoying themselves. "I think it'll take a while, but I think we'll be okay. Almost everyone we lost had a long amazing life here. Most of us would be long dead without this place, and I think once everyone realises that, we'll all move forward." I take another gulp of my drink and look over at him.

"When did you get so wise?" Jacob asks with a laugh and a drink from his bottle.

"The moment I was born. I am an old soul, making me the wisest person you will ever meet, and older than you." I smile.

"You wish." He laughs.

"No, I don't wish, I know." I chuckle.

"Sing, sing, sing, sing, sing!" the small group surrounding Tyler chants, interrupting Jacob from his next sentence.

"Nope. Not a chance, I'm not doing it again."

"Come on, you did it three nights ago. Give the people what they want, Ty," I call across camp.

"That was when I thought we were all going to die and no one would be around to torture me about it today. I'm not doing it."

"Sing, sing, sing." Everyone joins the chanting this time.

"Fine! Fine, I'll do it." He stands up, walks over to me, and holds out his hand. "But only if you join me in my embarrassment."

"What the hell." I down the last bit of my bottle and take his hand. "But I pick the song and you better know it."

"Pick away." Ty smiles and motions me to the middle of camp.

"The second part of *Give Me Love* by Ed Sheeran. I think it fits pretty well."

"How the hell do you know that song?" Jacob asks with a laugh. "Keeping up on modern-day music?"

"I've loved music my whole life. I keep up with the 'newest hit music' in my spare time. This is hands down my favourite song, and it is the only song I know well enough to sing right now."

"I don't know it . . . the point was a duet. It can't be a duet if half the pair doesn't know the song."

I grab Ty's hand and give him the lyrics. "There. Now you know and it fits, right?" I smile.

"Perfectly. First you, second together, third me?"

I nod, and the rhythm of the song fills the air from every direction. I take a deep breath and start:

> *Of all the money that ever I had,*
> *I've spent it in good company. . .*

Ty takes a deep breath and joins me for the next verse.

> *And all I've done for want of width*
> *To memory now, I can't recall. . .*

I leave him to finish.

> *A man may drink and not be drunk*
> *A man may fight and not be slain. . .*

I pick up for the last line

Good night and joy be with you all

Halfway through the last verse, Jacob brought Ty and I a glass with a tiny bit of alcohol. Everyone joins us in raising their glass. I feel tears rolling down my cheeks as I down the glass.

Ty wraps his left arm around my shoulder and gives a quick squeeze. "That was good." He smiles. "We should do it again, under less depressing circumstances next time."

I let out a laugh and step away from his grip. "Never again. You were right that was mortifying, and I never want to do it again."

"Oh, come on now, Ze, we all know you love being the centre of attention. You'll do it again," Hunter says with a chuckle. He's leaning on a tree at the north side of camp next to Elena with a bottle in his hand.

"Oh, you're back. Damn, the only reason I agreed was because I thought you were gone, and I would be saved from the endless Hunter torment."

"You know I'm your favourite. I keep things interesting." He flashes his signature grin as he peels himself off the tree to walk over to us. Elena follows with a shy smile. I wonder what that's about.

"First part no, second part yes. But only because I can do things like this." I flick my wrist, and he flies across camp until he hits a tree.

"That's why I love you, Ze, you're so predictable." He laughs.

I drop him and laugh too. "You're right. How many times have I done that to you? It's always the highlight of my day." I smile as he brushes himself off.

"If you're done hassling my boyfriend, I'd like him back now," Elena says with her arms crossed.

"El!" Clover and I yell at that same time. We clear the rest of the distance between us and throw our arms around her. "I'm so happy for you."

"Can't. Breathe."

"Sorry." We let her go.

"If you guys are done, we have more drinking to do," Jacob says walking over and handing us another bottle.

I smile and take it. "Till it knocks us on our asses." I raise the bottle slightly. Jacob smiles back as I take a drink.

"And Ze does an encore!" Ty adds right before he takes his drink.

"If I'm doing one, you're doing one, so keep hoping, buddy. We'll both be up there making asses of ourselves." I laugh and bump him with my hip.

"I, like Hunt over there, very much enjoy tormenting you, so if I have to get up there with you just so you'll 'make an ass' out of yourself, I will totally 100 percent do it." He turns to face everyone. "All in favour of an encore raise your bottle!"

Everyone. Everyone raises their bottle. I laugh. "All right, all right. If you want an encore so bad I will, once again, introduce you to my awful voice."

"Shut up and get up there." Clover gives me a shove onto the log in front of me. "We all know you want to."

"I'm going, I'm going. What now?"

"How about the first part of the song?" Willow suggests. Within the same second, the music is playing and Ty is singing.

***

No one wrote on Ace's headstone. It's been almost a week, and it's still blank. I've been sitting on his grave for hours, every day, and the right words still haven't come to me. He was an amazing man. I can't find one thing that does him justice.

I lift the stone out of its placement into my lap and stare at it some more. I take my knife and chisel ACE at the top and add JASON underneath. I can't figure out what else to add, and it kills me. I have a million things to say, but none of them feel right; none of them will ever feel right.

"Can I help?" I don't jump at Jacob's voice behind me.

"Nothing feels right." I sigh and put the stone back in place.

"What do you feel in your heart?"

"That words don't do him justice."

"That's perfect, write that."

I look at him crooked. "But that's not good enough."

"I think it's perfect. By saying that, you're saying that he is something beyond us. He is so amazing that anything that can be written isn't good enough." Jacob sits down beside me. "Words were the greatest gift ever given to us. If he can't be put into them, that means he is greater than any gift that could ever be given to someone. And that is exactly what Ace is—the greatest gift ever given."

"I never thought of it like that."

He looks over and smiles at me. "I'm older, therefore wiser."

I laugh and bump him with my shoulder. "Only by eight years."

"You're forgetting, I have knowledge of the world long before us and long after."

"You're going to have to show me one day, old timer."

He chuckles. "When you're ready." He stands up and grabs the stone from its place and hands it to me with a smile. "Now chisel."

"Thank you." I take the headstone. "You always know the right thing to say, even when I hated you."

"That's because I know you. It's easy to tell you what you need to hear." He sits back down beside me. "You are one of the few people that actually listen when you're given advice."

I chuckle. "It's a gift really." I sigh when I look down at the headstone in my lap. "Even though I know what I want to say, I don't know how to say it. You know what I mean?"

"No, actually I don't."

"Well, when I say it—chisel it, actually—it means this is all real. When I chisel my words into the headstone, it's permanent." I look back at him. "It means Ace is really dead."

Jacob puts his hand on my right arm. "Even if you don't write it, it's still real. Ace is gone, and there's nothing we can do about it. All we can do now is honour his memory, honour him."

"I don't want to honour him. I want him to be here, alive and smiling. It's not fair that he's the one who died. I should have killed Hook or at least it should have been me that died."

"Well, if you're going by that logic. I should have waited three seconds our first time on the ship. Hook shouldn't have been able to get onto the Island in the first place."

"You're right. This is all your fault." I chuckle, unable to keep a straight face. "By all logic, the only person to blame is Peter."

Jacob bursts out laughing. "I thought you were going to say Hook, but I am all for any excuse to blame my brother. Now stop stalling. Chisel."

Chapter 19

Just When I Thought

Zylan

Ace stands on the other side of a field. He looks so far away, but I know if I take several steps I'll be able to reach him. He stands there smiling at me, but he makes no effort to move. My legs feel heavy as I take a step toward him. With every movement, my legs become more like lead. I'm only a few steps away when Ace's smile falls and blood begins pouring out of his mouth.

I try to run, but my feet stick to the ground. I stand there and watch as his face goes white and he falls to his knees. Behind him, the one-handed pirate is pulling a sword from Ace's chest. The pirate has a smile on his face as he looks down at Ace's fallen body.

The ground beneath my feet begins to shift. Now I'm sitting in camp, on a log, in front of the fire, cuddled up to Ace. We watch the flames flicker as Tyler sings to the music playing from Jacob's flute. When the song finishes, I feel Ace's body shift. I look up to see Jacob's hand on his shoulder. I move away from Ace so he's able to stand. I watch the dancing flames until I hear a scream. When I look behind me, Jacob is standing over Ace with a dagger and blood all over his hands. But there's still music coming from the flute. When I look over, I see Jacob drop the flute, staring at himself. It's not Jacob standing over Ace; it's Peter.

The ground around me began to swirl, and I find myself standing in the kitchen of my tree house. Ace is dancing around the kitchen with a smile on his face and a spatula in his hand. He looks so happy.

I walk to the counter and lean on it. When Ace sees me, his smile grows. He moves toward me, but before he can hug me, I grab a knife off the counter and stab him through the heart and watch him fall to the ground.

The ground begins to morph. When it finally stops, I'm sitting, tied up, in the captain's quarters of Hook Hand's ship. Ace is in the chair next to me, completely calm as he fiddles with his restraints. He keeps whispering to me that it'll be okay and we're going to get out of this soon. I want to believe him.

He manages to get his right hand free then his left. As he starts to get my right hand loose, two pirates open the door. Ace fights them both as I struggle to get my left hand free. By the time I'm out of my restraints, both pirates are down. He smiles and reaches for me, but Hook came charging into the room and pushes his sword through Ace's chest. I feel the air leave my lungs before I even get the chance to scream.

***

My eyes open as my body flies upward and I struggle to breath. I feel tears streaming down my cheeks. I haven't had a nightmare in almost two years. I've been sleeping good, being good, feeling good. How could they be back? Why are they back? And why all four in one night? That's never happened before.

Jacob sits up next to me and rubs his eyes. "Ze, are you okay?"

I swallow my thoughts and nod. "Yeah, I just . . ." I don't want to tell him I had another nightmare. I'm just starting to move on with my life. They don't get to come back after five years of Ace being gone.

"You're having nightmares again, aren't you?" he asks.

"Not having. This is the first time in almost two years. You can't consider this as 'having.'" I force myself to smile. "I'm okay, I promise."

He lifts his hand to my cheek and gently wipes the tears out from under my eyes. I close my eyes and lean into his hand. "I love you."

"I love you too." I smile as he kisses my forehead. "Come on, let's go back to sleep."

"Okay." I turn my back to him, and he wraps his arms around me. "Good night." He kisses my shoulder and pulls me closer.

"Good night," I whisper, not daring to close my eyes.

***

"Ze, get your lazy ass out of bed! The sun is setting; therefore, you must be up," Clover says barging into my room.

"What took you so long? My nap is long done." She looks over to find me standing at my dresser, fully dressed and brushing my hair.

"Pan said you were still asleep." She rolls her eyes. "No matter, hop like a bunny, my maid of honour has lots to do tonight!"

"Really?"

She smiles, nodding her head. "Come on! We're getting Elena next!"

I put my brush down on the top of my dresser. With a quick check in the mirror, I'm ready to go. Clover drags me out, I barely have time to say bye to Jacob. He waves with a laugh as I disappear out the door.

"Didn't you pass Elena on your way out of camp? Why didn't you just get her first?"

"I tried. She fell asleep and she wouldn't wake up." She rolls her eyes.

"That sounds like Elena." I laugh.

It takes about ten minutes to walk into camp. When we step in, everyone jumps out. "SURPRISE!" they yell. "HAPPY BIRTHDAY!"

In the middle of camp is a long table with lots of food. There's a huge cooked pig in the centre with an apple in its mouth, two large pots—I'm guessing soup—thirty-two plates, bowls, and glasses, an array of cheeses, crackers, dips, bread, and so much more. I can't believe Jacob did all of this. I never told anyone when my birthday was because I hated that day more than anything. He must have known from before.

Everyone comes up to me and hugs me before going off to eat. When Clover finally makes it to the front of the line, I cross my arms. "Liar! You get no hug!"

"Bitch please." She hugs me anyways. "It wasn't a lie. It was a twist of the truth. You do have lots to do tonight. It just has nothing to do with my wedding." She pulls away smiling.

"Still no hug for the truth twister!" I exclaim, sticking my tongue out at her.

"Just 'cause it's your birthday doesn't mean I won't smack you upside the head. The biggest truth twister here is you! You never even told us when your birthday was."

"What's the date today?"

"August 14, 20 . . . 12 . . . oh." She frowns. "Now I'm really giving you a hug."

This time I hug her back. "Go eat. I'm going to talk to Jacob."

She gives me a weak smile when she pulls away and joins everyone at the table.

"You did all of this?" I ask as Jacob approaches me.

"You needed this." He smiles and wraps his arms around me. "Happy birthday, Zylan."

"Don't think I don't know it's your birthday as well." I pull away and smile at him.

"What? How the hell did you know?" he exclaims.

"I used to follow you around a lot. Every year on August 14—after I got over the whole trying to kill myself thing—I would see you sitting in the middle of your camp, alone, with a candle and a cupcake. You would sigh and blow it out, and for a split second, I would remember that you saved me. I came to the conclusion it must be your birthday as well."

"That's slightly embarrassing. Please never tell anyone that story."

I laugh. "Your secret is safe with me, cross my heart and hope to die."

"Please don't die. We have birthdays to celebrate."

"This is true." I raise my voice for the people at the table to hear. "Hey, everyone! I want you to know that Pan didn't do this all for me. It's his birthday as well. I think he's 569 now!"

"Dude what? The two of you never bothered to tell any of us you had a birthday and now you're telling us it's the same day!" Hunter exclaims, piling his plate with pig.

"Of course we have birthdays. Did you think the two of us just fell from the sky, or do you still not know how babies are made?"

"Oh, I know how babies are—" he cuts off his sarcasm when he sees the look on Elena's face. That's the best birthday present I could have asked for.

"Now that Hunt's got his foot in his mouth, maybe there might be enough food for the rest of us," Tyler says scooping mash potato onto his plate. I take that back—that was the best birthday present ever. Tyler's face when we all start laughing is the icing on top of the cake. He can be clueless sometimes, but it's awesome.

"*Can you guys just get your food and move on! There's more coming after this,*" Jacob says motioning everyone along.

Once everyone has their food, Jacob and I make our way over to the table. I've had my eyes on the mash potato the whole time, praying no one ate the last of it. When I approach the table, it looks like no one touched it, but I know that's not true because everyone has some on their plates.

"*If I had known you would take that much, I wouldn't have refilled it,*" Jacob whispers passing behind me.

I look down at my plate. It's basically all mashed potato with a little bit of space for roast beef. "*Listen, my mom was Irish. We used to have potato every night for dinner, and I love it, especially mashed.*"

"*I know that's why I refilled it.*" He laughs, grabbing the piece of beef I was reaching for. "*Oops, did you want this?*" He puts the beef on his own plate and walks away.

"*Hey! It's my birthday!*"

"*It's mine too!*"

I sigh and grab a different piece. I grab the gravy boat and take it with me to where my friends are sitting. When I sit down, setting my plate and the gravy boat down, everyone stares at me. "*What?*"

"*Are you going to drink the gravy?*" Tyler asks before shoving a handful of mash potato into his mouth.

"*No . . .*" I imagine myself up a fork and start making a hole in the centre of my potato. Once I can see the plate I pour the gravy into it. Everyone is still staring. "*What?*"

"*What was the point? Why couldn't you just pour it on top?*" Clover says giving me a weird look.

I glare at them. "*It's my birthday, leave me alone. I like these potatoes more than you, so leave me alone with them.*"

"*She used to do that all the time. This isn't a new thing. Stop staring at her it's creepy.*"

"Says the one that followed her around for three years and never worked up the nerve to talk to her," Clover shoots back. I almost choke on my fork full of potato.

"You what?" Hunter exclaims.

"I forgot no one knew that." I laugh as well.

"Not to mention all the time he spent staring at her during our weekly dinners for as long as I've been on this island," Tyler adds with a mouthful of beef.

"So really, the creepiest person here is you," Hunter finishes standing up.

"You finished all that already?" Elena exclaims. Hunter shrugs and walks back over to the food table.

"Back to Pan being a stalker, why did none of us ever hear this story before?" Justin asks, laughing.

"It wasn't relevant. It still isn't. Therefore we're not having this conversation." I take a chunk of my mash potato and dip it in the gravy.

"But—"

"Subject is closed."

***

My eyes flutter open at the sound of Jacob's light snoring. I smile at the memory of my first birthday celebration on the Island. That was a fun night. I'm glad that my brain gave me something good to remember after the collection of nightmares I woke up to a few hours ago.

I wonder what time it is. I don't see any sunlight, but that doesn't mean it's not morning, considering there's no chance of sunlight seeping in here. Jacob is still fast asleep, so I decide to curl back up next to him instead of trying to wake him up.

***

"Zylan? We're going to be late. Are you ready?" Jacob asks from the other side of the door.

"Yeah, come in. I'll be done in a second."

I examine myself in the mirror as he walks in. We've had a huge change in wardrobe the last few years. Personally I like it better. Jacob's been watching the present world a lot lately trying to find the pirates. Upon doing this, he stumbled on to some modern-day fashion, which I—mostly—enjoy. We have lots of high-waist shorts, baggy large shirts, almost nonexistent shirt, long skirts, cardigans, jeans, and a lot more. Today I'm wearing jeans with a giant plain white T-shirt.

"The baggy shirt look really works for you," Jacob says, watching me through the mirror.

"It's really comfy." I take one final look in the mirror and turn, smiling at him. "Ready? We have a dinner to prepare and twenty-first century people to piss off." I chuckle as I walk to the door.

"I already set it up. Everyone should be just about done getting food now." He smiles. "I'm tired of waiting in a huge line while my mouth is watering for this food."

"Ah! Me too! That's the best idea I've ever heard." I close my door behind us. "So, what's on the menu tonight?"

"Why do you care? You're just going to go for the mash potato and gravy." He laughs and holds out his hands.

"True." I smile and grab them. I blink and we're standing in camp.

"Better late than never!" Justin yells from our usual spot in camp.

"Remember who provides the food here, asshole!" Jacob yells back grabbing a plate.

Justin shoots him a thumbs-up. "You win."

Jacob laughs and rolls his eyes. I grab a plate and head right for the potato and gravy. I take five large scoops onto my plate, grab the gravy boat, and walk over to Clover, Hunter, Justin, Elena, and Tyler.

"I still can't get used to that . . ." Tyler looks at my plate crooked.

"It's been almost a year that you have witnessed this, put a fucking sock in it," I snap pouring the gravy into the centre of my mash potato moat.

"Please, for me, next time pour it on top." He pouts moving closer to me.

"Just 'cause you asked so nicely—" I move away from him. "—no." He frowns and switches logs, so he's sitting across from me.

"Leave her be," Jacob says sitting down next to me. "Maybe you should try it. It's pretty good that way."

"Thank you. At least I know there's one sane person here." I shoot Tyler a dirty look.

Clover and Elena look at me the same way. They have their left hand over their chest, leaning slightly back with their noses scrunched up. "Ouch."

"Stop looking at me like I killed a puppy. All I do is make a hole in the centre of my mash potato, and all you people do is make fun of me for it. Let me be!" I take a scoop and dip it in the gravy. I have this every single time we've done this, but I have yet to get sick of it.

"It's weird!"

"Is not!"

"Is to!"

"Fine, I'll spare you the sight." I imagine myself sitting in my room, on my bed. I lean back against the head of my bed and take another bite of my potato.

"Is it safe to enter?" Jacob asks poking his head in the doorway.

"If you're alone."

"Just me, scouts honour." He enters raising his left hand and puts his right over his heart.

"What's a scout? Jacob, not all of us can see the world like you do," I say with a mouth full of food. "All I can do is hear the music."

"Would you like to?"

"Well yeah."

"Well, come on then."

***

This time I wake up to Jacob pulling his arm out from under my neck. I don't even bother opening my eyes. I know he's still asleep. It only takes a couple minutes for me to join him.

***

"Pan! Get that flute shit started. Ty's gonna sing for us!" Hunter yells across camp.

We're all getting ready for Jacob to start the bonfire. Hunter, Clover, Elena, Justin, Tyler, and I are sitting off to the side of camp while Jacob is in the centre standing over the fire pit.

"No fire, no flute, so shut up and sit down." Jacob has his hands in front of him getting ready to send the spark.

"I am sitting."

Jacob drops his hands and turns to face him. "Interesting," he says sarcastically flicking his wrist. Hunter hits the tree behind him with rope securing him to it. "Enjoy your time out."

"Really? Again? What is it with you people and tying me to trees?" he yells.

"It's entertaining for us. Now, unless you want me to knock you out, I suggest you take your time out in silence," I say.

He rolls his eyes at me but stays silent. "Wow, Elena, you've been training him really well," Clover says.

"I know! I'm really proud of myself." She smiles looking back at Hunter.

He doesn't say anything. He stays there in complete silence while we chirp him and laugh at him. He really must want to hold on to Elena. I'm glad too, there's been enough death without Clover and I throwing him into the mix.

"All right, time out's done." Jacob lets Hunter down. "Let's dance!"

Cheers begin as Jacob starts the flute. I almost never participate in this, I prefer to watch. The only time I join is when Ty guilt's me into singing with him. I move to the spot Hunter was sitting and I lean on the tree. Everyone is moving around the fire, getting a feel for the music before they start dancing. They all kind of just bounce around and sway; it's really entertaining.

"You look lonely."

I jump. "Jacob, what the hell! You nearly gave me a heart attack."

The music is still playing, and I was so focused on the fire I hadn't noticed Jacob walk up. "Sorry, I enchanted the flute to play itself when I saw you sitting over here alone." He sits down next to me and smiles.

"I always sit alone, and don't tell me you never noticed because I feel you staring at me all the time." I laugh.

"You caught me. This was the first time I worked up the nerves to ask you to dance." He looks down at the forest floor and turns slightly red.

"I appreciate the gesture, but I don't dance in front of people."

"So don't, let's go for a walk." He stands up and holds out his hand for me.

"But if we leave there's no music . . ."

"Trust me."

"Okay, let's go." I take his hand, and he leads me out of camp. We head left, toward the centre of the island. "Can you tell me where we're going?"

"I could."

"But you're not going to?" I guess.

He nods. We walk farther and farther, past centre island. I have no idea what's out this far. His tree house is east; we're headed west. The only thing this way is the beach, but I can't see why he would be taking me there.

"We're almost there," he says pushing a tree branch out of my way.

"Almost where?"

"Almost—" He grabs the low hanging leaves of a willow tree and pulls them aside, "—here."

"I should he known!" We're standing at the foot of the cliff. We must have been heading northwest. I can't believe I never thought of that. "So, are we walking or . . ."

"Hell no. That's all the exercise I need this year." He chuckles and holds his hand out to me.

"Amen to that!" I smile and take it.

At the top of the cliff, the night is clear. We can see all the stars and an almost-full moon. It's maybe three nights away from full. There's a warm breeze wrapping around me like a blanket. I watch as it moves the trees and listen to the rustle of the leaves. I close my eyes taking a deep breath, soaking it all in.

"I want to show you something," Jacob says when I open my eyes. He leads me around to the other side of the cliff. I've never been over there before; in fact, I never even knew this was here. He stops just before a wall blocks the path. "I've been working on this for almost three years now." He walks to the wall of the cave holding the waterfall. "I didn't want to use magic for it because . . . well, I wanted it to be special." He puts his hand on the wall, and a piece of it moves, like a door sliding open. "I know that my tree house was a little small for the two of us, and I know you want your own space, so I made this."

He steps out of the way and motions me forward. On the other side of the opening is a large room. There's a huge bed, *pushed up to the back wall. To the left of it is a nightstand with a stack of books and an oil lamp. On the right wall pushed in the back corner is a dresser with a full-body mirror. On the left wall, there is a gas stove with four cupboards under a marble countertop. In the centre of the ceiling is an oil lamp hanging down.*

"Wow." I step inside.

"You like it?"

I turn around and face him with a smile on my face. "I love it. Thank you." I wrap my arms around him. "It seems a little small though." I step back and look around again, studying every detail. He put so much work into this. That's when I realize, I'm ready. I'm tired of spending every night with him, waking up next to him, then spending the whole day together as friends. I want more. I want him.

"What?"

"I mean for the two of us. Where are you going to stay?"

He gets flustered. "W-what? M-me? I made this j-just for you."

I look at him crooked. "Why? Are you tired of living with me?"

"N-no. I-I thought you would want your own space. I thought you were tired of living with me . . ."

I take a deep breath. This is it. *"How could I be? I love you."*

Jacob's eyes go wide. "Y-you w-w-what?"

"You heard me," I say taking a step toward him.

He doesn't hesitate. He grabs my cheeks, pulling my face to his and kisses me. It's not like last time; no memories come flooding back. No guilt rips me away from his touch. This time, the only thing that matters is me and him, everything else just disappears.

He pulls away. "Are you sure? Because I don't want this if you're not ready."

"I'm sure."

He doesn't question it again. He moves his hand to my waist, pulling me against him, then he picks me up and carries me over to the bed. "Wow, this is really comfy," I say sitting down on it. I shimmy my way up to the pillows and lay down. "I could go to sleep right now."

He lays down beside me. "Wow me too. I out did myself."

I roll to my left so I'm facing him. "Is that what you want to do?"

"Absolutely not."

He kisses me again, pulling me on top of him.

***

This time I wake up to the light kisses being placed along the back of my neck and down my shoulder. I debate whether to roll over or let him continue. I decide to let him continue.

"Good morning, sleepyhead," Jacob mumbles into the back of my neck as he places his last kiss.

"I'm still asleep, keep going."

He chuckles and rolls me onto my back. "Do you know what time it is?" I shake my head. "Almost ten."

I groan. "So what?"

"It's September eighth, twenty-sixteen."

I shoot out of bed. "What are you still doing in bed! We have so many things to do!" Today's the day. Clover and Justin are finally getting married. After almost five full years of stalling, they are finally going to do it. The wedding is at seven, and there was so much to do.

"It's not like it's going to take nine hours to set up we have magic. Come back here." He reaches his hand out for me and I back up. "Ze," he whines. "Don't make me come over there."

"So scary." I roll my eyes. "Jacob get up!" I grab my hairbrush and whip it at him.

He snaps his fingers, and it falls to the bed right before it would have hit his face. "Oh, now you've done it." He throws the covers off himself and walks toward me. The look in his eyes has one-half of me stuck in one place and the other half wanting to run.

"What is it that I've done?" I ask. The half that wants me stuck in one place is currently winning.

He doesn't answer. He just keeps walking toward me, slowly. When he's millimeters from me, pauses. "This," he whispers closing the gap between us.

I close my eyes as our lips meet. He pushes me against the wall, leaving his hands on either side of my head. "You win," I mumble as Jacob moves his lips to my jaw and down my neck. "Let's go back to bed."

I feel him smile. "As you wish."

***

"Sorry I'm late. We sleep in a little longer than I anticipated." I smile to myself as the events from this morning play in my head.

"IT'S GODDAMN TWO IN THE AFTERNOON. WHAT DO YOU MEAN YOU SLEPT IN!" Clover screams. "WE ONLY HAVE FIVE GODDAMN HOURS!"

"C, calm down. We all have magic. It's going to take like twenty seconds." I sigh.

"IT'S SUPPOSED TO BE MY DAY! I WANTED YOU HERE AT TWELVE!"

"C, I love you, but if you don't shut up, I will freeze you until it's time to get into your dress." She closes her mouth and turns bright red. She looks like Hunter when we tied him up to the tree and told him we were moving in. "Okay, now that that's taken care of—" I turn to Elena and Willow "—have you started yet?"

"Nope, we were waiting for you. Where should we start?"

"You start on her makeup, Willow start on her hair, I'll go set up the beach." I pause and lean closer so Clover can't hear me. "And whatever you do, do not let Clover put on her dress until it's six-thirty."

Willow and El chuckle. "Okay, can do."

"I'll be back around six." I wave to Clover and disappear to the beach. I'm not surprised when I find myself alone. The boys are too busy having fun to think about preparing. I roll my eyes. "Looks like I'm doing this all by myself."

I sit down on the sand and shut my eyes. Everything I need to set up is in a plié in the middle of the beach. I picture four legs and the back, meeting with the body of the chair, then I repeat twenty-three more time. I open my eyes to make sure they look right.

The twenty-four chairs are in one long line along the edge of the beach. I wave my hand moving one chair at a time to its rightful spot. I make three rows of four on each side. Once all the chairs are where they belong, I raise my arms, calling the vines to wrap around each chair. I admire my work for a minute before moving onto the platform.

When I see that the platform is still in pieces, I roll my eyes. "All I asked was that they put the damn platform together before they went skipping off to do God knows what! I hate boys."

I put all the boards together and move them a few meters in front of the chairs. Then I bring the arch of leaves over and place it in the centre of the platform. I add the flowers then smile and stand up, admiring my hard work.

I still have three hours to kill before I have to go back to Clover's craziness. I decide to head back to my cave. Before I can even picture the cave in my mind, Clover's panicked voice comes flying at me. Nothing making its way to my ears makes any sense. All I got was something happened and I need to find her right away. Great. So much for my three Clover-free hours.

***

"Okay, I'm here. What's—oh my god." I stop when she turns around. "I told you! The one thing I said was not to put it on until we got to the edge of the beach!" The whole front of her dress is ripped open. There's mud all along the bottom. She has tears streaming down her face, ruining her makeup, and her hair is pulled out of her bun with branches sticking out.

"I couldn't help it! I wanted to see it so badly."

"Okay, this is an easy fix." I wave my hand so she's wearing a T-shirt and jeans. Her dress is hanging off a tree branch in plastic wrapping. I focus my attention on the dress. "I wonder if the waterfall works on clothes." I tilt my head back and forth studying it.

"Can't you just poof me up another one?"

"I'm not stealing a dress from someone who actually takes care of it!"

"How do you know you'll be stealing it from someone?"

"Because I have no clue where it comes from! Jacob left the Island to get you this! I told you to take care of it because we're not getting you another one!" I take the dress off the tree and lay it on the forest floor.

I try to find a reasonable way to fix this. I know I can't get another one because it might come from someone who's about to get married and actually took care of her dress. I could magically sow it, but everyone would be able to see it and it wouldn't fix the mud stains.

"I have an idea, but you have to stay here and not move." She nods her head. "Call Elena to fix your face and Willow to fix your hair. I'll be back as soon as I can."

I picture the lake at centre island. I reappear, sitting with my legs crossed, on the shore. I stick my hands into the water and search. Jacob showed me how to work the pond a few years ago. I've been using it to search for any sign of Ace, completely unsuccessfully. Now I use it to look into wedding stores; at the tenth one, I find her dress.

It's pure white, slim fit until midthigh; from there the dress fans out. The sleeves are thick straps around her shoulders until her shoulder blades. The back of the dress is almost open but not quite. Over the shoulder blades, the straps connect and there is a line of beads connecting the top of the dress with the bottom. There's a really cool design covering the fabric. It's very tight together at the top, but as the dress fans out, so does the pattern. She picked a very beautiful dress.

I'm not sure what to do from this point. I wonder if I reach into the water, will I be able to grab it? It's worth a shot. I slowly stick my arm into the water; the picture doesn't waver. I feel my hands touch the hanger of the dress. *This is so cool!* I pull it off the bar and out of the water.

"Okay, Clover, I'm serious this time. Do NOT put this dress on until we get to the beach. Do NOT try and use magic to take it from me. And DO NOT use violence because I don't care if it's your wedding day, I WILL beat you senseless if you do something stupid." I appear in front of Clover, Willow, and Elena who are sitting on rocks. It looks like they just finished.

"I love you!" Clover squeaks jumping up. "We have to go now, it's almost dark."

We walk to the edge of the Island in silence. I can tell Clover is freaking out. Even after being together for as long as they have, plus the five years Justin waited for her to be ready, she still thinks he's going to back out. We pause at the edge of the trees so I can poof Clover, Elena, Willow and I into our dress. Once we're in them, I part the trees in the centre so we don't have another ripped dress mishap. It's a very dramatic entrance if I do say so myself.

Everyone turns to look at us. Willow goes first, carrying a basket of rose petals. Elena and I follow behind Clover holding her dress off the ground. When we get to the edge of the chairs, Willow starts dropping the petals.

Justin is looking at Clover like he is the luckiest man in the universe. He looks very handsome. Elena refused to let him show off his meaningless tattoos, so she took makeup to everyone that showed with his suit on. She also forced him to remove his piercings for an hour while this was going on. He looks really good.

Jacob, Hunter, and Tyler are standing on Justin's right all dressed in black suits. Jacob and Hunter have red ties to match Elena and me, and Tyler has pink to match Willow.

Willow moves off to her right once she's hit the stage. Clover steps up next. Justin is still staring at her like he can't believe she's his. As Elena and I set Clover's dress down, I whisper, "Take good care of her or I'll kill you."

He peels his eyes away long enough to give me a look. It says, "You're crazy if you think I would mess this up," then he looks back at Clover.

As I move to my spot directly behind Clover, on the left side of Elena, the setting sun gleams onto the ocean. The area around us turns orange. Everything is perfect. There's no way it could be any better.

Jacob moves to his spot in between Clover and Justin. As he opens his mouth, I hear a voice.

"Zylan," it says from right behind me. I know that voice. I would know it anywhere, but it's not possible. I think I'm hearing things, but it looks like everyone else heard it too. They're all staring in my direction.

I turn around slowly. Standing in front of me is a boy with blonde hair and blue eyes. He's beat-up, his lip is swollen, his eyebrow has a huge gash through it, and his left eye is black and swollen shut. He's hunched over holding his right arm to his chest.

"Ace?"

CPSIA information can be obtained
at www.ICGtesting.com
Printed in the USA
LVHW05s0158010618
579056LV00001BA/4/P